Praise for Jen
THE BET

"From the dirt trails of Stanley P̶a̶r̶k̶
lesque clubs that Vancouver once hosted . . . *The Better Mother*
is a pitch-perfect portrait of the city I grew up in. But perhaps
more importantly it is a skillful observation of the parts of us
that often refuse to be seen. With great tenderness and poetry,
Lee pulls aside the masks we wear to hide our raw emotions
even while we yearn for the compassion of others."

Billie Livingston, author of *Greedy Little Eyes*

"Complex and layered. . . . An ambitious and engaging read
with a wholly original premise and characters you have likely
yet to meet in Canadian fiction. . . . Straight-ahead page-
turning brilliance." *National Post*

"Lee writes with her pen attuned to every detail of sensory
experience. . . . My heart was with Danny and Miss Val every
step of the way. . . . Poignant and beautifully told."

Schema Magazine

"*The Better Mother* brilliantly invites us to see the forgotten
lives that have populated our cities—their vulnerabilities,
their luminous and indomitable energy."

David Chariandy, author of *Soucouyant*

"Lee is a fine storyteller. . . . More than a nostalgic montage
of times and places, *The Better Mother* is an evocative portrait
of two lonely hearts and their synchronized longings."

The Georgia Straight

"It's always good news when a great first novel like *The End of East* gets a strong follow-up. Obviously, Jen Sookfong Lee didn't use up her talent the first time around."

NOW (Toronto)

"Rousing literature. . . . A page-turning depiction of triumph over adversity." *The Vancouver Sun*

"Virtually oozing with sensuous and romantic longing. . . . Lee describes the contrast between wealth and poverty . . . with clarity and insight. . . . With remarkable facility, Lee breathes life into two characters who lead lives of relative anonymity." *Winnipeg Free Press*

"Beautifully written." *Vancouver Observer*

THE
BETTER
MOTHER

JEN SOOKFONG LEE

VINTAGE CANADA

VINTAGE CANADA EDITION, 2012

Copyright © 2011 Jen Sookfong Lee

All rights reserved under International and Pan-American Copyright Conventions. No part of this book may be reproduced in any form or by any electronic or mechanical means, including information storage and retrieval systems, without permission in writing from the publisher, except by a reviewer, who may quote brief passages in a review.

Published in Canada by Vintage Canada, a division of Random House of Canada Limited, Toronto, in 2012. Originally published in hardcover in Canada by Alfred A. Knopf Canada, a division of Random House of Canada Limited, in 2011. Distributed by Random House of Canada Limited.

Vintage Canada with colophon is a registered trademark.

www.randomhouse.ca

This book is a work of fiction. Names, characters, places and incidents either are the product of the author's imagination or are used fictitiously. Any resemblance to actual persons, living or dead, events or locales is entirely coincidental.

Library and Archives Canada Cataloguing in Publication

Lee, Jen Sookfong
The better mother / Jen Sookfong Lee.

Issued also in an electronic format.

ISBN 978-0-307-39951-9

I. Title.

PS8623.E442B48 2012   C813.'6   C2010-907642-7

Text and cover design by Jennifer Lum

Image credits: (woman) © Masterfile,
(fan) © Fuzzybearphoto | Dreamstime.com

Printed and bound in the United States of America

2 4 6 8 9 7 5 3 1

For Annelise

CONTENTS

PROLOGUE

1958

Danny is eight years old and skinny, a boy who fingers his kneecaps every night, wondering if the sharp bones will pierce through his skin if he gets any taller. It's summertime, and his black hair—thick and straight and glued in place with three generous dollops of Brylcreem—shines in the sunlight as he bobs and darts through late-afternoon crowds on Pender Street. A white woman in a greyish-pink straw hat (the colour Danny imagines is called *dusty rose*) stops to stare, her green eyes lingering over his cut-off jean shorts. He tugs at his almost-outgrown, striped T-shirt, but soon recovers; it's not he who should feel out of place, but this knobbly-faced woman. She is, he thinks, the kind of person his father complains about, the kind who comes down to Chinatown on weekends and holidays to gawk at the mysterious dried seahorses in the herbalist's window, taking in the stacks of Chinese newspapers on the street corners, the lined and tanned men leaning against the buildings, their fingernails yellow and split from cigarettes and weekday work.

Danny grins sweetly at this woman until she tentatively smiles back. She isn't to blame for being one of the many tourists who troop through the neighbourhood and hog all the parking spots big enough to fit his parents' boat of a car. Satisfied, he continues weaving between people until he spies his father's favourite café. Standing at the counter inside, he can see, behind glass, the rows and rows of apple tarts, their flaky tops sprinkled with sugar. But he knows that looking isn't any use. Money, it seems, is always tight and the family's curio shop always on the verge of closing. Besides, he had lunch at home with his mother and little sister just four hours ago: a bowl of bland but filling rice, that leafy green he can never remember the name of, a steamed pork patty dotted with the pickled snow cabbage he hates.

He waves at Mr. Gin behind the counter. "One pack of Sweet Caps, please."

"Sure thing, Danny. How's your dad?"

Danny shrugs. "Same as always."

Mr. Gin nods. "I bet all these tourists are making him grumpy, eh? All right then, here you go." He hands over the pack of cigarettes.

Danny digs in his pocket for the coins his father gave him, but it's empty. He checks his back pockets—nothing. Bending down, he searches his socks and the insides of his shoes—still nothing. He stands up and stares at Mr. Gin.

"I must have lost the money."

"Don't worry, Danny. The cigarettes will be here. You can come back later."

"No. Dad will be so mad! He always says that I have holes in my head."

"You'll have to tell him the truth. Here, why don't I give you this apple tart to make you feel a little better."

But Danny is gone, blindly rushing down Pender Street, spooking the live chickens on display in their cages. They flap their wings, peck at their own toes in anger. Maybe if he runs fast enough, he'll escape Chinatown altogether and never have to face his father again. Or watch his mother wipe away stray rice grains with her thin, mud-coloured sleeves. Danny makes a tight right turn into an alley. The trail of a woman's voice shouting in Chinese follows him: "Slow down, little boy! You'll knock down one of my customers. You'll get it then, I tell you!"

He slips into the shadows, hears the click and clack of mah-jong tiles from the third-floor windows echoing off the tall buildings. The air is damp, as if all the rain that fell during the spring has been trapped in the cracks between bricks and uncovered garbage cans, and sharpens the smell of barbecued pork and overripe fruit that stings the insides of his nostrils. He slows to a walk, keeping one hand on the exterior wall of the building on his left so he can trace the roughness with his fingertips, feel the mortar crumbling as he passes. Sometimes he thinks that he could walk all these back streets with his eyes closed, using the texture of the bricks and rhythm of his footsteps to find his way to the shop—or somewhere else far, far away.

The alleys are the only places left where it is almost always silent. Sunlight still filters through the power lines, but it is a very particular light, striped with darkness, sharply defined by the shadows it tries to burn away. Through the half-gloom, he sees a woman leaning against a wall, a line of

smoke with a familiar smell rising from her mouth and floating into the air.

He creeps toward her. With every step, more and more
of her comes into focus. The lines around her legs begin to
sharpen. She is wearing fishnet stockings and red T-strap
heels. Her hair is jet black like his, but hers seems to absorb
light, not reflect it, and her head is like a storm cloud, all heavy
and moody and maybe dangerous. A green robe hangs around
her, hastily tied and partially covering her black satin one-
piece. She crosses her left leg over her right, and a row of
green sequins around the tops of her thighs catches a wayward
beam of light.

When she turns to look at him his stomach lurches.
Instantly, he is aware of the toothpaste stains on his shirt, his
mismatched socks, even the tiny hole over the baby toe on his
right shoe. She is everything beautiful that he has ever imagined, more beautiful than Lana Turner or Rita Hayworth or
even the stars in the night sky. This woman stands before him,
breathing and shifting, more real than any actress or far-off
constellation, as real as his own mother, but so, so much more
dazzling. *She* would never pin up her hair without looking in
a mirror or wear her husband's old corduroys rolled up to her
knees because they're still too good to throw away. For a
second, he sees his mother in that same green and black outfit,
but he realizes she would still be the mother he has always
known, just squeezed into clothes she has no business wearing.
A familiar surge of disappointment rolls through his chest.

He imagines running down the alley and resting his
cheek against the smooth satin barely covering this woman's
body; he is sure her muscles won't give, that there will be no

extra rolls padding her belly. But he stands motionless, hoping that he will somehow melt into the grime and slick of the alley and that this perfect creature—so powdered, so fleshy—will not see him and the telltale signs of his unsophisticated life.

She squints through the shifting light, her face hard and suspicious, like she is bracing herself for something unpleasant but predictable: perhaps a stumbling, drunk man, or a woman from the nearby church, maybe even the same one who came into his father's shop two days earlier clutching a fistful of pamphlets and wearing plain brown shoes. When Danny feels her black-lined eyes travelling over his flushed, hastily washed face, he holds his breath, wondering if she will ignore him, yell at him, or, worst of all, pat him on the head like a puppy and send him on his way.

A pigeon waddles across the alley, stopping to consider a soggy piece of bread.

The beautiful, satiny woman suddenly smiles. Her face softens and she looks, for a moment, like she has just spotted her child in a crowd. Danny lets the air out of his chest and puts a brown hand on his forehead. Somehow, he feels swollen and light at the same time.

"Do you need something, little boy? Are you lost?" Her voice is like gravel crunching under the wheels of a speeding car. Danny feels sorry for her and wonders if the cracking in her voice is from sobbing into a pillow in the dark early morning, the way he once saw a light-haired actress weep in a sad, romantic movie.

"Are those Sweet Caps?" He wants to kick himself for uttering such an ordinary thing to this woman, who is surely a temperamental creature, one who might bristle at questions deemed too mundane for her bejewelled ears. But his words have already fallen like heavy bricks.

"My smokes? You're far too young to be thinking of putting one of these in your mouth." She smiles again, runs a painted fingernail across her red lips.

"My dad needs some, but I've lost the money. He'll yell at me unless . . ."

"Sweetheart, if you need some smokes to keep your dad from dressing you down, by all means." She reaches into a pocket on her robe and pulls out a full pack. "Here, take them."

"Thank you," Danny whispers, darting forward to take the cigarettes from her white, unlined hand. "Miss . . . ?"

"You can call me Miss Val. Although everyone around here knows me as the Siamese Kitten. Funny, isn't it? Pretending to be Oriental in the middle of Chinatown."

"Sometimes I think I would rather be someone else," Danny ventures, tucking the pack of cigarettes securely into the waistband of his shorts.

"Honey, we all wish we were something we're not. That club back there," Miss Val gestures toward the grey door behind her, "is full of men pretending all sorts of things." She laughs loudly, and it sounds like hundreds of bells, the kind Danny once heard being rung for dinner in the fancy house his mother cleans once a week. Because of her raspy voice, he had expected her to chuckle or half growl and he laughs with her in surprise. "I guess that's where I come in. Easier for them to forget their lives when I'm up onstage, shaking my can in their sad little faces."

Danny steps forward again, his hand outstretched and reaching for her shiny green robe, but Miss Val doesn't notice.

She blows a smoke ring and watches it dissipate into the air above their heads.

"There was a time I could have been a real, bona fide actress. The studios were interested, let me tell you. But that was almost ten years ago now, and I guess I can't complain. Better dancing and taking off my clothes every night than breaking my back raising five kids." She pats her hip with her free hand and looks down at the ground. A puddle shimmers with the tremor of cars and trucks passing at either end of the alley.

He is close enough to smell her perfume—woody and underground, like freshly turned soil and cedar in the rain. He wants to breathe it in deeply until he falls asleep. The belt on her robe is dangling from her waist and he pinches the end between his index finger and thumb. So soft and smooth. Slippery like water, if water were cloth. What if he wrapped the fabric around his wrist and twisted it up his arm? What would that feel like? Like a whisper on the ear? The breeze from a seagull flying overhead?

Miss Val looks down at his bent head, the concentration lining his small face. "What's your name, sweetheart?"

"It's Danny," he says, without looking up.

"Danny, that's real silk satin. Some of the new girls, they go cheap on the costumes, but not me. Here." Miss Val reaches around and pulls the belt from her robe. "Take this. You seem to love it even more than I do." She threads the long, narrow piece of silk through the loops on his shorts, passing it through twice and then knotting it in a symmetrical little bow at his belly, firmly over the pack of cigarettes in his waistband. Briefly, Danny feels her fingers in his hair, riffling the strands until goosebumps rise on the back of his neck. "You remind me of a little boy I knew once," she says. She straightens and laughs; her cigarette is now no more than a stub in her fingers. "Of course, you're much more special. I wouldn't give away bits of my costume to just anyone, you know."

"Thank you so much, Miss Val. I can keep this for real?"

"Yes, honey, for real. It's been a long time since any kid looked at me with those big saucer eyes, so that's your reward." Miss Val cocks her head at him and smiles, the sharp lines of her jaw and neck relaxing into a soft blur of skin that reminds him of the cheeks on his mother's face. She throws her spent cigarette into a puddle. "Look at that. I'm getting lost in memories, like an old woman." She runs a finger down Danny's left ear. "You should run off and deliver those smokes to your dad before he goes looking for you. Don't want to be caught with a used-up stripper in an alley, do you?"

Danny doesn't quite understand what Miss Val means, but nods anyway. He knows that these few minutes have changed everything about him, and that he will forever be a different Danny—maybe even a glamorous, salty, fearless one. If his father weren't waiting and likely pacing in the shop's front window, Danny would stay and ask Miss Val how she became this lovely, silk-covered being. Maybe she had to break free from something as boring and everyday as Chinatown with its fish tanks and piles of cloth slippers.

Impulsively, he grasps Miss Val's hand with both of his and kisses it, the way he has seen men who are in love with beautiful women do in the movies.

"Are you trying to get fresh with me?" she asks, her eyebrows knitted together in mock disapproval.

Danny shakes his head. He doesn't know how to tell her that they could be the best of friends if they had the time, or that he would like to go home with her and create his own little nest in a pile of her clothes where she could tell him stories about dancing and parties. He owes her so much, for the cigarettes and the belt and this glimpse into a life that must be exciting and always bewitching. But he has taken far too long already.

Danny says in his best grown-up voice, "We'll meet again. You've captured my heart forever." He shoots her what he hopes is a debonair look before running away, one hand clasped over his belly, the silk bow a ball in his small fist. Her laughter bounces off the buildings and multiplies, until he is sure he is being chased by church bells, ringing and ringing for souls both lost and found.

PART ONE

THE RETURN

1982

This neighbourhood. Crooked sidewalks cracked by tree roots, eroded from rain and the burdened feet of people hurrying to work or hurrying home. Garbage from the twenty-four-hour convenience store is piled around the bus shelter. A cat meows. The dampness in the air shimmers as it rises, and Danny stands, staring at his parents' house through the haze.

Everything looks the same, only greyer and smaller. The same windows fogged over with years of cooking grease. The same front steps that tilt to the right. The same gutters, choked with twigs and old leaves. He blinks slowly. When he opens his eyes, he is still here, his hand on the gate, sweat coursing down his back and pooling in his waistband. He might just pass out.

Fourteen years ago, he left this place in the early morning. Every sinew in his body was stretched taut as he rushed westward, headlong into the crush of buildings and traffic and the ever-present noise of downtown. He swore to himself, *I am never going back. That is not where I belong.* He stayed away completely, taking winding and circuitous routes whenever he came within ten blocks of this place. He had removed this yard and those windows from his head on purpose. And yet he is here, all because Cindy's eyes drooped at lunch last week describing their mother's sallow and soft face in the living-room window as she waited for Cindy to come home from a date.

"I can't do it by myself anymore," she said. "All they do is wonder where I am."

And he's back because maybe this visit will exorcise the reverberations of his father's voice in his ears.

"You're weak."

"What kind of boy are you?"

"A dog would be more useful than you."

In all this time, Danny has only heard his parents' voices on the phone when he called at Chinese New Year or Christmas. In person, he hopes his father will be less viciously articulate, and be round and jolly instead. He doesn't dare hope anything for his mother.

His eyes travel over the chipped wooden siding. He looks behind him at the cars speeding down Dundas, each revolution of their wheels making a rhythm: *run run run*. When he was younger, his dreams beat to the same pace. Unrelenting. Continuous. At eighteen years old, he hurriedly and silently packed a small suitcase. As he drove off in his best friend's car and counted every block they passed, it took all his willpower not to say the numbers out loud.

He had jobs, learned how to be a passable wedding photographer and lived in apartments in squat buildings that were half hidden by the high-rises blotting out the sky. He looked for and found lovers who asked him no questions. Living in a world of his own making and escaping from a house in which he never belonged are his two successes. He is, after all, not the famous photographer he thought he might be, or the spectacularly dressed owner of a high-rise penthouse on English Bay. But everything else he dreamed of at eighteen and worked for is his. His own apartment. A little bit of money. No one sitting in the dark when he gets home at night, asking him pointed questions about where he's been, or whose smell he carries on his breath.

Still, when he's being honest with himself, he remembers how he sometimes wakes in the middle of the night, groggily wondering when his mother will call him for breakfast, or if his father will hustle him out the door to help in the shop. These moments never last, but they are numerous enough that Danny notices them. Even as he tries to forget.

But right now, he can feel himself leaning toward the house, his feet stepping down the front path by instinct. He remembers the feel of his mother's hand on his feverish forehead, the baby-soft flannel sheets in which he cocooned on wet, windy nights. The grunt his father made every time he sank into his armchair at the end of the day. He closes his eyes and counts to ten. If he isn't careful, this will begin to feel like home, even though home was hardly ever nice or warm or peaceful. And he fears that, at thirty-two, he is now too old to twist himself free again.

Heart beating, he pushes open the gate.

Cindy stands in the small vestibule, her thin hands holding open the front door, her feet in red Chinatown slippers. He wonders if anyone from her outside life—her friends, her co-workers at the bank, even the homeless man who sits in the same spot at the corner of Robson and Burrard every day—would recognize her in this house. Is the real Cindy the sister he has been meeting for drinks once a week for the last thirteen years, with the glossy hair and wide smile, bright dresses and matching pumps? The one who only mentions their parents if she has four glasses of wine? Or this one, with the unpainted face and shoulder blades like arrowheads underneath her pilly blue T-shirt?

She hands him a pair of slippers, identical to hers but bigger. "Here, wear these," she says. "No shoes in the house, remember?"

"Cindy, I think I'm going to be sick."

She frowns. "You won't feel better standing here. They're waiting."

"I want to go. I want to leave right now."

She grabs him by the shoulder and gives him a little shake. "You can't. If you leave now, I'm never going to speak to you again," she hisses.

"We could leave together. Let's get the hell out of here." His voice rises to a glass-clear pitch.

She bites her lip. He knows what she is imagining: a twirling life, red shoes, drinks with condensation pooling on coasters in an apartment with high, wide windows. Something brighter, with music, where lovers laugh at the coming dawn and hold up their glasses for more. No pained looks when she comes home after eleven o'clock. No statements that seem small but are really about husbands and grandchildren and disappointment.

"Get your shoes. My car's right outside," Danny whispers.

Cindy's face resettles. Her voice is clipped, a businesslike tone that Danny has heard her use at the bank when counting out money for customers.

"They need me. Maybe you've forgotten, Danny: I'm not you."

She turns her head and moves down the hallway, the bottoms of her slippers slapping at the badly worn hardwood floor. She pulls on her ponytail and disappears into the kitchen. Danny takes in a deep breath, smells the unmistakeable scent of mildew that grows in the hidden crevices beyond his mother's reach. He sniffs again, and his nose fills with ginger and garlic. This house. Like no other.

In the living room, Danny's father, Doug, sits in a faded yellow armchair, his thick hands firmly gripping the armrests. The television sends blue and white and green light into the room, making Danny's eyes water. The news anchor stares fixedly. "A young man was found dead in Stanley Park early this morning," he intones. Danny jumps, but his father doesn't notice and merely drums his fingers against his thigh. The voice continues, "Police are not releasing any details, but already those who live in the area are saying the victim was targeted for being a homosexual." The newscast cuts to a shot of a heavily wooded area near Lee's Trail, cordoned off with yellow police tape. Danny can see a suede shoe with a tassel poking out from under a tarp. He saw a man with shoes just like that, walking in the park at night.

Danny chokes back the heaving in his stomach as his father turns his head and stares.

"Hi, Dad."

"Danny. Why do you look like that? Are you sick?"

Doug reaches for the half-drunk bottle of beer on the table beside him. A grease stain in the shape of a misshapen heart wrinkles on his thin blue work shirt as he moves.

"No. It's just warm out, that's all."

"So, you're back," Doug says.

Danny shifts on his feet. His father doesn't invite him to sit. "Just for dinner."

"Why?"

Danny thinks he hasn't quite heard. "What?"

"Why? Why are you here now?" For the first time, Doug looks at Danny's face, and his eyes twitch. The bottom lids are red and watery. Danny suspects it's from the beer and not his own long-delayed presence.

"I thought it would be nice to see everyone again. Cindy said you wanted to see me."

"You haven't visited once all this time. What makes you think I want to see you?"

Danny remembers those first weeks after he ran away, the fear that he might pass his own parents on the street or that they might descend on his best friend and nag him until he revealed Danny's hiding spot. When he finally saw Cindy again at a pre-arranged time at a bus shelter near the Granville Bridge, he was shaking with anxiety, eyeing every bush in case his mother might pop out and grab his arm with a resolution to never let him go. But Cindy said they didn't look for him. Doug yelled at his wife, saying, "This is all your doing," before throwing out everything Danny left behind in his bedroom. He shook his finger in Betty's face. "I don't want anyone to know. If people ask, we say he moved away for a good job. Understand?" Betty wept every night for a week, her head on the kitchen table. She cornered Cindy when Doug wasn't home, but not once did either of his parents drive or walk through the city, looking for their son.

"It's like they knew you would never stay, even if they found you," Cindy had said as she shivered in the early morning wind. "How could they make you come home? Besides, it's a big secret. God forbid any of their friends should figure out we're actually a completely messed-up family."

Danny puts a hand out behind him and touches the familiar, warm front window. If he could, he would launch himself through the single-paned glass right now. He pushes on it. The frame gives slightly but manages not to break.

His father mutters, "You're home now. Nothing I can do about it."

Danny reaches into his mind for the safe discussion topics he thought up that morning. "How's work, Dad? The store still busy?"

Doug grunts and scratches his lower back with his free hand. "You know, always the same. People look, don't buy. Some days, I sell nothing."

"That can't be true. Now that it's June, there must be people looking for souvenirs. When I used to work there in the summers, it was packed with tourists."

His father fixes Danny with a hard stare. "That was a long time ago. When's the last time you were in the store? Fifteen years?"

This is not how the conversation was supposed to unfold. Danny closes his eyes and focuses on the darkness. When he opens them again, his father is once more staring at the television, his hands clasped and resting on his stomach.

"Well, I guess I should go and see if Mom needs any help in the kitchen."

Doug nods. "Yes, you go and see. She's cooking a big meal, all for you."

The kitchen steams and spatters. Every surface is covered in food: snap peas, bean sprouts, thinly sliced chicken, butterflied prawns. Danny can feel the oil from the cast-iron wok hurling droplets through the air and settling on his hair and skin. He squints and his mother's outline emerges through the hot, greasy fog.

She looks so happy, he thinks. *She's smiling like she is about to crack in two.* Danny stares at her stained apron and the cheap polyester shirt she wears underneath and takes an instinctive step backward. *God, will she ever pull herself together?*

"My boy," Betty whispers in Chinese, "you're here." She rubs his arm with both her hands. "You're so thin. And look, wrinkles. How can you have wrinkles?"

"I'm older, Mom, that's all," Danny replies, laughing at his mother's chatter, despite himself. He feels strangely soothed.

"You're old enough for a girlfriend then, aren't you?" Her small eyes search his face. He shifts from one foot to the other and she taps a finger against his chest. "All you do is go out with your friends, isn't that right? You must make time for girls too, you know."

Cindy has turned around from the kitchen sink, her hands full of dripping greens. In her face, Danny can see his own—same full mouth and upturned nose, same smooth cheeks. The one difference is their eyes: while Cindy has the long, snaky eyes of their father—the kind that can hold secrets and laugh at you behind their thin, wrinkled lids—Danny has the eyes of their mother: round, dark and seemingly innocent.

"Mom, enough of that. Look, the water's boiling," Cindy says, pointing.

The lid on the noodle pot clatters and Betty rushes to the stove, forgetting that Danny hasn't responded. He looks up at a spider on the ceiling and touches his forehead. The nerves in his skin are outgrown and bare, tingling with a sensation that is more than pain, that is amplified sharpness, the bright of noontime and a sound like mice screaming in their traps. His mother was this close to unravelling it all, to picking at the right scab to see the baby-pink skin underneath.

Betty sprinkles sliced green onions on the last dish— braised pork belly—and brings it to the table. As they begin eating, she talks and talks. Her voice fills the room, rising and falling, asking questions that remain hanging until she answers them herself.

"Do you know what happened to Mrs. Chang? Her husband left her. It turns out he was having an affair with a younger woman. What sort of girl wants an old man like that? I'll tell you, a girl who's not right in the head. I said to Auntie May, 'Maybe this girl is retarded,' but she said no. She's a flight attendant and isn't in town much. So then I thought maybe she has an old man in many different cities. A very bad girl, I think. A good girl doesn't leave her parents for a job. No, she waits for the right husband and buys a big house that will fit everybody. A daughter can't be separated from her parents." Betty smiles at Cindy, who drops her eyes.

Danny thinks he might laugh and spray the table with rice and pork. Betty picks up an especially fat prawn and places it in his bowl, nodding as he pokes at it with his chopsticks.

Cindy leans toward Danny and says in a whisper loud enough for everyone to hear, "She's gone bonkers. She's so happy you're here, I'll bet she doesn't even know what she's saying."

Doug chews. The dishes in the middle of the table steam, blowing smells toward the ceiling. "Good daughters, good sons—no such thing," he says in English, eyes fixed on the tablecloth. "We should have had at least five grandchildren by now, all living under one roof."

Danny looks at his mother, whose face has brightened.

Cindy rolls her eyes. "Here she goes again. I swear: she hasn't talked this much in a month."

"Yes, grandchildren." Betty lays down her chopsticks and points around the table. "I know why you two don't get married. It's because you, Miss Cindy, are too shy. Always walking around with your head down. Who will see your face then? And you," she turns to Danny, "think no one is good enough. The right girl won't be perfect, you know. And it's not as if you're so perfect yourself. Always hanging out with your friends; never coming home to see your mother and father. How will you ever become a good family man?"

Danny was ready for the hard questions. That morning, he lay in bed, imagining all the ways his parents could say *you're not good enough, why don't you do what we know is best, we are disappointed*. Even so, their words sink like stones and he droops in his seat. All he can think of is the failure raining down on him and pricking his skin. Not a good son. Not a famous photographer. Not the love of anyone's life.

He can feel Betty's gaze on his face as he stares at his rice bowl.

"You will never be the man you could be, Danny, unless you try to change," she says softly. "You must try."

As soon as Cindy stands up and begins collecting the empty dishes, Danny rises. "I have to work tomorrow," he mutters. "One of the brides is in a hurry for the prints."

Cindy dumps the pile of plates and bowls into the sink and the crash startles him.

"What about dessert?" Betty rushes to the fridge and begins pulling out a dish of sweet tofu pudding.

If he doesn't leave now, his parents will ask him more pointed questions and he will lie at first, but eventually, exhausted, he will speak the truth. His parents' disapproval will break him, make him want to hide forever in his old bedroom, surrounded by the boxes filled with extra stock from the store. His life outside that front door will evaporate, and he will have wasted all those years he spent carefully building his uncontaminated freedom. He will grow immune to his mother's dowdiness and his father's sarcasm. The local schoolchildren will whisper about his face in the living-room window, pale and unsmiling, and make promises to each other that they will never approach, not even for trick-or-treating. His socks stick to the kitchen floor; perhaps it's the spilled grains of cooked rice, or perhaps the house itself is clinging to him, pulling on any available part of his body. If this is home, then home is not what he wants.

"No, I'm sorry, Mom. I have to go." He hurries toward the front hall, wiping his hands on his pants as he goes. He bursts outside into the humid air, not daring to look behind.

In that pre-dawn all those years ago, Danny took this same route, riding in someone else's Cadillac as it drove too quickly down these same streets. His body braces, anticipates the bumps and pits in the road. The railroad tracks run parallel to the street and abandoned train cars sit to the side, some rusting from the top down, others settling into the ground, surrounded by crab grass and salal. Shadows move in the doorways of the warehouses and shipping companies. Danny doesn't look closely at the people he perceives hiding in the evening dim. Men trading money for heroin or cocaine. Women trading all sorts of things for five dollars, sometimes ten.

He rolls down the window, and the smell of the fish cannery, drying weeds and salt blows into the car. He breathes it all in; after all, this fetid air means that he is driving away.

Turning down Davie Street, he sees that, even though the sun has not set, the night has already begun. Women stand on the sidewalk, fixing each car with looks of disdain or invitation. Their short skirts cling to their thighs and asses and stretch almost to ripping whenever they walk or shift their weight. In the doorway of a boarded-up restaurant, a group of uneasy men and women in walking shoes eye the prostitutes warily. One man fingers a stack of picket signs leaning against the wall behind him, seemingly unsure of the right time to begin marching up and down the street and screaming at the cars that slow down, "Shame, shame, shame!" Through the passenger window, Danny can make out one of the hand-lettered signs: JOHNS GO HOME! And the cars keep coming, one after the other, with heads swivelling to see better out the side windows. The drivers sit in shadows, but Danny imagines they look the same: unremarkable; hair, eyes and skin all varying shades of brown and beige. In the apartments above the storefronts, curtains sway, moved by the wind or by the tenants hidden behind them.

Around the corner, huddled in a small group on a side street, six boys stand in their white T-shirts and tight jeans, their hands stuffed into their pockets. They, too, eye the cars cruising past, but look directly at a driver only if the driver looks first. Like a flight of swallows, they seem to be one pulsing creature, until a single boy, tall with dark hair, breaks away to lean against a lamppost and light a cigarette.

These boys stand like his eighteen-year-old self, the one who slumped and slouched down the sidewalks, watching how others conducted their public, street-level lives. Years ago, he might have sidled past them, maybe even asked for a light just so he could more closely study the way their hair flipped along their collars.

He turns right onto Jervis and eases his way into a parking spot, tight between two other cars. Looking up, he can see the dark windows of his apartment. His neighbour has installed two planter boxes, both filled with begonias and pansies, and her curtains—yellow with blue dots—are backlit by a soft lamp. As he reaches down to roll up his window, a brief muggy breeze blows through the car, raising the hairs in his nose. He looks up once more at the third floor before pushing open the driver's door, stepping onto the sidewalk and walking in the opposite direction, away from the quiet of his apartment above.

This is Vancouver, the city that he loves for its very wetness, for the cool rain that trickles down awnings on November evenings, the slippery sidewalks, the inlet that promises escape to other, farther places if he should ever feel the need. This is the place where land and water meet, where the shoreline is forever shifting, waves ebbing over the rocky sand or crashing against the roots of rust-coloured arbutus, cold and wind tearing away layers of bark. The buildings of downtown rise above it all, winking through the mist, attracting boys and girls from the suburbs, the Eastside, the North Shore.

This is the damp Vancouver that Danny knows. The Vancouver he hurries across, where the shadows and crowds and fog provide cover for the men who populate his open nights. This is the Vancouver where he sometimes sees glimmers of old lovers through the rain; one stands ghostlike in half-lit alleys, blue eyes pulsing through the gloom.

Tonight the hot air opens his pores. He walks along the seawall in Stanley Park, under the shade of Douglas firs and cedars, avoiding the piles of fallen needles and dust that have collected in the dips and cracks of the concrete. He can hear a car radio through the trees. "This may be the hottest summer on record, folks. Temperatures will remain in the thirties for the next week at least. Watch out—1982 is turning out to be a scorcher!" Danny looks up at the dark sky—cloudless, with stars barely visible from this swath of green that flirts with nature but is really a city park, made and marked by machines and the humans who travel its paths. By the men who walk with disguised purpose between trees in the night.

He turns onto a narrow gravel trail and his stomach clenches in expectation. Branches brush his ears, poking the thin skin like sharp words. His shoes press down on the rocks and dirt, his steps making as little noise as a raccoon's pointed, furry paws. He wonders if the police tape is still there, past the trees on his left. A ripple of fear builds in the bottom of his spine and snakes its way up into his neck, his ears. He thinks about turning back. Perhaps the murderer is waiting for one more victim, maybe a nervous, jumpy Chinese man. He passes a group who look over their shoulders at every sound.

"Someone told me it was Wayne. You know, that short guy from back east."

"I heard it might have been someone he was sleeping with."

Danny shivers in a gust of warm air. And decides to stay in the park. If he left he would be scared and lonely. Here, he's only scared.

The first time he found this trail, he was living in a tiny, ground-floor apartment on Pendrell, where clouds of flies and the smell of cat pee drifted in through the window. For a week, he wandered from bed to toilet to stove, unsure of whether he should lounge in his underwear or clean the mould that grew on the sills. He finally went outside, where at least the streets looked familiar and walking from one place to the next was a simple decision. He stumbled on this path while exploring the park on an overcast, chilly night. His parents disliked the outdoors, especially in the dark, when fences and garages blended into the bush and the yellow eyes of unknown animals glowered from their perches between trees. And so Danny, restless, with nerves standing on end, decided to walk every trail he came across, touch each species of evergreen he passed. Eventually, he came to a clearing where three benches sat in a triangle. There, behind a thicket of vine maples, he saw two men clasping hands under branches that curved above their heads.

It was then that he began to come to the park every week.

Tonight, his nostrils twitch. He can smell the men, some standing in groups of two or three where the trail widens and forks to the left and the right. There's no mistaking the smell that collects in arm hairs, the smell that is musk and breath and cologne all at once. The smell that lingers on Danny when he returns home, a slight smile playing across his lips as he lies alone in his double bed.

As he walks, he begins to forget the news, the eyes of his plain-faced mother as he sat eating the food she cooked. He forgets that he rushed out of his parents' house unceremoniously. His muscles ache and his blood rushes, thinned by the heat around and within him. He continues to walk, and is exactly as he appears: a man who is as much a part of this protected, harbouring park as the decaying nurse log on his right, or the other men who lean against tree trunks, their bodies melting into the mass of vegetation around them. Even his name isn't important anymore.

A voice behind him. "I've seen you here before."

Danny turns, looks into the eyes of a light-haired man almost as tall as the trees behind him. Pressed polo shirt. Moustache and glowing teeth. Skin that looks pebbly to the touch, as if he has spent half his life working in a rough wind. He seems to carry his own spotlight, for how else could Danny see all these things in the dark?

There is, he knows, a spot accessible by squeezing through two oversized ferns, a spot that generates its own protective silence. He opens his mouth, but every word he considers is inadequate. All he can think is how hot it would be to have sex with this man, in the park where needles and dry grass are in danger of flaming up, where the slightest friction could cause treetops to catch fire like matchsticks. He thinks of sweat simmering between bodies.

Danny nods to his right and they silently enter the bush. In his favourite spot, there is enough air and ground for him and him on this sweltering night. Their outermost selves— the ones who drive to work in the morning, or who don't answer the phone because they know their mothers are trying to reach them—have fallen away, expelled because of this need to feel the velocity of their bodies together. Danny's breath emerges from his chest easily, without pain.

Branches crack in the quiet. If he leans forward, like so, he can rest his hands on the trunk of the tree in front of him. His narrow hips are grasped from behind and his body opens until he and this colossus of a man are no longer distinct as two separate people. They are an eight-limbed, brand-new creature, slick and burning, its double mouth closed in case a police officer happens to be walking on the other side of the trees. Danny relishes the feeling of another man's hands hold- ing him, encircling his body like he will never let go, like this one meeting will somehow turn into a lifetime of late brunches on Sundays. He wonders if he should ask his partner's name, then thinks better of it, realizing that, in the months to come, he would rather wordlessly remember him with echoes of these waves that push and pull. Besides, asking might spur this man to question him in turn, and how would Danny ever explain his compartmentalized self to someone else? This is something he has never done in the park and he doesn't want to start now. Please, not now.

For one second, a streak of moonlight falls through the tree cover, and their combined shadow, defined by lumps and the sharpness of joints, appears and is then gone. When they separate, the man kisses Danny on the lips before walking away, waving once before disappearing down the gravel path.

As Danny makes his way home through the downtown streets, he exhales in relief that neither of them had spoken. It's the newness he craves, the change from face to face to face, the constant march of men through his nights, none of whom ask for details or stories of the past, just this sliver of a moment in the hush of the park. The fulfillment of his wants helps him believe that he is not a failure, that he is still running and immune from capture; words will only suggest the opposite.

THE OBSERVER

1982

Sometimes he is convinced he can touch people through the camera, that the lens is a finger that grazes the backs of people's necks, smoothes down tufts of hair standing in the wind. He wonders if the simple act of pressing down on the shutter release means that he has left a trace of himself on his subjects' bodies—a filmic thumbprint, a flash of light that tans the skin ever so slightly. If he actually reached out and grazed them with his hands, they would turn around and stare, not comprehending how in a city this size, human touch is even possible. *How strange*, they might think. *How uncouth.*

He leans his body against the hot Orpheum wall on Granville Street. The day has just begun and everything is still new. Hurtful conversations have not yet started. Women still walk through the city with their blank, nighttime faces. He grips his camera tightly. Every week, he leaves his apartment trusting that he will take that one picture that will breathe other-worldly beauty into ordinary, unsuspecting things and people. He walks, looking for that moment that exposes what twirls inside, the secret loves or hates that shimmer through eyes and open doorways. The photo that will make him famous.

He had come downtown at eighteen, camera strapped around his neck, convinced that he would one day see his images in a white-walled gallery, that people dressed in black, holding glasses of wine, would tilt their heads to the side while gazing at his thought-provoking, visceral photographs. "So raw," they might say, "as if someone splattered their feelings right there." And he would smile because everyone would finally know how the world revealed itself when he saw it through his viewfinder.

He sees an abandoned bicycle, wheels upended outside a corner store. The blinking of a Pac-Man machine at the arcade down the street. A backyard bordering an alley that is unintended for casual observers and filled with the particular remnants of family: a burnt-out television, a stack of car tires, a one-eyed dog sniffing its own feet. He even sees the sun-shine, cutting diagonally across his viewfinder, yellow slashes on grey sidewalks.

But it's the people he looks for most.

He sees them walking, driving; sees them eating in the big front window of a diner across the street. Their faces move and wrinkle, their expressions fall or light up. They are lovely, touched by light and shadow, dwarfed by the tall lines of buildings, or made giant when their faces fill the viewfinder with pores and wrinkles, their eyes moving up and down with thoughts of what they might have done better, or what they did best. He stops in mid-stride at the sight of a woman with laugh lines around her mouth and a shiny, dangling handbag that he imagines her drawing tissues from. His breath catches in his throat and he wants to tell her story in one glorious, well-focused frame. But when he finally brings up his camera and looks through the viewfinder, this woman, like every person who catches his attention, turns away and he is left with a shot of the back of her head. Frame after frame of the permed, greying curls of older women, the hatted heads of businessmen, the barrettes of little girls.

His body curves in on itself and he lets the camera dangle from his neck. He must spook his subjects; they can sense his hovering presence and turn away even though he is across the street or behind a rhododendron. He might be a bloodsucker, and the men and women and children are simply protecting themselves. Perhaps he clings to the beat and thrum of other people to counteract his own pale, quiet self. He has spent years staring at his collection of images, and none of them pulse with the beat of human breath, or drip desire and pain and longing. They are pretty little pictures and no one ever made it into a New York gallery on pretty pictures alone, something even his more hopeful, younger self understood.

Now he sees a small figure leaping down the sidewalk, wearing a red-and-blue-striped T-shirt and brown shorts. The little boy comes closer, and Danny watches as he very carefully avoids the cracks in the sidewalk and mouths the words of the schoolyard rhyme. "Step on a crack, break your mother's back."

Danny lifts his camera and the little boy looks behind him in the direction of the rickety rental houses near the bridge, possibly checking for his mother's watchful eye in the living-room window. Grinning, he breaks into a run, taking advantage of the mostly empty sidewalk now that everyone has reported for work. His arms and legs pump like a marathon runner's, eyes closed against the wind tunnel he's created. He shouts into the street, "Watch me! I'm faster than an airplane!" Danny presses the shutter as soon as he can, but the boy speeds past him. The photograph will be a blur of arms and legs, a swirl to indicate the cowlick at the back of his head.

He begins to walk away, mentally listing all the things he has to do for the next Saturday wedding. Tomorrow he will buy film, pick up his suit from the dry cleaner, fill up the gas tank in the car so he can make it to the church for the ceremony, the park for photos and the hotel for dinner. He'll have to crouch in the aisle of the big church on Burrard, focus on a bouquet of lilies and gladioli and, of course, the heavy wooden cross hanging above the pulpit.

As he turns the corner on the way to his studio, he thinks about the bride, how she will see his pictures as her memories. She will not remember seeing out of her own eyes, not even that moment when she joins her groom at the altar and he brushes her cheek with his thumb. She will not remember having to pee and marching her bridesmaids to a tiny washroom stall so they can hold up her skirt, the toilet-paper roll digging into the back of her beleaguered sister. She won't even remember her father whispering to her during their dance, "Your room is always yours in case you need to get away." All these memories will be sucked into a vacuum where other, older things wait: the name of her first kitten, her favourite sandwich during her entire grade six year, the running shoes she saved her babysitting money for. One day, in a hospital room somewhere, long after her worn vocal cords have fallen silent, there will be a flood, and she will remember everything. But no one will hear.

All of this Danny understands and, strangely, loves. Years ago, when he first began looking for work, he was disappointed that he couldn't find anything more interesting to photograph than weddings. But soon, he began to see their beauty—the dresses, the light diffused and coloured by stained-glass windows, the flowers that cost hundreds but would wilt the next day. And the rest of it: the pinched face of a father not willing to let his daughter go. The hunted look of a groom who proposed because he thought it was time. The shifting of flesh underneath the big white dress, each chunk of skin manipulated to fit the shape the bride always dreamed she could be and not the shape she really was. What Danny ended up loving was the shiny veneer of glamour and happiness, and the human ache and smell and longing that always seethed underneath.

On the street ahead of him, he notices a bulky man with a shaved head and tattoos climbing upward from the collar of his T-shirt. Blue, green and red inks swirl into snakes and thorns, shiver slightly whenever the man looks from side to side. He walks briskly, turning down Smithe toward the Cambie Bridge. Danny hurries after him, fumbling with his lens cap as he goes.

The man stops for the red light and Danny puts his camera to his eye and starts shooting, zooming in on the tattooed skin, the way the snake undulates around the roll of flesh between skull and shoulder. The shutter clicks. The film creaks as it advances.

The man turns around, and Danny can see his small green eyes staring at him through the lens. Danny drops the camera and lets it dangle around his neck.

"What the fuck are you doing?" the man booms, taking a step closer.

Danny hesitates, but manages to choke out, "I was just taking some pictures of the buildings." He points at the law courts across the street.

The man scans Danny, toes to head, and sniffs. Danny wonders if he smells like a gay man, if there is some sort of pheromone that betrays him.

"You stay away from me, skinny boy," he says, pointing his beefy finger in Danny's direction. "If I catch you following me again, I'll smash that nice camera you've got there. Understand?"

Danny nods and turns around, walking away as quickly as he can without breaking into a run. The camera bangs against his chest but he doesn't notice; he is concentrating on the incline of the street ahead of him, and how long it will take him to reach the top of the hill and rush down the other side.

That afternoon, Danny walks down Davie on his way home from the studio. When he stops at the crosswalk, he sees a stocky Chinese man standing outside the corner store across the street, carefully unwrapping a Creamsicle and flicking the pieces of paper onto a browning strip of lawn. It's Edwin, of course, in a light-grey suit and well-shined, darker grey shoes, with a thin moustache lining his upper lip. Edwin's brushed-back hair is like freshly poured tar and so glossy that Danny wants to dunk his head in a bucket of soapy water. Danny exhales sharply and walks across the street.

"Danny, what a coincidence!" Edwin steps forward, grabs one of Danny's camera bags with his free hand and grins, his lips already turning orange from his quickly melting snack.

"How is it that I always run into you?" Danny asks, as they walk together toward his apartment.

Edwin grins. "We're meant to be together. It's fate, you know, the universe making sure we're thrown together as much as possible." He stops walking and lets out a bellowing laugh. "Don't look so scared, Danny. I'm just joking. God, you're not my type anymore, all right?"

It's never a coincidence, no matter what Edwin says. Whenever Danny sees him standing at a traffic light waiting to cross the street, or drinking a glass of Chardonnay in the window of a bar he's walking past, he always thinks that Edwin has somehow figured out where Danny is going to be and purposely waits for him, the surprised look on his face so practised it's almost believable. Danny thinks he can see a triumphant glimmer of *I knew it* in the lines of his mouth.

At the apartment, Edwin asks if there's any coffee ("What a day—I can barely stand up") and settles on Danny's couch, his feet resting on the table in front of him. Danny can see Edwin's eyes moving and then resting on the Lucite table lamp, the black leather armchair, Danny's own photographs hanging on the walls in geometric groupings of three and five. When the coffee is ready, Danny hands a mug to Edwin and stands, arms crossed, watching as Edwin sips noisily and winks over its rim.

"I saw you looking. What are you thinking?" Danny asks.

"Why are you so suspicious? I wasn't thinking anything."

"Liar." Danny sits down in the armchair and looks out the patio window at the building across the street.

"Fine. I was thinking that this place looks like a show home. One of those modern apartments we keep building around here. Do you even live here? Where's the dirty laundry, the crumbs on the table, the fingerprints on the window?" Edwin puts down his coffee and clasps his hands behind his head. "I could sell this place tomorrow, it looks so clean."

"Listen, not everyone's a slob like you. You live in that huge house with all that furniture your parents bought. Look at it now. It's a complete mess."

"True enough. If it weren't for my parents, I'd be a total failure. People remind me of that every day." Edwin closes his eyes and Danny is unsure if he is hiding disappointment or tears, or if he is simply exhausted.

"Did something happen?" Danny asks quietly.

Edwin laughs, his hand on his stomach. "My dear father called at seven this morning from Hong Kong to tell me that our sales aren't up to snuff and that if I don't turn it around in six months, he's going to close the Vancouver office. We're making money, lots of money, but not fast enough for the Hong Kong crowd. We can sell the properties, but it's not like Asia where they have ten bidders for every tiny apartment or roach-infested office." He rubs his forehead. "And then my mother picks up the extension and starts asking me when I'm going to get married. She's aching for grandchildren, she says, like having none is a disease or something. I should say to her, 'Ma, I'm never having children because I like to fuck men,' and then take bets on whether she has a heart attack, or falls mute and never leaves her bedroom again. What do you say, Danny? Care to wager?"

Danny leans over and pats Edwin's knee. "I know, Eddie, I know."

"Of course you do, my closeted friend. Maybe you should tell my parents and I should tell yours." Edwin throws back his head and laughs some more, until tears form in his eyes. "We're a little overwrought, Danny. We need a drink."

Danny stands up and starts to walk to the kitchen. "I have some beer and a bottle of wine. Let me get it."

"No, no, stupid. We need a drink somewhere else. Somewhere with eye candy. Somewhere I don't have to look at your sad face all night." Edwin jumps up off the couch. "Let's pretend we're in high school again, when we were ignorant and cute and thin, although I was never the thin one. Come on." He grabs Danny's sleeve and propels him toward the bedroom. "Put something nice on and let's get the fuck out of here."

This is a feeling Danny knows well: that combination of weed and gin, when the music in the club bores into his eyes and ears and belly button until his heart is beating harder than he ever thought it could. It rises and falls and rises and falls and he is breathless, leaning against a concrete pillar that is sticky against his palms with old beer and the fluids of others. He wants to scream above the driving music, slam his body into the crowd, fight or fuck or both, it doesn't matter. Edwin bounces across the dance floor, damp hair flopping against his forehead. Danny laughs and then emits a loud, deep belly cry that peaks above the driving bass line for one short, crystalline second. He is lost in the crowd, the men whose skin rubs against his, whose sweat dries in layers, one for every hour spent in this dark, airless club.

Edwin breezes past him and shouts something in his ear, but all Danny can hear is *hot, green pants* and *don't look now*. He watches him dance to the middle of the room where he shimmies to the irregularity inside his head, which is like no rhythm Danny has ever heard. Edwin looks over his shoulder and winks in Danny's direction, and it feels like an arrow burrowing into his gut.

There has always been something about Edwin that isn't quite right. He explodes with enthusiasm, squeezes kittens until they squirm and cry and wriggle out of his grasp. He smiles openly at strangers until they look at the ground. Instead of walking, he bounds down the street, his unbuttoned jacket flapping in the air behind him. When they were teenagers, he always offered to buy the beer, even though the clerks ejected him, their faces grim when he stuck his tongue out at them through the glass doors. These are the reasons Danny loves him, but these are also the reasons Danny wants to shake him until his head rolls loosely on his neck and he is mercifully silent.

No matter. There is music to dance to and men all around him with square hands and sharply lined jaws. He runs his finger along a tall man's stubble, his skin tingling as he feels one hair after another. Yes, this is why he's here. For this very thing.

Later, Danny walks down Richards Street, his hands and hips and spine still loose and warm from an hour in another man's apartment. He passes club after club, smiling to himself, sure that no one can see his face on this dark night. He can smell the spilled beer on the sidewalk, hear the sound of high heels on concrete. At the corner, he stops for the traffic light and turns his head to look into the lit window of a club on his right. Through the glass, he sees three men—all tall, all handsome—gathered around one woman in a purple dress. She holds a martini glass and balances expertly in her gold pumps. One of the men whispers in her ear, and she flips back her black hair and turns her face upward. Danny starts. It's Cindy—languorous, lean, smiling. The very same Cindy he saw three days ago shuffling through their parents' house. Her lipstick is glossy. Her hold on these men is iron-tight; they look at nothing but her.

Danny knows the pre-sex dance as well as anyone, and he can see that Cindy is poised for a long night. The fabric of her dress shivers as she moves, slides like water over her hips, her small breasts. She shines for the night, and the night loves her back.

He knows that Cindy will sleep with one of these men in a matter of hours, a man whom she will probably never see again, even if he phones, even if he asks to meet her parents and offers to take her far from the house on Dundas. He knows that tonight will be filled with deep core urges, and that tomorrow she will smile over her secret while twisting a piece of hair around her finger. But she will still have to sneak into her bedroom, shoes in hand, all the while listening for the sounds of their parents' breathing—Doug's snore and Betty's soft inhale and exhale, still alert because she has waited for her daughter's return, but is pretending otherwise. How long can Cindy keep this up, swimming in a different life after dark, in these downtown clubs where she can be the most beautiful woman in a room? In the morning, she is just Cindy, the daughter who says little to her parents before taking the bus to the bank. When she returns in the early evening, she changes into her sweatpants and dutifully sweeps the puddles of water off the walk and into the storm drain.

Danny looks up at the changing traffic light. As he walks away, he remembers that she is almost thirty, that one day she will be past the age that most men find attractive, and then what? She could be a caricature, a middle-aged, grinning version of herself in thick makeup who sips vodka tonics at a table for one in the back. Or she might fade away in her Chinatown slippers, white strands of hair growing at her temples as she rubs their father's back every night in the fall and winter. *Run away, Cindy*, he thinks as the cars rush past him. *Run now.*

Danny turns south on Seymour, feeling that the night is not quite finished. He looks ahead to the flickering green neon sign. Underneath, in crooked lettering, the club announces that it has THE BEST GIRLS IN TOWN!!! The fluorescent bulbs have a pulse of their own. Danny feels their buzz inside his body, that dark cavern in his torso where the blood echoes the sputtering rhythm of the flashing lights. Turning up his collar, Danny digs his hands in his pockets and steps from the sidewalk and through the front door, not daring to look up the street.

Inside, he is not the only person sitting at a table by himself. To the right, a tall man with bifocals and sparse, straw-coloured hair sits with rigid posture, his hands wrapped around a full glass of white wine. His expression never changes, his colour remaining an unhealthy yellow, even when the dancer onstage walks slowly toward him and bends over, holding her breasts together two feet from his eyes. He nods slightly, and she walks away, winking at him over her shoulder.

The waitress, wearing a red and black lace bra top and a faux-leather miniskirt, brings Danny a beer. Her frosted hair is carefully brushed away from her face. When she places the bottle on the table in front of him, she smiles. "Back again?"

Danny nods, holds on to the beer with one hand, waiting for that chill to travel up his arm and into his spine.

The waitress pats him on the shoulder. "At least you're well-behaved, even if you're a little quiet." She laughs and turns away, sauntering toward a table of college boys, who wave at her with two-dollar bills.

Danny is here for one complicated reason: this club—with its glossy stage and sticky tables—feels like home. Not, of course, the type of home where just-baked cookies cool on the windowsill, but a home where a fierce mother pulls you in for a hug that envelops you but also makes you gasp for air. A home where comfort and a crackle of excitement commingle. At his usual table, he waits for the stockinged leg to part the curtains with a kick, for the swish of satin as a dancer makes her way to centre stage, head up, back straight. He comes here because, every once in a while, a girl will make his heart swell. Sometimes it's the ribbon in her hair, or the coral lipstick she wears. Sometimes it's nothing at all that he understands, but even then he sits at this table, hope and dried liquor gluing him to his chair. There are nights when he sits here for hours and hours, and nothing catches his eye. He leaves dejected with a droop in his shoulders and the film of too many beers on his gums. When he returns home, his apartment feels colder.

Tonight, he doesn't like his chances.

The two spotlights spin, meeting in the middle of the stage and parting again. The curtain ripples slightly, like skin covering the breathing chest of a sleeping lover. The club is briefly silent. Everyone, even the fraternity brothers across the room, seems to be waiting on tenterhooks for the next performer, for the girl who will emerge with feathers and long gloves, for the girl who will crack jokes and sing a little as she peels off her gown and stockings, for the girl whom they imagine loving for her breasts and legs, but also for her smart mouth and knife-sharp energy. The spotlights come together once more, illuminating a narrow crack in the curtains. There are possibilities waiting to burst through, to overwhelm him with wit and shine and shimmy. He holds his breath.

The music starts, an up-tempo dance track sung by an aging rocker who has turned to disco in desperation. The tall lone man is bobbing his head to the unrelenting beat. The curtains part and standing on the stage is a small, compact woman with high breasts and bleached hair. She struts her way to the pole in front of a row of tables and quickly, with a beauty-pageant smile, she tears off her short plaid skirt, revealing a pair of sheer black panties. She twirls her fingers in her pigtails and launches herself into a spin around the pole, her legs held stiffly in a wide split.

The schoolgirl act. Of course.

Even from where he's sitting, in the middle of the back row, he can see that she has used heavy pancake makeup to hide the pockmarks on her cheeks. Under the spotlights, her skin wrinkles every time she smiles or puckers, and Danny notices the age in her eyes, in the way she holds her mouth as she unbuttons her blouse. As he does during each visit here, he searches her knee socks, the elastics in her hair, even the tattoo above her left breast for some trace of glamour. Perhaps a sequin or some glitter. A bit of metallic thread sewn into the straps of her bra. Nothing.

The dancer pulls at the shiny green tie around her neck, easing it through its loop. She brandishes it in the air like a whip, then saunters over to one of the college boys. With a lopsided smile, she wraps the tie around his neck, knotting it into a neat bow the colour of unblemished grass.

Danny coughs, cold beer dribbling out the corners of his mouth. He stands up, drops a five-dollar bill on the table for his two bottles of beer, walks through the maze of tables and stumbles outside. On the way back to his apartment, he doesn't see anything around him, not the homeless couple arguing over a half-smoked cigarette, not even the ambulance parked haphazardly on the sidewalk across the street, its lights flashing and reflecting on the dark shop windows. He is aware of the pounding in his head, the sensation that things long forgotten are smashing their way through the layers in his brain.

He runs up the stairs in his building while reaching into his pocket. His hands shake and he drops his keys before throwing open the front door and rushing into his bedroom. Memories churn.

"Frank?" he asks, and then shivers at the sound of his voice uttering a name he hasn't spoken in three years. Frank the handsome. Frank the strong. Frank the one he loved, who left him.

No, not Frank. Danny turns around and stares at his black-sheeted bed. *Underneath*, he thinks. *Look underneath*.

He lies down on the floor and peers into the darkness. The one flashlight he owns is at his studio and so he relies on his hands. His fingers touch the springs of the bed frame, the cool wall behind the headboard. But then they brush against something pebbly and large, something with loose fibres that tickle his palm.

Still lying on his stomach, he pulls out an old, sand-coloured suitcase, the one he brought with him when he ran away. His mother's Chinese and English names are written across the woven top in her light, spidery hand. When he undoes the latches and pushes open the lid, mothball-scented dust puffs into the air. He looks at the stained brown lining, the big rectangular space inside. Nothing.

He reaches into a pocket on the inside of the lid until his fingers touch paper. He is holding two department store catalogues, their pages stuck together with time and damp. He gingerly tries to peel one from the other and they fall to the floor. Muttering under his breath, he pulls them toward himself and feels something slippery between their covers, something altogether different from the slight tackiness of the catalogue pages, something that whispers on his fingertips like breath. He picks up a flat green square and it unfurls until he is holding one end of an emerald silk sash that blows the smell of cigarette smoke and female musk into the air.

The fabric shimmers along its wrinkles, ripples like the surface of water. He runs his thumb down its length and feels no loose threads, no seams, only the smoothness of silk, warmed by his own hand.

He spent so long forgetting his incompatible past that the rush of memory threatens to knock him over. All those childhood nights he spent dreaming in his twin bed below the damp ceiling had been carefully locked away. Up until now, he thought he had organized this perfectly, that his adult life was free of weights and burdens, that he was the Danny Lim of his own making, not the one shaped by his parents or the hours spent breathing in the air of the curio shop. He was the man who cruised without guilt and touched the hip bones of his partners with unshaking fingers. He stares at the sash in his hand and knows that he has failed, that his visit to the family house three days ago was a precursor to this moment. He never completely erased anything, only temporarily pushed his memories aside. All this time, they were waiting. He closes his eyes and groans. It has been a long, long night.

But he looks one more time at the sash lying across his lap and, slowly, his parents' house recedes and he remembers a specific alley during a warm afternoon twenty-four years ago. A beautiful woman stood in a puddle of sunshine and he knew he wanted her to cuddle him as she sang him her favourite song, about a lover who died, her hands resting on that tender spot between his shoulder blades. Right there, beside the garbage cans. Right then. Danny smiles.

The pounding in his head has disappeared. The past has arrived.

THE ALLEY

1958

He meant to stay awake, to wait up until his parents and sister went to bed and the house hushed under the weight of night-time, when the sounds were restricted to cars driving down the street and the neighbour's cat crying from its post on the lid of a garbage can. Danny imagined that the outside world after dark was full of skittering creatures brushing past and faraway laughter rolling through the air, thick with black. He squirmed in his bed and tried to ignore the urge to burst through the back door so that he could run and run and run, down the alley, around the corner and away, to New Brighton Park perhaps, or toward downtown, where the neon lights buzzed and men whispered to each other, the brims of their hats touching. Danny turned over and listened.

His mother was still padding down the hallway, her slippers simultaneously dragging and thumping on the scarred wooden floor. He could hear her walking from closet to back porch to closet again, the squeak of the rusty hinges on the folding doors. From the living room, the crack and hiss of his father opening another can of beer, and the fuzzy sounds of the late-night news. Even Cindy was tossing and turning in her bed on the other side of his bedroom wall, her small feet kicking the spot right by his head.

He waited and waited, but it was no use. He thought that he may as well rest his eyes until the low noise settled (his father burped, his mother dragged a chair across the kitchen floor), perhaps sleep—just a little—until the quiet finally came.

He stood in the middle of a ballroom, illuminated by one enormous chandelier that was the size of his father's Oldsmobile. Danny looked down. He was wearing brown corduroys with knees worn smooth, and his brown shoes, so small that he could feel his toes scrunching up under the leather. How on earth had he arrived in this place, with its mirrored walls and parquet floor, looking like this? He wiped his clammy hands on the seat of his pants.

In one of the mirrors, he could see a door (a fabulous door, decorated with stars made of glitter) opening and closing, and a slip of something green slid into the room. He turned around and Miss Val, the Siamese Kitten herself, stood in front of him, both her hands on her hips. She smiled and the painted beauty mark on her cheek lifted and then fell.

"My little Danny," she said, "what are you doing here?"

He felt himself blushing. "I guess I was waiting for you."

Miss Val laughed. "In those clothes? Honey, we have a ball to get ready for!"

Danny crossed his arms over his chest. "I don't have anything else."

"Well, we'll fix that, won't we?"

Miss Val opened the lid of a fantastically bejewelled chest in the corner. She rummaged through piles of silk and satin and muttered to herself, "I can never find anything in here." After a few minutes, she drew out a small black tuxedo on a hanger, complete with red bow tie and cummerbund. "There, you see? Now, put this on before anyone arrives."

As Miss Val was tying his bow tie into a fat knot, the double doors at the end of the room opened and a line of finely dressed men and women entered, their arms linked in couples, the women's skirts brushing the floor. Miss Val placed a hand on Danny's head and whispered, "Be yourself, sweetie, and everybody will love you."

While Miss Val chatted with the people in the crowd, Danny stayed as close to her as he dared, his nose on level with her gloved elbow. He stared at her green strapless dress, at the ruching on its sides and the slit up the thigh. *How wonderful.*

The music started and couples floated out into the middle of the room, the women with their necks held gracefully, like porcelain figures, the men smiling, close-lipped, over their partners' shoulders. It was all so flawless, without dust or pickles or the smell of bubble gum. Danny heard Miss Val laugh and he looked up at her clear, white face.

Gently, he tugged on her hand.

"Yes, honey?"

Danny bowed his head and, in as low a voice as he could manage, said, "Would you care to dance?"

Miss Val smiled and took his hand in hers. "Why, of course."

They spun out onto the dance floor, his left arm clutching the fabric around her waist, his right holding her hand. He peered down at his own feet, careful not to step on her toes. Gently, she said to him, "Look up. Only a fellow with something to hide doesn't look into the eyes of his partner."

And so they danced, slipping through gaps in the crowd, skimming over the floor as if they weighed no more than feathers. He could see their bodies in the mirrors, the whirl of movement that meant they were fast and smooth, like the wind Danny felt when he stood at the top of the hill in the school playground. When the music stopped, Miss Val embraced him and his face was crushed against the smooth satin of her dress. He put his arms around her and closed his eyes, wondering if he could somehow make this moment last and last, preserve it with perfume or shellac it with hairspray. He sighed, because he knew that this was impossible and he would have to return to his real life.

He said, "There's something I want to tell you." There was nothing she couldn't understand. She would know how it was to feel like a Martian. She would help him figure out why he always stood apart from the other boys as they played in the schoolyard. She would never look at him with disappointment or confusion. Or sound like she was sorry whenever she spoke. Or plod down the street in tan walking shoes when all Danny ever wanted was to see her in a pair of high heels.

Val knelt in front of him and touched his cheek with her cool hand. "I have a secret too."

And he leaned forward, his ear practically touching her red lips. She breathed in and he shivered, knowing the words were coming very soon. She would know everything about him and he would know everything about her.

Danny woke with a start, rubbed his eyes in the grey light of early morning. He stood and pressed his nose to the window. Even though his small room looked out at the house beside theirs (a newer, taller house, covered not in wooden siding, but in a fine layer of beige gravel with bits of granite that winked in the sunlight and grew shiny in the rain), Danny could see the reflection of the sky in the neighbour's window.

Usually, in this small square of glass, he tracked the speed of the clouds, the magical break in the mist when the sun shone for one second, long enough to illuminate everything and remind him that it couldn't possibly rain all the time. But now he squinted at the barely blue sky and listened, hearing nothing but the two-note song of the bird that lived in the scrawny birch tree across the street. He must have slept through the night, but it was just as well, because the house was still and he was sure everyone was sleeping.

He crawled under his bed and pulled out the pile of department store catalogues from its hiding place behind two shoeboxes in the far right-hand corner. Sitting on the floor, he opened the newest one—the one his mother saved for him two months ago by pinching it from the morning mail before his father saw. He traced his sticky finger along the lines of the long dresses, the dangling strands of imitation pearls, the gloved hands of the one lucky little girl modelling her white, rabbit fur coat. The thin, glossy pages were dotted with his fingerprints, and small clumps of dust had collected in the spine. He lingered on his favourite page, the one with the teen-aged boy wearing a navy-blue sweater vest and white shorts, his hair parted on the side. Like a real movie star stepping out to play tennis in a city with palm trees swaying in the warm breeze. Someplace far from here. He wondered if any of the boys he knew saved catalogues like he did, but of course no one else did. Of course he was the only one.

Outside, he heard Mr. Murray open his front door for his morning newspaper and Danny knew he had only a few minutes before his mother woke up and began gathering the dirty sheets for laundry day. He reached inside his pillowcase and unravelled a long, emerald-green silk sash. He folded it over and over again, pressing down each fold with his small hand until the creases were sharp and the belt was flat and no bigger than a handkerchief. He slipped it between two catalogues, *Winter 1957* and *Spring 1958*, and pushed the whole pile back under his bed, careful to slide his two shoeboxes into place again. Even in the middle of summer, the mornings were cold, and the floor beneath Danny's bare feet bit into his soles. He climbed back into bed and waited for his mother to knock on his door, whispering in Chinese, in that apologetic way of hers that he hated most, "Time to get up, Danny. Breakfast is ready."

The summer days began to blend together. Danny had forgotten how long it had been since he and Cindy walked to school in the cool mornings and pressed their shoes into the thick frost blanketing Mrs. Fratelli's lawn. He lay on the folding lounge chair on the back porch, the flesh on the backs of his legs oozing through the holes in the woven plastic cover. A cloud like a spooked horse and another in the shape of a feather duster passed overhead.

Cindy's face hovered above him. Her thick bangs were held back with a yellow plastic barrette and she shaded her eyes with her left hand. Her right hand held an old cookie tin.

"It's time for paper dolls, Danny," she said, shaking the tin so that they could both hear the scissors and coloured pencils bouncing around inside.

"Can't you play with Jeannie next door?" he asked, drowsy from the sunshine.

"She's at camp. And no one draws better than you. Please, Danny?"

He blinked against the harsh light and tried to remember the last time he rode his bike to Marcello's house two blocks away. Yesterday? It was too hot to play outside and, besides, Danny was never convinced Marcello really wanted to play with him. He was just too polite to say otherwise. Maybe it *was* time for paper dolls.

In Cindy's bedroom, they drew and cut out paper dolls from their father's used and carefully refolded brown wrapping paper. They giggled, marched their dolls across Cindy's bed, changing the dolls' clothes for brunch, drinks at the club, or a dinner date with a dashing young doctor. Through the thin walls, they could hear their mother wringing out the wet laundry in the bathtub and cleaning the floors with the grey, stringy mop that, when propped in the corner of the bathroom, looked like a skinny, dishevelled old man, the kind who insisted on holding your hand while he was telling your parents what a fine little boy you had become.

"They should go to a party, I think. Maybe Anastasia will wear the pink dress with the white bow. Glamorous, right, Danny?"

But Danny was busy making a new paper doll, one with black bobbed hair like midnight, and a green robe. Cindy, looking up from Anastasia's honey-blond head, wrinkled her nose and said, "She doesn't look like any paper doll I've ever seen." But Danny took no notice (little sisters, what do they know?) and propped up his new creation on a tissue box. He tried to remember what Marcello's teenaged brother told him about the women who danced at the Shanghai Junk. Danny wiggled the paper doll's bum and sashayed her around the stage while Cindy laughed and laughed, her chubby hands held up to her mouth. Finally, Danny pulled the doll's clothes off, piece by piece. He poked Cindy in the leg and whispered, "You have to clap, dummy. It's almost the end of her act."

And the doll bowed to thundering, appreciative applause before sauntering off, obscured from the crowd by one white tissue standing up in the box, in folds like a stage curtain.

As Danny was carefully re-dressing his paper dancer, their mother hurried into the bedroom. "Baba doesn't like to see the mess. Put the dolls away," she said, her eyes wide open and searching the room for any stray paper clothes. "Cindy, take them to your room. You shouldn't play like this with your brother anyway."

Generally, their father hardly noticed the house at all or most of the objects inside it. But Danny knew that the paper dolls were the one thing that might rouse his father out of his television, beer and armchair stupor, so he helped Cindy pile them into the box as quickly as his small hands allowed.

"Summertime," Danny heard his father mutter as he walked through the front door. "Nothing but tourists."

After dinner, Danny sat in the bathtub while his mother washed his hair, her thick fingers massaging his scalp. He closed his eyes, breathed in the steam rising from the water and the smell of soap and shampoo and his own wet skin.

"Wake up, Danny. It's very dangerous to fall asleep in the bath." She tapped his shoulder with a sudsy hand.

He turned his head and looked at her face. Small round eyes. Cheeks like brown apples. A wide mouth that smiled and opened for whispers and quiet complaints, but never for laughter that caught you off balance or blew through the house like a cedar-scented windstorm. He saw that her sleeves, once pushed up but now falling, were soaked. *What if we just curled her hair?* he thought. *She could wear real stockings and not those dumb white socks.* Maybe she wasn't always like this.

"Tell me a story, Mama. About you and Ba when you were young."

She clucked and poured water from an ancient, cracked rice bowl over his head. "Those old stories. I don't know why you love them so much."

"Please, Mama."

It was the same story every time, told in the same way, in his mother's soft voice. Doug Lim was a fast-talking Chinatown boy, one of the few born in Canada back then. He was the undisputed king of gin rummy and, many times, she saw him slam his fist on the table in victory as the cards flew up into the air and the glasses rattled. "Not everyone liked him, you know," she said frowning. "Young men don't like to lose all the time."

During the long evenings of summer, Doug used to race his father's produce delivery truck against the other boys' faster, newer Chryslers and Fords, the cars bought by the fathers who had managed to finish school and worked as notaries or salesmen or hospital technicians. Doug didn't win, of course, but the truck held up, never once spinning out of control or overheating in the sunshine.

"After I met him," Danny's mother whispered, scrubbing his back with a damp cloth, "I would tie my scarf around his arm and he would tell everyone, 'This race is for Betty.' Your father was very sweet then. He really wanted to marry me and have a son and daughter." She tilted up Danny's chin and said, "You should remember that and try to get along better."

He saw his mother in a red circle skirt, hair combed up into a bouncing ponytail. He wanted to ask if she had ever looked like that, but was afraid that she never had, and he would be left with an image of a less wrinkled, slightly thinner version of the woman she was now. Danny tried to imagine his father walking down the street with his hands in his pockets, his hips tilted forward in a teenaged boy's swagger, but all he saw was the same rounded, cranky man who ended up running a curio shop for the tourists he sneered at when they weren't watching.

Maybe everything changed when he decided to marry Betty, who had arrived in Vancouver from Hong Kong at sixteen to join her father. Maybe Doug fell in love with her quietness, with her wide mouth and round, sad eyes. Maybe he wanted this life, and hadn't fallen into it. Maybe, as a young man, he dreamed of having a little house like this one on Dundas, and maybe he didn't mind saving eggshells for fertilizing the garden, or layering sweaters to save on the heat in winter.

She dried Danny off with a large blue towel, mercilessly rubbing under his armpits and around his ears. The mirror above the sink was fogged over and Danny thought he might choke on the heavy dampness in the air. He looked at his mother's blurry reflection and imagined how beautiful she could look if she tried. She could wear some blush on her brown cheeks, even put on something with a low neck to show that she really was a woman underneath the shapeless cardigans and wool slacks. But he knew that if he even suggested it to her, she would knit her ungroomed eye-brows together and stare at him like she might stare at a two-headed cat.

"Have you heard enough for tonight?" Betty smiled, but her eyes didn't change, didn't crinkle up in mirth the way Cindy's did when Danny made a funny face. "Was that a good story?"

As he pulled on his pyjamas, he nodded and said what he always did: "Yes, Mama. The greatest."

The morning light hurt Danny's eyes and he curled up in bed, the covers pulled over his face. He could hear Cindy's voice, clear and shrill. "It's Thursday, right? We're going to help Ba at the shop today, right?"

The walls shook with his father's shout. "Don't you ever shut up? Every Thursday, it's the same thing. Mama goes to clean the big house and you and your brother come to the shop with me. You know how it works, so stop talking. All I want is a little quiet to eat my goddamned toast."

Then, silence. Danny felt sleep dragging him down, felt the warmth of his blankets pooling around his body.

His mother opened the door to his bedroom and put a hand on his forehead. "Are you feeling all right, Danny? It's not like you to be late for breakfast."

He peered up at her, his eyes rolling slowly underneath hot lids.

Doug's face peered around the door frame. "Is he sick? I can't have him spreading germs all over the shop."

Betty turned and said, "But I have to go to work. He can't stay home by himself."

His father began walking away, toward the kitchen. "Then take him with you. It's a big house. There has to be some place he can hide."

His mother pulled the blankets down and helped Danny get dressed. Even the act of stepping into his pants pained him, made his joints shudder with the effort. She rummaged in the cupboards for some crackers and an apple and packed them in her purse. Holding hands, they hurried down the street toward the bus stop, where the sun pushed on Danny's head and he shivered in the heat.

When they stepped off the bus, all Danny could see were the tall trees lining King Edward Avenue and the boulevard in the middle covered with grass. He stared, searching for one stray brown blade, but found only an even, unblemished green carpet.

As Danny and Betty walked up the street, they could see the house through gaps in the shrubbery. First the stone facade and double, panelled front door, then the high, peaked roof with the spinning, wrought-iron weathervane. By the time they reached the circular driveway, Danny's hands had grown cold, and his mother folded the one she was holding into the pocket of her skirt.

He saw dark shadows moving behind the windows, changing shape as they flitted past each diamond-shaped, narrow pane. The stones flanking the front door seemed obscenely alive—bulging, round, pushing out of the walls before receding again.

They knocked on the side door and a broad woman with blond hair fading to white answered. She nodded at Betty before glaring at Danny, who peeked around his mother's body.

"Why is he here?" she asked, in an accent Danny was sure he'd heard before, maybe in a movie.

Betty bowed her head before speaking. "He's sick today, Mrs. Lehmann, and can't stay at home by himself. I thought he could sit in the kitchen."

Mrs. Lehmann wiped her hands on her apron. "Well, he can't. What if he sneezes on the food? Better take him with you. The family won't be home until suppertime." And she walked away, her hips falling heavily as she stepped across the room.

Danny followed his mother from room to room, carrying her rags as she hauled the domed, shiny metal vacuum up the stairs. The children's rooms were first, and Danny, careful not to touch anything, sat at their desks, his eyes wandering over model airplanes, a silver tray covered with hair ribbons and barrettes, stuffed animals arranged precisely at the foot of each bed. When his mother wasn't looking, he traced his fingers over the wallpaper, the lions and tigers in the boy's room, and Little Bo Peep with her herd of fat, fleecy sheep in the other.

The master bedroom was dark; all four of its windows were covered in thick purple curtains. When Betty pulled them open, Danny could see the mess: the unmade bed with sheets wrinkled and twisted, the water glass overturned on the nightstand, the clothes all over the floor, sleeves reaching limply out like empty skin. And the smell. Even Danny, with his stuffed nose, could detect that tang of bodies, of wine gone sweet as it slowly evaporated into the air, of expensive, ethereal perfume wasted on the stale, motionless air in this silent room.

His mother, her face screwed up, opened the windows before she began to clean, pausing long enough to pat Danny on the head and whisper in Chinese, "My boy would never be this messy. You'll be the good kind of husband, won't you? You'll help your wife clean and not shout or argue. You'll be the nicest man, Danny. I just know it."

When they had gone upstairs to clean, Mrs. Lehmann had been kneading bread dough and listening to the radio. But in this bedroom, he couldn't hear anything that would suggest there was another living creature inside this house; only the swish and thump of his own mother as she cleaned, and the shiver of leaves outside in the wind.

"Almost done, Danny," Betty said, straightening up with her hand resting in the small of her back. "And then we'll go home, have some cool noodles with cucumber." She walked to the door beside the carved wood headboard and opened it.

Clothes hanging from racks on all four walls. Shoes arranged in rows on the floor, in shelves, even in drawers. A three-sided, full-length mirror and a hanging chandelier, the crystals sending out fragments of light, tiny rainbows that danced around the room.

"The lady's dressing room," Betty whispered as she pointed Danny toward a silk-covered stool in front of the mirror. "Pretty, don't you think? All these clothes though. I have to put mothballs everywhere." She smiled as she looked at Danny's reflection. "I know what you're thinking. So impractical. So silly. Right?" She paused as she looked at his wide-open eyes. "Don't tell your father you were in here."

He nodded absentmindedly as he stared at a row of evening gowns, the deep colours like jewels. Black, green, red, gold and silver. Danny wanted to bury his face in the skirts, tear the dresses off the hangers and jump into the silken pile on the floor. How would it feel if those long skirts were tangled around his legs, if he could run his finger along an expertly sewn seam? He could take one of these dresses home and keep it in his bed, where he could lie with it every night and dream that he was dancing in a ballroom, leading one of his paper dolls come to life. Afraid that he couldn't control his own fingers, he sat on his hands and kept his eyes on his dull brown shoes, the laces knotted over and over again because his parents couldn't afford to buy new ones. He told himself that he would be willing to miss out on another breakfast of congee instead if that would help save money.

As they were leaving, Mrs. Lehmann handed him a cookie in a paper napkin. "He looks pale, Betty. He'd better have something for the trip home. You were so quiet, Danny. I hardly even knew you were here." She smiled down at him, showing the silver caps on her teeth and the deep wrinkles around her mouth. Danny smiled back, and wondered what the lady of the house looked like, whether she wore silk every day and how she arranged her hair. He bit into the cookie— thick, dense and gingery—and Mrs. Lehmann nodded kindly.

He fell asleep on the bus ride home, his fists covered by the sleeves of his thin jacket, his head resting on his mother's arm. He dreamed that he was walking back toward the house and could see in the window the outline of a woman—curled hair, sharp shoulders protruding from a well-tailored dress. He called to her from the lawn and he swore that he saw the glint of her green eyes as she glanced at him through those tiny panes that distorted everything. Her shadow paused, as if considering this grubby little boy with the uncombed hair. He woke up to the bump of the bus and the odour of his mother, a smell like Comet and cooking oil, comforting but oh, so ordinary.

The last days of summer had crept up. Danny felt that autumn might arrive any minute and the long evenings would then recede, leaving the burning of leaves in backyards and the wearing of woolly socks in bed. Next week, school would start again.

On the way to the shop, Danny looked up through the open car window at the power lines, the crows sitting in a line, unruffled by the electricity pulsing under their feet or the wind blowing in from the west.

By ten o'clock, Cindy was dusting the shelves, carefully lifting and replacing the ceramic lucky cats, the small brass buddhas and the tea sets painted with cherry blossoms and bamboo. Danny saw her press her index finger to her upper lip, and knew that she was trying to contain a sneeze. Once, she coughed on a box of folded-paper fans and their father locked her in the storage closet for two full hours for contaminating the merchandise. "If you're going to cough, you run outside first," he shouted at her through the closet door. Danny could hear her sniffling (quietly, so Doug wouldn't notice from his perch behind the front counter), but didn't dare say anything. When she was let out, she simply sat on a stool at the back, rolling two metal worry balls in her hands.

Now, Danny unpacked a box of silk placemats, black with red Chinese characters that he couldn't read. As he was pulling out the paper stuffing, his father snapped, "Stop throwing that on the floor. The garbage can is right there. Lazy." Danny froze then hastily gathered up his mess.

The high, narrow windows in the backroom were open and he could hear the trucks that sped down the alleys, the sounds of men unloading crates of produce and pushing them along the concrete toward the back doors of the shops. He heard the cries of a colony of seagulls and, when he looked up, he watched the grey and white of their wings, the rapid flapping that meant they were fighting for the same piece of food, perhaps a glob of sticky rice or a squished banana. A conversation between two men floated in on the air and Danny, bored with the emptiness filling the shop, strained to listen.

"My wife wants to start her own produce store. Outside of Chinatown, she says, where people have money."

"Yeah? What does she know? Does she know how to run a business?"

"That's what I was thinking, but you can't say those things to your wife. She might clamp those legs shut for a month." Danny winced, but kept listening.

"You know, you can fix that sort of problem. Lots of girls around here willing to do what you need for a little bit of cash." Both men laughed and the sound was distorted and ugly, like a radio whining between stations.

"I feel guilty enough going to see the strippers. But boy, some of those ladies can dance."

"Have you seen the one they call the Siamese Kitten? Some legs on her. And she dresses up Chinese, so, really, it's no different than being with your wife."

"I wonder what she'd do for a little extra cash on the side?"

They laughed again and Danny stared at the empty placemat box. He wanted to run out the back door and throw garbage at these two men. Miss Val commanded a stage and wore satin. She could have been a movie star. What had they ever done? Slowly, as his anger cleared, he began to feel sorry for those men who spent most of their days staring at apples and wilted greens. They would never know the touch of Miss Val's hand on their hair, never see her red lips break into a smile that, to Danny, meant love and caring and held a little bit of weariness. After lunch, the shop filled with tourists and he saw that his father was busy juggling three white families who all wanted to buy the last jade monkey on the shelf. Danny tiptoed through the store, careful to duck so that he was obscured by the shelves and customers, and hurried out the front door.

He knew where he was going; there was no question, really. He didn't even look at the jars of candy in the newsagent's window, or stop to say hello to Clarence, Mr. Ng's son who helped his father change and clean the tanks in the fish shop. He headed a few blocks west, turned right and then right again into a familiar alley.

He stopped at a partially open grey door. He could see nothing from where he was standing, so he stepped closer until he could smell the cigarette smoke and hear, faintly, the tinny sounds of a piano being played with more force than finesse. Silently, he reached out and pulled the door open wide enough for him to slip through.

This had to be back stage; it was just like the auditorium at school. Danny could make out shapes hanging from the ceiling and stacks of boxes piled against the walls. He inched forward, his hands stretched in front of him until his eyes adjusted. Wires on the floor, coiling and stretching in all different directions. Sandbags weighing down ropes that hung from a catwalk above. To his left, a crack in the darkness. It took a few seconds until Danny realized that the sliver of light he was seeing was the narrow meeting place between two curtains. The stage curtains.

He desperately hoped that his shoes wouldn't squeak on the floor as he walked toward the gap. His heart was beating like a rabbit's, and his skin felt no thicker than a tissue. Every sound made him jump, but he kept walking. He stopped when he was behind the curtains at centre stage. The Siamese Kitten must be dancing steps away.

Taking a deep breath, he leaned forward and peered through the curtains. At first, all he saw were the lights—the bright spotlight, the other smaller lights in different colours suspended from the catwalk. But soon enough, he caught a glimpse of skin, the long, extended flesh of an arm, a glove being peeled off slowly, but not so slowly that the audience lost interest. He heard men whistling, could see one or two of them leaning forward in their chairs, their hands cupped around their mouths as they shouted toward the stage. "We want to see your fanny! Come on, give us a little bump and grind!" Danny was appalled. How could these men shout at Miss Val like that? Treating her like the bearded lady in a circus. How rude!

He pulled open the right curtain an inch so he could see Miss Val's costume. He wondered if she wore the same clothes at every performance, or if she rotated, pulling out a blue gown for Tuesdays and a red cape for Fridays. He tilted his head until he could see her clearly.

But it wasn't Miss Val. No, this was a different woman altogether, a woman with curly blond hair like Shirley Temple, a woman in a short, white dress with ruffles on the skirt and ankle socks and shiny black Mary Janes. In his surprise, Danny let go of the curtain and stumbled forward, just a step and a half, but it was enough.

The blond dancer's head whipped around and her eyes narrowed as she spied Danny. He stepped behind the curtain, his breath coming sharply, his head turning left and right, his eyes looking for the quickest way out. As he was about to run off the way he had come, he heard her voice through the curtains.

"Kid, you'd best get out of here. The manager won't like the looks of you." She spun on her toes and glared through the crack before turning back to the audience with a wink and a smile.

The wisest thing, of course, would be for Danny to slip away as fast as he could, but he couldn't resist leaning toward the curtain and whispering, "Where is the Siamese Kitten?"

The piano player pounded on the keys and, by the rise in volume, Danny knew this must be the climax of the act. He heard her shoes tapping on the floor.

"Val? I don't know, kid. She stopped dancing at least a month ago, at the start of the summer. I heard she's retired. Now scram before anyone catches on that I'm talking to someone back there."

"But I wanted to tell her something," he insisted.

The dancer pushed her hand through the curtains and waved him away, her fingernails—painted lavender and chipped on the sides—flicking the air. Danny stepped backward, then peered past her arm and into the crowd, hoping to

catch a glimpse of Miss Val in the balcony or maybe walking
up the aisle. The theatre was partially full and only the first
eight rows were occupied. An old man, bald except for a tuft
of white hair that stood up straight from the back of his head,
leaned forward in his front-row seat, elbows on his knees, his
face empty, his cheeks hollow like those of the toothless men
who continuously drank coffee in Mr. Gin's café. Behind him,
a younger man with black hair combed away from his forehead tapped his fingers on the back of a seat. He seemed to
be vibrating from head to toe while his squirrel-like amber
eyes remained locked on the dancer. His nostrils flared a bit
when she shimmied to centre stage and her skirt twirled
upward. Danny shivered because he was watching a man
watching a near-naked woman, which seemed naughtier than
watching a naked woman all alone.

In the back, underneath the protruding balcony, a lone
figure sat, half in and half out of the heavy dark. Danny
squinted. There was something familiar in the way the head
was tilted to the side, in the line of the shoulders leaning back
in the red upholstered seat. An usherette in a red and gold hat
shone a flashlight into the rows and the shadows disappeared
for one second, long enough for him to see that the figure in
the back with the small eyes wide open was someone he knew.
His mother.

He opened his mouth to call out to her, but clamped it
shut in anger instead. How could his practical, workaday
mother be sitting here, in this place, where women were supposed to shine like stars or comets? What did she care for
fancy clothes and fast music? He had come here to find Miss
Val, to be dazzled and awestruck, and to be somewhere else

besides the shop or their sad little house. He should run at his mother right now and tell her to get out. But then he remembered that he was supposed to be at the shop, counting his father's inventory of teacups. If she saw him, she might tell his father and Danny didn't need to hear any more shouting. He punched his right fist into his left hand and stomped into the darkness, shoulders quivering.

When he was past the sandbags, he stopped. Which way should he turn? A cool breeze blew past his left ear and he turned toward it, thinking he could smell the garbage cans in the alley outside. With every step, he felt the floor with the toe of his shoes, afraid there might be stairs or even a trap door that might drop him into the tunnels his father once claimed ran like rivers underneath the whole city. He shivered.

He was in a narrow hallway with a line of doors on each side. He looked up, down, in front and behind and still nothing looked familiar, only cramped and dim and strange. A triangle of light appeared at the end of the hall and Danny hurried in its direction, thinking it was sunshine. As he squinted through the dark he saw the light shimmer and gain shape, and he thought he saw a flash of green fabric and a sliver of cigarette smoke spill out into the hall. He heard high-pitched laughter and a crowd of ladies' voices, each layered on top of another. "Miss Val," he half called, "is that you?"

In the open doorway he stopped. Five heads turned and looked directly at him.

He stared at the women, at their bare legs and stockinged ones, the flesh spilling out over the tops of corsets, the shoulders sloped forward and criss-crossed with straps. He took a step forward and whispered, "Miss Val," without really knowing which of the dancers he was talking to. He was sure he had seen her while he was running through the hall. Was that the Siamese Kitten's dark hair? Or was it the bobbed head of his mother, shining in this room like it never had before?

The room was full, stuffed like the stockings that hung in the Woodward's display windows every December. Elvis Presley blared out of a radio set on the concrete floor. To the right, pink, blue, striped and sequined costumes dangled from a wheeled rack. Two brassieres and one stocking were draped over a pipe heater. To the left, a table was piled with lipsticks and creams, perfumes and hairbrushes. And directly opposite hung six mirrors, each lit by one bare light bulb. Danny counted six chairs.

All Danny could hear was his mother's voice, that sing-song tone she used whenever she was trying to tell him something very important. "Remember," she said to him yesterday, as she hurried him up the street on the way home from grocery shopping, "you must never wander off by yourself. Evil woman-demons are always looking for sweet little boys like you." He frowned. He was quite sure no woman-demon ever put this much effort into making herself look pretty.

One of the women stood up. A black feather escaped from her headdress and floated through the air, catching the draft from the ceiling vent. Danny remembered how cold he was and rubbed his left arm with his right hand.

"What are you doing here?" asked the woman with the heavily lined eyes and Cleopatra wig.

"The Siamese Kitten," he said, in a voice barely above a whisper.

"Are you looking for Val?"

Danny nodded. This dancer towered in her high heels, far taller than any woman he had ever seen. He could not see her face; instead, he stared at her black stockings and the feathers sewn into her romper.

"She left without much notice and didn't say where she was going. Sorry, kid."

He closed his eyes against the mirrors, the reflections that turned the five dancers into ten and then twenty and beyond.

"Did you come here all by yourself?" Danny felt the weight of her hand on his shoulder as he leaned against the door frame.

When he opened his eyes again, the women were crouching around him in a half-circle, so close that he could smell their skin, the dampness that collected in their belly buttons or under their arms. A ring with a purple stone flashed and he saw long fingers topped with bare ragged nails, the kind that have been chewed and chewed, the kind that picked dried food off dishes in scalding hot water.

He was silent.

"I don't think he speaks much English," one of the dancers said.

"He's clearly lost," said another.

Danny heard a giggle. "He's cute as a button though. I could use him in the act. He could carry my train for me."

"Watch out, that might be a hit. Some of those old guys out there like little boys more than they should."

A storm of laughter erupted around him and he turned and ran out of the room, down the hallway, behind the stage and out the grey door.

Danny blinked at the bright afternoon light. He walked through the alley and around the corner, his head down so that all he saw were the colourless sidewalks, filmed with fine dirt brought in on the dry wind. He had to go back to the shop—there was no question of that—but he wanted to sit on the curb and feel the sun soak into his black hair until he couldn't stand it any longer, feel the sweat that would inevitably drip down his spine and collect behind his knees.

He wanted to tell Miss Val all the things he had never told anyone else, about the secrets he had hidden under his bed, how his father was pleased with nothing, the time at school when he was picked last for the T-ball team and the other boys didn't even look him in the eye, the way his mother smiled as if she had never learned what smiling actually meant. Once upon a time, he thought he could tell rich and jolly Uncle Kwan a secret or two, but after letting it slip that he would rather take tap dance lessons than play basketball, Uncle Kwan started to ignore him, and simply nodded curtly in greeting when they met. Danny ached when he thought of Miss Val. He wanted to burrow his head into her stomach, listen to the blood pumping through her body and twist his small fingers into the satin of her robe.

"It's okay if no one understands you," she might have said. "I do."

After he nodded, she would continue, "We're the same, you know. We grow up wanting something different, something beautiful and glamorous. Who cares about mops and peeling potatoes? Everyone else, they're boring. We're the fascinating ones. You'll see."

And he would know she was right. They were the exception, the two huddled in the corner when everyone else crowded into the middle. Maybe if he had found her, he could have gone home feeling newly empty and free. Another person would know his secrets and he could look at his soggy house and sullen family without feeling that he was brimming over with dangerous, hidden things. Then his father might love him and his mother could be happier.

Maybe she would have told him all about her own secrets too. He could grasp her hand and listen to the flash and bang and buzz of her life story, one that he imagined was filled with lights and clothes that shimmered in the dark. And he would try to learn from what she said, because she was the one person he had ever met who smelled and looked real but whose whole self was dripping with star quality. She was impeccable, but not so much that he couldn't throw his arms around her waist and close his eyes against her belly. *Maybe one day*, he thought, *I'll be lovely and famous too*.

But it was one foot in front of the other on these streets he knew so well that he could close his eyes and feel his way back to the shop through the soles of his shoes. He would never find Miss Val now. In an hour and a half, he would see his mother at home, trimming the ends off bok choy and slicing chicken into thin strips. He wanted to rush into the house and beat his fists into her stomach. He had been looking for *Miss Val*, not her. She was there when he woke up in the mornings, there as he fell asleep at night, shuffling down the hallway and cleaning the floors. Even now, she was there, sitting like a brown lump in a club that should have been full of women who were glittering and colourful. But as he came closer to the shop, he knew he wouldn't say or do anything to betray where he had been. The truth meant trouble, so it would probably be an evening like any other: she would cook, they would eat and he would fall asleep. Except tonight, with his face turned toward his open window, his mind would churn because he knew Miss Val and his mother had set foot in the same place. His head ached with the strangeness of it all.

THE MOVIE

1982

Danny resents the hardness of afternoon sunshine, when the sky is so bright that it isn't blue any longer, only a thin, brittle off-white that is indistinguishable from the wisps of clouds or the exhaust trails of airplanes. He wonders if July in Vancouver has ever been this hot. He walks down East Pender Street, squinting behind his dark glasses. He doesn't need to look at the street signs or the numbers on the buildings; Chinatown is a place his body remembers. When he crosses Main, he sees it right away. The curio shop.

The same string of bells tinkles when he pushes open the door. Doug is standing at the back counter pulling out jade pendants for a customer. When he sees Danny standing awkwardly by the display of twisted bamboo plants, his face suddenly, inexplicably, brightens. He hurries the elderly woman along, saying, "This one is the best. I'll give you my lowest price." She grows flustered at his efficiency and buys whatever it is that he pushes toward her before turning, head down, and stumbling out the door.

Danny doesn't know what has happened. Now he sees his father coming toward him with something close to a smile, an expression that moves underneath the skin as if surprise and happiness and eagerness are fighting to break the surface. He wonders if it pains him, this almost-smiling, if those long-unused muscles are growing sore from the effort. This is the first time Danny has come to the shop since he was a teenager and he fidgets, his fingers rubbing at the lining in his pockets.

"Hi Dad," he says, wincing at the echo of his voice against the high ceiling.

"Danny, you didn't tell me you were coming! You should have said something at dinner. But it's okay. I can close up for an hour and we can go for coffee."

All at once, Danny knows that Doug thinks this is the real homecoming: the son returning to his father's business. He can see Doug's thoughts floating between them. *He'll take over the store. He's come back unexpectedly because he really wants to be here.*

"I need some parasols for a wedding. The woman getting married wants her bridesmaids to carry them instead of flowers. I told her I could get them from you."

"Sure, sure. We have lots of those. But you can stay for a while, right?"

He can't look at his father anymore, standing like that, eyes wide open like it's Christmas. He turns his head and looks out the window at the insurance company's neon sign across the street.

"No, I have to take off. Another time?"

Doug nods, his face falling back into its familiar lines of grump and irritation, and leads his son into the backroom, where the best stock, untouched by customers, sits wrapped in plastic. As he hands Danny parasol after parasol, he keeps silent, shaking his head whenever they hear the scratching of mice in the walls. Danny could stay, could even share a dough-nut and some coffee at the café down the street, but he feels the hairs on his arms stiffen and the muscles in his face tighten at the smell of damp in the walls, the sounds of haggling old women coming in through the open, barred window. He is afraid to look up at the shelves of miniature buddhas for fear that they know exactly what he's thinking and frown to show their disapproval.

On the corner table, beside the big roll of brown wrap-ping paper, Danny sees a pile of posters. He peers at them through the fluorescent light.

"Dad, what are those?"

Doug turns his head and grunts. "Those? A bunch of junky old movie posters. Uncle Kwan bought that whole stack in California the last time he went golfing. Said he thought they would be good sellers here, said all the kids are buying up garbage like that for their apartments. I don't even know how much to charge for them. Ah, they won't sell anyway."

Danny walks over to the table and begins to pick his way through the stack. "You've got *All About Eve* and *Some Like It Hot* here. These will sell for sure."

"You wait. All the good ones are on top."

Danny riffles through the pile, stopping at famous movies or obscure ones with funny titles. One poster from the middle stops him, a poster bordered with a stripe of bright poppy red. A young woman, all legs and tightly curled blond hair, hides behind a giant fan of feathers, coyly puckering her shiny lips. On her feet, glittering silver shoes.

"*The Dream Girl*," Danny reads. "A farm girl from America's Heartland, yearning to be a Broadway star, is forced to become an exotic dancer, bumping and grinding her way through New York City's raciest clubs. Will she escape this degenerate life, dignity intact? Or will she be eaten alive by drink, fast men and faster cars? Featuring newcomer Lily Jansen and a special appearance by none other than the infamous, bodacious SIAMESE KITTEN."

Danny stares. There, in a corner of the poster, is a small illustration of Miss Val herself, a cigarette held to her lips with one black-gloved hand. Her eyes are narrowed at the blond actress, as if she is wondering how a rookie like this managed to land top billing. The smoke winds around her forehead and hair. He traces his fingers over the line of her cheek, feels the thin paper wrinkling. He feels like he did when he was a little boy and stumbled on the Siamese Kitten in that dark, narrow alley. His chest is full with air and the staccato beating of his heart. He doesn't know what this discovery means and he is restless with the need to snatch the poster and hold it to his face so he can scrutinize every dot of colour, every oversized letter.

He hears his father's voice at his left ear. "You see? All these movies no one ever heard of."

Danny turns around, rolling the poster up into a long tube. "I have to go, Dad. How much for the parasols and the poster?"

"You want that? What for?"

"I like it, that's all," Danny stammers. He reaches into his pocket for his wallet. "Seriously, how much?"

Doug waves his hand and looks away. "Nothing. Free."

"Are you sure? You don't want anything?"

His father starts to walk toward the front of the shop. "You come for dinner again and be nice to your mother. That's what I want."

The film flickers, travelling from one reel to the next. It's a small room in the library, with a screen that the librarian pulled down from the ceiling before she left Danny alone. One after the other, frames whirl by. The eye can, barely, distinguish one still from another, those frozen images of surprise, heartbreak, desire. One strong blink and all these disparate parts become a movie.

The plot is simple. Lily moves from Iowa to New York, stepping into Grand Central Station with two brown suitcases and a small purse slung over her shoulder. She is lit from above and her fine blond hair is almost white; not one shadow obscures her smooth, pale face. She looks for work, walking from theatre to theatre in her red plaid coat and blue beret, at first hopeful, then desperate and begging. A musical director promises her a part, his moustache twitching as the camera lingers on his thin, pointed face. Later, as she lies in his bed, sheets twisted around her breasts and the curve of her hips, he mocks her.

"You're good for one thing only and it ain't Broadway." He sneers as she struggles not to cry, her lips trembling, full like a child's.

She wanders the streets alone in the rain, shivering, her small umbrella poor protection against the sheets of water falling on the set all around her. The rain is lit like another actor; lights glint off its surface; it shimmers and dances as it bounces off Lily's umbrella, the newspaper box she is walking past. And then, a warm neon light. She enters a shabby theatre with hundreds of seats. Near-naked girls teasing the crowd with peek-a-boo fans. Lily is shocked by the expanses of skin and the hooting men in the audience, but she is also hungry and tired, and she asks for a job. The manager brings her back stage, where an experienced stripper, the best in the business, looks with disdain at the young, nubile girl she is supposed to turn into a star.

In the movie, this woman is called Jade, but there's no mistaking her: this is Miss Val. Her black wig. Those red, red lips. Her costume, green and black.

She cannot act, this is clear. Her voice is too strident for film and distorts the sound, like a microphone turned in on itself. She holds her head tilted up, so that her nose seems enormous, and the lights cast deep shadows in the hollows of her cheeks, under her stiff and jutted chin. She delivers her lines with the same emotion every time: a mixture of contempt and sarcasm.

And yet she fills the screen with her presence, dwarfs the other actors around her. Their lines are barely heard, their faces barely noticed. Lily is nothing more than a simpering child compared with Miss Val. She is scared of this older woman, of the words she could utter if there were no script to follow.

Miss Val's scenes are few, and she performs one strip-tease, an elaborate number that is the first burlesque dance

Lily ever watches. She begins with her back to the audience, her tall body covered with a red and gold robe. When the first notes of her song begin with what sounds like a pan flute, she turns her head slowly. Miss Val wears a veil suspended from a fearsomely bejewelled headdress that bobs as she nods to the camera. The music picks up speed, and she twirls and pulls open her robe, revealing the bustier underneath. She extends one fishnet-covered leg slowly until it seems impossibly long. As she continues to dance, her face remains hidden for two full minutes until she rips the veil off, her nails like talons, pulling at the fabric. She smiles, and purrs like a cat. She doesn't sing. Instead, she talks in her halting, fake accent while peeling off her costume.

"I am your Chinese princess for tonight."

"I love to dance."

"My heart is broken. Maybe you can fix it?"

On film, the act is brash and loud. Miss Val is so brightly lit and filmed so close up that the texture of her foundation is visible, lightly crinkled, like the side of a nubuck shoe. She wiggles, holds up a painted bamboo fan to cover her G-stringed bottom and tasselled breasts. The camera is her audience and she tries to play to it, looking over her bare shoulder, staring straight into the lens as she runs her fingers over her stockings. It's easy to feel embarrassment, for it is clear that the Siamese Kitten's charms—her archness, the fluidity of her movements, the fluttering of her eyelids—are best viewed onstage, when her scent wafts through a theatre, when she looks directly at the loneliest man in the joint.

Later, Lily becomes more famous than Jade, and refuses to help her even when Jade is old and has lost all her money paying the debts of a gambling, drinking ex-husband. Lily grows hard and mean and her makeup becomes harsher, with sharp liquid eyeliner and overdrawn pink lips.

"I don't need anyone," she says when a nervous, hapless salesman asks her to marry him. "Not you, not my family. No one."

It is only when she discovers Jade dying in a grungy apartment—her unkempt brown hair spread out on the pillow beneath her, her hands trembling as they clutch the blanket— that she leaves the circuit forever. Jade takes one look at Lily's motionless hair and high, painted eyebrows, and stage-whispers, "You'll never be happy unless you let someone love you, Missy. See what's happened to me? It's sad, but at least I had a man once who loved me because of who I really was, and not who I was onstage."

Lily returns to her penthouse apartment and packs all of her glittery, expensive clothes in boxes and drives them to a homeless shelter where the bedraggled women stare, open-mouthed, at the evening gowns and high heels she pulls out to show them. In the last scene, Lily walks through Grand Central Station again, carrying those same two brown suitcases, and looks behind her once, her gaze travelling past the camera to something the viewer cannot see, before boarding a train bound for her hometown.

But the movie is really all about Miss Val, and everyone can see that. Who cares about her overacting, her large hands that flutter dramatically against her chest? It is Miss Val who sucks in all the light, who stamps her almost-real self on this strip of moving film.

—

Danny clutches the arms of his plastic chair. Behind him, the full reel of the projector is still spinning, the ends of the roll flapping in the airless room. In front, a blank square of light flashes on the screen. He can hear the noises of the library through the door—shuffling shoes, opening and closing filing cabinets and card catalogues. When he exits, clutching the film to his chest, the light forces itself in through his eyes and fills his head. He stumbles backward until he is leaning against a wall.

His younger self whispers, *Remember when you met her? Remember how she gave you those cigarettes and patted you on the head? There's no woman in the whole world like Miss Val. You looked for her once, maybe you'll find her this time.*

Now that his past has come to life, there is no shutting it out. He rubs his ear, but the voice is still there. One week ago, he would have silenced his old self immediately. But as he walks to the librarian's desk, he thinks of his return to his parents' house, Miss Val's belt, and the old curio shop whose unchanging, musty smell snaked through his childhood. Danny the child has emerged, newly feral and disobedient, determined to take down what the grown-up Danny thought was his previously fetterless, adult existence—lovers, clubs and all. That was the life he loved, one that he purposely created, conveniently carving off whatever parts of his past he didn't need. He looks at his reflection in the floor-to-ceiling window, expecting to see a little boy with uncombed hair and a rip in the knees of his jeans staring back at him. But he is relieved when he sees a transparent, pale version of himself, exactly as he remembers from this morning, with his short-sleeved shirt neatly tucked into his pants, his white tennis shoes spotless as always.

By the time he reaches the librarian's desk, he is able to smile.

"Thanks for all your help," he says.

"Oh, you're welcome. It's not often that someone asks for something out of the ordinary." She fiddles with a pen and looks up at Danny's face.

He's not sure how to end this conversation, so says, "I like your earrings. They warm up your face."

The librarian blushes and looks down at her desk. She tugs on her left earring before tilting her head to the side and saying, "Is there anything else you need?"

"Do you have any books or old magazines on burlesque here?"

"That movie is all we have, but I wonder if you might find something in the archives at the public radio station. It's worth a look if you have the time. The person you want to talk to is Jerry."

Danny nods and thanks her again. Even as he steps out into the street he can see the planes of Miss Val's face, the sharpness of her cheekbones and the square tip of her chin. Her eyelashes fluttered to the rhythm of her words. In the heat, the library's chill evaporates. Men and women walk past him on the sidewalk and their faces seem to bear the features of more familiar people. His parents. Edwin's grandmother. Cindy as a little girl. Frank. And, most of all, Miss Val.

When Cindy picks up the phone, Danny realizes that he has one thing to ask her. There is no way of padding his question in a different sort of conversation, one that is casual, that touches on the weather, or each other's workout regimens. But if he doesn't ask, he will be caught in a circle of worry and his own monologue, one that will rise and fall and whisper words like *mistake*, *forget*, *he was never yours to keep*. It's not just his childhood that is breaking up the surface. Other, more recent pasts have made their way through the veneer.

"Cindy, it's me."

Her voice brightens and Danny feels sick at the sound. "Danny! What a day. I thought you were Head Office; thank God you're not."

"Hard day, then?"

"You have no idea. Sometimes I think I should do something else, go work in the Cayman Islands or something, you know?"

He is having difficulty hearing her, and processing her words so that he can utter a logical response. He can hear the voices of the bank tellers and customers in the background, the monotonous hum of an office. How long has it been since Cindy spoke? He tries to remember her last remark.

"The Cayman Islands," he says. "There aren't any taxes there."

"Exactly. And lots of beaches and ocean. Do you think Mom and Dad would insist on going with me? Think of Dad in bathing trunks."

There's no time, he thinks. *Get it out.* "I need to ask you something."

Cindy pauses, but says cheerfully, "Sure. Go ahead."

"Does Frank ever ask about me?"

"Oh, Danny," Cindy whispers.

"I mean, I know it's been a long time, but I've been thinking about him because, well, I don't know why. But here

I am, calling you, asking you a question you probably can't answer in a way that will make me happy. I'm sorry. I'm sorry I called." Danny is ready to hang up the phone, to put an end to this humiliation masking as conversation.

"Wait. I'll tell you if you really want me to. Do you?"

He takes a deep breath, counts to ten, and lets it out. "Yes."

It was a few years ago that Danny had met Frank. Back then, Danny had often wondered if he was going to meet someone; the city itself seemed like such an unlikely meeting place, so separated into pockets where people walked and ate and worked, but never seemed to look into each other's eyes. Even when hidden behind the dark trees and enveloped in the blanketing silence of Stanley Park, where he shuddered with satisfaction at the heat generated by him and these other men, conversation seemed impossible. They held him, ran their hands over his body in the ways he wanted them to, whispered strange secrets into his ear sometimes. Still, when it was all over, he left alone and walked through the downtown streets with his collar turned up against the night-time breeze. No one followed. Until he met Frank, that was all he wanted.

Danny was at Cindy's twenty-sixth birthday party. They sat in a corner booth of a loud, full-to-capacity restaurant. Lights blinked on and off. Donna Summer beat mercilessly through hidden speakers. On the walls, fabric panels undulated in the slight draft, like skin stretching and relaxing.

He sat beside a blond woman from Cindy's aerobics class, who kept whispering into his ear that she loved to dance. Danny smiled and nodded, but avoided looking into her sharp grey eyes, fearing that she might never let his own eyes go once she locked on to them. Forty-five minutes into dinner, he heard a booming voice. "Cindy, I'm so sorry I'm late. The dog threw up in the hall, and I had to mop it up and then spray the whole place with Lysol to get rid of the smell. Is there a place for me to sit?"

Cindy gestured at the end of the table and the empty seat across from Danny. "Make room for Frank!" she shouted as she tightened the post on one of her dangling gold earrings. "Danny, be nice!"

What Danny saw was a tall man with thick brown hair and light blue, glow-in-the-dark eyes. His grey shirt was impeccably ironed and his teeth shone white and straight in the dim light. Frank reached across the table and offered his hand.

"I'm Frank. I work at the bank with Cindy. You must be her brother?"

Danny grasped his hand—warm and dry, with tiny hairs at the base of each knuckle. "Yes. I'm Danny."

"Nice to meet you, finally. She tells me all about you, all the time. It makes me wonder sometimes if she's trying to set us up."

A roaring started in Danny's ears and he wondered if the restaurant had suddenly shut off all the lights except for this single one suspended on a wire track right above Frank's head. He stared at the wave of his hair, the span of his shoulders, the joints visible under the skin at his wrists. *Now everyone here knows*, he thought, but he smiled, and the crowd seemed to recede into the surrounding darkness.

Slowly, as Frank and Danny talked, the room reappeared in his peripheral vision. Frank remained in the centre of it all, seeming to grow until his body took up all the space, looming and somehow benevolent. Danny was dimly aware that the blond woman beside him had shifted in her seat and turned her head to the right to concentrate on an accountant from Prince George. Danny laughed before he could stop himself.

Everyone could see him and Frank talking, staring at each other with eyes wide open and hands inches apart. They were the two gay men in a room full of people who knew why they were laughing, ordering drinks for each other, talking to no one else. And still, he didn't care. He wanted to reach across the table and cup Frank's face, feel that tender skin on his cheeks and chin and pull the two of them together. What if he stood on his chair and sang a wordless, godless hymn? What then? He wondered if this freedom might last forever.

They saw movies and went for dinner, talking until their tongues hurt. Eleven days after they met, in Frank's bedroom, with the curtains drawn against the streetlights outside, Danny folded himself into Frank's arms. They lay, Frank's stomach curved around Danny's spine, for hours, breathing in tandem, inhaling deeply into each other's skin and hair. When dawn filtered through the leaves on the red alder outside, they began to move together, their bodies slowly reaching for lips, thighs, hips. Danny ran his finger down the curve of Frank's jaw, whispering, "You're so beautiful." That afternoon, Frank saw Danny's photographs for the first time. "We should get these into a gallery," he said. "I'll help you." And even though Danny knew his images weren't good enough to be shown anywhere, he felt invincible, Frank's words like armour against his chest.

—

Through the phone, Danny can hear Cindy clear her throat. "Once in a while, he asks me how you're doing, if you're happy. He does it nicely, like he's interested, like he really wants the best for you." She pauses. "Does that help?"

He bursts in: "Does he still love me?"

"Danny, how would I know that? Since you guys broke up, I never ask about his personal life."

He feels ashamed. "I know. I don't know what I was thinking."

"I tell him you're happy."

Danny lets loose a rupturing laugh that is part cry, part scream, part release. "Thanks for that, I guess."

Cindy pauses before taking a breath. "Are you happy?"

"What?"

"Seriously, are you happy? I mean, maybe you are. But do you have everything you want?"

"I don't know, Cindy. Maybe I want to have my pictures shown in a gallery somewhere. Maybe I want to move to New York. Maybe I want a dog. Stop asking me. I don't even know what I'm going to do tomorrow, for Christ's sake."

"You know what your problem is? You keep too much inside. What do you do most of the time? Where do you cruise? How can you live like that, with your life so separated?"

"You should talk. Do Mom and Dad know what you do outside of the house?"

Cindy laughs roughly, but it soon dies away into silence. "Fine. I get it. We both have secrets. But you work yourself into fits, worrying about how it could all go wrong. It's not good, Danny, not at all."

"Thanks, Dr. Cindy. I've wasted enough of your time this morning."

"Yes, you have," and her laugh, a real one this time, trills over the phone line. Danny smiles, half in love with the version of his sister who can laugh like this, who can coquettishly twirl her hair around her finger. "Maybe I'll call you later."

When he sets down the phone, he turns and picks up his camera bag and folds his tripod under his arm. Before he leaves, he scans the apartment. *Like an empty eggshell.* His eyes wander over the clean surfaces, the chrome and glass and leather, resting on the iron, the stove and coffeemaker to make sure that he hasn't left anything on that could burn down the building. If Danny were watching himself, he wouldn't see any difference in this pre-studio ritual he performs four days a week. No, he has done everything in the same way, with the same neutral expression on his face. But inside, an unstoppable rush has started, and he is submerged by Frank's puffy, sleep-crusted eyes first thing in the morning, by the roll of flesh Danny once saw on Miss Val's thighs where her costume bit into her skin, even by the coolness of his mother's hand on his forehead when he was feverish. The deluge is beyond his control, and the fear of it washes over him; without control, his life bleeds together and he is no longer the Danny of his own creation, but a nerve-ridden, guilt-racked man who will never please his parents and never have sex again. He calmly closes his apartment door behind him and locks it, but each muscle and brain cell churns, remembering touch and smell and sight, old memories that he thought were irrevocably lost.

THE FIRST TIME

1968

It was the summer after graduating high school that Danny worked at the Exhibition, operating the rickety roller coaster. Part of the thrill, his boss told him, is that it looked as if it could splinter apart any minute, as if a nine-year-old constructed the rises and falls out of paper glue and balsa wood. On hot days, he baked in his uniform; on rainy days, he hunched over in his standard-issue yellow slicker. He hid his camera in a gym bag and took it out when the lineup was short, when no one would notice his hands winding and clicking, the lens pointed at long hair whipped back by the wind on the steepest fall, or hands held upward, stretched straight, the fingers trying to escape the rest of the body.

The year before, his art teacher had pulled a small camera from her desk and tossed it to him, muttering, "If you're going to stare out the window all day, then take some pictures of what you're looking at and maybe I can give you a passing grade."

He brought the viewfinder to his eye and something curious happened.

Through the lens, the world resettled. He saw the angles of shadows, the fall of light on walls, faces, shoes. He saw the tetherball hanging alone in the school's concrete court and understood that its meaning in a photograph was more than a ball on a rope. It was loneliness and hope and the promise of play, all in one. Absolute, wordless sense.

He didn't know it until then, but this particular silence—where even the innermost meanings were revealed—was what he had been looking for. Danny could stare at an unremarkable sidewalk with ordinary pedestrians walking past and see nothing, but when he looked through the camera, he saw that there was fear and joy and frustration drawn like lines on the walkers' bodies. And he knew exactly who these people were and how their footsteps—punishing, light, slow or uncertain—spoke what they probably would never dare. *I love my wife. I'm scared of this city. What am I doing?* There was no confusion, and he felt warm and happy because it meant that, one day, maybe somebody would turn their lens on him and see Danny for what he really was. And then explain it all to him in a way he might understand.

Today, the last day of the Exhibition, a little girl, waiting for her older brother to disembark, stood to the side and stared at Danny, her eyes just visible over the top of her pink cotton candy. Danny wondered what she saw in his face, if his restlessness from the night before was branded on his skin somehow. Or perhaps she was simply scared and realized the one thing preventing her brother from being flung off the very top of the roller coaster was this unsmiling young man.

Her head moved slightly to the left and Danny saw that she was looking at the control box. He pushed a red button and the line of cars came to a sudden stop at the bottom, the people inside tossed around as if they were only flesh and not bones. One woman, sitting in the very front, laughed and laughed. She wiped her eyes with a handkerchief and adjusted her pearl necklace. Danny squinted through the smoggy air, thinking that there was something familiar in her red-painted mouth, or the upward tilt of her head. He heard her say to her male companion, "Well, honey, that'll liven us up for the rest of the day. What do you say to a nip of whisky?" And she pulled a flask from her purse while a mother with two young children gasped and hustled them away.

But then a chubby boy threw up beside the control booth and Danny had to reach for the sawdust and broom. By the time he looked again, the woman was gone and the lineup for the roller coaster had snaked around the metal barriers and down the fairway.

On his day off, Danny took the bus aimlessly through the city, ringing the bell whenever he thought to and boarding the next bus on a different route. His camera dangled from his bony neck, resting against his equally bony chest. He stood at street corners he had never noticed before: 2nd Avenue at Main, Alberni at Bute, Beach at Gilford. "Perspective," he whispered to himself. "That's what it's all about."

Ahead of him lay the great expanse of English Bay with barges anchored on the edge of the horizon, the water churning at the shore but barely rippling in the distance. If he had been an extraordinary swimmer, he could have reached the open ocean eventually, and, from there, turned south to California, or west to Hawaii, or perhaps farther to the Philippines, even China, if he wanted. But here—the western edge of the city's core, only eight kilometres from the family house—was possibly just far enough. There was something he loved about the salt air in his nose, the burn that filled his throat and lungs. He looked down at his own feet and wondered why he wasn't running, why he wasn't pounding the sidewalk, smiling so widely that his face might never recover, laughing when he stopped to catch his breath because he was on the way to somewhere else. He looked to his left, where a man and woman were helping a little girl build sandcastles. All three were covered in a fine grey-brown dust. Danny slipped behind a maple tree and began shooting.

The little girl had dug a hole with her bare hands. A collection of brightly coloured spades and rakes lay in an abandoned pile beside her. The woman offered her a bucket to help shape the mound of sand, but the little girl frowned and slapped at her hand. Face reddening, the man yelled, "Don't you ever hit your mother like that!" The girl looked up, startled, and began to cry, her wails floating over the sand and water, travelling swiftly through the air in all directions. Danny winced.

And then, both parents crouched forward and began murmuring. Danny could see the father saying, "I'm sorry. I didn't mean it," while the mother fumbled in her purse for a tissue. Danny wasn't sure who was more upset, the tiny four-year-old or her furrowed, anxious parents. He didn't stop shooting. Each frame was this whole story in miniature.

Inside, his stomach was churning; the ham and pickle sandwich from lunch had become a brick-solid mass. He could hear his father's voice booming.

"I'll teach you to steal one of my beers."

"Give me that look again, I dare you."

"Your mother might think the sun shines out of your ass, but I sure don't."

"Not such a smart-mouth now, are you?"

The words all pointed to the same truth. If his father

could have chosen a son from a lineup, Danny would have remained unpicked, standing by himself, staring at his own shoes. Waiting for the right family.

When Danny looked again, the little girl was drinking from a nearby water fountain and her parents were sitting on a log, staring out at the water, their hands hooked together, each finger woven with the next. Danny pressed the shutter release one more time before walking off the beach to the corner of Denman and Davie. He took three buses to get home and when he arrived, his parents were both waiting for him in the living room.

"Am I late?" Danny asked, checking his watch.

Betty, sitting in the far corner of the couch, looked at Doug, who held a beer can on his lap. "Not this time," he said.

His mother scratched her nose before speaking. "Your father wants to talk to you about your plans."

"Plans? For what?"

Doug sat up straighter in his armchair and stared at Danny until Danny looked down at his sand-covered shoes. "When the Exhibition is over, I want you to work at the shop full time. You're old enough now to learn how to run things. We don't have the money to send you to school anyway." He ran his hand over his face. "Not that you or your sister could even get in."

Danny didn't say anything. He turned his head toward his mother, who nodded at him gently. For a moment, he wanted to shake her, bounce her head off the wall behind her and yell, *You should know better. You should know that working at the shop will be the end of me. You should know this is nothing close to what I want.* But her eyes were so blank, so blandly accepting and quiet that he knew it wouldn't be any use.

After a minute and a half of silence, Betty stood up and took one of Danny's hands. "Auntie Mona's friend has a daughter about your age. Maybe we could invite them over for dinner."

Danny looked from his father to his mother and back again, and saw that they both had set jaws and unshaking hands. He patted his mother's shoulder and stepped around her toward the hall.

"Well?" Doug said. "Is it a plan, or what?"

Danny paused. "Sure. Whatever you want." When he reached his bedroom, he closed the door as quietly as he could before shaking the sand out of his socks and shoes onto an old newspaper. The itch would have bothered him all night.

Two weeks later, Danny lay awake in the middle of the night. When he was sure everyone else had fallen asleep, he got up and changed out of his pyjamas and into a sweater and jeans. He stuffed his final paycheque from the Exhibition, which he had collected that morning, into his wallet. As quietly as possible, he opened his dresser drawers and pulled out socks, underwear and T-shirts. He listened, unmoving, for the sounds of his parents walking through the hallway to investigate the noise. But all he heard was the wind blowing through the unruly patch of bamboo in the backyard. He pulled out four pairs of pants and his winter coat.

He filled up his mother's old suitcase, the one she brought with her to Vancouver twenty-five years ago. He was careful not to overstuff it, for fear that the tattered corners would not hold. He stood in the middle of his room and looked at the single bed, the blue floral curtains with the hole near the hem that could be from moths or maybe even mice. He wondered if he should feel nostalgia for the years spent here or if relief was acceptable too.

He pushed down the thought that he was *running away*. If he allowed them, those words would burrow into his head and remain forever. His parents' friends would whisper, "That Danny, he's a runaway," and they would shake their heads and cast their eyes skyward. He scurried around his bedroom, moving from closet to bed to dresser, not daring to stop in case he imagined his mother crying into her apron, her face buried in the grease and pork juice and rice flour embedded there. And beside her, sitting in one of the hard kitchen chairs, his father, hands in fists on the table, his usually slicked-back hair hanging over his forehead in one damp, drooping lock.

Leaving was one of two choices. He could stay, and work in the curio shop for the rest of his life. He would marry a girl he barely knew or barely tolerated, and live in this house with his parents, eating the same food, staring at them staring at him. If he left, no one would notice him. He would be invisible, moving around this city or another one, one body among many—life unseen, life unplanned. If he left, he could be anonymous for a time, observing and quiet. And then he could create a new Danny, one who took the world's most famous photographs, one who never thought of his parents at all.

There was no in-between. He couldn't stay in this house and work where he wanted. He couldn't leave and still come home once a week for dinner without his father shouting at him for neglecting his duties or his mother staring at him with her eyes half filled with tears. Leaving now meant leaving for good.

There was one more spot he needed to look. He lay down on the floor and peered underneath the bed. Two shoeboxes, filled with smudged paper dolls that looked dishevelled, like women who had been drinking champagne and allowed their dates to smear their lipstick over their faces and spill caviar on their long silk skirts. A stack of department store catalogues crusted over with dust that had mixed with the dampness in the air and then dried. He ripped the dolls into small pieces and placed them back in the boxes, piles of green and red and purple confetti. He took two issues from the middle of the pile and threw them into the suitcase. *For company on a lonely night*.

The hands on the bedside clock pointed to ten past four. He wanted to leave well before his mother woke up at five. On his desk sat a pile of hockey cards, a collection his father added to every birthday and Christmas, even giving Danny the thin plastic sleeves to protect the cards from dirty fingers and the disintegration brought by time. Danny left them where they were.

He pulled on a pair of socks and crept, suitcase and shoes in hand, down the hallway, past his parents' bedroom. Holding his breath, he slipped a folded note under his sister's door. *Tell them not to look for me. I won't come back no matter what*. He knew the precise location of the squeaky floorboards and stepped around them, wincing each time he had to shift his weight from one foot to the other. The front door was the hardest part and he twisted the knob slowly, making sure he didn't rush, that the door didn't rub against its frame. Once outside on the front stoop, he put on his shoes, grabbed the suit-case and hurried down the stairs. Across the street, a white Cadillac started its engine and Danny threw his bag into the back seat before falling into the passenger seat, shutting the door as silently as he could. He slid down so that his head was no longer visible through the window.

"What took you so long?" Edwin pulled out, steered through a U-turn and sped westward. "I've been waiting for an hour."

Danny wondered if he had breathed at all this morning. "I found some more stuff that I needed to pack."

"Well, you'd better tell me where I'm taking you because if I'm not back in bed in about forty-five minutes, my grand-mother will have a hairy conniption and start screaming at the neighbours."

"Keep going," Danny said, "and I'll tell you when to stop."

They stood in the middle of a single room in a downtown hotel where the occupants of one floor shared a single bath-room. A strange combination of people walked the halls and through the lobby: working men who had rolled into Vancouver from Campbell River or Williams Lake; women who crept up the stairs four or five times a night, each time with a different man; and young people who were determined to escape to the big city.

Of course, he hadn't come very far, only from the house on Dundas in East Vancouver to this hotel on Seymour. But it felt like he'd travelled around the world and was now in a place his parents never once thought about, a seedy establishment where those with shattered reputations nursed their watered-down beer in the ground-floor bar. A building that you noticed only if you needed it. Danny carefully placed his suitcase on the low dresser and grinned.

Edwin talked without once removing the cigarette burning between his lips. "God, did you look into the corner here by the nightstand? I don't even know what that black crud is. Mould? Dirt? Hair? I'm getting the willies, Danny. You can't stay here."

Danny parted the curtains. "This is temporary."

"You should go to New York," Edwin said, sitting down on the single chair and then standing up immediately and brushing off the seat of his pants. "There's nothing happening here. Vancouver is dull, dull, dull."

"I don't know where I'm going. I might even stay in town. But I'll get an apartment after I find a job. This is okay for now."

Through the window, Danny could see the pearl-grey light of dawn growing brighter around the edges of clouds. He turned and saw Edwin lying on the bed, eyes closed, his cigarette still in his mouth.

"I thought you had to go home," Danny whispered.

"Grandma can wait. I don't care. I'm tired." He pulled out the cigarette and, without even opening his eyes, stubbed it out directly on the cracked nightstand top.

Danny lay down beside him. Even here, in the middle of downtown where the stunted trees were forced to grow out of tiny plots cut into the sidewalk, he could hear the singing of birds, the rise and fall of their chirping. As he fell asleep, he heard no other noise, not even the rush of a car or voices from the hall.

He felt like he was being pushed awake, crashing through a single-paned picture window into the cold morning. He sat up, breathing hard, and wiped his eyes with the back of his hand. He could hear the splatter of raindrops as they hit the sidewalk and ran together into the gutters.

As his vision cleared, he looked down and saw Edwin's head between his legs, his own pants in a puddle by the side of the bed.

Why. Off. What the fuck. These were all the words that sat behind his teeth, ready to be shouted. At first he retracted, his body like a hand in a sleeve. His knees jerked and he was poised to jump up and shake off all of this, everything, that is, except the outrage that hissed through him.

But wait. This felt good. It was a mixture of pain—the sharpness of nerves coming to life, crackling under his skin—and warmth, as if his entire body was radiating heat, wave after wave after wave. He thought he might suffocate; every limb was heavy with simmering blood. His mouth was now too dry to ask Edwin anything; he simply sighed an exhalation of hot air. No one knew they were in this room, not even Cindy. They were alone, with strangers on the other side of the wall. Knowing this, Danny tilted his head back and breathed.

Moving so slowly that it seemed he wasn't moving at all, Edwin crept up the bed and pulled off Danny's shirt, every touch like a small explosion on his skin. The mattress creaked and, briefly, Danny wondered how many people had fucked on this very spot, on these same sheets and blankets.

He felt the weight of Edwin's body. For half a minute, the pain was vicious, like a scream that ripped across time and space, but Edwin's right hand was still stroking him and, soon, the pain dissipated, leaving Danny feeling like a melted human candle, a humid pool of liquefied flesh and hair. He shuddered and buried his face in the rough sheets.

They might have been lying there for hours or minutes; there was no clock in the room and the light through the window remained an overcast grey. The rain thickened and the individual drops falling on the pavement couldn't be distinguished from the roar of water rushing down the street. Neither of them was asleep. For the first time that Danny could remember, Edwin didn't speak, only breathed deeply, his arms thrown over Danny's chest. Danny shifted and brought the covers up over his shoulders, but Edwin still didn't move, his naked body half obscured by the tangle of blankets. Finally, his voice rose from the pillow.

"I love you."

Danny hadn't been this close to crying since he was a little boy. His mouth felt glued shut, but the silence was growing thicker by the minute.

"I can't," he said, breathing deeply through his nose. *How inadequate.*

"But, I thought—"

"You never leave me alone, Eddie." Danny was surprised at the force of his voice, at the way his words echoed in this small room, shrill and clear as glass. "Why do you need me to be with you all the time? Why can't you make some other friends? Did it ever occur to you that sometimes I just want to be alone?"

Edwin was silent. Danny knew that he was thinking about the unfairness of this outburst. It was Danny who had asked

Edwin to drive him to this place, Danny who had accepted his touch and enjoyed it. But still. He couldn't be Edwin's lover. At night, Danny drifted to sleep buoyed by images of blunt fingers tracing a line down the side of his body and the fleshy smell that men have nestled in their clavicles, the smell that reminded him of the dirt floor in a dark forest. Edwin's substantial thighs and sour breath were so real, so solidly part of his everyday life that he felt sick.

Edwin sat up and turned to face him. "I'm gay, Danny. Get it? Maybe that's something you should try saying one day."

I'm gay. Danny thought those words were like unexploded bombs, potentially lethal, but still only words. But he knew that they were the right words, ones that had been circling inside him for years and that partially propelled him to leave his parents' house. Still, he wanted to grab Edwin by the shoulders and ask him, *How do you know for sure? How do you know this won't go away? How do you know you're not crazy?*

Edwin had already begun putting on his clothes. He left without saying another word.

Danny walked down the hall to take a shower. When he returned, he crossed the room to open the window. He breathed in the damp air, so wet that he swore he could feel the invisible mist coating the inside of his nostrils. The morning was halfway over and people hurried past the hotel, careful not to look directly into the bar where dedicated drunks were hunched over on their stools. Edwin paced back and forth directly below Danny's window, his hair soaked and shiny with rain.

He looked up and waved at the open window, jumping up and down. Danny scanned the street, wondering if someone else might be witnessing Edwin's strange dance in the middle of a puddle.

"Danny!" Edwin shouted. "I'm sorry I left!"

Danny waved his hands, tried to hush him.

"I didn't know what to do," Edwin continued. "I know you and me can never work!"

Half hiding behind the thin curtain, Danny yelled, "Shut up!" Then, lower, "Everyone will hear you. Come upstairs."

"No, I have to go. My grandmother is probably freaking out. I just wanted to tell you that it's all right! I know you don't love me. It'll be okay, Danny." Edwin gave a thumbs-up, nodding and smiling.

Danny watched as Edwin ran across the street to his car. The headlights of the Cadillac cut through the gloom as Edwin nosed the car into traffic. He was gone before Danny could shut the window.

THE PLAGUE

1982

There's something creeping through the night, a faceless monster that breathes, damp and quick, on the back of Danny's neck. At first he thinks it's just him, that his visit to his parents' house has disconnected him from his carefully structured life. But the feeling that something menacing is following him has been increasing for months, long before the family visit, and it will not disappear. He begins to notice a skittish, unsettled look on the faces of the other men at the bar, on the trails in the park at night, at a birthday party for his friend Jack.

On a Friday afternoon, Edwin, perched on Danny's couch, turns to him and says, "Marco is sick. It's that gay disease." His head droops on his chest.

In a flash, Danny knows what is chasing him, or at least he knows the shape of it. The havoc it creates with a touch of its invisible finger. Their friends are sick, shivering through pneumonia, a mysterious cancer, cold after cold. The monster, nameless and undiscriminating, captures a body and then another, felling each by a different method.

"But there are only two cases in Canada," Danny protests. He feels panic rising up his legs, into his stomach. "I heard it on the radio."

"People are getting sick all the time, but no one's counting, or no one really sees what's going on," Edwin mutters. "James stopped coming to the bathhouse months ago, and we don't know where he's gone. And Sean. I saw him last week. He was wearing an overcoat and toque in this weather. It won't take long, Danny, before everyone begins to freak out."

"What are we supposed to do?"

Edwin grimaces. "Nothing. Live harder. What else?"

Danny walks down Davie Street with this new awareness and sees that men move with their heads down, not looking up for fear of seeing yet another man newly infected, newly spotted with Kaposi's sarcoma. In the nightclub, the dancing has become feverish, panicked, as if these nights of shaking their asses and arms to New Order could be annihilated mid-song. The night progresses, and the men move sombrely through the crowd, some drinking quickly, some doing lines in the bathroom until their faces reconfigure into a forgetfulness that doesn't obliterate the confounding circumstances, but dulls their feelings, which is second best, but perhaps acceptable for now.

The gay community newspaper has been publishing reports since last winter, and is now punctuating the low-level panic with actual words. *Gay cancer.* No one knows how it jumps from one body to another. Danny wonders about sex but shakes the thought free. What he does with other men doesn't belong to the doctors and the journalists, only to the park and cry-muffling bush.

He returns to the park after an absence of a few days and begins to notice how everything has changed. The needles on the trees have turned rust brown; those that have fallen to the ground are half powder now, crushed by the passing feet of humans, coyotes, even the sharp paws of raccoons. All thirsty, all searching for fresh water. Danny walks by a sign. FOREST FIRE HAZARD HIGH. NO FLAMES IN WOODED AREAS. Ahead, he can see the lit ends of cigarettes bobbing in the evening light. He wonders what sound one-hundred-year-old trees make when they burn. He imagines coarse, scratchy screaming, the whoosh of branches lighting from the bottom up. The nerve endings in his fingers twitch as he aches for a fast blaze, instant combustion. If he doesn't touch someone soon, he will slowly smoulder.

The fucking is sad and deliberate. Danny is grateful for the silence, for the tangled clumps of bush that darken and conceal. Sex is a consolation when nothing is certain. Though the men hold each other briefly, it is better than being alone in your apartment, where there is no protection against the shadows that fall across your skin until you are convinced you are dying. Here, in the park, everyone knows everyone else's thoughts. They don't need to be spoken.

The movie with the Siamese Kitten has been lingering with him for over a week. He hears Miss Val's voice wherever he goes, that purr and growl offering advice to the film's novice dancer. "Now, sweetie, remember to look those fellows in the eye. If you want tips, you have to make each one feel like he's the only guy in the room, like the two of you are going to go off and mate like bunnies." Even now, as he stands on his balcony in a patch of shade, he laughs at her delivery—part world-weary dame, part concerned mama trying to make sure her kids are treated fairly, part bad actress shouting lines when there's no need.

He replays the shake of her backside, the way the camera zoomed into her face until her fake eyelashes cast shadows wider and longer than his index finger. He swears he could feel the pounding of her heels, as if she were dancing on his chest. If he closes his eyes right now, he could smell her—that combination of cigarettes and cedar and clean, dried sweat. He can feel her fingers in his hair, her long painted fingernails gently grazing his scalp. If he could have revealed every one of his secrets to her years ago, he might never have run away. Even now, Miss Val might still be the person who understands him, who makes him see he isn't the only one who dreams of being just as he is but lovelier. And then maybe he wouldn't want to scratch off the parts of his face that he shares with Doug or Betty or even Cindy. She was the mother he could never have. And he loved her for it.

—

He stands in a musty basement room below the radio station. The once-white walls have been so assaulted by damp that they are now yellowy grey and strangely shiny. A short man with a crewcut stands with his arms crossed over his chest. He squints at Danny, who forces a smile. The man doesn't reciprocate.

"Who sent you here?" he asks, his forehead wrinkling.

"I was at the library and the woman there told me to ask for you. You *are* Jerry, right?"

He huffs. "Yes, that's right. But why are you here?"

Danny resists the urge to roll his eyes. "I'm looking for anything you might have on a dancer who used to perform in Vancouver in the fifties. You know, radio interviews and things like that."

"Why should I help you? The general public isn't even allowed in here," Jerry says, his voice short and clipped.

There really is no reason for him to help. Danny is asking a total stranger for a favour. His intentions are quite straightforward: Danny wants to roll around in Miss Val's voice again, let its roughness scratch his ears while he pictures her red-painted lips and long neck. But this is not something that he can explain to someone else. He stares at Jerry.

"The librarian told me that you're the only one who can find what I'm looking for. She said you're the best archivist in the country." Danny smiles at the man.

Jerry shrugs then turns toward a card catalogue against the near wall. "The best, eh? All right then, what's the name of this dancer you were talking about?"

—

Danny sits in a rickety wooden chair at a scarred chrome and laminate desk, his headphones connected to a tall reel-to-reel tape recorder, his hands twisting in his lap as he waits for a sound. Jerry said nothing about what he found, simply pointed Danny to this chair and handed him a pair of puffy headphones. The tape scrapes along for half a minute, silent.

Then a reedy, Upper Canadian voice cuts through the silence. In this interview, the reporter explores Vancouver's reputation as a sin city. "Here," he says, "tourists and locals alike can partake in the vice of their choice, be it drink, cards or women." The year is 1956 and the reporter walks down Granville Street. "The ladies wear chic raincoats and mince down the sidewalks in high heels, while the men tip their hats forward and guide their paramours around puddles and dripping eaves. It's ten o'clock on a Saturday night and everyone seems to have a place to go. The Cave Supper Club. The Orpheum Theatre. And a little place called the Penthouse where we found an experienced stripper known around these parts as the Siamese Kitten."

Miss Val's voice spills out from the headphones, warm and rough. What whisky would sound like if it could talk. Her words tumble and spin and Danny smiles at the sound.

"It's a gas whenever we have a full house. I have a lot of fun with the other girls here, and if you have the right customers, they can really show their appreciation." Her peals of laughter tumble into Danny's ears, clear and undistorted. Brilliant. "You learn how to spot those fellows pretty quick, I can tell you."

Before the reporter can ask another question, Miss Val continues: "Lots of people, they don't understand what we do, but being a stripper is like any other job. We work and we get paid for it. Besides, where else could we wear costumes like this? I don't see too many secretaries running around in beaded G-strings."

"Why are you called the Siamese Kitten?"

Miss Val laughs again and Danny holds his breath. "I needed a hook, see, and I thought why not be Oriental? In the act, I'm a Siamese princess who is exiled and has to dance to earn money for her family. Lots of action. Lots of skin too, of course. But it's a real show, real spectacular. Even the ladies love it!"

The reporter's earnestness breaks through his voice. "But most little girls don't dream of becoming a burlesque dancer when they grow up. It's not all fun and games, is it?"

For several seconds, all Danny can hear is the background noise of the club: the clink of glasses, the murmur of voices. She takes a deep breath and then speaks. "It's hard work. You can see it in the faces of the girls, you know? When we take off our makeup and you can see what we really look like, we're like old ladies. I mean, I'm not even thirty yet, but I look ten years older. The girls never last very long. No one strips until she's sixty-five, if you catch my drift. We burn out—fast."

The weariness pools in Danny's ears and he wants to take Miss Val's hand and lead her to a chair where he can serve her a cup of tea and a sugar biscuit. He has never thought of her as tired. Whirling, yes. Kicking her way across stages, spiking the ground with her high heels, winking at men who gape at her on the street. How can she be tired like an ordinary woman?

The reporter leaves the Penthouse and walks to a seedy bar in Gastown where he begins a conversation with a bartender. Danny pulls off the headphones and stares at the stained wall in front of him. *She was real*, he thinks, *like everyone else.* She washed her underwear in the sink, rubbed her sore feet and slept with curlers in her hair. It pains him to think that she might have been like his mother, a woman who counted and recounted her spending money and squeezed oranges in the grocery store. Then again, who says that her real life wasn't spectacular too? When she had to slice bread, Danny guesses, she did it in style.

He tries to sleep, but heat has infected everything. He feels sleep rolling over him in fitful waves, brushing his damp skin. Danny dreams that he is a little boy again, sneaking his way through the alleys in Chinatown. On every utility pole he sees the same poster, like an endless hall of mirrors. "The Siamese Kitten stars in the first-ever Oriental Sextravaganza made for the burlesque stage: SEXILE IN SIAM! One-of-a-kind dance numbers, chorus girls, heartbreak and, of course, plenty of Shake and Shimmy!" In the grainy, mimeographed photo, Miss Val holds one large fan in front of her body and wears a Chinese princess headdress that dangles beads and chains in her eyes.

Young Danny runs and runs until he reaches the club where he first met Miss Val. He sneaks in behind the legs of a man who walks with a cane, and darts into the theatre. He sits in the back, under the shadow of the balcony. One row ahead, he sees a black bobbed head nodding slightly to the beat. A crash of cymbals erupts and he stares, wide-eyed, at the stage.

First, Miss Val is a young princess, picking flowers in the garden, attended to by servant girls who dance in costumes slit high up the leg. She strips to a lilting Oriental melody played by a single flute and one violin. In the next act, she's in the middle of a war, standing centre stage while musicians pound drums. Pieces of foam, painted to look like the debris from bombed-out buildings, fall around her. She strips as she recounts how her family was forced to leave the palace for a cave dwelling in the faraway, snowy mountains. By the end of the scene, she is wearing rags that are tied and torn in strategic places.

Danny claps enthusiastically, joining the thunderous applause all around him.

The Siamese Kitten's father dies, and she and her mother make the long journey from the mountains to Bangkok, where the poor princess supports them by dancing in clubs frequented by foreigners. She falls in love with an American and dances a special routine created for him alone, a slow, seductive striptease with fans made of peacock feathers.

When her soldier leaves Bangkok, the Siamese Kitten secretly follows him to America and discovers his wife and two children. She begs and begs, but he does not leave his family. Instead, he hisses at her to get the hell out of town before everyone puts two and two together. Tears streaming, she boards a bus for Los Angeles, where she dances again and where hundreds, nay thousands, of American men love her at first sight.

The act ends with the Siamese Kitten lying on a red silk chaise, a gold cigarette holder in her fingers, wearing nothing but a G-string and an embroidered shawl around her shoulders.

"Who would you rather be, my friends?" she asks the audience. "The wife at home who has no idea what her husband is up to?" The crowd roars with laughter and stamps its feet on the club floor. "Or me, the Siamese Kitten, wearing the finest silk, adored by not *one* man, but more than I can even count?" She winks as the curtains begin to close. "The choice seems crystal clear to me." She blows a series of smoke rings that float up toward the stage lights, dispersing as they rise.

Danny wakes up covered in a long lick of sweat. It's still dark and the street is quiet. He wonders how he will get through this summer.

The phone rings and rings. Danny checks the clock—ten thirty in the morning. He's slept in.

Naked, he hurries to the living room. The curtains are still closed and an otherworldly light filters in. Danny swears he can see a quiver of anticipation shimmering through the air—perhaps the room itself is waiting for the action to begin. Or maybe all he's seeing are wayward fruit flies, circling the one beam of light that has managed to force its way in.

He picks up the black receiver and clears his throat. Before he says anything, he hears a familiar voice.

"Danny, it's Frank."

Danny sits on the floor; his joints have turned to mush. Almost instantly he imagines a reunion, Frank's arms around im again, the warmth of sleeping with someone whose body is a visceral, nerve-tinged memory.

"Frank," he says, his mouth immediately recognizing the shape of his name, the catch in his throat for the ending *k*. "It's nice to hear from you."

"I need to see you."

"See me?" He wants to shout, *But it's been three years, why now, why are you calling me now?*

"I just need to talk to you about something. It's just that, well, things have changed." Frank's voice trails off into a crackly, not-quite-silence.

"I don't know what you mean."

"We have to talk, that's all. Can you meet me next Thursday? Maybe for lunch?"

Six days away, Danny thinks. *How can I wait that long?* "Sure. How about the diner on Denman?"

"Fine. I'll see you there at eleven thirty. Bye." The line goes dead.

He stares at the receiver in his hand, at his own bony knees splayed out on the living-room floor. He remembers the light, almost blond hair on Frank's arms and legs. The way he used to brush his hand lightly over the tips until Frank shivered and grasped Danny's wrist to stop him. When they were lying in bed, while the light in the bedroom brightened from black to grey to dawn, Danny felt immersed, as though Frank's body were absorbing his so that they would become something else together, a creature both angelically beautiful and reassuringly real. One winter day, they stood together at an art show and Danny turned his head and saw Frank lit from above, the white beam from a ceiling bulb diffusing all the shadows around them. Frank seemed precious, exquisitely pristine and still. If Danny could have folded up that image and pressed it into his own skin, he would have. He is tempted to rummage in his night-stand for the old photos of him and Frank together, but he resists. Now that he has constructed a life accommodating Frank's absence, there can be no room for him. None.

He makes it to the bathroom, where he splashes water on his face, feeling the chilly floor tiles radiate cold from the bottoms of his feet to the tips of his ears, touching every part of his body on the way.

THE WEDDING

1982

Saturday, Danny stands on the bride's parents' front lawn, sweating into the collar of his white dress shirt. He hopes he has not soaked through his jacket.

The bride's mother, with carefully curled blond bangs perched on the top of her head, is hustling a group of people outside and pushing them to a spot in front of a multi-coloured wall of dahlias. The heavy-headed flowers droop in the full sunlight and Danny viciously hopes that the blooms will snap under their own weight and bury the muddled relatives in drifts of orange and purple and yellow. He is shocked at his inner rage but blames it on the heat. He silently promises that he will spend the rest of the day smiling. Overhead, a seagull flies sluggishly, turning and turning in the same circle.

One after the other, groups of people—some red-faced from the heat, others squinting against the sunlight—walk slowly to their designated spots, smile at Danny's camera and walk off again, their hair glistening, their clothes hanging limply from their bodies.

A woman in her fifties, whose presence in the doorway seems to signal a shift in the atmosphere, steps out into the sunshine. Hair set in glossy brown curls. Red lips to match a red dress. Long, still-shapely legs visible through a modest slit in the skirt. She saunters toward the dahlias, each hip sliding her body forward deliberately so that she seems to be slithering. Hers is a walk that could be described as *liquid, languid, effortless*. She looks around at the family members shading their eyes with their hands, at the respectable men and women shuffling from one inadequate spot of shade to another, and her body resettles. Swiftly, visibly, she crumples in on herself, pulling the slit in her skirt closed. It seems that she has thrown on a cloak of age, one that suggests respectability, decorum, Sunday dinners with a discreet glass of sherry.

And yet, in her hand, a lit cigarette is burning sweetly and disseminating its smoke through the humid air.

She has changed (it has been twenty-four years, after all, and she is heavier all over, her ample bosom weighed down by its own bulk), but her face still glimmers with mocking humour, and her mouth still blows out little uniform puffs of smoke. Danny feels a surge through his body.

"Auntie Val!" The bride steps out onto the lawn, her white dress like a porcelain doll's. Danny thinks she is blandly pretty, in her blond, safe and creamy whiteness. He watches as Val gazes at the young bride, at her tiara, her pearls, the sash wrapped around her waist. Val's smile is turned down at the corners, revealing nothing. Danny thinks he sees her hand reach out, but when he looks again her fingers are resting on the curve of her hip.

"Auntie Val, you have to stand over here, beside Mum. I want a picture of you together." The bride waves Val over, her ring finger glittering with a high-set diamond.

Val drops her eyelids and smoothes out a wrinkle on her skirt. "I don't know that your mother wants to stand next to *me*. She might catch something."

Three elderly men, standing in a circle on the lawn, guffaw.

The sun begins to burn the tips of Danny's ears as he waits for the two women to finish arranging themselves so that each is presenting her best side. Finally, Val and her sister are ready for the camera. Both smile, but Val's lips are closed, her chin down so that the lens can capture the full effect of her direct green eyes. Danny snaps, unable to speak. Val frowns and looks, for the first time, at the red-faced photographer kneeling in the grass.

Danny stands and feels her eyes boring their way into his body, past his grey suit, past his underwear and socks, through his skin and into his organs. What is she seeing? His body's parts—marrow, blood cells, lymph glands—or something else? Perhaps his real self, like a small, hard kernel hidden under layers of muscle and fat and illusion. Silence stops everything around them. If someone is speaking, he can no longer hear it.

She blows out a smoke ring, contemplating his slightly shorter-than-average frame. Her lips purse and she smoothes down a stray hair that has curled up in the humidity. He shivers and wonders how feeling a chill is even possible.

The air seems to part between them, making a narrow path of clear, damp-free air along which her smell—cedar and lipstick, leather and hairspray—floats toward him. She grins, places a hand on her hip and winks.

Slowly, he hears a low buzz: people's voices, the hiss of air that follows a car driving down the street, doors opening and closing. Blunt ends of grass prickle his neck. Sunlight illuminates the insides of his closed eyelids.

And he remembers.

He was watching Miss Val; in fact, he was on the verge of speaking to her when a stifling heaviness descended on his shoulders and he felt his spine buckling under the pressure. Before he could look around for help, his neck weakened and his head fell to his chest. He had two thoughts before his body hit the ground.

If I fall backward, I can save the cameras.

What if Miss Val disappears and I never see her again?

He opens his eyes, sees a crowd of faces peering down at him.

"Danny, thank God you're all right."

"It must be heatstroke, and you in that dark suit."

"Come on then, let's get the boy something to drink."

He sits up on the lawn and sips a glass of water. The mother of the bride holds an umbrella over his head, shading him from the early afternoon sun. A bridesmaid, holding up her blue skirt with one hand, sets down a plate of crackers beside him. He searches the crowd for Val, for her red dress, for the smirk he would recognize anywhere. Nothing. He sees only a sulky flower girl, wedding guests in tasteful suits and pastel dresses, and the bride, wilting beside the rhododendron, dabbing at her eyes with a tissue. He looks down at the grass stains on the palms of his hands, at his tripod lying on its side in the garden, at the limousine waiting blackly by the curb. A mess.

At his eye level, a pair of long legs, encased in seamed, sheer black stockings, walks toward him and stops inches from his nose. A voice, throaty but feminine, says, "All right, folks, let's all go to the church now. We're running behind, so why don't you beefy men over there make yourselves useful and help this poor kid up?"

Danny grabs her hand with both of his as she starts to walk away. She turns and stares in confusion at his flushed face.

"Please, Miss Val, you remember me, don't you?" His voice cracks.

Val squints, purses her lips. "No, I don't think so."

She tries to pull her hand away, but Danny pulls it closer.

"I'm Danny. From the alley in Chinatown, behind the club?"

Val manages to shake off his grip. Her smile is tight, sitting on her skin like a disguise. Her eyes dart left and right, at the family members clustered around them.

"What club, sweetheart? I was never much of a club gal, you know."

And she walks away, clutching her purse to her stomach, seeming like an old lady as she carefully steps across the uneven lawn.

At the church, Danny stands to the side of the altar, snapping photographs of the bride's tearful face and the looks of bemusement and resentment on the faces of her bridesmaids. He sees, through his viewfinder, Val standing outside, watching the wedding through the window, her right hand pressed against the glass. His eyes prickle and he blinks hard until the half-formed tears stop brimming and dissipate, until there is no evidence that he might have been crying. He focuses on Val and releases the shutter. She looks directly into the camera, her eyes like sharp pinpoints—assessing, measuring.

The vows are almost over and soon the couple will kiss. If Danny misses this moment because he is staring out the window at the bride's vaguely embarrassing aunt, the photographs will be ruined. He has no choice but to look away.

The day has been long. One photograph after another. Speech after speech. Nothing makes this wedding any different from the others. Except, of course, Miss Val. Danny has spotted her out of the corner of his eye all day, her tall body wrapped in red, visible one minute and gone the next, never stepping directly in front of him or his lens. Maddeningly elusive.

After finishing the evening with a few shots of the dancing guests, he packs up his camera and light meter and skirts along the edge of the ballroom. Only the bride and groom's friends are left, dancing in a mob in the middle of the parquet floor. Trampled corsages are scattered throughout the room, brown and flattened and emitting an off-sweet smell, the bruised odour of fruit left too long on the tree. Danny squints, trying to separate real bodies from shadows and strobe lights.

One long arm shoots up from the middle of the crowd. The bridesmaids and groomsmen part and Danny sees that Miss Val, the lone relative still there, is dancing, her right hand above her head, surrounded by men who are thirty years younger than her. But this pulsing light is forgiving and she is, right now, no older than the girls who giggle behind their hands at her shimmying hips. Danny can't tell if Val sees them. The dance and the men who watch her are all that matter. He laughs to himself. There are some things even the Siamese Kitten cannot hide.

All of a sudden, he realizes how silly he has been. He turns and walks to the coatroom, where he picks up his equipment and jacket. His face begins to flush from the tips of his ears down, skipping whole sections of his neck but fiercely spreading around his Adam's apple, on either side of his nose and the knob of his chin.

Miss Val will never recognize him. He might look familiar and he can creep around the ballroom all he likes, but it will never happen. He was only a little boy. She was a stripper who saw thousands of faces in theatres and alleys too. "Stupid," Danny mutters. "You're just a crazy wedding photographer."

He bends down to fold and pick up his tripod and swears under his breath when one of the tripod's legs refuses to retract. He is turning a loose screw with his fingernail when a rush of cool air blows against his ears. He turns around and Miss Val stands in the doorway, a lit cigarette in her hand. He reaches for the wall behind. She looks evenly at Danny, at his camera bags, at his glossy black shoes. "Well, little man, let's figure this out. Who are you and what do you know about me?"

The moment is here. He could walk away, pretend that he's never seen her before and perhaps his eight-year-old self will be quiet again, settle back into his childhood. But a howl has started in his head.

Danny straightens, wipes his hands on his pants and looks directly into her eyes. "I saw you once, outside the Shanghai Junk, in the alley. I was a little boy then. My name is Danny."

"Listen, Danny, I've met a lot of people in my time, and a lot of my past has been forgotten. The people here, at this wedding, they know nothing except what I tell them, and I don't include the Shanghai Junk in too many conversations, if you know what I mean." Val steps forward, places a wide hand on Danny's shoulder and smiles, showing all of her small, yellowing teeth. "You can keep your memories to yourself, if you please."

Danny can see the slight quiver of rage building under her makeup. But the roar in his head is receding and he is now struck with the desire to jump and giggle like a giddy child because Miss Val, the Siamese Kitten, is touching him, holding his shoulder here, in this coatroom, on this sweltering July evening.

"You gave me the belt from your robe. Green silk. I still have it."

She steps back, flicking the ash from her cigarette toward a pair of leather oxfords on the floor. "Sweet Caps," she mutters, smoke floating out from between her lips.

Danny steps forward, close enough to smell her again, close enough to stare at the smooth fabric of her dress. "Yes, you gave me a whole pack for my father. I was scared of him."

"You reminded me of a little boy I knew once," she says. "Those big eyes." Smoke surrounds her head, and she peers at him through the swirl. "That was a long time ago."

He doesn't know where the words are coming from, but

he has to get them out. "A few weeks later, I went back to find you, but you weren't there. I used to think about you all the time. I guess I must have fallen in love with you, like I was your son, or your best friend. I loved your costumes and your makeup. Everything about you." He is out of breath, deflated. His thin chest heaves and he bows his head, resting his chin on his shirtfront. "I watched your movie."

When he looks up, he sees that she has dropped onto a chair and leaned her cheek against the wall. Her profile hasn't changed. The lines around her nose and lips are unblurred and still sharp. He wonders how it would feel to run his fingers down her jaw, if her skin would be soft, or if the muscles underneath would feel like steel, the hard structure holding up everything else. Her cigarette has burnt down and she is left holding the filter.

"No one talks about the Kitten anymore."

Danny swallows. "We could leave. We could get a drink somewhere. My car's outside."

Val turns to look at him, an unpractised smile on her face. "Well, I haven't been in a strange man's vehicle for some time. It's nice to know I still got it."

When they are in his small blue car, he is acutely aware of her presence, even when she says nothing, even when his eyes are on the road and he can see her in his peripheral vision. Danny feels that he may never understand this day, that he will stumble through it with his mouth half open in awe. All those years ago, he had hoped that he would be elegant, maybe even a little bit glamorous, when they met again. He had always thought that he would be wearing a pressed tuxedo with tails, smoking a cigarillo, a snifter of cognac in his hand. He would show her what a fine young man he had become, that his glimpse of her all those years ago had pointed him toward a well-dressed life far away from the curio shop or the smell of Chinese cabbage in his parents' house.

They drive over the Cambie Street Bridge. To the left, English Bay and the barges in the distance, their twinkling lights the only break on the nighttime horizon. To the right, False Creek, its shores dotted with flat, empty lots ringed by chain-link fencing and abandoned shipping containers. Wind whips in through the open windows and Val, her hair whirling around her head, closes her eyes and turns her face into the rushing air. Danny glances at her and sees that she looks both young (with her skin pulled tight from the wind) and old (the white roots of her hair, the low-hanging earlobes pressed flat against her jaw). She holds a hand out the window, pushing against the current.

"A disco," she says as she turns toward Danny.

"Sorry?"

"A disco. I've never been. Can we go to one?"

Danny checks his mirror, turns west. "I guess. Which one?"

"Whichever one you go to. I want to hear some music." She closes her eyes again and leans her head back against the seat.

At the door to the club, Danny takes Val's hand. He expects that her grip will be strong and decisive, but she holds his hand like a little girl would, her fingers loosely curled inside his palm, her whole fist weighing practically nothing in his. He leads her in through the dark hallway and past the coat check. Before they step into the main room, she stiffens beside him and peers around the corner, her neck tense and straight.

Lights pulse on and off, swoop around the room so quickly that all Danny can see are flashes of people; their faces illuminated one second and then blanketed by darkness the next. The long bar at the end of the room is lit from below so that the bartenders are like jack-o'-lanterns, their grins malevolent and Joker-like. At tall tables, men stand and drink. On the dance floor, they twist and spin, their drinks held high above their heads, their eyes sometimes closed, sometimes open and locked on someone else. Danny can smell the musk of all these men, and wonders if this odour is singular to the club, or if it changes every time someone new enters, or every time someone, tired of the throb and thump, leaves for the night, his jacket rolled and under his arm. He swears that the floor itself is vibrating to the beat.

He finds them a low table on the edge of the dance floor. A waiter takes their order, a gin and tonic for Danny and a whisky sour for Val. A new song begins with a driving, synthetic rhythm and Val claps her hands.

"This is gorgeous, sweetheart. Look at all these handsome boys. Exactly what an old broad needs." The waiter hands her a cocktail and she takes a dainty sip. "Now, this is the life."

Danny sits beside her, watches her eyes as they follow the dancers. She is focused on their moves, on how they dance alone and then with each other, on the give and take between partners whose arms and legs and pelvises are opposite and complementary. Her fingers tap on the tabletop, keeping time. He counts the wrinkles on her neck, wonders if her swollen finger joints make it impossible for her to take off her rings at the end of the day. So many years, so many possibilities for undiluted joy, for tragedy, for lines in the skin.

He closes his eyes briefly and allows himself to sink into the memory of his childhood self, the one who wanted to both dance a tango with Miss Val and be wrapped within her strong arms, the stones in her rings winking as she held him tight. Tonight, breathing in the tang of Val's smell, he thinks that maybe, just maybe, some parts of the past might not be so bad.

The music changes again; it's a slower song but one that still pounds the walls with a bass line that gracelessly punches its way into Danny's chest. Val slams both hands on the table and looks him in the face. "Listen, are we going to dance or what?"

He begins by holding on to her hands, placing one on his shoulder. Looking at her face, he is unsure of how to start, how to apply the waltz he once learned from his mother in their kitchen to this club and this recorded song, sung force-fully and richly by a woman he imagines to be both over-weight and fearsomely tough. He hesitates, and then takes one step forward, out of time.

Val shrugs off his hands and punches him lightly on the arm. "This is all wrong, Danny! You're going to shake your rump if I have to shake it for you. Come on." She slaps him on the ass and laughs wickedly, wiggling her hips to the beat.

He lets her lead him into a raucous dance. She twirls and bounces, gesturing for him to do the same. Under these lights, his arms and legs appear fluid and refined, not gawky and sinewy. Val smiles at him.

"You're a natural," she shouts. "A born dancer."

Danny dances until he vibrates with the beat of the music. Val's laugh cuts through the song and he reaches out for her, grasping her arms, holding and releasing her into the pounding, dark room. He hears his own laugh meeting hers. This is the very thing he has been waiting for: this dance in the middle of a club with the woman he dreamed of, whose voice filled his imagination when his own mother's fell silent. Maybe he and the eight-year-old version of himself have become one—lighter, wiser and leading this dance with the twirling Siamese Kitten.

Danny drives Val home through the quiet streets of the North Shore. This is where voices and cars and the hisses of city life are buffered and absorbed by untouched firs and cedars, by the rushing of unnamed creeks, by the thick walls of small, self-contained houses. She turns to him, reaching across the handbrake to grasp his arm.

"Thank you."

Danny grins. "Same to you."

He parks the car in front of a low-rise apartment building with wood siding and sagging balconies. All the windows are dark and he hears a cat crying. He walks Val to the front door and, as she searches in her purse for her keys, he says softly, "I'd like to see you again. Maybe somewhere quiet next time."

She holds a cough candy up to the light above the door before dropping it back into her small beaded purse. "I don't know, Danny. That old life doesn't fit in so well with the one I have now."

"We don't have to talk about what happened before. We can do things, go anywhere you want."

"Anywhere?"

Eagerly, Danny steps forward. "Yes, of course. We could see movies, or go to the beach if the weather's nice."

"There's a particular beach in Kitsilano," she says with a thin layer of excitement in her voice. "I haven't been there in a long time. It's near a boarding house where I used to live."

"We'll go. Whenever you want."

She pulls out a key ring chained to a shiny gold lipstick tube. She nods. "Come by on Wednesday morning around ten." She reaches up and pats him on the cheek. "Danny, you're one hell of a good time."

He watches through the glass doors as she walks slowly to the elevator, one hand on her right hip. A little unsteadily, she steps into the elevator and turns around. As the doors to the elevator close, Val blows him a kiss and he swears he can feel it landing like a moth on his cheek.

In his darkroom two days later, Danny moves and mixes, his hands adjusting the focus on the enlarger one minute, fishing out a wedding print from the developer the next. One by one, he pins the prints from the wedding on the drying line. They sway in the breeze from the ceiling fan, like bedsheets hanging in the sun. His fingers travel over their edges lightly, fondly. Sometimes he even smells them, sniffing that faint residual odour of developer, stop bath, fixer. He thinks of it as a clean smell, the smell of genesis, of birth without the mess.

Other prints sit on the counter in four neat rows. Men and women hurry away, their bodies dark against white buildings, light flooding the frames so that it seems to be consuming the figures, eating up the visual space they tenuously inhabit.

A young boy, his ears sticking out like handles on a trophy, cranes his neck so that the very tip of his nose is visible beyond the curve of his cheek. His hair, black and heavy, obscures his right eye. Danny visualizes these prints even when they are out of sight; they feel heavy with their stark blacks and pure whites. They are colourless and bloodless, pictures of feature-less people without skin and hair and breath. With their faces turned away, the figures are unknowable. No eyes. No sweat, oil, food. Frank always said that Danny should exhibit his work, and called two galleries and a dealer before Danny stopped him. "They're just pictures of people retreating," he said, piling the prints into a box. Maybe they were beautiful, but he knew then as he does now that they're also empty.

He watches as one wedding print in particular floats in the developer tray, watches as the whites become shapes defined by shadows. A picture of the bride at the altar, her face occupying the right third of the frame. Her eyebrows are knitted and a tear is frozen in place halfway down her cheek. She is the kind of beautiful that men take home to their moth-ers. The kind of beautiful that, sometimes, is easy to forget.

In the corner of the window, a small black blur.

He drops the next print into the tray. Here it is: a full frame of Val standing in the window, watching the wedding from the outside. As he looks closer, he sees that the corners of her mouth are turned down, that her head is tilted just so. Her eyes droop at the edges and she seems in danger of fading away, her face slightly more distinct than the background or the panes in the window. He sees it clearly now, the look that he has seen hundreds of times before on the faces of brides-maids, grandparents, mothers. It's that moment when you are about to lose control, when you know the tears are coming and you are still, fruitlessly, trying to hold them in. He hangs her story on the line, touches the edges gingerly.

The hot sand stings the bottoms of his feet. He has rolled up his jeans as high as they will go, and they are now bunched around his knees, collecting sweat and sand. Val walks ahead of him, gracefully avoiding the splinters from driftwood. She unfolds a Mexican blanket and arranges it in front of a large, bleached-white log. Squinting into the sun, she lights a cigarette.

Danny settles onto the blanket and empties the sand out of his shoes. When he looks up again, Val has taken off her shirt and skirt and is standing in a black swimsuit, the neck cut low, almost to her waist. Her cleavage is tanned brown, with freckles dotting the space between her breasts. She stands straight, one long leg in front of the other, and surveys the beach, challenging the other people to look at her, admire the lines of her body. When an elderly man behind them, dressed in walking shorts and a Panama hat, stares at her and then stumbles on the path, Val smiles brightly and sits down, her back against the log.

"You see?" she says. "I've never let myself go." She smoothes down a wrinkle in her swimsuit. "I've been dying to wear this. It just came in at the store."

Danny nods before closing his eyes. The light glows red through his eyelids. "What store?"

"I didn't tell you? I work at the big department store downtown. Selling lingerie. I guess you can say I have a lot of experience with underwear." Her laugh, loud and ringing, spills out into the air around them. Danny wonders if the sound waves will ripple across the ocean and tickle the ears of someone in Japan.

Staring at the sandflies hopping around the blanket, Val says in a matter-of-fact voice, "You're alone, aren't you, honey? Why?"

It's a question that people ask him all the time, but it's a surprise nonetheless. His body feels jolted and goose-bumped; his spine tingles. He looks out at the beach and ocean, at the buoys bobbing in the distance. Val stretches and digs her red-painted toes into the sand.

"Well? Out with it. I don't have much patience these days." Val lets out an exaggerated cough and lightly pounds her chest.

Danny tells her of the evening he first met Frank, how everyone else in the restaurant receded into the dark. The falling-in-love part was quick and complete. No questions. No doubts.

"How long were you together?" Val asks, rubbing tanning lotion on her legs.

"Eight months."

"And then what?"

After months of spending nights in Frank's apartment (because Frank couldn't bring his dog, Barton, over to Danny's, even though Danny offered to sneak him up in a suitcase), there came a time when things began to descend and spin until Danny seemed to be tripping over his own feet wherever he went.

At first, it was little things. Frank not answering when Danny asked him a question, and looking out the window. On a Friday afternoon, Frank would announce that he was spending the weekend at his parents' so Barton could romp in their double-wide lot. "I want to leave before traffic gets bad. There's no time for you to pack your things," he said, while stuffing a canvas bag with Milk Bones and squeaky toys. "My parents love you, but I think it's better if I go alone this time." Once, Danny waited in his apartment for an hour and a half, with a special dinner congealing on the table, before Frank showed up, his face stony and hard, his apologies clipped and monotone.

He tried to convince himself it was his own paranoia, but he knew it wasn't. Danny wondered if he should ask, sit down with Frank and hold his hand until something—anything—was revealed. Maybe it was the way Danny drooled when he slept, or his habit of saying nothing unless the words were brilliant and awe-inspiring. Because he could fix all that. If only Frank would tell him. If only Danny wasn't so afraid to ask.

A few weeks later, after a long wedding during which the ring bearer refused to walk down the aisle and was carried, bawling, by his embarrassed mother, and the cake collapsed under the weight of its melting butter cream, Danny went back to Frank's apartment to find Frank sitting on the sofa with his dog in his arms. He was stroking him slowly, down his unmoving flank.

"He's dead," Frank whispered.

Danny rushed over and put his arms around Frank, kissing the side of his head as Frank sat limply, bent over the body. "I'm so sorry. What happened?"

"He seemed sluggish all week and wouldn't eat, and I thought maybe he was overheated. But then, a few hours ago, he crawled into my lap and began breathing funny.

I held up his head, but it didn't seem to help. When I tried to get up to call the vet, Barton gave me this look, and so I didn't move and kept patting him. He stared at me the whole time. And then he shuddered and it was over." He paused and fell back into the cushions. "What am I going to do?"

Danny held Frank's hand all night, sitting on the couch with the dog between them. He didn't know what time he fell asleep, but when he woke up, bright sunlight was pouring through the window and Barton was gone. Frank stood in front of him, his hands on his hips.

"I wasn't sure if we should have this conversation now, but why the fuck not? Danny, where is this relationship going?"

Danny, confused and groggy, said, "But where's Barton? I don't understand."

"I took him to the vet this morning. They'll call me when the ashes are ready."

"Come here and we can talk about it."

Frank pounded his fist against the wall. "My dog is dead. I want to talk about *us*." He swallowed a sob and wiped his nose with the back of his hand.

"I thought we were happy, just like this."

"Danny, I'm thirty-five years old. I would like to buy a house someday, have a home with *you*. My parents are on board. There's nothing to stop us."

Danny rubbed his hands together. "You know about my parents. What am I supposed to tell them?"

"That you're *gay*, for fuck's sake!"

"They'd be so angry. I couldn't ever see them again. My father—"

"I don't understand why this is even an issue. You never speak to your father anyway. If you come out to them, the same thing will happen to you that happened to all of us. Your father will rage and shout and then ignore you for months and months. Your mother will cry and try to be brave. Everyone gets over it eventually, and even if they don't, then at least they know, and we can live our lives without hiding anymore, without being afraid we're going to run into them on the street. God!" Frank slumped against the wall.

Danny stood up and put his hands on Frank's shoulders. "Can't we talk about this later? You're still upset and maybe this isn't the right time to have this conversation."

Frank shook him off. "No, this is the only time. Don't you see? The longer you hide from your parents, the longer it'll take you to get on with your life." Frank waved at a stack of photos on the coffee table. "Those pictures are just sitting there, Danny, waiting for you to *do* something."

"I know, I know. I just have to figure out a plan."

"A plan that does what exactly? Makes your parents disappear? Makes me disappear?" Frank's face was wet and shiny with tears. When Danny moved to wipe them away, Frank stepped back and turned his head toward the wall. "Did it ever occur to you that while you were trying to avoid being a good Chinese son, you became a gay stereotype instead? Look at you: well-dressed, skinny, afraid of commitment. It's almost funny."

"That's not fair. I want you. I want us," Danny whispered.

Frank laughed, even while his nose was running. "If that were true, you'd want a different life. Maybe it's all too domestic. Maybe having happy Christmas dinners with my parents is too weird for you. Not that it matters. We want different things. That's all there is to say."

"I can do anything you want. Really. I just need time."

"Sure, whatever you say. Listen, why don't you go home and call me later when you've thought some more, okay? I need to sleep." He walked to the front door and opened it. "Why are you so afraid, Danny? When will you stop running away?"

Danny didn't answer.

The next morning, Frank called to say that unless Danny could come out to his parents, it had to be over. And, just like that, it was done.

Val leans back on the log behind them. "Very sad, honey. Do you think about him much?"

"Every fucking day," Danny says, drawing a line in the sand with his fingers.

"Do you ever see him now?"

"No. Although he called me out of the blue and we're meeting for lunch tomorrow."

"What do you think he wants?"

Danny looks up at the glittering sky. "I have no idea. Sometimes, I think he wants to get back together. Other times, I think he wants to tell me something totally unexpected, like he's getting married."

Val chuckles. "That would be a punch in the gut, wouldn't it?"

"What if I see him and fall in love all over again?"

"Well, then, I guess you'll get what you deserve."

When Danny looks over at her face, he sees his reflection in her oversized black sunglasses. Without her eyes, her expression is unreadable.

Danny drops Val off at her apartment after an early dinner of fish and chips, and he hands her the photograph from the wedding. Val stares at the print for a few minutes before slipping it into the pocket of her jacket. "I don't photograph so well when I'm not posing," she quips. "That's an old lady in that picture, my alter ego."

"I think you look beautiful. Human."

Val snorts. "I took some publicity shots when I was younger. Talk about beautiful."

"You look like you're going to cry here. What were you thinking?"

She opens the door and steps into the lobby before answering. "Who knows? Maybe I was wondering what my own daughter would look like." She frowns. "Maybe I was remembering what it was like to be young."

She props open the glass door with her foot and looks at him, no hint of a smile on her face. "All right, don't just stand there. Come on up for some tea and maybe I'll tell you something about it." She points her finger at his nose. "But only because you took me to the beach. Otherwise, I wouldn't care about you at all." She winks and chuckles.

Her hands tremble as she reaches out to press the elevator call button, and he knows that soon he will be sitting on the sofa in her apartment, listening to the fine gravel of her voice as it travels through the years of her childhood and the flash and bang of her youth. He imagined this moment years ago, that moment before the Siamese Kitten would reveal all her secrets because he was the one who could understand. Because he was a child who woke up every other morning expecting that his life had magically transformed overnight into a glittery, musical adventure, and was disappointed when he realized he was in the same old house on the same old street. Danny steps into the elevator beside Val. As it begins to rise, he realizes he is holding his breath.

PART TWO

THE HOUSE

1938 to 1946

It was a small house, a clapboard shack really. It sat on River Road, on a wooded lot choked with wild blackberry and dogwood. Even though there were other houses nearby, it was easy to believe, when standing on the porch or on a boulder in the backyard, that this was the only inhabited house for miles and miles and that they were the only family. From the kitchen, Val could just see the Fraser River through the trees. When she was a little girl, she spent hours staring at its winking, grey-blue surface. Once, right after her eighth birthday, she took her father's axe, the one with his first name, Warren, carved crudely into the handle, and tried to slash her way through the bush and down the hill to get to the shore. After a half hour, her mother discovered her, covered in scratches from the thorns, dead leaves stuck in her dull brown hair, her hands covered in rust from the blade. Her mother said little, and finished cleaning Val's scratches before sitting with her by the kitchen window in the late afternoon light, listening and watching for the fishing boats and logging barges.

"I love the river, Mum," said Val, resting her hand in her mother's lap.

"Yes. Me too. If you cross it and pass the island, you'll find the city," Meg said softly, as she waved her hand at Annacis Island, blue and blurry in the sunshine.

"Have you been to the city?"

"Once. Before you girls were born. It was lovely, you know. We saw a vaudeville show and looked at diamonds in a shop window."

Val imagined her mother as a young woman with sparkly, lively eyes, sauntering down a glittering street lit with tall, wrought-iron lamps. She wore a white fur coat and high, shiny black shoes. She stopped at a bright window, pointed at a necklace winking on a blue velvet cushion. Val's father, dashing in a black hat and coat, strutted into the store and came back out, necklace in hand. Val leaned her head on her mother's arm as the story came to an end, the rough cotton tickling her cheek. She fell asleep to her favourite lullaby.

Her father promised that he would cut a path to the river the following weekend, but instead spent those two days sitting on a stump in the backyard, drinking beer with his old logging buddies, talking about the wild days they used to spend in the bush and the wilder nights they spent in the city. Before there was no more work to be found, before all a family man could do was line up for relief and take whatever was given to him.

Val and Joan were fifteen months apart and inseparable. In school, they were known as "Those Wild Nealy Girls." Teachers sent home notes complaining that the sisters picked on the other girls, cutting off their braids with pocket knives, chasing them with dead rats they found in the schoolyard. Once, Joan took exception to another girl's pristine white gloves and quickly but silently drove a sharpened pencil through the creamy leather and into the back of her hand, where it stuck into her flesh as the little girl howled.

Joan—small and small-boned with white-blond hair and blue irises ringed in black—only stared blankly at the teachers and the other children when they were angry with her, sometimes allowing a perfectly formed tear to course slowly down her pale cheek. Val—taller and bigger with arms capable of killing field mice by throwing them against the schoolhouse wall—yelled back, her head vibrating with so much raging energy that her brown curls shook and stiffened from the sound of her voice.

Meg, in her faded cotton dresses, took the notes they brought home and left them on the kitchen counter, where they remained unread and eventually multiplied into a pile of meticulously folded foolscap, which Warren used to start fires in their ancient woodstove. Neither parent ever asked why the other children never came to the house to play or why, on sunny Saturday afternoons, Val and Joan stuck close to the house, holding hands as they lay on their backs in the yard and watched the clouds shift and blow through the sky. Perhaps Meg and Warren heard the whispers when they went to the general store for flour and salt and seed, those whispers spoken behind hands, with eyes averted.

"Those girls never speak to anyone besides each other."

"I invited the mother over for tea two years ago, but she didn't drink or eat. All she did was stare at me with those empty eyes. It gave me the creeps."

"The blond one pushed my Jimmy into the duck pond and tried to hold his head down. Would have drowned him if Mr. Lumby hadn't heard the ruckus."

"Men who don't help themselves only punish their families."

Val knew that money was tight for everyone these days and that, years ago, when she was a baby or maybe even before she was born, times had been better. The stories her father told his friends were always the same: he was once the bravest logger in the whole province, and could climb the tallest spruce in his spiked shoes without even a shiver of dizziness or fear. Some men never got the hang of it and were relegated to sawing the logs into pieces after they came crashing down to the damp, mushroomy forest floor. But not her father. Sometimes he'd climb higher than he ever needed to, just so he could sway with the skinny branches and feel his whole body bobbing in the wind. The other men hollered up at him that he was as crazy as the crow they once saw eat her own chick, but he didn't listen, only grinned wildly at the sunshine he never felt while on the ground.

They had been on relief for as long as Val's memory stretched, but she knew that other children's fathers had started to work again now that the sawmills were expanding and the trains were stopping to pick up wood and fish to ship east, and that the other girls in school were wearing new hair ribbons and sturdy boots. But Val didn't care as much about those things as Joan, whose eyes flashed meanly when Beryl showed off her cashmere stockings at recess by dancing the Charleston in the schoolyard.

"My dad is the new foreman at the lumber mill," she said as she smoothed down her sleek, dark hair. "He bought my mum a jar of special cold cream that cost a whole three dollars."

That afternoon, Beryl went home crying, her legs bare and her arms tied behind her back with one ripped stocking. The other was tied around her head, with the foot stuffed unceremoniously into her mouth.

Once in a while, Val watched her father leave in the morning for a pickup shift at the rail yard, his lunch pail half full of bread and butter, an apple and beef jerky. He came back before bedtime, his face covered in a fine layer of dirt and his work pants covered in paint or smelling like whatever he had been loading and reloading into the cars. Other days, he would simply sit in the backyard or on the front stoop in an old kitchen chair, watching as people walked by, as the occasional car or truck rumbled down the road. Eventually, by dinnertime, two or three or four of his friends, those who had no children or wives and couldn't get relief, would show up and Meg—her shoulders drooping with exhaustion, or perhaps disappointment—would have to search the house for more scraps of food to make a big enough meal for everyone. Val particularly hated the soup, which was dense with potatoes and not much else, and she felt sick every time she walked through the kitchen and saw it bubbling thickly on the stove, its smell seeping through the house like dirty clothes wet with rain. She swore she would never be like her mother. If she married, he would be rich. If she didn't, she would take care of herself.

On nights like these, Val and Joan huddled together in their makeshift play tent made from fallen branches and an old tarp of their father's, and pretended to cook a meal—Val doing the cooking while Joan organized their imaginary dishes.

"I'm going to make a lemon chiffon cake."

"What's a chiffon cake?"

"I think it's a cake that has lots of bubbles in it; one that floats in your stomach when you eat it."

"Oh. What else?"

"Bacon and toad-in-the-hole and roast chicken and jellied salad and champagne."

"I think I would like some beef pie too, please."

"All right, Joanie. Beef and mushroom pie it is."

The other children at school were buzzing, their small heads bent together in class or at lunchtime. But this time, they weren't whispering thoughts and observations (both true and untrue) about the Nealy girls. They were talking about war.

Words that Val and Joan had never even considered before became part of conversations they overheard wherever they went. *Germany. Enlist. Fighter plane. Commonwealth.* The older brothers of the other children at school were enlisting and, every morning, another girl or boy would brag about how Jimmy or Willy or Fred had made the decision to leave home and shoot Nazis. Once in a while it was even somebody's father, usually a man who hadn't been able to find work and whose children were as poor as Val and Joan. At home, however, the discussions were still the same, which meant that Warren still talked about the old days with his buddies, and Meg softly told the girls about her one visit to the city, a story they knew so well that they repeated it silently whenever they had a quiet moment.

But news has a way of infiltrating even the most isolated house, even the one drowning in bush and the scent of decaying raccoons and squirrels, long dead and hidden in layers of salal and creeping Charlie.

One evening, their father sat down to dinner (trout from the river, small knobbly carrots from the garden and the last jar of applesauce from the autumn before) and smiled broadly at his family. His lips stretched far past his teeth and showed what Val thought was an unseemly expanse of gum. Banging his fork on the table, he announced, "I've found a job."

Meg gasped and Joan gaped.

"You see, I told you it would happen," he said, spearing a carrot. "There was never any need to worry."

Val couldn't remember if her mother had ever said she was worried. Then again, her mother didn't say much.

"Where?" Meg asked, her hands resting on the table-cloth, her plate of food steaming in front of her. "How?"

"They're reopening the fish cannery downriver. It's going full steam, Meg, with shifts around the clock. The pay isn't as good as I was hoping for, but I'm glad to be off relief. It hurts a man's pride to take handouts like that." Her father thumped on his chest with his fist.

Her mother said nothing, but Val sat up straight and looked around the table. "It's because of the war," she announced. "They need to feed the soldiers and they're going to send them canned fish."

Joan nodded and said, "That's right. The war."

Their father ignored them and nodded at Meg, who was lifting her first forkful of food to her mouth. "Bake us something sweet. The boys are coming by tonight to celebrate. It'll be a party."

Later, Val and Joan sat on the back porch, hidden by the holly bush that grew by the stairs. Warren and his friends smoked and drank, passed around bottles and stories, and threw rocks at the furry shapes that scurried around the perimeter of the yard. Crouched around a small fire, each man was indistinct and Val couldn't tell whether the one closest to the outhouse was Johnny or Oliver or Buck. Their clothes were faded or stained the same shade of brown, and each of them had the same scratchy voice, a voice scarred by yelling, drunken singing and the sharp-edged whisky that clawed at their throats on the way down. The one she recognized was her father, with his narrow shoulders and scrawny neck, his outline sharp against the wavering firelight.

"What about the logging then, Warren? Canning fish sure isn't the same thing now, is it?" Their laughter lifted the hairs on Val's arm. So loud. Tinged with that meanness that swells in groups.

Val saw her father lean back and tip his face toward the night sky. She wondered what he was looking at because there were no stars tonight, no moon. Nothing but the dun undersides of clouds, one shade brighter than the sky itself.

"Meg won't have it. She told me so this afternoon. Said she wasn't going to stand for me disappearing into the bush for weeks at a time, no matter how good the money was. I tried to reason with her. The war will be eating up all sorts of things, not just canned fish, but lumber and steel too. I told her, these next few months could be the richest of our lives, if she'd let me go. But she doesn't like the danger. And, of course, she doesn't want to be alone. Once a lady has had a taste of this," he said, gesturing toward his crotch, "there's no turning back."

The laughter rose up again and Val rubbed her ears to empty out the sound. When had she ever heard her mother say those things?

Joan leaned in toward her and whispered, "I don't think Mum would notice if Daddy went away."

One man, whose voice sounded smoother than the rest, as if he had been chewing on duck fat, boomed into the air. "Come on now, Warren. Maybe you're getting old and scared of what those trees could do to you, hmm?"

Warren stood and threw his bottle at the man's head. He missed, but his target rose as well and began pushing up the sleeves of his shirt.

"Lost your temper with your balls?" the man hissed.

Val craned her neck to see better, but the light from the fire skipped over the men's faces and all she could see was their two standing bodies, dark and tense. She held her breath, waiting for another word, for the sound of fist hitting flesh, but everything was silent. No small animals rustling in the bush, not even the breaking of water on rocks. Joan put her thin hand on Val's knee.

Their mother stepped out of the kitchen and onto the back porch, not noticing her two daughters crouched behind the railing. She held a plate with a flat, plain cake. Blinking against the darkness, she said softly, in a voice that wavered on the air, "Cake?"

The other man sat down with a thump. Warren strode over, pulled the plate out of Meg's hands and dropped it on the tree stump in the middle of the yard. "Eat," he said, before disappearing into a narrow gap in the bush and stomping toward the river.

—

By the time Val was fourteen, she and Joan had stopped going to school altogether. Their mother said nothing about it as she let down the hems of their dresses and sent them on errands to buy milk and flour. It didn't even matter when the truant officers came to the house and knocked and knocked. Meg simply turned her head creakily at the sound while continuing to knead the bread or wash the windows. Eventually it became Val's job to feed the chickens and make sure they had enough air and light. It was Joan's job to weed the garden and harvest what could be eaten. But these things took little time, and by mid-morning the girls had nothing to do, so they started to dance.

In the attic, they found an old record, *Hinky Dinky Parlez Vous*. In their bedroom (where their father couldn't see or hear them and complain about the noise), they set up the ancient phonograph and danced, each taking turns high-kicking, twirling, doing the splits. In the beginning, Meg told them about the show she saw in Vancouver, describing the routines at her daughters' prodding. When Warren went to work, they pulled their mother into the bedroom and danced for her. She laughed until she cried, her hands clasped over her belly.

"You two will never be famous hoofers, but at least you try," she said, wiping away the tears on her cheeks.

After two years of selling eggs for pennies and accompanying their mother on intermittent cleaning jobs, Val came up with a plan. One night, as she and Joan were lying in bed, awake because their father was outside drinking again with his friends, she whispered the details to her sister.

"We'll run away, see? We'll hitch a ride to Vancouver

and we'll audition for the Orpheum. They'll take us for sure. And then, maybe we can get all the way to New York! Mum said the vaudeville shows were full of dancing girls like us. Come on, Joanie. What do you think?"

Joan pulled the quilt up closer to her chin. "I don't know, Val. We don't really know anything about Vancouver, do we? Mum hasn't been there in almost twenty years."

Val grew angry. "What's the matter with you? When did you become such a wet blanket?"

"I'm not! I want to leave this place as much as you do. I just don't know that running away is the best thing to do."

"Do you have any better ideas?" Val asked scornfully.

"No," said Joan. She turned to face the wall. "But I'll think of something."

A few weeks later, Val woke up in the middle of the night, feeling strangely cold. She turned over. Joan had disappeared.

Val pulled on her housecoat and padded through the house in her bare feet, listening for her sister's voice or the creak of a floorboard. She peered into her parents' room, where her father lay on his stomach, his face squished into his pillow. Her mother was curled on her side, taking up less room than a small child. Outside, Val could see the deep blackness of the river.

She heard a murmur and a slight thump coming from above. In the hall, she saw that the ladder to the attic had not been pulled up. "What on earth is she doing up there?" Val whispered. She had thought that speaking would dissipate the heavy silence, but her words fell and disappeared, making no impact whatsoever on the quiet around her. As she climbed the ladder, she heard the squeak of the unfinished wood floor. *Is she dancing?*

Moonlight flooded in through the uncovered window. Against the walls, boxes of old clothes and toys and tools sat in uneven piles. In the corner, an armchair was covered with a white sheet. And there, right on the floor, on top of their dead grandmother's quilt, was Joan, naked, her back arched, her white breasts pointed toward the ceiling. Underneath her was a man Val only knew as one of her father's friends. His brown hands were travelling up and down her sister's body as she rode him, moaning with her eyes closed. A pool of moonlight illuminated the curve of her hips, the paleness of her skin. The man was barely visible; he was, to Val, shades of brown and clumps of black, curly hair.

He lifted his head. Val stepped backward, looked behind her for the trap door. Before she could step down onto the top rung of the ladder, she heard his voice.

"You can be next, big sister, if you like."

As Val climbed back down, Joan's giggle floated after her.

In the early morning, Joan crawled back into bed beside Val, smelling of flesh rubbed together, like the odour of burning hair and sour milk. Val kept her eyes shut and pulled the blankets up to her nose until dawn, when she quietly left the bedroom and went outside to the henhouse. She checked their nests, her ears filled with the sound of clucking chickens.

At breakfast, her mother set down plates of toast and poached eggs. Val's stomach was unsettled, tightening and loosening every time she tried to swallow. As she choked her food back, Joan wandered into the kitchen, still in her nightgown.

"I'm starving," she announced.

Meg nodded and pointed to her congealing egg.

With a mouth full of yolk and toast, Joan eyed Val from across the table. She swallowed loudly. "Have a good sleep?" she asked, a grin starting in the corners of her mouth.

Val sat up straight. "No, actually. A couple of rats in the attic woke me up."

Joan stared sullenly out the window.

Val felt strangely rooted to her chair, listening to the sounds of her sister and mother chewing their breakfast. She kept her head down, eyes fixed on the scarred wooden table-top, at the crumbs that had, over the years, collected in the scratches and dents.

Joan stood up to bring her plate to the basin. On her way, she whispered to Val, "You have your own stupid plan to get out of here, I have mine. He'll marry me, you'll see." And she flounced out, her almost-white, uncombed hair like a cloud in the morning sunlight.

That winter, the baby was born, squalling and slimy and wrinkled. Val stared at the child as he lay on Joan's chest, clenching his fists and wailing. Joan's eyes were closed and she was breathing through her mouth as Meg, with an old sheet, tried to clean up the blood and fluid slowly soaking into the girls' mattress. Everything seemed wrong to Val: Joan's skinny frame that had hardly appeared pregnant at all, the baby's bluish skin that barely contained his small, bird-like bones, her mother's tentativeness in telling Joan when to push and for how long.

As Meg wrung out a cloth in a basin by the window, Val

whispered to her, "I told you we should have gone to the hospital."

Wet strands of hair clung to the sides of her mother's face, and Val could see her body wilting as the exhaustion crept from feet to spine to neck.

"Better to keep it quiet," her mother said. "That Lumby girl is a nurse, and then everyone around here would know." She turned and looked Val directly in the face. "Do you think I don't know how they talk about us? If word gets out that Joanie has a baby, those self-righteous women will start saying Warren is the father or that we're making you girls part your legs for money. Maybe they're even saying it already."

And Val knew this was true, that eyes watched their every move and not just because of curiosity. She looked back toward her sister and realized no one had yet cut the umbilical cord. She picked up a pair of sewing scissors from the windowsill, took a deep breath, and stepped toward the bed.

When Val walked into the kitchen to fill a pail with hot water from the kettle, her father nodded at her and said, "You remember to tell your sister she's to name that child Warren. I don't usually ask for much, so it seems to me Joanie can humour me this one time." And he stood up and walked out the back door, his work boots leaving behind a trail of dried mud, flecked with the mirrored remnants of fish scales.

Val cleaned the baby with warm water, poked her finger into his armpits and the creases around his thighs. Quiet for now, he stared at her with round, teddy-bear eyes, searching her face for, perhaps, something familiar. She thought she saw him reach for her as his tiny hand brushed the fabric of her grass-green dress. She knew he couldn't possibly control his arms, but she smiled anyway and wrapped him in an old flannel blanket. Drowsily, he fluttered his hands and fell asleep.

Joan lay on her side, her hands between her legs. She stared at the faded wallpaper beside the bed. The blood was mostly gone (only faint pink streaks remained on the wall and on the floor) and Meg had replaced the soiled sheets. Val tucked the baby into his basket by the window.

"Does he have to sleep in here?" Joan asked, the words coming out like groans.

"Where else is he going to sleep? In the henhouse?"

"Shut up, Val. You don't know what it's like."

Val laughed. "No, you're right; I don't. Why don't you tell me then?"

Joan traced a crack in the wall with her finger. "You're talking so loudly, it hurts my head."

Dropping her voice to a whisper, Val leaned closer to the bed. "Tell me: which one is the father? Or do you not remember?"

Joan rolled over to face her sister. "I know exactly who the father is, you stupid cow."

"Really? Where is he, then?"

"Stop talking! I need to sleep. Leave me alone."

"Why isn't he here, Joanie? Did you say something to make him mad? Did you drive him away?" Val wanted to slap Joan, take her by the shoulders and bang her blond head against the wall until she admitted she was wrong, that she had miscalculated her escape.

"He's with his wife! He wouldn't leave his good-for-nothing, lazy wife. Satisfied?" She sat up abruptly, thumped her fist on the mattress and jumped to her feet, her arms out like she was ready to grab Val by the hair. Val was about to yell something back at her, sleeping baby or no, but Joan turned pale and her mouth twisted in a strange half-smile, half-grimace.

She wavered in place until Val caught her and helped her lie down. As she pulled the blankets up to cover Joan's chest, her arm brushed her sister's cheek. Red hot, like the rocks their father used to ring the firepit in the yard.

All that night, Meg sat by the side of the bed on one of the hard, wobbly kitchen chairs, wiping Joan's face with a cool, damp cloth and murmuring that same story over and over again.

"The lights. You should have seen them," she said softly. "Like a night sky, but so much brighter."

For three days, Joan tossed in a fever, gripping the sides of her stomach with her long white hands. On the fourth day, Warren went to the neighbours' to telephone the doctor, who examined Joan for ten minutes before taking her in his own car to the nearest hospital, a one-hour drive away. Meg, with Joan's head in her lap, went with them and left Warren, Val and the baby home alone.

Val had been worrying over the baby all this time. When Joan, groggy from oversleep, tried to feed him, she cried that her breasts hurt too much, and no milk came out of her swollen, bright-red nipples. It wasn't long before she stopped trying altogether, and she seemed to forget his existence entirely. It was up to Val to clean him and soothe him, to prepare the diluted cow's milk every two hours and feed him.

He seemed all right for the first little while, and he often stared at Val with a contented look. Whenever Warren held him, the baby screwed up his brow and scowled at his grand-father, fussing until Val cuddled him close to her chest and hummed a made-up song. Soon, she thought she could see his eyes searching the room for her, and she said to herself, "I'm the one he can trust. I understand him like nobody else." When he was awake and quiet, she sometimes wet his scalp and spent a half hour gently arranging and rearranging the fine, dark hair, pretending that she was a barber with a tub of Brylcreem. And as he fell asleep in her lap, he pulled at her skirt and clutched it in his fist so tightly that she closed her eyes and slept with him in the chair by the kitchen window for as long as he needed.

But three days after Joan left for the hospital, he changed. He napped in irregular spurts and hardly seemed to notice Val at all. He began to spit up every drop of milk she fed him, coughing and choking until the front of his chest was sour and damp.

Still, she kept trying, and still, he couldn't keep it down.

After five days, Joan and Meg hadn't come back. The baby was yellow and listless, barely waking when Val tried to rouse him to eat. She and Warren stood at the side of his basket, staring at his small, peaked face.

"I don't know what to do," she whispered.

Her father wiped his hands on the seat of his pants. "I can't afford the doctor again. If I ask for another advance, the cannery will fire me. Every day that Joanie is in the hospital means more money." He didn't say, *It's Joan or the baby*, but Val knew that, stripped down, this was the choice they were both making, even though it felt like no choice at all.

The next day, as Val was holding the baby, trying to tease his mouth open with the nipple on the bottle, he reached up with his shrivelled hands and looked past Val's shoulder at something in the distance. She looked behind her and saw nothing except shadows on the bare wall, dust motes floating in a ray of sunshine. She held his little hands in hers and murmured, "You don't have to be scared. Shhh." After a few minutes, she even brushed the sleeve of her green dress against his cheek in the hope that he would grasp it like he always had before. But he didn't seem to notice her at all and continued to hold his arms out stiffly. When Val began to worry they would never relax again, he sighed, dropped his hands and died, his life escaping like a whisper, the straight black hair on his head wavering slightly in the draft. Eventually Warren discovered them in the kitchen chair. He took the baby from a motionless Val, wrapped him gently in an old white sheet and carried him into the bush, where Val knew he would bury him.

For the rest of the afternoon and evening, she sat on the front stoop, but Joan and Meg didn't come home. She thought, *There's no hurry now.*

She cleaned the house for days afterward, starting at the attic and working her way down. She threw out everything that hadn't been used in a year and scrubbed her way from room to room. Her father, for the first time, went to work clearing the bush around their house, cutting and slashing and digging in concentric circles for hours after his shift at the cannery. In the evenings, Val made dinner, usually potatoes and salt pork, with blackberry preserves from last summer for dessert. She and Warren said little; as he washed the dishes, she swept the floor. Afterward, they went to their separate bedrooms and slept dreamlessly, their arms and legs and backs aching with work. In the morning, she found the trails of dried tears on her cheeks, but never remembered crying in the night.

When Joan and Meg returned, her sister appeared older and sharper, the lines on her face clearly defined—eye, jaw, cheek. She no longer looked like a doll, but like a tired, beaten woman whose body seemed on the verge of collapsing under its own meagre weight. Her eyes darted from left to right as she came up the front walk, until they rested on Val's face.

"How are you? What happened?" Val held on to Joan's elbow and guided her to a chair.

Meg stepped in behind them. "It was an infection, they said. Something she caught before she was pregnant." She paused. "She won't be able to have any more children."

"I'm sorry," Val said, her hand resting on Joan's shoulder.

"Where's the baby?" Joan asked. "Is he sleeping?"

Val tried to be gentle, tried to impart that he had died quickly and didn't suffer, but Joan didn't appear to be listening as she raked her fingers through her stick-straight hair. When Val finished, Meg was sitting on the floor in a corner of the living room, sobbing into her hands.

Joan stood up. "The doctors said he might not live without me. I half expected it." She walked down the hall and into their bedroom, not bothering to close the door. Val could hear the springs in the mattress groan as she lay down.

THE CITY

1946

About two months later, Val started to dream again. One night, she saw herself dressed in a fine, floating white gown, standing at the edge of the river, overgrown bushes and trees behind her, blocking her view of the house. The surface of the water sparkled, catching light on the edges of waves. Val saw a salmon leap and twist in the air before disappearing again, its return to the river making barely a ripple.

She stepped onto a passing barge, a fantastic barge, decorated with blue velvet and painted paper lanterns. As she floated away, she could see past the bush and into the attic window, where Joan's face was twisted, whether in pleasure or pain, she couldn't tell. Joan's eyes watched as the barge drifted downriver, as Val arranged her skirt to billow more gracefully in the breeze. Her lips moved and Val could swear that she was saying, *A curse, a curse.*

Then, a voice: "Across the river, Val. We have to get across that river."

Val struggled to open her eyes, groped for the wall, something solid to bring her back to waking life. "Joanie?"

Joan's back was resting against the headboard. She turned toward Val, who could just see her glimmering hair in the dark. "You remember your plan, don't you? We have to get out of here, go across the river and get to Vancouver somehow. Val? Are you listening?"

Val sat up and shivered as the cold air hit her shoulders.

"I didn't think you liked that idea."

Joan shrugged. "I didn't. But what else is there to do? Either we run, or we stay here and watch Mum and Dad crumple and die and dry up." Her voice cracked a little and she paused, waiting, Val thought, for inconvenient feelings to evaporate. "Come on, Val. We've always done everything together."

Val had a vision of her and Joan, high-kicking on a stage with a dapper man dressed in a top hat and black tails between them. How beautiful they would be in their sequined costumes, their high-heeled shoes, their curled and set hair. She wanted to hear new music. The only popular songs they heard were on Mr. Ladner's radio when they went to buy supplies at his general store; that is, when they had enough money to buy anything at all. She wanted fast music, the kind that made you stand up and dance, by yourself or with a partner, it didn't matter.

She knew that if they stayed, they would grow older and stranger, like a pair of mad and isolated witches. They would pace through the damp, silent rooms, each keeping her eyes averted for fear of seeing evidence of their own slow disintegration—liver spots, dark circles, caved cheeks—in the other's face.

Val turned to her sister. "We'll go. Tomorrow."

They left a note for their parents, waiting until their mother had gone to the Ladners' big square house, looking for some housekeeping work. Their father, whose industrious streak had fizzled, was still asleep, cocooned in his own particular cloud of stale beer and tobacco.

The note, written on the back of a circular that had come in the mail, sat on the kitchen table, propped up against the sugar bowl.

Dear Mum and Dad,
We've gone to Vancouver to look for work. We'll write when
we get settled. Don't worry and take care.
With lots of love,
Val and Joan

Joan quietly slid a cracked soup tureen from the top shelf in the hall closet. Inside was a small roll of bills, which she stuffed into a brown leather pouch that Val held open. Along with the money they'd made selling eggs, it was all they had.

As they walked down River Road, glancing behind them for a car, any car, to flag down, Val's stomach contracted with a rush of guilt as her mother's money grew hot in her dress pocket. She knew that, without them, the house would be perennially silent, filled with only the sounds of eating, defecating or working. She tried to imagine the rooms without Joan or herself and saw nothing to take their place, just bare walls and limp linens, a smear in the air that could be the ghost of baby Warren. If left to its own devices, the bush would creep slowly toward the house, eating up the garden, then the dingy, muddy lawn and finally, the back porch. Soon, no one passing would even know that a house and a little boy's grave existed under the thorns and dead leaves and birds' nests. And inside, her parents would suffocate, helpless to do anything about their darkening lives. Her parents rarely talked to each other, and she couldn't remember the last time she saw them touch or smile across the table. How could she leave like that, sneaking away with the household money? *At least*, she thought, *they no longer have to feed us.*

She looked at Joan's small body trudging beside her, her right shoulder drooping under the weight of her carpet bag. When Val saw Joan's face, she stopped thinking about her parents altogether. There was Joan: bright and smiling and so glitteringly happy that Val was afraid anything doubtful she might say would shatter this thin veneer of joy, and Joan would be nothing more than tiny shards of brittle skin and bone and hair.

The road twisted around a corner and, finally, their old house was hidden by a group of thin black cottonwoods leaning dangerously over the embankment, their branches almost grazing the surface of the river. She could hear the clang and hum of the canneries to the southwest and the distant horn of a tugboat, sounds that receded as they walked inland. Val took Joan's free hand and squeezed it. Behind them, she heard the faint growl of a car. Val turned and waved. The faster they were gone, the better.

In Vancouver, soldiers who had returned from the war wandered the streets, differing levels of trauma on their faces and in the way they held their bodies. Some were straight and tall and so, so thin. Others wilted under the weight of normal life: their almost-forgotten livelihoods, girlfriends who were no longer girls but women grown tough with waiting. Some drank in the pubs all day and then spilled onto the sidewalks at night, where they seemed to carouse only with one another. The well-adjusted ones offered their services to shops and businesses or allowed their families to lead them around to see all the changes in the city—the new mall across the inlet, even the new supper club downtown.

"They're everywhere," said one waitress they met at a diner. "If you're looking for a husband, you're in the right place at the right time."

The soldiers reminded Val of her father, with his ill-fitting pants, the expression on his face that was half empty, half lost. She wondered if the Depression might return now that the war was over. Perhaps a new generation of children would have to wear underwear sewn from old flour and sugar sacks, as Joan and Val had done, the fabric scratching and scratching until they cried.

The girls found a boarding house not far from the water, on the south side of the Burrard Bridge. They shared one room, with one bed, but they loved it all anyway. The carpeted floors were clean and dry and the hallway smelled like cinnamon and Sunday roasts. Through their window, they could see the lights of downtown winking at them. From here, the aimless soldiers were too small and too far away to be seen.

On their first full day in the city, they ventured across the bridge, writing down the names and addresses of the top theatres, taking note of the kinds of shows they were playing, examining the posters glued to the windows. They ate in a café, carefully counting out the coins from Val's leather pouch. Joan had coffee and a glazed doughnut, while Val limited herself to a bacon sandwich. After lunch it rained, and the people around them hurried from awning to awning, ducking into buildings with their dripping umbrellas and hats. Val and Joan continued to walk the streets with their faces turned up, their

eyes fixed on the limestone lions perched on the tops of buildings, the street lamps with their carved iron bases, even the
streetcars that snapped and rumbled as they sped past. The
ghostly soldiers faded into the shadows.

They spent their whole second day trying to decide what
to wear and how they should fix their hair. The next morning,
they walked into the Orpheum, the most important theatre on
their list, and asked to audition.

A man emerged from a back office and looked them over,
head to toe. "Do you girls have an agent?"

"No," Joan said. "We moved here a few days ago. But
we can dance really well. You just need to see us."

The man smiled and stroked his moustache with one
hand. "I'd love to see both of you, sweetheart, but the shows
aren't doing so well. In case you haven't noticed, it's all movies
these days. No one cares about live entertainment anymore."

Joan stared, wide-eyed, at the manager's face. He looked
away and bent down to tighten his shoelace as her chin
trembled.

Val stammered, "So you won't even let us audition?"

"Listen, I've got plenty of experienced dancers coming
by every day looking for work. I've got agents calling me
every other minute, begging for a show, any show. To be
honest, even if I did have a spot for you two, which I don't,
there are lots of other dancers I would choose first." He
reached past them and opened the door to the street. "Thanks
for stopping by, ladies. Good luck."

As the girls walked past him, he whispered in Val's ear,
"Burlesque is still going strong, I hear, especially now that the
soldiers are back. You look like you've got good legs and a

strong stomach, so if you're willing to show a little skin, you can try the Shangri-La in Chinatown." She gasped and stared at the man's round, red face. "It's a suggestion, honey, that's all. You don't have to take it if you don't like it." He nodded at Joan's retreating body; her arms were wrapped around her chest. "Don't take her along with you, though. Stripping can kill a girl who isn't cut out for it."

They tried every respectable theatre in town. Each manager said the same thing. Shows were closing; the theatres were converting their stages to movie screens. When Val looked into the managers' faces, she saw limited sympathy. They would continue to have jobs, even if all they did was screen movies. Dancers and comics were the ones who would have to find other ways to pay the bills. It was too bad, but what could the managers do about it?

One evening before dinnertime, they walked by the Palomar Supper Club. They saw through the open door that it was full and that couples and single men waited in the lobby to sit at the bar. Val heard the music—clear and fine with a pitch like ice cubes rattling in a glass—and thought that dancing to that backdrop would be magical. If she could just keep her clothes on. She glanced at Joan's body, which seemed even thinner in the city, and kept her mouth shut.

Joan cried when they got back to their room, her shaking hands fingering the blisters on her feet. When their landlady called them for supper, Joan refused to go, even though Val reminded her that they were paying for the food as part of the rent, and she should eat it. Val went to the dining room alone and sat in the only empty seat, between two young men. They said they were students at the university, and brushed her breasts with their hands while passing the dishes. She forced herself to eat the roast potatoes and ham, the soup with crackers, even the sponge cake—as much as she could. Later, she lay on her side of the bed, her hands cupped around her too-full and distended belly.

The day before their weekly rent was due, Val walked through downtown, stopping at every restaurant, shop and hotel to see if they had any work for her. Nothing. The managers and shopkeepers looked at her faded, floral-print dress and her scuffed shoes and simply said, "No." As she walked down street after street, she thought of Joan, lying in bed in her nightgown, refusing to move even when Val grabbed her ankle and tried to pull her to the floor. Despite the February drizzle, Val began to sweat, and her face flushed with hot, angry blood. She kept blindly walking, bumping into men and children as she went. When they first arrived, both she and Joan had examined the face of every stranger they passed. Now, Val didn't want to look.

Maybe they should have never left their parents' house. At least there they didn't have to pay the rent.

The streets began to change around her. Buildings were narrower, with balconies on the second and third floors. Red- and green-painted pillars rose from the street. Val, her eyes misted over with anxiety and rage, noticed none of it and plowed forward. When she spotted another restaurant, she took a deep breath and plunged inside.

In the dim, she saw vinyl booths, a few loose tables and chairs and a lunch counter. The smell of coffee and frying pork surrounded her and she felt hollow. They had run out of money for breakfast and lunch two days ago and had been eating only the supper that their landlady prepared. She put her hand to her stomach and heard it rumble. Embarrassed, she looked around at the customers to see if anyone noticed.

Chinamen. Sitting in almost every booth, at the counter, in the chairs. Some methodically ate their food, while others chatted to men at their tables or yelled across the room. *So angry*, thought Val. *Why are they shouting like this?* A man wrapped in a white apron stood behind the counter, wiping it with a damp cloth. Through a window in the kitchen door, Val could see more men cooking in the back. She looked behind her at the rainy street, at the purposeless soldiers huddled under awnings and in doorways, wearing coats inadequate for this biting late winter.

A girl, a few years older than Val, with tightly curled red hair, walked toward her, a tray in her hand. "Here for something to eat?" she asked, her head cocked to the side.

"I came in to see if you need any help. Maybe you need another waitress?" Val stumbled over the words, unsure if this was appropriate, if a restaurant run by Chinamen expected different things from girls and women.

"Well, as a matter of fact, Marge quit this morning. Mr. Chow," she shouted to the man behind the counter, "this girl's looking for a waitress job. You want to talk to her?" The man nodded and the girl pointed to a table by the window. "Sit over there. He'll be with you in a minute."

Val rubbed her hands together under the table. She sniffed deeply, smelled butter and eggs, toast and doughnuts. How could a place like this smell so familiar? Her stomach rumbled again.

Mr. Chow wiped his hands on his apron before sitting in

the chair across the table. "What's your name?" he asked.

Val was confused; she had expected this man would barely be able to speak English. But he sounded like everyone she had ever known, like her father, like the young men at the boarding house. "I'm Valerie."

"Do you have any waitressing experience?" He looked over her face, narrowing his eyes to a squint. His thick black hair was brushed away from his forehead and neatly parted on the side.

"No," she said, "but I can do the job. I used to help out a lot at home, you know, with the dishes and getting meals."

"Hmm," he said, rubbing his chin. "I don't know. A lot of girls have more experience than you."

Val's eyes started to water, but she took a deep breath and forced herself to answer calmly. "I know that. But I really need this job, Mr. Chow. My rent is due and my sister isn't feeling well and," she paused, "it smells really good in here." She blushed and looked down at her lap, readying herself for the rejection.

Mr. Chow stood up, pushing his chair backward. "You look hungry."

Val stared. "I'm sorry?"

"You need something to eat, don't you? I'll get you something right now and a bag for you to take home to your sister." He disappeared into the kitchen.

The waitress put her hand on Val's shoulder. She was covered with freckles, all the way down her arm to her fingers. She nodded and shifted her tray so that its edge was balanced on her hip. "He'll hire you, don't worry. He only feeds people for free if he likes them."

Val smiled and held out her hand. "I'm Val."

"My name's Suzanne. Welcome to the Chow family." She patted Val on the head and walked off, swinging her tray in time to the music coming from the radio behind the counter.

Mr. Chow brought her an egg salad sandwich, brown beans and a small bowl of carrot soup. He set a paper bag on the table. "This is for your sister."

"Thank you," she whispered, staring at the food.

"When you're done, I'll take you around and introduce you to everybody. You'll start tomorrow morning at seven thirty, for breakfast. We'll see how it goes from there." He looked at her hesitating, his brown eyes (lighter than Val would have thought; everything here was a surprise) lingering over her hands as they lay on the table, waiting. "Go ahead, eat. I'll come back when you're done."

When Val returned to the boarding house, Joan was sitting at their small table, looking out the window at the boats on the inlet, some simply floating in place, some sailing through the rain as white-crested waves tossed them back and forth. Silently, Val set out the food and watched as Joan, with her thin, pale hands, brought the sandwich to her mouth and ate, faster than Val had ever seen her.

Before Joan could speak, before she could ask where the food came from, or why Val looked so pleased with herself, Val smiled widely and said, "A Chinaman has saved us."

The mornings were busiest. Val buttoned up her blouse and scratchy wool skirt in the darkness, her fingers cold with the damp air that accumulated in the room overnight. She filled the wash basin with water and scrubbed the sleep from her face, shivering the whole time. As she laced her shoes, she looked at Joan, still asleep, a line of dried drool on her cheek. When Val left, she didn't try to be quiet.

The café hummed with activity. Omelettes, bacon and oatmeal went from kitchen to Val to customer. She poured coffee after coffee. Suzanne nodded at her from across the room, sometimes whispered in her ear when they passed, "Make sure you smile. They tip bigger if you're pretty." Val noticed the Chinamen's hungry eyes that lingered on her body as she walked away, that measured the distance between her and them, watching to see if she would move closer, drag her fingers on their shoulders. At first, she was shocked and nervous, wondering if one of them would wait for her to finish her shift and jump on her in the street. But she saw, soon enough, that these men were afraid of her—of the whiteness of her skin, the kind of man her father might be, the riot she would inspire if she ran out into the street screaming.

And so she let them watch her, knowing they would take her image into their beds with them.

A barber whose shop was down the block became her favourite customer and he talked to her as much as he dared. "Where are you from?" he asked, stopping her rush to another table with a thin, lifted hand. "A small town like me?"

Val balanced her tray on her hip and smiled. "Not even a town, just a string of houses by the river. It was pretty quiet. Not like this."

"Yes, living here is sometimes very hard. So many strangers. And so few friends. It makes people old before their time. Did you know"—he leaned forward and pointed at his greying, receding hairline—"I'm actually twenty-one?"

Val let out a belly laugh and walked away, looking back at his strangely crooked yet handsome face. She smiled again, over her shoulder, almost coy. When she turned her head back, she saw that Mr. Chow, a roll of dimes in his hand, was watching, his forehead heavy like a thundercloud. She looked away, confused, but when she saw him again, counting the change in the till, he seemed to be his everyday self.

Sometimes a returning Chinese soldier came into the café, and the men would crowd around him, asking him if the stories were true, if the Canadians and British used them to infiltrate enemy lines, if they were spies in the wilds of Burma.

"Was it exciting, Jack? Like in the movies?"

"Those mosquitoes are vicious. Look at my scars."

"Things are changing, brothers," said an older man who had been listening to the soldier all afternoon. "I can smell it."

Val could hear them arguing over the influence these new veterans could wield in Ottawa, parlaying their loyalty to the Commonwealth into the right to vote.

After work, if it wasn't raining, she walked north to the waterfront, through the smells of wet lumber and salted fish, so she could stand as close to the waves as possible. As the evenings grew lighter, she could see across to the shore of North Vancouver, the mountains looming, blue in the fog, green in the sunshine. To the west, she knew that the inlet opened into the ocean, which led to Japan and China, places she knew nothing about but created in her mind. Lacquered red. Gold dragons. Ancient pagodas somehow untouched by war. Rich incense that smelled of cinnamon and cloves. The feel of silk on bare, clean skin.

When she arrived home, Joan was dressed and waiting.

Not once did she go down to the dining room alone. If the bell rang before Val came home, she didn't eat at all.

It was a gloomy and drizzly Monday morning one month later, and the men were grumpy. One or two smiled at her as she poured them coffee, but the rest either nodded or didn't acknowledge her, staring at the newspapers in front of them or the scratches on the tabletops. *It's understandable*, Val thought. *I don't like this weather either.* Earlier, as Joan slept with her white hands folded over the quilt, Val had had just enough time to run the comb through her hair once, button up her plain cotton dress and shove two bobby pins over her ears. Now, as she half ran to the kitchen to pick up an order of cream of wheat, she put a hand to the side of her head and swore under her breath when she realized the pins had disappeared. She hoped they hadn't fallen into somebody's scrambled eggs.

Outside, the city had woken up, startled out of sleep by car horns and the beat of footsteps on the sidewalk.

Val rushed past Mr. Chow on her way to the kitchen, carrying a tray piled high with dirty dishes. He stood beside the door, his checked shirt free of food splatter, his apron tied precisely at his waist (never crooked, never bunched or wrinkled) and drummed his fingers on the wall. Val wished he would pick up a rag and clean something, or perhaps make a fresh pot of coffee; he was taking up precious space with his tree-like body. As she kicked the kitchen door open, Mr. Chow turned his wide head and said, "You look pretty today."

She walked to the sink as if he had never spoken, acted like his smooth and quiet voice had never launched those words. Her shift continued, her wrists aching like they always did at lunchtime, the curls in her hair drooping in the humidity that blew from the stoves. That night she listened to Joan chatter about the young couple who had walked by their window in the afternoon. And then she bathed and lay down in bed, eyes closed.

But she did not sleep. All she could hear were those same four words, breathed to life by Mr. Chow's barely moving lips.

Night air. She remembered the hiss of cold wind that used to sneak in where the walls of her parents' house didn't quite meet, those gaps that grew wider every year until Val and Joan slept with their arms and legs twisted together for warmth, even after every girlish fight. Even after the baby died.

Late one day, she walked home from Chinatown through the side streets, taking unpaved lanes, sometimes walking through vacant lots choked with tall grasses, wildflowers that might have been yellow last summer but were now brown and mouldy from months of winter and early spring rain. She followed narrow trails, carefully placing one foot in front of the other and swaying through the tangled weeds.

When she came within sight of the boarding house, she saw a slight figure fifty feet ahead. She squinted through the darkness at its directionless walk; two steps to the left were followed by one step to the right, and then a jolting hop forward.

Val looked up at the sky and saw a break in the clouds. There, the moon.

The awkward, marionette-like figure wore a pale dress and dark shoes. Val knew that cornflower pattern as well as

she knew the sharp point of that nose. It was Joan wandering
through this cold, damp night—coatless, with her face turned
up toward the lit windows of the houses around them. For a
second, Val wondered how little Warren might have fit into
this picture if he had lived, whether they would have stayed
at their parents' house, whether he would be holding his mother's hand and toddling down River Road, his round eyes
searching the night for owls and mice, or whether Joan might
carry him, her narrow spine buckling under his weight.

Val took a step toward Joan, and then stopped. Joan had
ventured outside alone, had decided it would be a good idea
to explore without the help of anyone else. Val's lips tightened.
Fine. Let her do something on her own steam for once.

But as Val turned to walk through the boarding house's
gate, she craned her neck to see where Joan was headed. Her
slight form stood at the corner as she looked up and down the
street. To the right, a steep hill leading south. To the left, the
beach and Burrard Inlet. She seemed to quiver, like a nervous
sparrow. Just when Val thought she was going to turn left and
follow the sound of the ocean, Joan spun in place and began
walking back to the house.

Val slipped past the front gate and hurried through the
double doors. When she arrived in their room, she pulled off
her coat and shoes, then ran to the bed, where she sat, breathing as slowly as her heaving chest allowed. As she waited for
the sound of Joan's shoes in the hallway, she closed her eyes
and saw her sister's face from two minutes before: teeth held
stiffly in her small mouth, her nose twitching, testing the air
for impending danger or a whiff of her next prey, her eyes
focused on a point. Val had seen that look before, in a similar

pool of moonlight, under those blackened attic rafters. She pressed her closed fists to her eyes. The doorknob turned, and she was sickeningly afraid.

Two weeks passed and Val never mentioned seeing Joan wandering the street. She left her alone, talking only when necessary and avoiding her eyes whenever possible. It was when she reached the narrow sidewalks of Chinatown that she finally stopped clenching her fists.

One evening, Val arrived home from work and could hear music playing through the door to their room. She wondered if perhaps the window was open despite the spring rain and the teenaged boy across the alley was playing his radio too loudly again. As she opened the door, she saw, in the middle of the room, Joan twirling and dancing, her left foot first in the air and then tapping on the floor. Joan laughed, held her arms out in the fading grey light.

In the chair by the window sat one of the university students, his hand resting on his own radio. He smiled and nodded at Joan's dance, watched her skirt as it ballooned above her knees.

"Joan?" Val said, quietly.

"Val!" Joan stopped dancing and ran over to her sister, taking both her hands. "I was showing Peter our old routine, from when we were children."

Val nodded at Peter and pulled off her coat. She couldn't bear to look at his smug face, which was wide with a broad, lumpy nose. As she turned to hang her hat on the hook behind the door, he stood and walked over to her, his long legs covering the distance in three steps.

"I'm glad you're here, Miss Nealy. There's something I would like to discuss with you."

The politeness. Val was confused, but began to feel angry at his carefully worded greeting. *He wants something I won't want to give him.*

"Joanie and I were talking, and we think we would like to get married. I've got two months of school left, and I'll be going to work for the Crown. We could have a wedding this summer. A small one, of course, but Joanie will ensure that it's nice. What do you say, Miss Nealy? What about giving us your blessing."

Val leaned against the wall, the damp hem of her skirt sticking to the backs of her legs. She felt insubstantial, like she might dissolve into a puddle of jelly. She looked to her left and saw Joan smiling widely, her hands clasped in front of her.

"My blessing? Do you need it?" Val stammered.

Peter spoke again. "Yes, of course. We would like you to be the maid of honour too, if that's all right."

The silence from Joan was unnerving. Val wanted to run across the room and shake her out of this act, this pretend innocence that seemed to have materialized out of the crumbs and shards of their past. But she felt pinned; Peter's pale, sharp eyes locked her to this spot beside the door.

"My blessing is yours. I'll do whatever you need." Val looked past Peter's looming body at Joan. "Congratulations, Joanie. I hope you'll be happy."

That night, as Val lay beside Joan, she felt Joan's cool hand on her shoulder. Val opened her eyes, felt rather than saw the presence of the white ceiling, the moulding that cast shadows in streetlight, the crack that ran westward in the plaster.

"Is this what you want?" Val whispered.

"Of course. Why else would I do it?" Joan sounded impatient and tired.

Val turned on her side and stared out the uncovered window. "Do you love him?"

She felt Joan fidgeting beside her. "He's nice enough. He'll have money one day and we'll be as happy as anyone, I guess."

"What about children?" Val held her breath in this moment of silence.

"I'll figure something out before he needs to know."

Before Val fell asleep, her body anticipating the work and hustle of the next morning, she imagined what little Warren might look like now. An unruly thatch of black hair. Long fingers. Eyes that seemed far too innocent for a real human face. A reluctant smile that grew slowly and could disappear in an instant. He'd be the sort of boy who'd feel embarrassed every time his shoelaces dragged in the mud. She could see him seeking her out in a crowded room and, when he found her, reaching for her skirt, his face opening up with relief and contentment.

Even now, with Joan breathing heavily beside her, she could feel the weight of his small body in her hands. Reaching through the blankets, Val gently touched Joan's neck, but Joan grunted and rolled away.

Val stood at the rocky shoreline, kicking pebbles with the toe of her shoe. Seagulls circled, their small black eyes on the shallow hole she was inadvertently digging. The piles of sulphur on the opposite shore gleamed weirdly. Val wanted to fling her coat into the frigid water. She wanted to scream until blood bubbled up in her throat. She wanted to pull out each of her fingers, one by one.

The sound of crashing waves pounded at her ears, seemed to stir her thoughts into a teeming, brackish swamp. She was the one who cared for Joan, whose body was once broken. Each day that Val had gone to work at the café, it had been for Joan, so that her little blond head would have somewhere to sleep. It was Val who kept them from starving, from having to take jobs that traded on their young skin and narrow waists. Their escape to Vancouver had been a plan for both of them; they were supposed to dance together, live together, share everything they had. And now Joan was leaving to marry a man who looked like a cauliflower on legs.

A sharp rain began to fall, but she didn't feel it. Anger, at least, was warming.

PART THREE

THE INEVITABLE

1982

This street is one of his favourites. Mature maples line the sidewalk; neat little apartment buildings stand in the shadows, their walks lined with bright annuals and ferns. He feels refreshed here, protected from the sun by large leaves, enlivened by the dampness of the grass. These few blocks south of Denman are a part of the city that isn't quite city. This is a place that blurs the line between merely surviving in a humid, outgrown mill town and really living in a place that coddles you with gentle sea breezes until you fall asleep.

This damned city, in Danny's experience, is often both at the same time, in the same place.

He turns right and starts to cross the street, mindful of the mothers taking their children to the beach, mothers whose ears and eyes are trained on the hungry, whining children in the back seat and not on the men in the crosswalks. A blue sedan speeds past and a face turns to look at him from the back seat. He flinches. Maybe he isn't as invisible as he thinks.

In the window of the diner, he sees the back of Frank's head, the collar of his blue-striped T-shirt. Danny's stomach turns over violently, and he pauses to steady himself at a newspaper box. Its metal top is burning hot from the sunshine, but

Danny leaves his hand there anyway, almost savouring the sizzle of his skin, the numbness that washes over him once the first wave of pain dissipates.

"I am not a fuck-up," he whispers. An ancient woman, her hair permed, turns to stare at him and then hurries away, pulling a wire shopping cart behind her.

When he steps into the restaurant, it takes a minute for his eyes to adjust to the cavernous gloom. Most people sit alone or in pairs, some silently eating, their mouths full of ham and toast and french fries, some talking with barely touched plates of food congealing in front of them. One wall is completely covered with a frameless, tinted mirror intended to brighten up the place, but all it does is extend the sense of being underground in an endless suburban basement with a fuzzy television and a table-tennis set.

Danny waves away the hostess who comes to seat him and makes his way to the small table by the window where Frank is sitting, his face partially covered by the hand that props up his head. Danny sits down opposite him and picks up a menu. He hasn't any idea what to say or where to look, so he stares at the list of sandwiches, hoping that all these letters will coalesce into some kind of sense.

"Aren't you going to say hello?" Frank's voice is soft, teasing.

When Danny looks up, he braces himself for the inevitable image of the Frank he dreams of, the Frank with wavy, abundant brown hair, the Frank with eyes that laughed and laughed and sometimes blazed, the Frank with broad shoulders and perfect posture.

But this is not the Frank he knows. This Frank sits there,

hunched over a cup of coffee, his hands holding the mug as if he needs the heat to keep his blood moving. His eyebrows seem to have collapsed into his eye sockets. Slowly, he reaches up and scratches a dark red spot on his cheek, and then, like he is thinking better of it, drops his hand and rests it on the table. The stubble on his chin is grey. And his eyes. His eyes tell Danny everything in a way that spoken words can't, in a way that is understood without thinking.

"I wanted to tell you before you heard it from someone else. Before it got so bad that other people started to notice."

Danny wonders how anyone could miss this. Frank is not himself. Frank is indisputably, undeniably sick. Danny feels his hands twitch on his lap, but doesn't reach over the table to grasp Frank's arm. He simply stares. Frank smiles, lips closed.

"I feel pretty good right now. I haven't lost much weight, and I only have a couple of these Kaposi's spots. I hide them with makeup when I have to go to work."

Outside, a mother, wearing a mint-green tank top and matching shorts, carries a screaming toddler, stopping once to shake him slightly, to glare directly into his eyes. The child continues to scream, to kick at his mother's stomach.

"I don't know how long the bank will keep me on. I've been telling them I'm getting over a lung infection, which is true, but not completely."

The mother drops the toddler on the sidewalk, snatches away his brown stuffed bear and slaps him on the cheek. Danny jumps.

"I know it's scary," Frank says.

The child gulps in air, his mouth wide open, his eyes

shut. Danny wonders if he is crying silently or if he hasn't yet inhaled enough to make a sound.

"Have *you* been feeling all right?" Frank continues. "Because if you haven't, then you should definitely go see a doctor, not that anyone knows anything right now, but still. Maybe the key is to go in before you start to feel even a little sick."

The mother snatches up the toddler again and hugs him, holding his chubby body close to hers, her hand on the back of his head. He sniffles, nods when she speaks, and they are off again, heading toward English Bay.

"Danny! Say something!" Frank slams his fist on the table, rattling the forks and knives, spilling the coffee.

There are many things Danny could say. He could say that Frank falling ill is another indication that his worlds are collapsing into each other. Ever since they met, Danny has carried within him a miniature Frank who understands Danny like no one else. And now the most intimate participant in Danny's life is a news story, his gayness a headline that invites public commentary. Danny is dizzy with the wrongness of it all. He could say, "I love you," but he doesn't know if this is true anymore, or if he would be saying it to comfort them both.

Danny stares at the menu, runs his eyes down the list. "A club sandwich," he says. "I haven't had one of those in years."

Frank starts to laugh, but Danny sees the tears welling.

"I guess there's no other response, is there? What can anyone say about a disease that has no name, that no one knows how we catch? Club sandwich is as good a reply as any."

Danny waves the waitress over and places his order.

Frank asks for meat loaf and mashed potatoes, and then he relaxes into the seatback. When the waitress leaves, Danny looks out the window again. The sunshine is directly overhead and so bright that there are no shadows, only pockets of shade in recessed doorways.

"I'm sorry," he whispers. "I'm so sorry."

Frank brings his coffee to his lips and takes a tiny sip. "Sometimes I think I might drown in everyone else's apologies. Maybe that would be easier."

The fear has gripped him, and he knows that escaping it is impossible. When he is sleeping, he writhes in his sheets, turning until he can no longer work his arms and legs free, until he is trapped in a straitjacket of his own making. Something sharp and stinging travels under his skin; he imagines it's the infection slowly pumping through his body. He can see it, painful and clear, whenever he closes his eyes—tiny pulsing organisms floating in a thick red soup, multiplying as they bounce off the walls of his arteries.

The fear has many features—inexplicable scabs, bleeding gums, bowels that leak. But the one he returns to is this: if he gets sick, there will be no hiding it from his parents.

He opens his eyes, sees the reassuring whiteness of his apartment ceiling. Turning over, he reaches into the drawer of his nightstand until his fingers brush the edge of a small box. He sits up and opens the lid. Inside is a pile of photographs. On the very top sits a portrait of Frank, his eyes like half-moons as he laughs into the camera, at something Danny has said. They had been hiking on a fall day, and, even though the photograph is black and white, Danny can see the shades of grey in the leaves behind that mean red and orange and yellow. He lifts this picture out and, underneath, another. Frank at the beach. Frank with the dog. Frank standing beside a sign in a diner window that reads, "Holiday special: franks and beans, $1.75!"

Their first Christmas together, Frank took Danny back to his parents' house, a ninety-minute drive away in the Fraser Valley. There, his mother insisted on serving Danny her favourite wine, a sweet, syrupy drink that reminded him of powdered Tang and coated his tongue. Frank's father pointed at the newly constructed back porch and said, "That's some fine cedar decking. If you ever need to buy some, I can get you a deal." Danny couldn't imagine when or how he would ever need cedar decking, but he nodded anyway and politely sniffed the planks when Frank's father told him to. "Clears out your sinuses, I'm telling you."

At dessert, his mother held up her mug of chamomile tea and said, "A toast to the newest member of our family."

"He's not the prettiest daughter-in-law I've ever seen, but he'll do, Frankie," boomed his father.

And everyone laughed, except Danny, who stared at the popcorn ceiling, his feet itching like they were about to burst right out of his shoes.

During the drive home, Frank reached across the console to pat Danny on the thigh. "I'm sorry my parents were acting like we were about to get married. They're just excited. I've never brought anyone to meet them before."

Danny nodded and kept staring through the windshield at the black highway. *Just follow the white lines. No need to think about it.*

"Did it bother you?"

"Did what bother me?"

"That stuff my parents said about welcoming you to the family."

How was Danny going to pretend like this night never happened if Frank didn't stop talking? "No, it was fine. They were just being parents."

Frank looked away and out the passenger window. "Okay. As long as you know that I didn't put them up to it."

But Danny knew that nobody's parents said things like that unless they had seen a quiver of want in their child's face. Maybe Frank had told them—years before—that he wanted a house, a partner, a garden where he and his lover could grow beans and squash and cook it all together on a stove they bought after haggling with a salesman at a discount appliance store. Danny had never told his parents what he wanted. And they had never asked.

Danny kept his love for Frank to himself, underneath an expressionless, silent face.

Tonight, the photographs are nothing but paper in his hands. Frank is in another bed, perhaps feeling the spots on his body with his trembling, square-tipped fingers. Danny is light-headed and places the box back in the drawer. He lies down again, blinks at the ceiling. If only he never had to sleep.

Danny sits in his car, the windows rolled down to catch the warm breeze that slithers in from the street. He glances nervously at his side mirror, afraid to see his own red face staring back at him. Through the windshield, he can see the entrance to the bank. A security guard paces inside the glass doors. Finally, the last customer leaves.

Frank emerges from the bank, a binder in his hand and his jacket wadded up in a ball under his arm. He slowly walks west on Robson, away from Danny. He can see that the seat of Frank's pants is starting to sag. Danny's hands grip the wheel, but he stays inside his car.

After twenty more minutes, Danny watches as Cindy talks to the security guard. She laughs as he unlocks the door and holds it open for her. Danny waits until her camel-coloured pumps hit the sidewalk before he stirs. He stands up, half shielded by the open car door. He has to grip the top of the frame in order to stand up straight enough that he doesn't appear deflated. The outside air washes over him and he feels dizzy.

"Cindy!" he croaks, reaching with one hand toward her.

She looks up and down the street, oblivious, and starts to cross.

"Cindy!" This time it comes out shaded with desperation.

She turns her head, sees Danny and rushes forward.

"Danny! Are you sick?" She grasps him around the waist. "Here—can you make it to that café over there? You need to sit and have a cool drink, that's all."

She helps him to the café and props him up in a chair near the back, away from the sunlight streaming in through the big front window. She goes to the counter and orders two iced teas. Danny leans his head back and wonders whether, if he stares long and hard enough, a picture will begin to form among the stains on the ceiling.

"Drink this," Cindy says, sliding an iced tea to him as

she sits down. "You look like shit."

Danny gulps half the drink in one swallow. The cold liquid travels, sharp like broken glass, down his throat. He smiles at his sister, at her face tanned from hours of lying in the sun at Kits beach, her thick hair in a long ponytail, her glossed lips. *So pretty*, he thinks. *What a waste.*

"What's going on, Danny? Did you come here to see me?"

"I—" He pauses. "I need you." It's out, but the urgency is gone. All that's left is his own voice, boyish and soft.

"What do you mean?"

"I saw Frank." He tells her the story, about the unnamed disease, the fear. He pauses to drink and looks away, for he sees that her eyes are changing: from sympathy to fear to anger to overwhelming pity. The ice in her untouched drink melts and a pool of water forms under her glass.

He had thought that talking to Cindy would somehow clear his confusion, would separate his thoughts so that he could consider things one at a time, like he used to. His family. His work. Cruising. After Danny finishes talking, he gulps down the rest of his iced tea and shudders.

Cindy pushes hers across the table. "Go ahead, I don't want it."

"What am I going to do?" he asks. *Please*, he thinks, *give me an answer. Any answer.*

"Do you need to see a doctor?" she says, scrutinizing his face with narrowed eyes.

"I don't know. I don't have any spots or anything. I feel all right. Well, scared and sleep-deprived, but all right."

"Maybe they can give you a blood test or something, or an immunization." He begins to hear an undercurrent of desperation in her voice, a thin line of brittle panic, yet her face remains smooth.

"There's nothing. They know nothing."

"You can't go out and cruise anymore, Danny. You can't go to the clubs or the baths or anything." Her voice breaks, and she brings her hand to her throat. "What will Mom and Dad say?"

Years ago, on a still Saturday morning, Danny was polishing the insides of the shop windows with newspaper while Doug grunted in the back, unpacking a pallet of Chinese comic books. The sky was overcast, and there were no shadows on the street. Danny stared at the tiny fingerprints near the sill and wondered which child Doug had allowed to touch the glass. A pair of feet in grubby sneakers appeared outside the window. When Danny looked up, he saw a freckled face on the other side of the glass, grinning.

Danny knew this boy, whose father used to work mixing paint at the warehouse by the water. He was one year behind Danny at school, but swaggered through the halls as if he were student body president. At lunch, he sat by himself in the baseball diamond, digging holes into home plate with his penknife and smiling. Danny searched his brain for a name. Eugene? Gerald? No, it was George. George Mason. He frowned at George's diabolical face. What on earth was he doing here at the shop?

Seeming to read Danny's thoughts, George reached behind his back and pulled a can of spray paint from his waistband. They were so close that Danny could see the colour printed on the label—Midnight Black. Danny stepped backward from the window and looked around for his father, but he was in the backroom. George, grin still in place, pulled the cap off. Desperate, Danny waved both arms in front of him and mouthed, *No*.

Everything seemed to happen slowly. Danny watched as George deliberately sprayed the words CHINKS GO HOME across the front window with a fine workmanship that was disorienting. George paused to admire his work before adding a smiley face with two slanted eyes. Even through the glass, Danny clearly heard the singular pitch of George's laugh, like coyotes mating in the park.

From behind, Danny heard his father's voice. "What the fuck is going on here?"

Doug rushed outside to the window and glared at the words, now dripping down the glass and pooling around the row of bricks underneath. George, crossing the street, turned and waved. Doug pounded his fist against the wall and shouted, "Come back here, you little prick!"

Danny picked up the wad of newspaper he had dropped. When Doug came back inside the shop, Danny timidly said, "Maybe if I try to clean it now, while it's still wet, I can get most of it off."

His father cocked his head toward him. "Do you know that boy?"

"Yeah, he goes to my school."

Every word that came out of Doug's mouth seemed forced. "Younger or older?"

Danny shrank, just a little. "A year younger, I think. But he's pretty tough. Once, I saw him in the alley and—"

Doug waved his thick hand to silence him. "Why didn't you go outside and stop him? He's no bigger than you.

Why are you standing here like a sissy?"

"Dad, he's tough. I've been trying to tell you," Danny started, but Doug was already across the shop, opening the closet where they kept the cleaning supplies.

He turned back to look at Danny's face. "You're useless. How I ever had a son like you I'll never understand."

Danny now looks at Cindy's face, the impeccable makeup shading her cheekbones, the precise blue eyeliner. "There's nothing to explain to them, is there?" he says. They're answering questions with questions, and Danny wants to laugh at the way this mysterious disease has turned even the words they speak into something shifting and thin.

Cindy says, "Still, do you want to come home with me tonight? At least you'll get some of Mom's cooking, not that it necessarily does anyone any good." The dry edge to her voice is back, and Danny allows himself a small smile.

"No, I'm going back to the apartment. I haven't been sleeping much."

"Oh, Danny," Cindy whispers. Tears are starting to form in her eyes. "I don't know how to help you."

"I guess I have to wait and see."

He places his hand over hers, their identical brown hands. He realizes that waiting is the very thing that will allow him to wake up to another day. Without it, the lines of his life are final. For now, waiting is the best part.

This problem, this invisible disease that manifests in sores and coughing and germs that settle in their bodies and multiply, like unthinned mint in a small garden. Danny stumbles toward the dry cleaner, wishing he could shut his eyes against the sharp sunlight piercing his face. *I want rain*, he thinks. *Where has all the rain gone?*

He considers calling Edwin, but he will be no help. He will bring Danny a six-pack of beer and drink it all himself until he falls into a restless sleep. Besides, Edwin will repeat the whispers on the street, the rumours he catches and then releases.

An old woman totters past him, pushing a walker. Their eyes meet and she looks afraid. Surprised, he wonders if she is scared of him; if she thinks that he will try to snatch her purse and knock her down. But after she is a half block away, he realizes that the fear in her eyes was a reflection of the fear in his own, that blazing fear that others can instantly recognize and be repelled by.

He walks by a clinic on Davie Street. In its large window, his body looks so thin that it appears transparent. His eyes focus on something reassuringly solid taped to the window, black type on white paper.

"New disease affecting gay men and IV drug users now called AIDS. Information inside."

It's that tension of knowing and not knowing. He can hold what he knows in his head and pass it from one side of his brain to another. He can prepare. He can grieve. What he doesn't know is less tangible than dreams, more like the shreds of dreams, what dreams would be if they were clawed at by raccoons. With not knowing, all he can do is stifle his horror at the possibilities, but also breathe with relief that the worst hasn't happened yet. Stepping into the clinic will change everything.

Danny pushes open the door to the waiting room and stands awkwardly in a square of sunshine. The other people (small, they all seem, bodies crunched like discarded pieces of paper) stare at him. The receptionist looks up at him with dark eyes ringed by purple liner. She smiles.

"How can I help you?"

He steps up to her desk and leans over so that he is as close to her as possible. "The paper in the window," he whispers. "It says you have information."

She looks confused, and Danny points discreetly to the sign. "Oh," she says. "Yes, we have some sheets typed up. Would you like one?"

He nods, and she hands him a photocopy.

"Thank you," he says. He grasps her hand and shakes it. She smiles again, her lips frozen into an expression he imagines she settles her face into dozens of times a day.

He rushes to a bus stop bench and sits down, holding the paper as still as he can.

It's simple: AIDS attacks the immune system. No one knows why, and no one knows how. Infected people are vulnerable to opportunistic infections and diseases, like Kaposi's sarcoma and pneumocystis pneumonia. Doctors think it's passed through bodily fluids, like semen and blood, but they're not sure. There are only a few cases reported in Canada, but doctors suspect there are many more that have been undiagnosed.

By the time Danny has finished reading half of the sheet, it becomes clear that all these words are meaningless, for there is nothing anyone can do. No one knows how to prevent it from spreading. Like an advancing tidal wave that you watch coming toward you, knowing it will consume you.

A bus stops and people stream off, their eyes fixed on

the sidewalk or the displays in the shop windows. None of them allow their gaze to fall on his face. Even the passengers on the bus look straight ahead, at the power lines, perhaps, or the crows gathered on the rooftops.

Life and death are printed right here, in words that will define things to come: the silence of nightclubs, the drying-up of bathhouses, even the emptiness of the park at night. The weight of the words and his thoughts seem to have rendered him immobile. What if his parents have already heard of AIDS? Seen it on the news, discussed it with Cindy? And if Edwin dies of a mysterious illness his grandmother never names, what questions will his parents ask then? He holds the back of his hand to his forehead.

When he looks up, he sees a blond man hovering outside the clinic, staring at the same sign in the window. The fear is visible in the line of his shoulders, the quick steps he takes as he paces back and forth. Despite himself, Danny reaches out and his body forms itself into a half-hug. *I may as well give him my sheet.* As he stands and takes a step toward the clinic, the man turns around. Familiar eyes. A moustache he once gazed at in thin, shifting moonlight.

Danny could laugh hysterically or run away. He grips the white sheet with both hands and watches as the tall, blond man looks at Danny's face, the paper he holds, and then back at the clinic window. Before thinking twice, Danny hurries forward and grasps the man's sleeve. "Here," he says. "Take mine. I don't need it anymore." Danny stuffs the paper into the crook of his ex-lover's arm and walks away. He feels worse with every passing pedestrian, every shiny car that speeds down the street. He turns up Jervis, remembering there are prints to make and film to buy for the next wedding. He stumbles toward his own particular silence in his contained studio.

That evening, Danny steps onto the walk leading to his apartment building. The laurel shrubs on either side have grown taller than him and lean inward, their branches brushing his shoulders, their tops connecting like a roof. He is overwhelmed by the feeling that he is being swallowed by the bush, and he puts his hand out to swat away the glossy leaves.

A quacking duck flies through the dimming sky. Danny looks up at the sound and squints. As he pushes his key into the lock of the front door, his foot brushes a paper bag beside the welcome mat. He sees the message, FOR DANNY LIM, written in black marker across the front. He crouches down and unrolls the crumpled brown paper, so wrinkled it appears to have been used and reused, folded and stuffed into a drawer between uses. Inside is a glass pickle jar with its label scrubbed off. On the lid, a piece of paper reads, "Danny, some soup for you. From, Mommy." He picks up the bag, one hand supporting the bottom, and carries it into the building. The jar's vaguely green contents slosh as he steps into the elevator. He stares ahead at the textured light pink wallpaper, striated to look like linen, or, he supposes, Thai silk.

In his kitchen, he pours the soup into a pot and sets it on a burner, watching as the coils turn red. The empty pickle jar stands on the counter, residual solids from the soup lining the bottom. Danny wants to pick up the jar and fling it across the room, watch it smash into shards that fall to the hardwood floor. He can imagine his mother, wearing a pair of long walking shorts and a short-sleeved, button-down shirt, riding the bus to the West End. The backs of her legs stick to the vinyl seat. Her thickly knuckled hands cradle the soup in her lap. She switches buses, walks down streets she memorized earlier only because her son chooses to live here and presses the buzzer by the front door to his apartment building. He can imagine her waiting patiently, buzzing once, maybe twice more. After several minutes, she carefully places the bag by the welcome mat, where Danny is sure to see it. She hesitates then tightens the lid once more so the raccoons, with their strangely human hands, won't be able to pry it open. And then she walks to the corner and boards the bus to return home, where Doug will be silent and brooding because dinner isn't ready yet, where she will lie and say she was visiting Auntie Mona and lost track of time.

His mother was here, standing at the front door to his building, peering through the glass doors, watching to see if Danny might step out of the elevator into the lighted lobby. He grips the counter with both hands. His mother has stepped into his carefully constructed life, bearing a gift that will taste like his childhood, those days he spent helping her in the kitchen, his skin absorbing the ginger-scented hot oil until he was sure if he sniffed himself, his nose would recognize each dish his mother cooked.

One particular Sunday, Danny walked into the kitchen, blinking against the blazing lights. He wore the new pyjamas his mother had bought him for his eighth birthday. It was the winter solstice, the darkest day of the year, and he still wasn't sure if it was morning or night. Betty moved from stove to sink to table, her hands covered in rice flour. A patch in her hair released a fine white dust whenever she stepped forward or turned around, as if she were slowly shedding her outer self in small puffs. Danny sneezed before the thick smell of pork broth coated the inside of his nose.

"You must help me or I won't finish before the solstice is over," his mother said. She took Danny's hand and pulled him toward the kitchen table. "You make the balls," she said, pointing to a mound of white dumpling dough in a bowl. She pulled off a piece the size of a Ping-Pong ball and began rolling it between her hands until it formed a sphere. "You see? Like that."

The dough—thick and elastic, like drying glue—stuck to Danny's palms, leaving a thin white layer that settled into his lifeline and the other spidery lines that snaked across it. He placed each ball on a floured cookie sheet, making rows and rows of smooth white spheres. When he looked up at the window, it was finally daylight.

"Such a good boy, Danny," Betty said. "Your sister would never sit here for so long. Look at that, all the same size too." She turned back to her cutting board, piled with peeled daikon waiting to be julienned. "We will have the luckiest solstice feast ever because you did such a good job."

He could have left the kitchen, gone to join his sister who was outside in her puffy coat, looking up at the low sky, her mouth open in the hope that a few flakes of snow might fall. He could have cocooned himself in his room, rearranging his collection of department store catalogues by preference, his favourite one in the middle so it was protected from dust and damp. He could even have watched television with his father, who was sitting in his armchair as he always did on the one day of the week the shop was closed.

But Danny sat at the kitchen table, his legs folded underneath him, the hot steam from the boiling pots penetrating his thin wool sweater. He knew that the kitchen was the one warm room in the house. Everywhere else, the single-paned windows seemed ready to drop out of their rotting wooden frames. Doug could promise all he wanted, but they knew he would never get around to replacing them, so they huddled in their beds at night and wore layers of clothes as they hurried from room to room. In the kitchen, the warm air seemed to wrap around his body, and sitting near a simmering pot of pork bones was as comforting as sitting by a blazing fire in a stone fireplace. Danny sighed, and his small torso relaxed.

Betty placed a bowl of palm sugar lumps and hot water in front of him. "Stir until it melts," she said, resting her hand on the top of his head for the briefest of moments before she turned away to shred the napa cabbage. Danny ran his fingers through his hair, and rice flour floated around him. He wondered if this was what it would be like to sit amongst the clouds, where everything was seen through a veil of white that softened edges and blurred lines so that each person appeared younger and prettier. His mother turned back, and Danny smiled at her. She nodded, and he picked up a spoon and started stirring.

Now, as Danny watches the pot on the stove, he smiles at the memory. He realizes that not every moment with his mother was painful. Still, it would be simpler to leave it all in the dusty cracks of his mind. It's his fault for returning home. With this one jar of soup, he understands how bad a son he really is, how he is no longer happy to sit with his gentle-voiced mother in a steamy kitchen. Now, whenever he thinks of her, he is devising ways to avoid her completely. And here she is, travelling for an hour and a half in the heat, just for him. He wants to shake her, yell at her that she should take a bath or read a Hong Kong tabloid, anything that will keep her away from her particular cycle of work and bloodletting that leads to this pool of guilt Danny flounders in.

He thinks of Val. She feels, she rages, she can say, *You're a fucking idiot.* When, as a child, he had met her, he knew in an instant that she was not a woman like his mother. Val could slice open your cheek with a twist of her fingernail and kiss you afterward, love and hate commingling in the air like a heady perfume. She is the mother who would have understood the confusion that twisted within his belly when he thought of other boys, the longing to burst out of his humdrum shell and emerge as something new and wonderful. If you hated her or didn't want to see her, Val would smile slightly and saunter away, every step seeming to say, *If you don't want me, I don't want you either.* His own mother is a turtle, sometimes poking her head out to watch the world with small black eyes, careful to upset nothing. Her smell speaks of work, days in the kitchen and cleaning other people's homes, nights on her knees in her own narrow hallway. She doesn't ask to be acknowledged, but the results of her drudgery are everywhere and speak for her when she is silent.

He rubs his eyes and tries to remember how he felt the first time he met Val in that alley. Awestruck. Comforted. For a second, his mother's face hovers as he visualizes the stage curtains he hid behind, the spotlights that circled through the gloom. Now that he knows Val came from a small house like his parents', her glamour is that much more impressive. If he thought she was strong before, he had no idea.

As the soup begins to boil, the phone rings. Even though she hardly ever called in the years after he ran away, he knows it is his mother, who has likely been calling every hour to see that the soup is safely in his apartment. The ringing is like a siren, persistent and unrelenting in its volume and shrillness. He reaches over to pick up the receiver then stops. He turns off the stove and grabs his keys from the hall table.

The dancers grind and spin, their platform shoes squeaking on the stage. The lights shine red on a girl's belly, blue on her thighs. Some are barely awake, their eyelids drooping from a long day followed by this long night, or for a chemical reason. Danny no longer looks for the track marks, and he doubts that the other men in the club ever notice. Whether they are asleep or awake their breasts still bounce when they sashay up the stage, and the space between their legs looks the same.

Danny looks at his watch and realizes that he has been sitting in this chair, absorbed in examining every costume and every shimmy, for three hours. His head feels stuffed with cotton batting, and his mouth is dry from the beers he has been mindlessly sipping. He wonders what Val is doing, but can't get past an image of Frank's newly sunken face. He leaves his money on the table, nods at the waitress and leaves.

The night air blows thick and slow. Even here, standing at the mouth of an alley beside a strip club, Danny thinks he can taste the salt from the ocean, those tiny crystals that tickle the raw red tissue of his throat. He scratches his head, trying to slough off the dullness of beer. Thin clouds move across the surface of the moon. When he was a little boy, he always thought the moon had a woman's face, the craters and shadows like the age spots spreading across his mother's left cheek, the criss-crossing lines like the deep creases around her mouth. Not a face subject to the whims of makeup. Not a face that smiles unless she means it.

Behind him, the side door to the club opens, and a dancer steps out, dressed in a pair of light blue jeans, running shoes and a kangaroo jacket. When she hurries past him, he steps to the side, hoping that she doesn't think he's a pervert waiting in the shadows. She turns and he sees her face, lit from above by the street lamp, pale and young, freshly washed. Her eyelashes are blond and her chin is a small knob, tensed against the dangers that lurk in the street. It is the lines of her face, the smoothness of her cheeks that fascinate him. She's like a little girl who pours imaginary tea for her grandmother and rubs rouge from her auntie's vanity table on her round cheeks when no one is looking. This stripper, without makeup and looking faintly afraid of Danny's gaze, is ready to break, as though she grew up only yesterday and has found that she is already cracking under the weight of adult responsibility.

Danny turns down the street, leaving the dancer to dash across the road and disappear into a waiting car. The next night, he returns with his camera. He waits in the side alley, his lens pointed at the backstage door of the club.

A girl with dark feathered hair steps out into the alley and pauses against the contrast of street lamp and dark night. Danny, his fingers itching, waits for a car to approach before he presses down on the shutter release, hoping that the glare from the headlights will make the sudden brightness of his flash unnoticeable. Tires squeal up the street. The camera flash is blinding, but only for a fraction of a second. By the time the dancer turns and looks around her, Danny has retreated into shadows and there is nothing to see but a line of speeding cars. She looks around once more before climbing into a cab. He lets out a breath and grins to himself as he advances the film.

All night he stands there, waiting for the girls to leave, hiding behind a Dumpster when the bouncers turn his way. It is easier than he thought, this lurking and snapping, capturing their faces, the faces he imagines they had when they were small, when they sat at desks in school and smiled openly at the teachers in front of them. These pictures will show them in their moments of transition and prove that none of them are inhuman, blow-up dolls come to life. On his way home, he walks with feather-light feet and fights the urge to skip down the sidewalks and swing his camera by the strap, singing as he goes.

In the morning, when he develops the contact sheets and brings them into the front room of his studio, he sees that he was right. The women look uncomplicated, like the ones you see at the corner store. And yet there is something about their beauty. Like moonlight, they are ghostly and transitory, as if they might disappear during your next blink. Behind them and above, the flickering neon sign of the club is solid and unmoving, the same in every shot, ugly in its explicitness, yet necessary—without the club, these women might be hairdressers or students or social workers, and their fragile beauty might never be seen.

Danny is euphoric at how clearly he can see their eyes, the arc of their lips. He can feel their breath on his cheeks, that rhythm that says, *This is just me*. No costumes, no makeup. These are their real and thin-skinned selves, as tangible to him as Val's throaty laugh and be-ringed hand on his arm.

This is why he returned to the strip club again and again. It wasn't for the glamour onstage. It was for this: flesh and despair, the things that make up these women, each neatly contained in one glorious shot. He looks up at the sunshine streaming through the skylight and thinks, *Finally*.

The next morning, he hurries to a Catholic church in Shaughnessy and then to a lunchtime reception at the bride's father's house. By four o'clock, he's exhausted, and he drives to the studio with his eyes half closed. There, he handles negatives and contact sheets automatically, not even looking at the tiny images that emerge from the developer. All he can hear is the groom's mother saying sweetly, "We need the proofs tomorrow. I'll have the cheque ready for you when you drop them off." He arrives at his apartment at three in the morning. Before he can submit to a wave of unconsciousness, he feels smothered and panicked, so he fights it, flicking at it limply with his open hand. But the sleep pulls him under, and he stops struggling as he realizes that this relinquishment of his day-to-day senses is what he really wants.

For the first time in years, he sleeps dreamlessly, floating in his own special, complete darkness. It pulses, and his heart pulses. It expands, and he feels his body stretching.

Breathe. It's the only thing he has to remember here.

He could be in an ocean, the tide rolling over and under his body. He swats at the waves, irritated with the interruption. Then he hears it. A ringing, growing louder and louder.

With each ring, the darkness dissipates and sleep recedes a little more until he can see the sunlight, bright and unrepentant, through the open blinds.

He stumbles out of his bedroom. *What would happen if I dropped the phone out the window and never left the apartment again?* He picks up the receiver and holds it to his ear.

A woman's voice explodes, "Danny? What took you so long?"

"What? Who is this?"

He can hear her clucking in disapproval. "Have you forgotten me already? It's only been a week since I saw you."

Confused and foggy, Danny reaches for the wall to steady himself before he remembers. "Miss Val."

"Well, that took you long enough."

He stands up straighter and smoothes the front of his undershirt. "I'm so sorry. I was sleeping, and I'm a little groggy right now."

"Sleeping? Danny, it's two o'clock in the afternoon."

He smiles. "You know, for a second there, you sounded more like my mother than a stripper."

"You little bastard." She laughs. "And here I was phoning because I was worried about you. You were supposed to phone me two days ago so we could go out again, or do you not remember?"

"I've been a little preoccupied."

"Sure, whatever you say, honey. I need to go somewhere today, and I was hoping you could give me a ride. What do you say?"

He knows if he simply delivers the wedding proofs and then returns home, he will want to replay memories: him and

Frank in Banff, his mother combing out the tangles in his hair, the last time he embraced someone under a tree in Stanley Park. If he calls his sister, or goes to see his parents, he will risk the silence that inevitably descends on his family gatherings; the silence that would be too tempting to break with *I am gay*, or *I think I might be dying*.

"I'll be there in an hour," he says. "Wait for me out front."

THE SUBURBS

1982

They drive east down the highway, toward the sprawl of the suburbs. Danny holds his left hand out the open window, and the warm air brushes his forehead. To his right, Val sits with her eyes closed. Danny can see the layers of her eye makeup: the liquid liner, the champagne powder near the tear ducts, the gold-flecked violet on the upper lid. Impeccable, with the ghost of her real skin showing through.

After twenty minutes of driving, he pulls up to a house with a familiar wall of dahlias. The garden where he saw Val for the second time.

Val opens her eyes and sits up straight, grasping her green, patent-leather handbag. "Here already?"

"You still haven't told me why we've come," he says, unbuckling his seat belt.

"Well, come in with me and you'll find out." She steps

out of the car and saunters to the front door.

Val's sister opens the door. Joan is dressed in pink slacks and a white sleeveless blouse. Her blond hair is pushed back from her smooth forehead with a plastic headband, also pink. Danny wonders if this is how Val would look if she had married an unremarkable man and lived in a big house away from downtown—calm, coordinated, with a face that betrays nothing, not even her age.

When she sees Val, Joan frowns. "Val, you could have called. I'm in the middle of cleaning out Kelly's room." She looks up and sees Danny hovering behind Val, trying to blend in with the lilac bush at the side of the door. "Oh. Hello. Do you need something? Has Kelly not put in our order for the prints yet? I have to apologize. She's sometimes a very thoughtless girl."

"Let us in, Joanie. He's with me."

Joan tilts her head to the side and narrows her eyes before walking down the hall toward the kitchen, leaving the front door ajar. Danny follows Val into the sunken living room and sits beside her on a tan leather sectional. As Val straightens her tucked-in blouse, she whispers in his ear, "Can you believe this place? Everything's so meticulous it gives me the willies."

Danny looks at the thick pile of the carpet, at his feet flattening and soiling this collection of fibres. He decides to sit as motionless as possible. Val is unusually silent, and Danny watches as she twists her hands together, over and over again.

Joan walks in with a tray of glasses. As she passes them to Val and Danny, she says, "Grapefruit juice and soda." She eyes Val suspiciously. "I think it's a bit early for anything stronger."

"Joan, you're a miserable bitch."

Danny squirms in his seat.

"Did you come here to pick a fight, Val? Or is there something else?" Joan stands in the middle of the room and sips her drink, staring out the large picture window. The back deck is bordered by potted plants. A finch stands in the middle of a faux-marble bird bath.

Val leaves her drink untouched and looks at her sister. "I came to pick up those boxes I left here."

"Boxes?" Joan's voice is light and noncommittal. "What boxes?"

"You remember. Before Kelly was born I brought all my old costumes and things here. I never did find an apartment that could fit it all."

"Ah, those boxes. I hate to tell you this, Val, but we had a flood in the basement some years ago, and I had to throw them out."

Val's face grows pale under her makeup. "You didn't."

"Well, I had to. They were going to get mouldy."

Danny swears he sees a fragment of a smile on Joan's lips, but her face soon resettles into its powdered serenity.

"Joan! You could have told me!" Val clenches her fists.

"I don't remember exactly, but it's possible the flood happened when you were off somewhere, and I couldn't reach you. I haven't always known where you were, Val, and that was entirely your choice."

"I haven't left Vancouver in years. You're lying."

Joan laughs. "Now, why would I do that?" Her eyes travel slowly over Val's painted-on eyebrows, the gloss on her lips.

Val stands and turns into the hall. "I'm going to look for myself. It would be just like you to hide my things and then lie about it."

Danny hears a door slam and the sound of high heels hurrying down a set of stairs. He wipes his hands on his pants, reaches for his drink, but then retracts his hand, remembering the white carpet between him and the coffee table. Joan sits still, one leg crossed over the other. He stares at her trim body, the clear skin of her cheeks, and thinks, *A woman with a face like that either never worries or she buries the worry so deep inside that she's forgotten it even exists.* He wonders how long they can sit like this, each pretending that the silence is comfortable.

"Have you known Val long?"

"No. I met her at the wedding," he mutters. "Well, actually, I first met her when I was a little boy, in Chinatown."

Joan's eyebrows shoot up. "Really? I never spent much time there. Not like Val."

Silence.

Val storms into the living room, a small purple suitcase in her hand. "I found this, at least," she snaps, waving the suitcase in Joan's face.

"I guess that's one of the things that didn't get wet."

"Or you missed it when you threw everything else out. I found it wedged behind the hot-water heater." Val winks at Danny. "I think we all know that she got rid of the boxes on purpose."

Joan stands up and collects the almost untouched glasses. "I really do have to get back to work. Kelly and Derek will be here tonight to pick up the rest of her clothes."

Val grasps Joan's elbow with her hand. "Why don't you ever say what you mean?"

Joan tries to pull her arm away, but Val tightens her grip until Joan's skin grows white between Val's fingers. "I don't choose to broadcast every thought I've ever had to the entire world, that's all."

"Tell me the truth, Joan. Did you purposely throw out my boxes?" Val stares at Joan's now watery eyes.

"Yes."

"Why?"

Joan wrenches free and says quietly, "I don't want to talk about this now, with him here."

"Loosen up, for Christ's sake. He knows I was a dancer. He's hardly a wide-eyed innocent."

"Fine. If you want to air our dirty laundry in front of strangers, then that's what I'll do." Joan picks up the tray, holding it between them like a shield. "I didn't want Kelly to know. She grew up thinking you were a real dancer, Val, the kind who dances in musicals and at Radio City Music Hall, the kind you and I once wanted to be, remember? We agreed, years ago, that only you and I would know about the clubs and the circuit. We kept it from everyone, from Mum and Daddy. Everyone. What would happen if Kelly came across those disgusting costumes? How would I explain them, Val?" She starts to walk into the kitchen. "Now, you have to leave. When I come back from washing these glasses, I expect to see an empty house."

Danny picks up the suitcase and takes Val's hand before she can say anything. They hurry to the front door and out. *Thank Christ*, he thinks. *I could barely breathe in there.*

He starts the car and looks over at Val, who sits with her hands in her lap, her purse thrown haphazardly by her feet. "Where to now?" he asks.

"Any place," she says, "where I can see the water."

He drives north toward the eastern edge of Burrard Inlet, where it meets the narrow waters of Indian Arm. In the distance, he sees a tree-covered mountain. Even here, the wild landscape is dotted with electrical wires strung from tall steel towers.

He turns onto an unpaved road and follows it until they reach a small parking lot. They walk across grass, past picnic tables and groups of children playing on blankets, until they come to a narrow, rocky beach. Val walks straight to the water's edge and stops, squinting at the ocean. It winks in the light, churns around rocks. To the right, trees have rooted precariously on tall stone cliffs.

"I've never been here," she says, bending down to dangle her fingers in the water.

"I took some wedding pictures here once. Whenever I'm out this way, I try to stop here."

"I don't get out to the suburbs much, you know. I mostly stay in the city, any city, really." She looks around and begins to walk back up to the grassy area. "We should find a place to sit."

She settles herself on the grass under a tree and smoothes out the wrinkles in her cotton pants. Her toenails, visible in her black sandals, are painted coral. Patting her hair, she leans her head against the trunk and folds her hands on her stomach.

Danny is grateful for the absence of city noise—the screeching brakes, the hum of air conditioners, the chimes from doorbells, the buzzing crowds.

Until now, he wouldn't have cared about anything other than the spinning spotlights, the hiding and revealing of fabric and skin, the way a dancer captures the attention of an entire room of men and plays it like a violin. But he thinks of the photographs he has left drying in the studio, of dancers looking simultaneously like the children they once were and the women they have become. He wants to know how the feisty little girl who lived on River Road transformed herself into the Siamese Kitten and then became a woman who rummages through basements for scraps from her past.

Val tugs on her earlobe and frowns. "I haven't said much to anyone about the circuit in a very long time. When I die, Joan will keep it to herself. And when she dies, there won't be anybody left to remember. Except for that suitcase, everything I had is gone. " She turns to Danny, her eyes round like a trapped child's. "It never bothered me before—being forgotten."

"What changed?"

She wraps her arms around her body. "I don't know. Maybe I had to meet the right person. It's like you've been a part of my life since the very beginning, even before I met you in that alley." Val's laugh subsides. "Maybe you're the one who deserves to know."

PART FOUR

THE CAFÉ

1947

Val stood in the café window, watching as the men left work, locking doors behind them, folding their stained aprons and tucking them under their arms. The streets of Chinatown, like they did every evening, would soon transform. The drab fish shops and diners would be abandoned, making way for the preternatural colours and sounds that unfurled in the night. Red-clad prostitutes leaning against doorways. Men, their faces hidden by brown brimmed hats and a navy darkness, scuttling through doors that went unused during the day. Music spilling out of the neon-lit clubs in booms and tinkles. Val slowly turned back to the empty restaurant and began stacking the chairs on the tables so that Mr. Chow could mop the floors.

One by one, the cooks left, nodding at Val as they walked out the door. Suzanne was the last of the waitresses to leave. A scarf covered her curly hair, and she winked at Val as she hurried through the room. "Hugh's taking me out again tonight. Wish me luck."

In the back office, Val took off her apron and hung it on a hook. The floor, wet with soapy water, shone in the light like the slick of sweat on hot skin. She looked down at her brown skirt and picked off a crumb clinging to the rough fibres.

As she pulled her handbag from a shelf above the desk, Mr. Chow walked in, his shirt sleeves rolled up, his apron balled in his hands. Val felt caught, like he had disturbed her while she was changing her stockings. She clutched her bag to her stomach, wanting an extra layer to hide behind.

Mr. Chow looked equally startled. "I'm sorry. I thought you had left. Am I interrupting something?"

"No. Not at all. I'm just leaving." The office was small, and Mr. Chow was standing in front of the door. His broad chest and the light-blue checked pattern on his shirt seemed to fill the room.

It was like the pure, bright crash of lightning, that moment when Val understood there was nothing she wanted more than to taste this man and feel his body on hers. She might pant from the heat seeping outward through her skin.

When he placed his hands around her waist, she tilted her head up and stared at the stubble on his chin. His lips were parted the tiniest fraction of an inch. She closed her eyes long enough to let out a small, barely there breath. She knew he could feel her exhale on his neck, trailing around his Adam's apple like a finger on fire. Funny how the smallest movements can churn the depths of a body.

Their lips together blew a wind through her, a wind flecked with the dampness of their tongues, a wind that shot straight from her throat and arched her back. She reached for the tail of his shirt and pulled it from his pants. When he touched the backs of her thighs beneath her skirt, she shuddered at the jolt. This was the simple feel of body on body, when she could be rewarded by the goosebumps on the side of this man's neck as she brushed him with her hand.

He smells like pancakes.

The desk rocked as he lifted her onto its edge and steadied himself. His hand was between her legs, pulling at her underwear and skirt and she thought, *There*. She unbuttoned her blouse and he licked her nipple, a long hot graze that left a damp crescent on her skin. His eyes simmered like hot tar under an unforgiving sun. He pushed into her, the desk banging against the wall, his shoes slipping on the wet floor. She was being torn in half, but she pushed back in a rhythm that made no sense to anyone but them. Val cried out, clenched her teeth, and Mr. Chow, his hair now fallen forward over his eyes, pulled away from her, shuddered and spoke one word: "Christ." She looked down at her warm, wet belly before he collapsed against her, his pulse pounding like a snare drum against her skin.

Val wanted to say something, wanted to whisper words that he would remember for the rest of his life, but she knew "I love you" was wrong and, in some ways (but not all), untrue. She sucked in the smell of them together—rust and breakfast and the earthiness of moss. The silence grew thicker.

Mr. Chow zipped up his trousers and tucked in his shirt. Val cleaned her stomach with a paper napkin and re-buttoned her blouse, her eyes staring at her shoes, still tied securely to her feet. She was afraid to look up in case she saw disgust or shame or disappointment (yes, disappointment would be the worst) on his face. She wondered if she should leave, even run. *This silence*, she thought. *Lord help me.*

"My first name is Sam."

Val looked up. He gazed steadily into her face, the lines of his jaw set.

"You can call me that if you like. But not in front of the others, if that's all right."

Val smiled, took his square hand in hers. "Sam," she said, "I'm hungry."

Every night, Val waited with a cleaning rag in her hand for everyone else to leave the restaurant. After locking the door behind the last employee, she met Sam in the office. There, his brown eyes travelled over her body as she undressed. Afterward, they clung to each other as if they depended on the weight of each other's body for survival.

She stopped going home for dinner, telling Joan that the café was now providing an evening meal for any staff who helped close up. Sam cooked for her, using the leftovers in the icebox for simple sandwiches and warming up soup. After a few weeks, Val asked him to cook Chinese food, the kind that he remembered his mother making. And so, in the dark restaurant with a single candle burning on their table, Sam brought her stir-fried greens, pork short ribs in black bean sauce and buckwheat noodles tossed with soy sauce and green onions. She ate it all as Sam smiled at her from across the table. When she was full, he massaged her feet, rubbing out the stiffness from the long day.

Late at night, through the windows of the café, Val watched the streams of people walking from club to gambling den to brothel, mostly stumbling men with half-closed, drunken eyes, or sober ones with a speeding walk who focused their eyes straight ahead, perhaps concentrating on the possibility of arousal and the give of soft flesh under the thumb. But she saw the women too. The dancers walked with their overcoats tied tightly around them, but the sequins and glitter still peeked out from underneath hems and around collars.

One night, a trio of black women hurried through the wet street, their heads lowered against the rain that fell in heavy drops.

"They're dancers from the all-black club around the corner." Sam's voice made her jump. When she turned around, he was standing in the dark, holding a steaming bowl of chicken congee. "We could go, if you want. I know you're bored staying in the café all the time. I'm sorry my room at the boarding house is so small."

She imagined the clubs to be hot and damp, with the odour of dancers and men alike, the floors sticky with spilled rye and whatever else the crowd brought in on their shoes. It would be warmest close to the stage, where the lights cut through the gloom and where high kicks spun the humid air. Maybe she could go, just the once.

A thin woman, her cheekbones like sharp rocks, staggered down the sidewalk. Her dress was pulled to one side, exposing a bony shoulder. One stocking pooled around her ankle. Val could see the makeup streaming down her face, black streaks from eyes to jaw. A man ran after her and pulled her arm so roughly that she spun into his arms. "You're to give me what I asked for," the man shouted, and she collapsed on his shoulder. He dragged her away, her body limp.

"Well, do you want to go?" Sam's voice was soothing.

Val shook her head.

That night, well past midnight, she took him to the waterfront. As she began to lead him toward the waves, he hesitated, whispering, "I can't swim." She gently untied his shoes, peeled off his socks and rolled up his pants before taking his hand and walking him over the sand and rocks. He stood in the cold water up to his knees and shivered, his lips set in a grimace.

"How can you live here and never touch the water?" Val asked, but Sam didn't answer and briskly rubbed his hands together.

She kissed him and felt the chattering of his teeth against hers. He held her tightly and pushed his face into her hair. As big and tall as he was, the water reduced him to a cold sliver of a man. Val wanted to laugh, but she stroked his back and led him to dry land. He reached into the paper bag he had left on a flat rock and passed Val a packet of sticky rice wrapped in bamboo leaves, the pork in the centre still steaming.

She woke up the next morning in her room, warm and smug with the cobwebs of happy dreams still clinging to her. Today Joan might sulk over the fabric of her wedding dress, or drag Val to look at potential apartments, but none of it mattered. For the first time in her entire life, Val was finally, deliciously full.

The wedding took place that June in the front garden of the boarding house. Joan and Peter said their vows under an arch covered in purple clematis, and the guests stood in the grass in a small circle, smiling and nodding as the two said their vows and kissed. Val's eyes narrowed. *Like brother and sister*, she thought. *If they're in love, who could tell?*

She was acutely aware of her parents standing beside her. When she met them at the train station, she was shocked at how old and brittle they seemed. They stood waiting with their suitcases on the floor between their legs, looking confusedly at the crowds. But it didn't take long for her to realize they hadn't changed at all; rather, in the year she had been away, she had grown used to their absence. With time and distance, her memories of them, now small and indistinct, had become smoother and more loving. Cleaner. The sight of them reminded her of Joan's baby, his sharp bones, the way he clutched her skirt whenever she held him on her lap. She wondered if her parents ever visited his grave, but she didn't ask. On the way to the boarding house they spoke about her father's job at the cannery, where he had been downgraded to working half-shifts, like a lot of men. The foreman never said why, but everyone supposed it was because the war was now over, and they could hire cheaper men from the Chinese and Japanese crowds that were begging for work each day.

"They'll take over soon. Mark my words," he mumbled. When an Oriental walked past, Warren spat in the street.

At the wedding, Meg stood with her hands behind her back, her unfashionably long dress blowing against her ankles. Val could see that her father had been drinking, but he was sober enough to lean himself against the cherry tree and keep his hands clasped so that others would think that he was praying, not dozing in and out. His face was tinted with layers of dirt that had accumulated over the years and repelled water and soap, no matter how often he washed.

Peter's parents, who had travelled all the way from Toronto, wore dark clothes and stood to the side, inches apart from each other. His mother silently wiped the tears from her face. They stared straight ahead, not daring to look into the eyes of Meg and Warren or to look too directly at Joan, in case one of them spoke, forcing a response. Val could sense their disapproval in the way Peter's mother pursed her lips and in the sound his father made when he cleared his throat every few minutes. It was easy to imagine the conversation they might have had with each other that morning.

"Have you seen her parents? Hicks. They probably don't even know how to use indoor plumbing."

"Well, what are we supposed to do? He loves her, and she *is* a pretty girl."

"Pretty! All you see is that blond hair and those blue eyes. She has no class. Just a step up from your common whore."

"Come on now, that's cruel."

"Mark my words: she'll never make him a proper wife. When we sent him out here for school, I didn't think he'd get married for a long time. Or at least not to a girl like this."

And there's so much they don't even know, Val thought.

A crow began cawing from its perch on the roof. Val watched as it opened and closed its sharp beak, its neck pulsing with the effort. The crow's talons, curled over the shingles, glinted in the sunlight. It emitted one last caw and flew off, the shadow of its body floating over the lawn, changing shape as it drifted over the bushes and trees.

After lunch was served on the veranda, Val sat with Suzanne on a bench by the lavender bush at the very edge of the garden, both of them enjoying the day off from the café. They could see Joan floating over the grass in her white dress, touching guests on the shoulders as she passed, holding her skirt away from the dirt in the flower beds. Suzanne smiled.

"She looks pretty."

"Yes, she does," said Val, trying to keep her voice light.

"Hugh and I, we're going to get married with no fuss. Just the minister and us, I guess." Suzanne spun the plain gold band on her ring finger with her other hand. "My parents couldn't come anyway, not in the summertime when there's so much to do on the farm."

"That's too bad." Val watched as her mother smoothed a wrinkle on Joan's skirt. Joan turned around and stared at the fabric their mother had touched, looking, Val knew, for a dirty handprint.

Their landlady, dressed in yellow with a white hat, bounded across the lawn. "You must be so proud," she boomed at Meg.

Val thought her mother was in danger of blowing away, her body small and dry, no match for the landlady's generous bosom and wide smile.

"Proud," Meg answered in a loud, strained voice, as if trying to match the merriment around her. "Yes. Very."

"And you, sir, are you a little sad at marrying off your little girl?"

Warren nodded slowly, his eyes wandering from tree to guest to the landlady's rouged cheeks. "I was sad when she left home last winter. She's got a good husband now and doesn't need to worry about herself anymore. Between you and me, I was never much of a provider. Shiftless, my father always said." He laughed and spilled half his wine on the grass. Val leaned forward, ready to rush across the lawn and coax her father into a chair.

"The café will be busy next month," Suzanne continued. "I'm leaving, and Mr. Chow is off to China again."

Val turned and stared at Suzanne's freckled face. "He's going away?"

"Didn't you know? Yes, he's going to visit his family one more time to tie up some loose ends in the village. His wife and kids are moving here next spring, he told me. They've been apart for so long. I don't think he's been back in at least two or three years." Suzanne laughed lightly. "I wonder sometimes if he even knows the names of his children."

Val felt a throbbing behind her right eye and wondered if Suzanne could see the muscles of her face stretching and contracting.

"Children?"

Suzanne turned and looked at Val, her eyebrows knitted together. "He never told you, did he. I think there are three. One set of twins and another little girl? I can't remember." She paused and tilted her head to the side before speaking more quietly. "I do feel sorry for his poor wife, though, raising those kids alone back in China all this time and not knowing what her husband is getting into. I don't know how she does it."

"His wife."

"He doesn't talk about the family much, so I'm not surprised you've never heard of them." Suzanne opened her mouth to say more, but the living-room clock chimed, and she turned her head at the sound. "Lord, is it three o'clock already? I have to go. Hugh is waiting for me. Make sure Joanie gets my gift, will you?" She stood up and put a hand on Val's shoulder. "He's still a good man, sweetie. Try to remember that."

And Val was left sitting alone, smelling the off-sweet scent of lavender. She thought of the sweetness of dried sweat that comes from two people, the taste detectable only after the salt has been kissed away.

That night, she lay in bed beside her mother and felt the heat coming off her body in a way that was unfamiliar; Joan was always cool, her feet clammy. Val kicked the covers off and turned to the open window. Across the room on the floor, her father mumbled in his sleep and pulled his blanket up over his chin.

If it weren't for her parents, she would walk down to the beach in her nightdress and step into the cold, churning water. Soak her body until she could no longer feel anything. She could hear the waves breaking on the rocks, followed by the whisper of water as it ran down the length of the sand and through tide pools that would be empty by morning. She could float face-up, her nightdress both billowing and flattening around her, and see nothing but the night sky.

She knew exactly how naive she had been. She had never asked, and he had never told. He had watched her undress, night after night. There were no secrets, only truths she hadn't discovered yet. Her own fault for never guessing that a man his age—a man who owned a thriving business and yet lived in a single room on the second floor of a boarding house—would have a family to save his money for. Ridiculous. Stupid, stupid girl.

She sat up in bed and leaned in closer to the scissor-sharp air cutting through the open window. Even if she were swept away or chilled to the bone in that unforgiving ocean water, she would never forget the way he sucked her fingers or the hours they spent breathing in tandem or his bemused face watching her eat plates of food like she had never eaten before. She chewed on her fingers, remembering. There was no doubt about it. His cooking had left its mark.

THE STAGE

1947

Warren and Meg left the next day, their suitcase repacked with Meg's worn stockings and Warren's one white shirt. When she returned from the train station, Val changed the sheets, her hands smoothing out the depressions in the mattress from her mother's body. The pillowcase her father had been using smelled of his hair. She had never noticed before how feral they smelled, their oils and other discharges mingling in the air and sticking to the chairs and towels. She was ashamed of her disgust, the roiling of her stomach when she swept up their stray hairs. But she cleaned and scrubbed anyway, erasing their presence with rags and brushes.

At breakfast, they had asked if she would be back for Christmas. Her mother had even smiled and said, "We could get ourselves a ham." Val tried to remember if her parents had ever served a ham before; all she could recall were sludgy stews made with three pieces of a gristly oxtail and turnips discoloured from weeks in the cellar.

Val said, "I don't know how much I'll have to work. So many of the men here are away from their families at Christmas, and they'll want a good hot meal from the restaurant."

Her father had continued chewing his toast.

When she left them at the train station, they had looked shabbier and smaller than when they had arrived. Val watched until the crowd closed around them. For a brief, panicked second, she felt like running forward and pushing people aside until she found them again. She wanted to burrow into their dingy, faded clothes, touch their dry skin and listen (carefully, for the cavernous station was loud and voices echoed) to her father's uneven breathing and the whistle from her mother's nose. But before she could take even one step forward, the crowd surged toward the trains, and there was no trace of her parents, only hundreds of people who could have been them but weren't.

That night, in her bed, she held herself beside the newly empty space. She missed the shape of Joan: sharp and angled, with cold radiating from her bones. And she missed Meg, who curled up like a kitten while sleeping. Sam had held her gently; his strong arms were surprisingly smooth. She didn't dare admit that she missed him. Val listened to the rustlings of the old man who lived in the room next to hers. She imagined herself rushing into his room and climbing into bed beside him, holding his skinny and wrinkled body in her capable hands. The old man's bones would jab at her, and he might have icy feet, but it wouldn't matter. She would feel his chest rising, stroke the remaining hair on the top of his head, whisper her fears for Joan and herself and this wild city, knowing that his deafness and poor memory would never betray her. She wondered if he would be afraid or silently grateful, unable to put into words his relief at discovering that another human being was willing to touch him, look at his drooping face with unflinching eyes. She hugged a pillow to her stomach, the darkness in her head like the black water of the ocean outside her window.

There was a time when she dreamed about Vancouver as a glittering city, bright with electric lights and the glinting of diamonds worn by languorous women. She had always known it wasn't very far, that it was a trip that could be made in the course of a day; still, it was a place that might as well have been across an ocean instead of the rolling, thick-watered Fraser River.

The morning after her parents left was her day off. She stood in front of the Orpheum in a circle of summer sunlight. She tilted her head back to see the theatre's sign in its entirety—the glowing white letters, the border of light bulbs that would have been ordinary in a regular lamp in a regular house, but not here, above the fanciest theatre in town. She loved Vancouver and, until yesterday, loved the fog in the early mornings as she walked to work, the sound of rain bouncing off the sidewalks as she rushed around the café, even the shouts and beats from the nearby nightclubs as she and Sam sat at a back table after closing, feeding each other with chopsticks shiny with oil.

It was his fault she was now thinking about leaving.

The rest of that morning, Val walked through the downtown streets, touching the walls of buildings with her palms, feeling the roughness of brick or limestone, the warmth they had already absorbed from the first half of the day. People walked past and around her, some bumping into her as she stopped and bought a bag of roasted peanuts from a street vendor. She savoured the sensation of their bodies so close to hers, the hum of blood and digestion that rose through the air. She licked her fingers.

At ten minutes past noon, Val walked into the café and cornered Suzanne as she was hurrying to the back with a tray full of dirty dishes.

"I'm quitting today," she whispered, keeping her voice low in case the customers heard.

"What? But how are we going to find someone else in time for tomorrow's shift?"

"I don't know. I can't stay another day because," and Val hesitated, hating the quiver in her voice, "things have become too complicated. I might leave town. I don't know."

Suzanne looked at her with sharp eyes and nodded.

"All right, honey. You'd better go tell the boss."

"Can you do it for me? Please? And could you collect my pay too? You can send it to Joanie when it's ready. I just need to leave."

Suzanne shifted to the right, and Val could see through the open office door. Sam was hunched over the desk, his wide shoulders curled around whatever he was reading. She felt sorry for him, for the contradictory thoughts that must be swirling around his head, the voices that whispered *family, this is home, money, my hands on her young body*. She thought of rushing into the office, beating on his chest with her fists and then crying as he made love to her one last time. His wife and children were the entire reason he lived and worked in this city. The café was for them, not for Val, not for the nights they spent crushed up against the office wall together. She was eighteen and had spent three months with a forty-year-old man who was also her boss. His wife (Val imagined her as thirty-seven and practical, saving pennies because she knew they would add up) had his three children. There was no use in forcing him to answer her demands. If Joan couldn't force an unemployed logger to leave his lazy wife even when Joan was pregnant, Val knew Sam would never cut off his entire family to marry her. Val knew that when a child slipped out of your grasp, the pain lingered, like razors slowly cutting away at your flesh.

Val looked down at her knees and wondered if they would even carry her to the office forty feet away. She waited for Suzanne to write down Joan's address and then left, turning the corner as the lunch rush began. She stopped half a block away and leaned against the wall of a building. No tears came, only a sharp, quick gasping that made her feel that her lungs might burst right out of her chest. She shivered in her summer coat, despite the heat from the sidewalk rising up around her. *Pork dumplings*, she thought, *in soup with egg noodles. And a plate of steamed greens on the side*. Her stomach rumbled, and she could feel Sam's hands on her waist.

A man's voice boomed behind her. "You a dancer?"

She jumped and, turning, saw a short, thin man with a full beard and a tall, brown hat. "I'm sorry?"

"Are you a dancer? I need someone for tomorrow. One of my girls skipped town. If you don't have a costume, I got some old ones in the back."

Val backed up two steps and stared at the sign in the window. THE SHANGRI-LA. THE BEST BURLESQUE IN THE WEST.

"Well? Are you in or out?"

"No, no. I was just resting here for a minute."

"Suit yourself."

He turned and pushed open the door. Val looked past him into the dark theatre. Even in the dim light, she could see the plush seats, the stage with its red curtains and string of turned-off lights. If she were onstage, eyes would be watching her, assessing the smoothness of her skin, the curve of her legs. She would see the desire in men's faces, in the flush around their ears, in the way they sat, hunched forward, waiting for her to peel off another piece of her costume. She could almost hear the music, the driving beat, the swells and peaks of a pounding piano that would drown out any doubtful words. Sweat would pour down her back from kicking and grinding, from the stage lights too. In that theatre the humidity of different breaths and damp skin would glide over her arms and legs, clinging like a film. Perhaps, if she went onstage, she could close her eyes and imagine that she was a chorus girl, dancing behind Bing Crosby, beside a younger and more innocent Joan.

She had been watched by a man before. How different could this be?

"Wait," Val said. The manager turned to her again, scratching his beard. She straightened up and looked down at him. "How much are you willing to pay?"

Two weeks. Only two weeks. It was a chant, comforting her and keeping other, more troublesome, thoughts at bay. The dancing was just an experiment that could make her some good money until she could find another waitressing job. But Val also wanted to satisfy the little girl who used to high-kick in her thin-walled bedroom; after it was over, she could start another, more regular life.

An orange striped cat. A front porch with a rocking chair. Children. Chicken and pound cake in the oven. Sunrises in the summer. Snow angels in the winter. All the things other families had that hers never did.

The manager handed her a leftover costume before leaving her in the windowless dressing room. She pulled the dress over her head, settling the fabric around her hips and smoothing the tear-away skirt over her thighs. The dress skimmed and contained her body, showing and revealing all at once. She fingered the blue sash and tried to fluff up the faux-crinoline underneath the blue skirt, but the dress was irredeemably limp, too tired to look acceptable. She was afraid she would smell another woman in its folds or, worse, the scent of a woman and man together. Looking up, she saw ropes hanging from pipes running below the ceiling and long cobwebs that swayed in the draft. Piles of mouse droppings littered the concrete floor. Her eyes grew dry and her vision blurred; she could barely see herself in the frameless mirror that leaned against the wall. She could make out a dim outline of her familiar shape, but she was dressed in a costume meant to transform her into a countrified Alice in Wonderland; Alice's older, dumber cousin. She might have drawn one eyebrow too high, or powdered her face so white that the men would recoil at her pallid presence. Her hands riffled through the dusty pile of eye pencils and rouge. Briefly, she wondered how many girls had touched these compacts and puffs, but she knew such a thought wasn't productive. "Two weeks," she muttered, her lips sticking together from the pink lipstick.

Val had walked to the Shangri-La that morning, taking a winding route so she could avoid the café. She wondered if her act might send ripples of electricity down the block and around the corner until Sam looked up and sniffed, the hairs in his nose twitching. *Screw him*, she thought. *If he finds out, so what? I was never going to be his wife anyway.*

She stood in the wings, waiting for her cue, peering out past the edge of the curtain at the rows of plush seats, the empty balconies. This early in the day, most of the men in the audience were loggers on their week off and old men with canes and neatly brushed hats. She had hoped that the theatre would be so dim and the stage lights so bright that she wouldn't be able to see the faces of anyone in the crowd, but as she stood there, one hand holding tightly to her sash, she could pick out each individual head. A white-haired man in a leather jacket who looked like he might once have been a pilot. A lanky Indian boy who couldn't be any older than fifteen. The usherette in her red-and-gold jacket in the back of the theatre. She wanted to cry with fear, but she didn't want her makeup to run.

She turned away from the crowd and forced herself to watch the stage. A clown with a crooked, painted mouth rode a unicycle, juggling bananas, and she could hear one man laughing, a slow chuckle she was familiar with, thick with rye and barely audible. As the two shabbily costumed clowns bantered back and forth onstage, a man with a dark moustache in the front row nodded off, his chin resting on his chest. One of the clowns spied her in the wings and blew her a kiss before tumbling into a somersault. She suppressed a laugh, closing her eyes so that she didn't notice when the MC ran past her onto the stage.

With his tall red hat in his hand, he smirked through his moustache and, with a cocked eyebrow, announced, "How about another round of applause for Jules and Bubbles? I tell you, folks, those two could make a joke out of a pair of old bedroom slippers." A tepid wave of clapping barely rippled through the seats. "Ah, but we have something coming up that I know you'll all love. Plucked from the farmlands of the Canadian West, I bring you the prettiest little girl you'll ever see dancing on a burlesque stage. Gents and gents, put your hands together for Val the Small-town Beauty!"

She shivered and rubbed her hands together to stop the shaking. Pulling on the ends of her hair (braided in two pigtails, tied with ribbon, the way she thought an innocent girl would fix it), she stepped out into a warm puddle of light.

The tidal wave of fear pouring out of her skin was so palpable she could smell it, like the odour of horses' sweat after they have been whipped or shod. When she closed her eyes, she could feel it: the electricity that crackles off you because *you are just so damned scared*. She swore the audience must be able to see the fear encasing her body. They could get up and leave, or throw their shoes at her, and then this whole experiment would be a failure, a huge disappointment for the younger Val who had only wanted to dance. She would be walking the streets sooner than she had planned, asking every restaurant in this stranger-infested city for work. She tried to repeat to herself, *Two weeks*, but instead she thought, *I hate this place so much. Why did I ever agree to this stupid dancing thing?* She suddenly realized that no one had really told her what to do onstage, or even how to dress and make up her face. The manager had simply made her watch two of the more experienced dancers and then vaguely waved his hand. "Do something like that, sweetheart. Don't strip too fast and make sure you shake what you've got."

Val walked to the middle of the stage and stood there trying to remember how she had intended to start her act, how she had visualized this first moment. But she froze and the spins she had practised fifteen minutes ago were totally forgotten.

A piercing whistle sliced through the air. For her. Someone was whistling for her.

Her arms and legs began to tingle from the heat radiating off the lights. One lone man started to clap, the echo bouncing around the theatre until it sounded like a dozen pairs of hands clapping. Others joined in, and she was cosseted by applause, by how it felt like the crowd was holding her up or patting her on the head, murmuring, "It'll be fine, Val. Don't you worry."

She heard her own laughter as a little girl, her voice coaching Joan to kick higher, to twirl longer on her toes. She remembered her father taking them to a calm part of the river to learn how to swim, his hands under her arms, holding her up, his whisper in her ear, "You'll learn. I'll just let go." And the water was so cold, but she swam and grew to like the chill.

With her mouth set, she pulled off her skirt and kicked one leg high into the air.

The men roared and banged on the wooden backs of the seats in front of them. She smiled widely at the audience, then kicked and twirled to the drums, all her limbs filling in the gaps between beats, her feet pounding the stage in perfect time. She flashed her bum, her breasts, even bumped and ground when the piano trilled the bluegrass tune meant to go with her costume. Her doubts and fears disappeared and she was simply a dancing girl, half naked, hot under the lights, pushing and pulling against the music that drove her. When she left the stage, she clung to the curtains in the wings and peered at the men, still cheering, calling her name.

She heard the MC's brassy voice close to her ear. "Listen to that, sweetheart. They love you." If she wasn't smiling so hard, she could have wept.

The two weeks were over, but it hardly mattered. The applause shook between her ears even when she wasn't performing, and she could hear the men's voices calling for her or their feet stamping on the floor. The rhythm of the single piano and the thump of her own high-heeled shoes on the floorboards of the stage lulled her to sleep.

And the money. The paycheque was fine, but men were throwing bills and coins onto the stage as she danced, and they threw more when she bent down, ass out, to pick up the money and stuff it into her panties. When she returned to the boarding house early in the morning, she counted each night's earnings and packed them in one of Joan's discarded shoes at the back of the closet. She washed her face while making lists of all the ways she could spend that roll of cash. New clothes. A nice apartment. A meal in a fancy restaurant once a week.

One night, as she stepped out of the back door of the club, a man in a grey hat emerged from the shadows and gripped her hand. He smiled and his little pointed beard bobbed up and down as he spoke. "Val. Have I got a proposition for you." He took her to an all-night café and outlined the acts he represented. "I handle all of Ann Corio's bookings on the West Coast and Yvonne de Carlo—she was one of mine before she went Hollywood. I've watched you dance. You've got strong legs and a big stage presence, plus that star quality any girl would kill for. You can't do better than me, little miss. I got girls asking me to represent them every day, but I always say, 'You have to be picky or else you're an agent with no credibility.' You follow?" He ordered another jelly doughnut while he watched her face with his small eyes.

Val nodded. An agent. She could travel and get out of this city that reminded her of the café and Joan. She saw her two weeks at the club stretch into years at real, respectable theatres, maybe even one of those new supper clubs that were opening in San Francisco or Cincinnati with their velvet curtains and champagne. She took a mouthful of coffee and gazed calmly at the agent before speaking.

"When can we start?"

Within the week, she was booked for Los Angeles, Toledo, Des Moines and Chicago, leaving before the end of the month. "New costumes," her agent told her, "and it's about time you got yourself a better stage name. Something with a hook. Something that'll grab 'em by the balls and never let go."

He took her to choreography sessions at a Water Street studio with an ex-dancer named Portia, who had taught himself to strip with his penis tucked between his legs. During rehearsals, he screamed at Val, "This is a strip*tease*, child, not a Halloween dance at an old folks' home! Step it up before I fall asleep."

At first, she had no idea what sort of act she should perform. One girl danced in a costume strewn with Christmas lights. Another wrapped a white python around her body. When Val asked a dancer at Portia's studio what made for a successful gimmick, the woman cocked her head to the side and said, "You have to go with what's natural, sweetie. If you like birds, go with some parrots. If you feel gorgeous with a blond wig, then wear the biggest, baddest blond wig you can find. I'm the Bazoom Girl because of these." She gestured at her breasts and then moved one independently of the other before laughing out loud. "Figure out what you're really all about and turn it into an act. It'll work. You'll see."

That night, Val lay awake in her bed at the boarding house. She saw gold and dragons and long, curling fingernails cupped around painted teacups. She could taste Sam's food—the sharp, clean ginger, the tooth-coating fermented black beans—but then she focused on the paper lanterns she used to see swinging from the third-floor balconies across the street from the café. They glowed through the dark winter afternoons, exotic pockets of light that dissipated the gloom and the ordinariness of the city around them. In the morning, she walked to the big fabric store on Hastings Street and bought yards of green and black and red satin, packets of sequins, and fishnet stockings. She took the fabric and trimmings to a Chinatown tailor, who nodded and smiled at her instructions and asked her no questions. Red lipstick, tassels, a black wig and nail polish in five different colours. The glossy bottles twinkled and shone in her drawer.

She told Portia her idea, and he threw back his head and laughed. "Now, that's a gimmick we can work with! This act will make you more famous than chocolate cake."

Two weeks later, an hour and a half before she was

expecting her agent for a final inspection, Val carefully painted her face in her boarding-house room, using the brushes exactly the way the girl at the department store told her. Next, she taped the tassels to her nipples and slipped on the black satin corset, the sequined G-string and the fishnet stockings. She attached the green skirt embroidered with lotus blossoms and two swimming, circling goldfish, smoothing it down so that it hugged her hips tightly. Then, the high-heeled shoes. Last, the black bobbed wig with heavy bangs. She looked at herself in the mirror, at the polished sheen of her nails, the length of her legs, the suggestive pull of satin tight over her ass and laughed.

"Why hello," she purred. "I am the Siamese Kitten."

She heard a knock and arranged herself in the doorway, sweeping the fabric of her skirt to the side so that her agent could get a good look at her stockings. With one hand, she threw the door open and posed, leaning up against the frame, her back arched.

Joan gaped in the hall.

"Damn it," Val whispered.

Val grabbed Joan's hand and dragged her inside, wrinkling the sleeve of her sister's dove-grey suit. She pushed her into the chair by the window and stood, hands on her hips, staring at her suddenly mute sister.

"What are you doing here?"

Joan blinked.

"You have to go. I'm expecting someone."

Joan managed to ask, "Who?"

Val told her everything, about the dancing, the stripping, the gigs in other cities, the agent who said she needed a hook. And, of course, the money.

"I'm going to save it, Joanie, and then I'll never have to worry again. I won't need a man to support me, that's for sure."

Joan nodded, her eyes wandering over Val's costume, her red, red lips. She touched her own mouth and then patted her blond hair. After a minute, she stopped and dropped her white-gloved hand back into her lap, underneath her handbag.

After a long pause, Joan said, "Have you written Mum and Dad?"

Val looked away. "They don't need to know."

"Don't you think they should know if you're travelling?"

"Listen, Joanie, you'd better not say anything to them. I'm going to be doing this for a little while, not forever, so there's no need to go telling everyone. Don't tell Peter either."

Joan sighed. "Why would I tell him? Do you think the neighbours would believe me if I said, 'My sister's a stripper?'" She leaned forward. "I just want to know: is the dancing like we imagined?"

Val looked at Joan's face, still so pale, with those icy eyes that could burn and burn. She smiled. "Sometimes. I high-kick like we used to. The men like it."

"They do? What else do they like?" Joan rubbed her lips together.

"Lots of things. They like it when I look at them over my shoulder. I don't know why, really. They like it slow, especially when I take off my stockings and pull off my gloves. It's not what I expected, you know, not all tits and ass."

Joan's face was flushed. She had taken off her gloves and was wiping her hands on the sides of her skirt.

Val touched her shoulder. "Is everything all right?"

"Yes, of course. Why are you asking?"

"I don't know. You look like something is upsetting you."

Joan uncrossed her legs and stood up. "It's nothing." Her voice rose to a high pitch Val had never heard before. "It's just— He goes at me every night. Hard, like he hates me. He wants children, he keeps telling me, as if I didn't already know."

"Joanie, I'm sorry. You could leave him." But even before Val said it, she knew her sister never would.

"I should go. I have a hair appointment." The expression on Joan's face had changed, hardened into knife-edged angles.

"Don't forget: you can't tell anyone. You promised."

"I didn't promise anything."

Val watched as Joan crossed the room, her black shoes like a new doll's—shiny and unscratched. When Joan opened the door, Val said, "Remember, Joan, I know exactly why you can't have children, and I can tell Peter anytime I like."

Joan paused in the doorway and half turned. But then she straightened her shoulders and continued out the door, wiping her feet carefully on the rug in the hall.

THE CIRCUIT

1947 to 1958

The act was the main thing. Without it, she was just a girl taking off her clothes to music; with it, she was a star.

The band began playing and she shuffled through the curtains, her eyes cast down, her hands clasped in front of her. She wavered uncertainly in place and the audience fell silent, perhaps feeling shame that such a shy Oriental girl needed to strip for money. Men cleared their throats, and Val could hear them shifting in their creaky, fold-down seats. Slowly, she lifted her head and looked out over the crowd through her thick black bangs. Here, in a dusty theatre in Chicago, lights were bolted to the walls haphazardly, and, even from the stage, Val could see the electrical cords dangling from the sconces. The wood on the balcony walls was poorly carved, no better than her father's drunken whittlings on scrap lumber. But no one was there to gaze at the construction of the place.

The music picked up speed. The drummer played a driving, impossible-to-ignore beat. The piano tinkled. Val began to tap her right foot in time.

She bowed low to the audience and said, "Hello, I am the Siamese Kitten. Tonight, I dance for you." And then she smiled, throwing off her red silk robe and purring to the crowd.

The applause. It came at her suddenly every time, so deafening that she inevitably stepped backward, rippling the curtain as she steadied herself. But she felt the audience was holding her close, buffeting her from the sharp winds that blew in toward the city. In this theatre—the moth-eaten red curtains, the cold dressing room, the candy and cigarettes that littered the makeup table—she was nothing like what she had been before. Not a waitress, not a girl from a thin-walled house on the banks of the Fraser River, not Valerie Nealy, not the mistress of a handsome Chinaman. No, she was the Siamese Kitten, the dancer whose posture never slackened, whose long, lined eyes held the audience in her inscrutable gaze, whose costume fell away so regally that the men who watched her imagined her to be a Chinese princess who had lost her way.

Eventually, she was left wearing nothing but her green G-string and red pasties with gold tassels. She held a large fan in front of her, flashing her bum, then her belly button and, finally, the under-curve of her breasts. She finished by pulling her robe back on, one shoulder at a time. When she took her final bow, her hands in front of her chest, palms together, fingers up, she said, "I am the Siamese Kitten. Thank you for watching me. I see you again sometime." As the spotlight faded, she could feel the collective flutter of disappointment that meant she could have danced forever, and these men, some of them lonely, others unfulfilled, would gladly have watched. Inevitably, one of the other girls or the night's MC came to her and said, "I've never seen a new dancer work up a crowd like that. They couldn't get enough!" She wondered if it was the gimmick or her choreography or the way she talked to the crowd as she danced. Several times, she stared at herself in the dressing-room mirror and searched her face for that special something. *Maybe*, she thought, *I really am a star.*

Before she left the theatre, she wiped off all her makeup except for her red, shiny lips. She didn't care that they were shocking when combined with her light brown hair and grey overcoat, that they marked her as a woman different from the wives and daughters of respectable men. Without them, she was no more than a once-rejected waitress, and she could bear anything but that.

In some cities, it was hotel rooms. Small hotels that had once been run by respectable families but were now staffed by surly men who eyed her bum as she walked up the stairs, carrying her own luggage. Other times, if the run was a long one, she let a room at a boarding house. She arranged her bottles on a chair and propped her makeup mirror against the wall. In these unfamiliar rooms, she sang to herself or read the five-cent magazines that she bought in every city and town. She tried to learn how to knit, but her very first scarf ended up as a confused knot of cheap yarn, and she threw the whole thing, needles included, into the garbage at one of the theatres, maybe the one in Wichita, she couldn't be sure. The other girls who travelled with her were lonely too, and they some-times spent early mornings in each other's rooms.

But she was bored most days, and her thoughts often turned to Sam. She imagined her hands running through his thick hair one more time, the bones of his pelvis pressing against hers, the taste of his skin in her mouth. She touched herself, pretending that her fingers were his, that her touch was really the brush of his lips. This usually worked for fifteen minutes, but afterward she could smell herself, undiluted and uncombined, in the sheets that were twisted around her.

She thought she might weep at the idea that she had been in love once, but even then everything about that love was false, for the presence of his wife hovered above them whenever they were together, even though she didn't know it at the time.

Men waited for her on the sidewalk after every show, in every city. At first, when they invited her to dinner or offered her a bouquet of flowers, she hurried away with her eyes firmly fixed on her shoes, holding her breath until she was sure no one was following her. But one night, during a week-long series of shows in Reno, a man's voice, smooth but with a hiccup of hesitation, made her look up. He stood underneath a lamppost with his hands in his pockets, his dark brown hair combed away from his face.

"What did you say?" Val asked, still holding open the door to the theatre, in case she needed to run back inside.

"Would you join me for dinner? My apartment is a few blocks away. I could cook for you, if you like."

She sat in his kitchen while he made her spaghetti with meatballs, which she ate quickly, sucking up noodles with so much enthusiasm that droplets of sauce flew in every direction, landing on the wallpaper, the tablecloth, the front of her blouse. Later, in his narrow bed across the room, he did exactly what she told him to do, caressing and sucking the parts of her body she presented to him. She felt heavy and sweetly full. She relished how the thin layer of spit he left on her neck and chest dried in seconds with the parched desert air blowing in the window, each breeze sweeping her skin clean.

When she left in the morning, he didn't ask to see her again or request her address so he could write. He gave her a meatball sandwich, wrapped in brown paper. Surprised, she cradled it in the crook of her arm and then walked through the grey dawn light to her hotel room.

Weeks later, she walked into a doctor's office in Idaho to be fitted for a diaphragm. When he asked if she was married, she laughed and said, "Not a chance. But if you don't give me that diaphragm, then I'll be a stripper with a baby, and I don't think anyone, not even the church ladies, wants that."

Soon there were other men. Electricians, judges, travelling salesmen in rumpled suits. She believed that these men, whose heads were buried between her legs, were happy enough, at least until they returned home to their wives, who, Val thought, must be able to smell another woman on their husbands' collars. But by the time they figured out it was her, she was gone, on a bus or a train to another city where another man would wait for her outside the back door of the club, clammy hands twisting together to calm his nerves.

Val had never liked Sacramento, not now, and not the first time she danced there three months before. The ground was dry and yellow, nothing like the wet black dirt of home, or even the dusty brown roads of Des Moines or Saint Paul. She couldn't help thinking that everything here was the colour of urine, like the spot you shovelled dirt over whenever you had to move the outhouse. Even though nothing smelled bad (beyond the odour of manure that drifted in from the surrounding farms), she still breathed through her mouth when she walked to and from her boarding house and the theatre.

On her last night, she danced and shook and wiggled, and the men shouted the usual things.

"Show us your tits!"

"Sit on my lap right here, little missy."

"That's some backside."

Tonight though, she could also hear another kind of heckling, the mean-spirited kind that grew from desperation, the kind that men, usually angry and drunk, engaged in when jobs were scarce and they had to dilute their children's milk with water. From her position, it sounded like a low hiss or the roll of drumsticks on a snare. Disjointed words floated toward her.

"Mother."

"Shame."

"Home."

But she continued to dance. She knew she couldn't be a star everywhere she went, but she had performed in every city on this circuit at least once, and she knew how to handle herself.

After she changed into her street clothes, she slipped out the back door, not stopping to see if anyone was waiting for her. She began walking down the street, past empty and dark grocery stores and diners. She liked these solitary walks back to her room; she never asked to walk with one of the other girls. She craved the way the night wrapped itself around her, the silence of the sleeping city or town like a warm, fluffy towel waiting as you step out of the bath. It was three and a half blocks to the boarding house, and the harvest moon was shining orange and huge in a sky that was not quite black, just the darkest shade of blue possible.

She shivered. Surely the heckling wasn't bothering her now? She turned around, but saw nothing behind her. A striped chipmunk skittered up a small, skinny tree as she walked by, and she jumped at the sound.

When she turned the corner, a man stepped out from behind a car. He wore a hat and a light coat. Val stopped and looked around at the dark, empty street, at the small abandoned playground behind her. "Shit," she whispered.

She braced herself for the assault. When he grabbed her and pulled, her feet remained on the ground, her hands in fists. She could hear him grunting, smell his armpits. Turning, she looked into his face. She saw the roughness of his skin and the dark stubble lining his cheeks and jaw. *A hard life*, she thought. She squirmed in his grip, and he swore. She was stronger than he had thought.

He said, "Fine. You don't want to move? We'll do it right here." He pulled open her coat and thrust his hand between her legs. He smiled.

She looked him in the eyes and spat, spraying saliva on his nose, his upper lip. He let go but didn't run away, only stared at her coldly. She planted her feet on the pavement, ready to scratch or slap or bite.

"How dare you? You've been flaunting yourself on a stage all night long. I've already seen everything you've got, Kitten."

He rushed at her and knocked her to the pavement. He grabbed her by the ankles and dragged her into the playground and behind the small, wood-sided playhouse. The blunt ends of cut grass were too short for her to grab. He struggled with her stockings and panties and with his own trousers (nicely pressed, how incongruous). She balled her hands into fists and punched at his head, but he didn't seem to feel it. When she screamed, he pressed his thumb into her throat, and she choked, angry that tears were filling her eyes. He positioned himself on top of her, and she realized that his weight on her body was too much and she couldn't push him off. She tried to will her body to be as heavy as possible, letting her arms and legs go limp and cumbersome so that anything he tried would cost him too much effort. She felt him pressing against her, felt that familiar sensation of unaired genitals touching each other. He muttered to himself, and she stiffened, waiting for the inevitable push and burn of unwanted sex.

But he stood up, zipping his fly. His face seemed swollen, angry in the moonlight. Val's underwear was still down around her ankles, but she felt nothing—no pain, no dry soreness.

"You see? You're just a used-up hag. I wouldn't do it with you anyway." He lifted his foot and stomped on her belly with his brown, well-worn boot.

Val stayed curled up in a ball on the grass for a long time. She cried silently through the night, barely seeing the light change as the stars faded into a daytime sky. He had winded her, and she thought she might have some broken ribs. She pretended the playground was her mother's lap and that the smell of the dirt was the smell of her mother's hands, like soap and dry, thick skin. If her mother were there, she might sing to her. Maybe "Hush, Little Baby," while she stroked her hair. Val remembered how light Joan's baby had been in her arms and how carefully she had bathed him, as if he had been a thinly painted porcelain doll with fine, breakable hair. Val even wished for her father, for the comforting smell of his tobacco, his curt nod whenever she cooked dinner.

At dawn, she heaved herself up and stumbled to the boarding house. In her room, she lay on the covers, panting like a cat. She was to get on a bus that afternoon for a performance in San Diego. If she missed the bus, she would miss her gig the following night, and they would have to replace her, which meant that they might use the substitute dancer for the rest of the week. The Siamese Kitten was never late and had never missed a show. Her agent once said she was the most reliable, least-bitchy dancer he had ever met. *I can sit on a damned bus*, she thought. *I'll sleep the whole way there.* She checked the clock on the nightstand. Six hours before she had to leave. For now, she could stay still.

When she woke up, every breath was an explosion, and the bones in her chest felt like they were splintering each time she inhaled. She crept down the hall to the bathroom and rinsed her mouth out with cold water. She coughed, and a splatter of blood stained the sink. "Shit," she said, before walking slowly back down the hall, where she pounded on another dancer's door. "Where's the hospital around here?"

Eight years later, during a sunny and pleasant fall, Val returned to Vancouver. She had been back before, of course, to dance in the theatres and clubs, and to see her agent in his office on Granville Street. There were too many loggers, too many mill workers, for her to ignore the place altogether. This time, however, she was back for a whole two weeks, staying in a downtown hotel with a view of the mountains. She didn't think she needed such grand accommodation, but the manager at the Cave Supper Club insisted. "We don't get stars of your calibre every day, Val. It's been four months since Lili St. Cyr came through town and the boys around here are ready for more. Maybe you don't remember," he continued, "but Vancouver is one of the few cities that treats its talent right." When she checked in, the man at the front desk asked if she would sign his pocket square so he could prove he had met her.

She thought about Joan, about the house she and Peter had bought outside of the city, with the fish pond and wall-to-wall carpeting. In her letters, Joan seemed consumed by the house, by the creaks in the floors, the steepness of the staircase, even the colour of the grout between the bathroom tiles. Val, lying in bed at a boarding house in Indianapolis, laughed while she read. She could just see little Joanie tumbling around alone in a gigantic house, a gin and tonic in her hand, fluffing up the pile of her carpet, staring at the other houses in the cul-de-sac through the big front window but not stepping outside to speak to one of her neighbours.

Joan never asked what Val was doing on the road, and Val didn't tell her. She wrote of the impossibly tall Chrysler Building; the groves and groves of oranges on the side of the highway in California; the flatness of the American Midwest; the deadened eyes of the travelling salesmen she saw at train stations, the elbows, knees and seats of their suits shiny with wear and filmed with dust. But they both knew other words lurked behind her written ones: *circuit, cabaret, the strip*.

In her hotel room, she picked up the telephone and dialled her sister's number. It rang once before Joan's crisp voice answered.

"Joanie, it's me. I'm back in town." She heard Joan snort. "Back? For how long?"

"A couple of weeks. I'm having Mum and Dad down to the city for a few days. I thought it would be a nice treat, especially now that Dad's not working much anymore. Maybe you'd like to have dinner with us or walk with us in Stanley Park."

Joan clucked her tongue against the roof of her mouth and Val wondered how a woman so small could make such a sharp, gunshot-like sound. "It's a busy time here for us, Val. Peter's working long hours, and I really should be home to make sure he has a good dinner so he can keep up his energy. I'm sorry. It's not a good time."

Val looked at the fresh flowers on the side table, the shiny mirror across from the bed, the jug of cold water on a silver tray. This life—so much like their dreams of living in the big city, the ones they whispered to each other when they were little girls—or the bland interior of Joan's house and dinners with Peter, his stout face reflected at suppertime in the dining-room mirror.

Val said, "Suit yourself," and didn't wait to hear Joan's response before she hung up.

That night, the standing ovation at the Cave drowned out Joan's words, and Val was glad she had returned.

The second week, she walked through Chinatown, wearing her navy cashmere coat and chocolate-brown shoes. She told herself that she was simply visiting a neighbourhood in which she had spent so much time. Her hair, set in full curls, was brushed away from her face and carefully tucked behind her ears. On her right index finger she wore an emerald set in gold, a gift from a movie producer she had met in

Los Angeles, who had moved her into his cavernous house before casting her in one of his pictures. But as it turned out, Val was the kind of actress who made audiences cringe with embarrassment; she was too loud, too fast, too *big* to be contained by the screen. After the premiere, the producer patted her hand and said nothing before dropping her off at a nice hotel. When she walked into her room, all the clothes and makeup and jewellery she had left in his house were there, packed in a neat little luggage set made of purple leather. To her relief, the movie came and went with scarcely a whisper. Most of her audience was more interested in live flesh anyway.

She walked down Pender, and the bright neon signs, more numerous than she remembered, blinked palely in the thin, grey daylight, announcing clubs, restaurants and butchers. Her face was turned up, like she was catching snowflakes instead of marvelling at the buzzing, multicoloured pigs, buddhas and seahorses.

Across the street, a little boy was sitting on the curb, spinning a wooden top on the concrete. She stood still for a second, thinking that this black-haired child in the worn brown sweater and corduroys could have been young Warren. From where she was standing, she could see those round eyes that seemed to take in everything at once, even those things no one else could see. He was hunched over his faded top; his shoes were nestled in the garbage and fluid flowing beside the sidewalk in the gutter. Val stopped herself from running through traffic and snatching him up, taking him with her to the house by the river where she could feed him better, hold him longer. Change how it had all turned out.

A woman with crudely bobbed hair emerged from the doorway of a souvenir shop and spoke to the little boy. He stood up into a beam of sunshine, and Val saw that he had olive skin and a smooth, open face. He stepped off the curb, and Val heard the woman sharply lecture him in Chinese before pulling him onto the sidewalk. Val wanted to smack herself in the forehead for being so sentimental and delusional. If Warren were alive, he'd be twice that boy's age. *This city*, she thought, *makes me crazy. Always will.*

As she walked on, she found that she couldn't keep the memories from flooding in. At first, she pretended that she wasn't thinking of Sam, but she soon saw that pretending to no one but herself was ridiculous. Every familiar crack in the sidewalk reminded her of him. Over the years, she hadn't dared to think of him as often as she might have wanted. She sometimes imagined him in the front row during one of her shows, although she knew this was impossible. Sam was a family man, after all, one who never went to see strippers, but one who kept his out-of-country wife a secret from his barely adult mistress.

She recognized some of her old customers: Chinese men squatting in the alleys, chewing on tobacco and pumpkin seeds, mostly unchanged but now smaller, their sockless ankles fragile under the rolled-up cuffs of their pants. She peered into the barbershop, wondering if her favourite customer from the café was still there, cutting hair, trimming beards with long razors, tenderly scraping a sharp edge against the thin skin of someone's neck. She saw no one except a lone man, hair falling over his ears, waiting in a chair by the window.

Tired, she turned around to begin walking back into downtown, to her hotel with its deep tub and piles of pillows. As she looked west, she saw a couple—a man in his fifties, with a slightly younger woman—walking toward her. She blinked. It was Sam.

She made no pretence; she stood in the middle of the sidewalk and stared. There he was, still tall, still broad in the shoulders. What did she expect? After all, he could hardly have shrivelled up and been driven mad by her absence. His hair was still thick, but it was growing white around his ears and temples, and his face was beginning to fall; the wrinkles were hardly visible, but Val could see the old man he would become, pushing through his skin like roots through cement.

The woman, of course, must be his wife. The top of her head was level with his shoulders. She stooped a little, and her clothes were subdued: a grey raincoat, a faded yellow print dress, black shoes that laced up. Val could see the traces of multiple pregnancies, the fat that pads a woman's thighs and belly with each succeeding child. And her face—drawn, tired, hopeless.

Just then, she felt a touch on her sleeve. Sam looked her in the eyes, said, "Excuse me," and edged past.

He smelled the same: that sweet and doughy smell of pancakes. After his scent had disappeared from the air around her, she continued walking west. She replayed his gaze over and over again as she drew closer to the downtown core. Dark eyes, straight eyelashes, fine wrinkles in the corners. But one thing was different. His eyes showed not a glimmer of recognition and she knew, then and there, that she had truly become someone else.

—

It had been a hard night in Kansas City, the sort of night when the comics were too tired to deliver their jokes with any enthusiasm. Outside, dust covered everything—the beat-up cars, the screen doors, even the farmers' wives, who walked by the theatre with a mixture of fear, condemnation and shame on their faces for wanting to enter, to see what the fuss was about or to be dazzled by the lights and beading. Val was sure that these wives, dressed in clothes that made them look like the shapeless and boring potatoes they grew, would immediately leave the grime and kitchen grease forever if they could, just once, sit in the padded seats and watch as the possibilities were revealed before them, glove by stocking by brassiere.

As the dancers slouched and shrugged their way through the show, they each had a sinking feeling that all anyone cared about now were their naked bodies. No one listened to the jokes, hardly anyone clapped for the tease, for the flash of skin that signified more than it showed. Burlesque was growing old, and Val, with the added flesh on her thighs and the roll she had to suck in during every act, was almost thirty and perhaps growing old too. But she gave them the best show she could, day in and day out.

After her act, she hurried through the sharp wind, back to her boarding house. She paused and looked into the drugstore window, at the soda counter, the abandoned soda jerk hat on a stool near the front. So clean, so red and white. It was easy to imagine the rosy cheeks of the girls and boys who worked there, the smiles of the teenaged couples sneakily holding hands while they sipped their shared egg cream—two straws, of course. Val turned away. *Bad nights at the theatre always trigger the stupidest thoughts.*

In her room, she changed into her nightgown and pulled on thick woollen socks. As she padded to the closet, she saw a letter on the floor inside the door to the hallway. From Joan, of course. Her parents never wrote Val with such regularity.

> *Mum and Dad are gone.*
> *I don't know how to deal with it.*
> *The house is a mess.*
> *The funeral is tomorrow.*
> *Please come home. I need help.*

It was impossible to comprehend. Her mother, with her downturned brown eyes and knobbly legs. Her father, with his dirty undershirts and unkept promises. Joan must be mistaken.

But there it all was, in Joan's neat, small handwriting. It was a lung infection, one that developed quickly from a small, dry cough until they were lying, hot and damp, in their bed, unable to move, and only picking up the new phone that Val had paid for when they couldn't speak anymore. When Joan arrived, it was too late. A neighbour had cleaned them, and they lay like sleeping children, fresh-faced under white sheets.

I would have phoned you, Val, but you never gave me the numbers.

It had been three years since Val had seen them. They had come down to Vancouver for a few days, staying in her hotel room, marvelling at the indoor plumbing they still hadn't installed in their own house. She applied makeup to her mother's small, sharp face, draped her own clothes on her body and took them out for dinners and shows and shopping.

"All this," her mother wondered, "on a chorus girl's salary?"

Her father ate his steak in huge bites and hunched over his plate, probably expecting that someone would take it away from him.

Val crawled into her boarding-house bed and pulled the covers up to her nose. The wind whistled outside, and she couldn't decide if it was wolves she was hearing or the howling of the dry air, blowing itself through the gaps and cracks between buildings and trees.

She could have stayed with Joan, in her green and white spare bedroom with its line of porcelain dolls on the window seat, their glass eyes blue and grey and brown and unfocused. Instead, she took the train to the house by the river.

The water seemed to have crept closer to the house. When Val walked in, dragging her two trunks behind her, the smell of her family was gone, replaced by the fishy, woody and turbid smell of the river. Already, the remains of their lives were being claimed by the bush and air and water.

Joan arrived the next morning, spent one night crying and sniffling in their old bed, and left the next morning in her shiny green car, saying that Peter needed her for a company cocktail party. Val didn't try to stop her. It was better to be alone with the silence of the nighttime. She sat in the backyard, smelling rain from across the river, her hands folded over her knee. It was quieter than she remembered; the great logs floated by without a sound. The rough men who used to work and live here were slowly being replaced by young families who painted the houses white and planted flower gardens along their front paths. In the dark, when the one remaining cannery and rail yards were closed, the river lapped up on the shore, and Val could hear the occasional splash of a fish jumping and falling back.

It took her five days to clean everything out, not because Meg and Warren had accumulated much during their marriage, but because mould was creeping up the walls, mice skittered across the floors and vines were growing into the siding, slowly unfurling tendrils into the cracks by the windows. The landlord never came to see the damage. A letter arrived in the mailbox one morning, informing all remaining occupants that they were to vacate by the end of the month. Val read the letter with wet fingers, the front of her dress (her mother's old housedress, with her mother's large blue apron) damp with soapy water.

On her last day at the house, she pulled her father's axe out of the shed and walked through the backyard and down to the blackberry bushes, now a wall of thorns and twisted, impenetrable brambles. She wore her father's coveralls and work gloves and her mother's rubber boots. The darkness of the bush, even in the middle of the day, was complete. The wild plants rose above her head and blocked the sun. As she chopped and pushed, the thorns scratched her face and neck, catching on her hair and the tips of her ears. She stomped down the damp, fetid-smelling dirt and kicked the carcasses of dead rats and crows to the side. The mosquitoes rose around her in clouds. But she kept moving forward, cutting the path that her father had promised he would make when she and Joan had wanted nothing more than to dip their hot, sweaty feet in the cool water.

About halfway through, she found a pile of stones, polished and round as only rocks battered by the river could be. She knelt down and felt the ground with her palms, and she thought she could detect a slight warmth through the dirt. She swallowed hard. After a few minutes, she stood up again and swung the axe ahead of her, her eyes hard against the flickering dark.

Finally, she emerged on the other side, the Fraser River rushing fifteen feet from where she stood. She slipped off her boots and coveralls. Wearing a blouse and panties, she walked over the rocks and beached logs to the pebbly shore. She waded in until the water was up to her knees. The current pushed at her, but she dug her toes into the gritty sand and watched as fish, big and small, swam past her. Bending down, she dipped her hands into the cool water and washed her face, rubbing off the dried blood and grime. When she stood up again, she felt a breeze in her damp hair, like Joan's breath on her skin when they shared a bed. Now, over the sound of the running water, she thought she could hear the soft buzz of her father snoring in the other room, the creaks of the bed frame when her mother woke up in the middle of the night and had to walk the floor to dissipate the pins and needles in her legs. She wondered at what point memories became ghosts, clinging to the body like the anchoring threads of a spider web. Across the river, another town. And beyond that, the big city. She could see it all clearly.

Behind her, the path she had made rose up the hill, and she saw the house, no longer white, with its small windows like blind eyes in the afternoon sun. She sat on a large flat rock and waited for her feet to dry before pulling on her boots and trudging uphill.

THE ACCIDENT

1958

Finally, she left the house and returned to Vancouver. The number of families had grown in her absence, and three-bedroom houses had sprung up in pockets of town Val had never even heard of. Everywhere she went, there was more construction. She supposed 1958 was proving to be a profitable year for the husbands and fathers who commuted across the bridges into downtown. Still, desperate girls worked the streets. Val wondered if men came in every weekend like they used to, fresh from months of hauling logs out of the bush or netting fish off the Gulf Islands, their pay burning in their pockets, their bodies hungry for booze and women. Perhaps it was now salesmen and managers who drove to Georgia or Davie or Main after their babies had been bathed and put to bed, and their wives were watching *Perry Mason* in their flannel pyjamas. Not that it mattered. Sex and the paying for sex remained unchanged.

After she found an apartment downtown, she began dancing regularly at the Cave Supper Club and the Penthouse and, later, at the Shanghai Junk, where she was always the final dancer onstage. "And now, ladies and gentlemen, it's time for the last, but not the least, act of the night. Please welcome the world-famous Siamese Kitten. She might scratch, but if you treat her right, she'll have you purring all night long!" The club managers said that her presence elevated the tone of the show, bringing a precious glamour to the evenings that made the audience forget they were living in a wind-blown city built on logging, drink and soil spongy with rain. When she stepped onstage, she could see the men sniff, as if she brought with her a whiff of the Orient, a smell of cinnamon that allowed them to dream about pale-faced, dark-haired women tangled in silk sheets, without the wife ever knowing. While she danced, the warmth of the spotlight swaddled her, and the gruff, low-voiced shouts seemed to propel her arms and legs forward and back, around the stage and toward the ceiling. She flashed a sequined pasty, and the club exploded. Always, she smiled at the noise because it meant the same thing: they wanted her.

After she had been back for several weeks, her eyes began to travel over the faces of the men in the crowd, the ones sitting alone with a single bottle of beer, the groups of businessmen who shouted at the girls and cupped the waitresses' bums with their meaty hands, the college boys who giggled and threw up in the washroom. There were women, too, women who sat alone at the bar in clothes that glittered in the darkness of the club. They eyed the men, walked over to those who seemed loneliest or who shouted the loudest at the dancers. Even with the bright lights between her and the audience, Val could see how these women pulled their chairs closer to the men they were talking to, how the shadows on their faces deepened as they smiled, and how some of them tried to hide the bruises and burns on their arms and legs with scarves or makeup that faded as the night beat onward.

Hard, she thought, *with eyes like stones.*

Throughout the night, they left, arms linked with flushed, sheepish men, or men with set jaws and narrowed eyes. As they passed her, she didn't look directly at their faces.

Before closing, she heard one girl say to another, "I have to get up early to drop my kids off at school," and Val flinched.

She soon saw that the dancers were changing, coming out in skimpier costumes that took no time at all to take off, dancing longer without their tops, squeezing their breasts together while they thrust their pelvises into the faces of the men in the front row. Val supposed they made more in tips that way. She could see the expressions on the men's faces, the damp, oily look of arousal. They were not teased, they were simply erect.

For the first time since she started dancing, she felt tired, as if the audience were sucking her dry. When she asked her agent if he thought the circuit was changing, he blew out a line of smoke and said, "Sure. We had some good years there, but the movies are really taking a bite out of the business. Who needs expensive burlesque shows when you've got cartoon movies with Technicolor and singing and dancing? That damned Walt Disney. I should have been *his* agent."

Val could see that the men expected more. If they were going to spend the money on a live show, they expected to see everything the girls had; the longer it took to get down to the tits and G-strings, the higher the frustration. It was like a slowly building tidal wave of discontent, one that rose from the back of the room and eventually engulfed the dancers until they all, except Val, took off their clothes to get it over with. Only the Siamese Kitten kept to her original act. No one expected otherwise.

One night, three months after her return, a young man sat at a table of college boys. His blond hair was not combed back with Brylcreem, but long in front, almost covering his eyes. He slouched in his chair, his chin half hidden by the collar of his white shirt and yellow sweater. Val could feel his eyes on her, their sharp blueness burning as they travelled up her legs and over her breasts. She saw the tremor underneath the surface of his smooth face, an electric and involuntary twitch of the muscles. She clenched her jaw to keep herself from visibly shivering.

After her act, she stayed in the dressing room for longer than usual. She imagined those eyes slicing through the air in a dark bedroom, and her own legs liquid and weak. He was not the sort of man who did as he was told. Rather, he got what he wanted and refused to wait. His hands would pull at her clothes, shift her arms and legs until he was satisfied with what he saw. He would say little, offering a small, serious smile that could turn ugly in a minute but was, right now anyway, pleased with the woman he had chosen and shaped.

When the club emptied that night, Val carefully left through the back door and stepped into the alley. There he stood, alone, leaning against the opposite building, his hands in the pockets of his brown trousers.

"You're the Siamese Kitten," he said. It wasn't a question.

She began to walk briskly down the alley. "My stage name," she muttered.

"I'm Carl." His long legs easily kept pace with her. She considered that it might be useful to own a pair of flat-soled shoes. "I really liked your act."

Val stopped and turned to face him, although she kept her gaze on his nose and not his eyes. "How old are you, Carl? Shouldn't you be going home to your mother?"

He stopped and stared, his tall body quivering. After a few seconds, he began to laugh, throwing his head back; his blond hair fell away from his forehead. "Is that what you say to all the guys?"

In the darkness of the alley, he stepped closer to her and put his hand between her shoulder blades. Val felt his body looming like a shadow. Everything about him dwarfed her— the vastness of his shoulders, the long trail of his veins down his arms. *I could sink right in*, she thought. *He could carry me off. How easy that would be.* She didn't pull away, staring at his beautiful, smooth face, the crooked asymmetry of his long, thin mouth. He kissed her, and she sucked in the feel of his tongue—the wetness, how quickly he needed to discover what she tasted like.

He drove her home in a rusty car. "It used to be my father's," he said, grinding gears as they accelerated up the street. "You should see the Lincoln he drives now. The colour of champagne, he always says."

Val nodded, not really listening to the words, but allowing his voice to swim around her, each syllable ringing and echoing. She closed her eyes and wondered if he would sound this young forever, or if that adolescent hitch in his voice would disappear when he married, when he was driving home on a foggy Tuesday night to a family house forty minutes outside of the city. But when she opened her eyes to look at him again, she forgot the boy in his voice and thought of the man underneath those clothes.

One day he would have a pretty wife. Would she ever understand this moment?

When they arrived at her apartment building's front door, Carl said, "I've known about you for a long time. I remember when I saw your movie."

"You might be the only one who did," she said as she pulled out her keys. "The past. That's all it is." She smiled and cocked her head to one side. "I only worry about tonight."

He filled her bedroom with his tall, thick body. She ran her fingers down his chest, each short hair pricking at her goosebumped skin. Waves pulsed through her when he grasped her right hand and kissed the inside of her wrist. Naked, he was as she imagined: skin transparent but burning to the touch, the line of his arms and legs clearly defined against the dim of the room. His tallness was like a command, a physical manifestation of the fucking he wanted and was going to get.

As she lowered herself onto the length of his body, her red lipstick appeared on his nipples, the insides of his thighs, the side of his neck. Without this one bit of makeup, she was, for the first time in years, not the Siamese Kitten, even in this small way. Only Val.

He stayed with her for the next two days and nights, hardly moving when she toasted bread and brewed tea. He lay there, the sheets twisted around his legs, his pale skin gleaming in all lights: in the greyness of morning, the thick sunshine of afternoon, even the crisp darkness of midnight, when the streets were so quiet they could hear the skitter of a dry leaf on the sidewalk. She forgot about shaving her legs or finding her diaphragm and worried instead about how much longer she might have with him, or how quickly she could respond to his lips on her ear. When she went to the bathroom in the morning, her hip was red with his handprint, and the spot was still warm from his night-long grip. She called the Shanghai Junk to tell them she was sick, and Carl laughed as she stood naked by the side table and croaked into the phone.

On their last afternoon together, they drank cheap red wine. Val put the palm of her hand against Carl's flushed cheek and felt the heat coming off him in waves. She could see the blond stubble when a stray beam of sun struck his chin at a precise angle. The lines of his jaw glittered hard, like diamonds.

"I'll have to go back to my dorm soon," he said.

Val nodded. "Of course."

He rubbed her earlobe between his thumb and index finger. "I could come back next week, take you out for dinner. I know a nice place downtown with the best steaks you'll ever eat."

As she stroked his bottom lip, Val saw herself in the house Carl would eventually own: a big house, square and white, with black shutters and petunias lining the driveway. Her face reflected in the long mirror on the wall in the dining room, scooping out mounds of mashed potatoes to three fair-haired children. And Carl—late because of traffic and a last-minute memo at the office—would rush in, kiss her on the cheek and remark, "This dinner smells so good, I drove home following my nose."

But she looked again at his face, his round cheeks masking the man he might one day be. Perhaps he meant what he said, and he really did want to see her again. Maybe he wanted to engage in that courtship dance that he understood with the cheerleader, or the girl with the glasses who sat at the same table in the school library every morning. Val knew that while the lines of her face were sharp against her jaw and pulled tight against her cheekbones, her body was the opposite, growing softer every year past the age of thirty, her breasts blurring into her belly, which blurred sideways across her hips. Today, she noticed; five years from now, everyone would.

She wanted him to stay and never go back to school, where he would soon see she could never attend a fraternity party or neck with him in the back seat of his car. If he stayed, she could curl into him every night and feel his weight when he threw his leg over the curve of her hip. She could teach him to dance, and his bulk would be hers.

Stupid, she thought. *Why would I think anything so stupid?*

Val took both of Carl's hands in hers. "Just remember me," she said.

And by the fall of his eyes, she knew he understood what she meant.

She danced, and the audience applauded and seemed satisfied, but at the end of every night, she sat in front of the dressing-room mirror and let her mind wander. It hadn't occurred to her in a long time that she might want something besides the shimmy and lights and costumes. Could she be a secretary or cook or nanny? She didn't know, and this was what frustrated her. There wasn't anything else she was good at.

One afternoon, before her first dance of the evening, she stood in the alley behind the Shanghai Junk and smoked a cigarette, blowing rings toward the blue sky, which was hot and liquid with the summertime sun. She stared at the grime on the buildings and ground around her, the scars on the door to the club that meant someone had tried to break in. She kicked at the gravel and watched the stones skitter and bounce, stopping to rest beside a pile of rotting onions left behind by the produce merchant next door.

When she looked up again, she saw a little boy standing in a patch of sunshine, staring at her. Her stomach lurched. His bones had grown longer but were just as sharp, his eyes still too large for his face. If she touched him and ran her finger down his cheek, he would know it was her and recognize her smell; he might even smile as she held his thin body to hers. She thought she might cry.

The sharp sound of squealing brakes at the end of the alley caused her to close her eyes against the whine. When she opened them again, she could see that he was a small Chinese boy with a grubby face and a stubborn cowlick at the back of his head. It was the eyes, she realized. The eyes had tricked her. Again.

"Are those Sweet Caps?" he asked, inching toward her, his body tense with apprehension.

She smiled and pulled out a full pack. By the time he ran off, she had given him the green silk sash off her robe. It was the way he held it in his hand, as if there was nothing more magical than this slip of fabric, coloured like grass but smooth. He was just as she remembered.

—

When she realized she was pregnant, she wept. In that white room with those bright lights and plastic blinds, Val sat hunched over in a bucket chair, the doctor's hand on her shoulder, and cried—shaking, coughing, tears and snot in her mouth, a rippling sensation through her lungs like she was drowning. She had never cried like this, not when her parents died, not when she had let go of Joan's baby so their father could bury him.

The doctor smiled and said, "A surprise, is it?"

Val wiped the tears off her cheeks with the back of her hand. "I always wanted this baby."

In her apartment, she moved her dresser to the opposite wall, stared at the empty space below the window and imagined the sunlight lingering across the face of her sleeping infant. Their life together would be quiet, punctuated by the smell of baking bread, neat piles of clean laundry, Val's smile reflected in the face of her baby. She knew what kind of mother she would be: wise, patient, understanding. The mother everyone wished they had. This baby would right everything that had gone wrong. She felt full at the thought.

She went to her agent and told him to stop booking shows. "That's it, I'm done," she announced in his smoky office. "Nobody wants my style of act anymore, and besides, there are other things I should be doing with my life."

He sat up straight and spat his cigarette into the ashtray on his desk. "What things? What's more important than the Siamese Kitten, eh?"

"I'm pregnant, all right? So I'd better quit, unless you think there's a small group of weirdos out there who get off on that sort of thing."

Her agent said nothing then lit another cigarette, his eyebrows knotted together. "Well, that's a kick in the nuts. Are you happy?"

"You don't even know how much."

He swiped a hand over his eyes. "Then good luck to you, Valerie Nealy. And if there's ever a time when you want to come back, you know how to get a hold of me. There'll always be a place for you, even if the circuit keeps changing." Gently, he patted her arm. "It'll be great, sweetheart, I know it."

When she returned home, she gathered up her costumes and props and packed them in boxes. She left her most special things for last, packing her first full costume—wig, fishnets, green satin robe—into a small suitcase and setting it on the pile. Outside, she could see the honey bees flying in and out of her neighbour's flowers; she wondered how long it would take to plant a container garden on her balcony.

In the taxi on the way to Joan's house, Val thought about names, about the woman she wanted her daughter to become. She knew she was having a daughter; she pictured a tiny, floating baby, with skin like paper and blue, blue eyes ringed with pale gold eyelashes. Donna. Bree. Lisa. Michelle. She looked out the window at the tall trees bordering the highway, the tops that seemed to touch the flat grey clouds, the lower branches that swayed, dropping needles on the unpaved shoulder.

Joan stepped into the front yard, wearing a baby-blue shirtdress tightly belted at the waist. She seemed no older, only pointier. Val saw that she was well-preserved, a woman who stared in the mirror every morning, coming up with ways to hide the barely perceptible lines feathering outward from her lips. Silently, Joan watched the driver struggle with the boxes up the walk and carry them into the foyer.

"What's all this, Val? Surely you're not moving in." Joan spoke crisply, waiting for this visit to be over.

Val laughed and put her arms around Joan's shoulders. Joan stiffened, but relaxed enough to collapse a little into Val's embrace. "No, honey, nothing so horrible as that. I've given up dancing and need you to store my old costumes and things for me. My place is too small."

Joan looked eager, and she clapped her hands. "Really? Well, it's about time! Come on in, and we'll have a drink to celebrate."

"I really shouldn't. I'm pregnant, Joanie."

Already on her way through the hall to the kitchen, Joan turned to look at Val. "Pregnant? Val, how did this happen?"

The kitchen table was smooth and shiny. In the window, a small box was filled with fresh herbs. But still, with all this— the red-and-white checked placemats, the potted fern hanging from the ceiling—the house smelled of Joan and Joan alone. Her orange-scented shampoo, the lavender water ironed into her dress.

"It just did. He's a young man, too young, maybe. He doesn't know about this, and that's all right."

"Who is he?" Joan asked, rinsing out a tall glass.

"His name isn't important."

"Don't tell me that you don't even know his name," she half whispered, half hissed.

"I'm having a baby, Joanie. That's all."

"Yes, but whose baby?"

"It doesn't matter. I need a change, a big one." Val paused

and leaned forward, her elbows on the table. "I need this baby, do you see?"

Joan sipped at a gin and tonic, her face still. She said, "I know. I understand. I really do."

Together, they had survived shattered dreams and the unexpected. Joan looked at Val, both hands tightly wrapped around her glass.

"What will you do for money if you're not dancing?"

"I have some money put away. It should last me a year, maybe two, if I'm careful."

"Peter and I will help out. I don't want you skimping on food or anything like that, not now."

Surprised, Val sat back in her chair. "It's not necessary, Joanie. I can get by."

"Well, we can help you in other ways too, you know. You can use the extra car so you don't have to take the trolleys everywhere. You should come over for dinner, you know, so I can fill you up."

"Honey, thanks a lot, but I'm not a charity case. I made good money."

Joan stood and walked to the glass-paned liquor cabinet. Her voice was strange, like a violin string on the verge of snapping. "Of course, I know that. Charity isn't the point. I want to make sure my niece or nephew gets the very best, that's all."

That night, Val stayed for dinner, leaving in Joan's second car before Peter arrived home from work. As she drove away from the house, she could see Joan's thin silhouette in the doorway, her long arm raised in a wave, the light of the hall pushing itself into the night through her legs, around her sides and over her head.

—

Val dreamed of the baby every night. She saw the baby's pale face, her small, elf-like body, even her round toes. Sometimes the baby cried, a quiet, barely there plea that ceased as soon as Val picked her up and held her, her small chin resting on Val's shoulder. Other times, she sat on a sheepskin rug on the floor, clapping her hands as Val danced in front of her, a goofy version of the strip she used to do in the clubs with a towel on her head for a wig and an old sheet wrapped around her body for a satin gown.

When she woke up, she was warm and round and unworried. Through the window, she watched the birds flying between the downtown apartment buildings. She lay on her side until the sun rose past the railing on the balcony. She sometimes looked in the mirrors in shops, or in her own mirror at home, and was surprised by her bare, makeup-less face, which seemed, oddly, younger than it had in years. The flowers she planted on the balcony nodded at her through the window, and she nodded back. For once, she felt quiet, like an undisturbed, clear-as-glass lake.

One afternoon, Joan appeared at her door, her tweed skirt peeping out the bottom of her tan trench coat. She held up a paper bag filled with groceries.

"Fresh fruit and veggies for the baby," she announced, walking straight into the kitchen where she began putting the food away in the fridge. "I bought you a nice steak too. You need to keep up your iron, you know."

After Val settled Joan on the balcony with a cup of tea, Joan smiled. "This is really nice, Val. You've done a good job of making this little apartment into a home. I can see you had some pansies over the summer."

Val nodded and waved her hand over the yellow and red trees lining the sidewalk. "The summer was really great, but it looks like the fall might turn out to be even nicer."

"You're getting big." Joan let her eyes linger on Val's belly. "When's the due date again?"

"End of December."

"Like I said, the apartment looks very homey," Joan said, her voice rising to a clear, precise pitch. "What are you doing to get ready for the baby?"

"I've been looking at cribs, but I haven't found the exact right thing yet. I wanted something in a natural wood, you know, and everything these days is covered in white laminate or some such thing. I've started a quilt, in all different colours." Val laughed, rubbed her needle-pricked fingers together. "I'm not much of a seamstress, but I try."

"Are you prepared enough, do you think?"

"I think so. No one is ever really prepared, you know."

"No, that's true." Joan paused. "What about afterward? What are you going to do for money?"

Val twisted a finger in her hair. "I'll figure it out. I always do. I could waitress, of course, or I was thinking I could be an agent for other girls. You know: make sure they're treated fairly and all that."

Joan turned and looked into Val's eyes so intently that Val had to look away. "Is that wise? If you waitress, who will look after the baby? And if you're going to work with those girls again, aren't you exposing the baby to that crowd? Do you want to do that?"

Val put her hand up to her hair. Below, a car with a mattress tied to its roof drove slowly past. Val thought she could hear a polka drifting from a building across the street. "I never thought of it that way, I guess. I'll do what I have to do. We'll get by."

Joan tapped her fingers on her lap. "Don't you think, Val, that the baby deserves more than just getting by? What about music lessons, or summer camp? Have you even thought about university?"

"That's thinking really far ahead."

"Yes, but that's what mothers do. They plan. They make sure their children have everything they could possibly need."

"What are you saying? That I won't be a good mother?"

Joan leaned forward and gripped Val's knee with a thin hand. Behind her, the sky seemed far too bright for morning, far too blue and sharp for the coming of fall. "No, of course not. But your baby deserves the best, that's all. Now, Peter and I, we could give any number of children the best lives possible."

"You and Peter?"

"You know how we've wanted children for years and years. It's been the hardest thing, not being able to give him the family he's always wanted." Joan's voice broke and her lips trembled. "When I told him about you and your pregnancy, his face went all hard and, that night, he didn't even come home from work. Sometimes, I don't even know where he is."

"Joanie, I didn't know."

"It's been so hard all these years, thinking about little Warren and what he might look like now. I'm going to love your baby, Val. I really will. If I had one of my own, he or she would have everything and grow up in a real family with a father and a house in a good neighbourhood with lots of other children. It would be so ideal."

Val stood up, pushing her chair with so much force that it crashed against the glass of the patio door. "*My* baby, Joan, not yours." She could feel Joan's eyes travelling over her swollen stomach. Empty eyes. Eyes that could bore through skin and blood.

Joan grabbed Val's sleeve. "No, that's not what I meant. It's just that I have everything, except a child. And you"— she choked and swallowed and deep frown lines creased her cheeks—"you have nothing, except this baby. Even you, without a husband, without even a real home, can have a baby while I sit by myself in the living room every day, staring at the goddamned lawn. Maybe I should have been a stripper too and fucked men whose names I don't even know."

As briskly as her belly allowed her, Val hurried through the apartment and opened the door to the hallway. "Get out, Joan. I'm not listening to you anymore."

Slowly, Joan walked to the door, her eyes pink and wet. "I need to love your baby, Val."

Val remained silent and watched as Joan made her way down the hall and to the stairwell. After locking the door, she went straight to bed, pulling the covers over her face until the heat from her breath warmed the pocket of air around her head. Almost buried by blankets, she fell asleep, her fists clenched, ready for the fight that might come to her in a dream.

—

In the hospital, Val held her baby in her arms, smelled the fine fuzz on her head and stroked her cheeks with one finger. It was when the baby was coming out (she wondered how she could stay whole while her body was sundered, push by push, and she was almost blind with effort and throbbing) that she realized the perfect name.

Dawn. For the morning and the transition from the dark dreams of night to the relief of day.

There was no surprise. Dawn arrived exactly as she should, looking as Val had always imagined—pink and white and blond. Val held a finger on a pulsing blue vein in her tiny forehead.

A nurse walked into the room, carrying a pile of diapers. "When is your husband coming, my dear?"

Val looked up. "There's no husband. Just me."

The nurse's forehead wrinkled, and she looked away, peering into the closet. "Well then, you'll need more wash-cloths," she muttered as she hurried out the door.

But Val barely heard her, only watched as Dawn put out one small hand and fluttered it in the air.

"I promise you everything," Val whispered. "All you need to do is ask."

THE DEBRIS

1959 to 1980

The baby would not stop screaming. Everywhere Val went in her little apartment, she could hear the echo from her cries bouncing off the walls until it sounded like a dozen babies were trapped in the bedroom, shrieking for help. Her milk wouldn't come in, and she was tired, so tired, of pushing her nipple into Dawn's mouth and watching her suck until Val started to bleed. No milk, just oozing scabs.

She scorched the bottles, slept fitfully, her body tensed and anticipating the cries from the crib. Every sound, every change of light woke up the baby, until Val took the phone off the hook and kept the curtains drawn at all times. She was trapped in a stuffy cave, with nothing but this squalling child for company.

In the mornings, when Val crept up to the crib to see if Dawn was sleeping, her heart rose and swelled as she gazed at the purse of her mouth, the flutter of her eyelids as she dreamed in her sleep. This was the best time.

One evening, Dawn cried and cried, the wails consuming all of the air inside her small lungs. When she inhaled, she gulped and hiccupped and coughed. Her cries shuddered and skipped. Val walked with her from the kitchen to the living room and back again, whispering, "Shush now. Shhh. It's all right." But she knew that Dawn couldn't even hear her over the screaming, or see her through those tightly closed eyes.

She was afraid to leave, afraid that wherever she went, the baby's cries would alarm passersby until someone tried to take her away. There was no place where the baby's cries would be muffled by the encroaching bush or the crash of waves. There was this tiny apartment and the two of them, their voices circling and rebounding into their ears. How long before she couldn't stand it anymore? Before she thrust the baby underneath the sofa cushions until her breath shuddered and stopped? Val wrapped the still-crying Dawn in her home-made quilt, lay her down in her crib and shut the bedroom door. She hurried through the living room, a glass of sherry in her hand, and out onto the balcony, sliding the patio door shut behind her.

The smell of frost rose up from the grass, and Val breathed in deeply, savouring the nip of cold air in her throat and lungs. In the streaky January sky were the remnants of a sunset. On the bare maple in front, a crow sat unmoving, its wings held close, its shoulders hunched. Her glass was soon empty, and she stood up to refill it.

On the other side of the door stood Joan, meticulously dressed in a cashmere sweater and plaid skirt, holding the baby and gazing evenly at Val through the glass. Val pulled her milk-stained robe closed and slid her left slipper behind her right to hide the hole over the big toe. She patted the tangle of hair at the back of her head but there wasn't anything she could do to fix it. She dropped the empty sherry glass behind her onto one of the chairs.

When she opened the patio door, Joan smiled at her. "The door was open, so I walked in. You should lock that, you know."

Val stared at Dawn, whose eyes were wide open and fixed on Joan's pearl necklace. Dried tears stained her cheeks, but she appeared calm, happy even, as Joan rocked her slowly from side to side. "She settled right down when I picked her up. It's like she already knows who I am."

In the shadows of the living room stood Peter, his doughy body skulking and blending with the gloom so that he seemed to be a more substantial shadow than the ones surrounding him. He nodded at Val, his face unsmiling.

"I tried calling, but I think you must have ignored the phone," said Joan. "Understandable, of course, when you have to deal with this new baby all by yourself."

Val couldn't move or speak. Her palms rested on the cool glass of the patio door behind her.

"What did you name her, Val? You never phoned when she was born."

"Dawn," she croaked and then flinched at the unused sound of her voice.

"Dawn? That's a modern name, isn't it? Don't you think, Peter?"

Peter nodded again and clasped his hands behind his back.

"You look tired, Val. How about I stay for a few hours so you can get some rest?"

Val slumped a little. Her bones felt so full of exhaustion that they were threatening to buckle under the weight of her skin and flesh and hair.

"I can even spend the night, and Peter can pick me up tomorrow on his way home from work." Joan watched as Val dropped onto the sofa by the window. "It's settled then. Peter, why don't you run to the grocery store and pick us up some baby formula? And get a couple of pork chops and maybe some bread and broccoli as well. I'll make supper before he has to drive home, Val. Don't you worry."

That night, Joan arranged extra sheets and pillows on the couch and moved the crib to the living room. She tucked Val into her bed, pulling the covers right up under her chin and smoothing Val's hair away from her face before silently backing out and closing the door softly behind her. Val waited for the sounds of Dawn's crying to burst through the wall, but heard only the padding of Joan's stockinged feet as she moved through the apartment. Slowly, she fell into a dreamless and unmoving sleep.

When she woke up, Joan had cleaned the apartment and dressed Dawn in a pretty little pink dress with a white collar. "I brought it with me," she said proudly. "Of course, I didn't know if she was going to be a girl or a boy, so I brought a little blue sailor outfit too." Joan laughed and the trill filled the room; Val winced.

But she felt good. Better than she had in a month. Her joints didn't feel as if they were grinding together, bone on bone. She was aware, again, of her whole body—the way her legs moved and her neck swivelled—instead of just the soreness in her breasts. At Joan's suggestion, she drew a hot bath and soaked until lunchtime, when Joan made sandwiches. Dawn slept peacefully, cried out briefly when she was hungry or wet, and settled down again as soon as she was satisfied. Val watched Joan, her serene face, the light way she caressed the baby's cheeks, the brightness of her eyes when she held her. She was suspicious, but forced herself to think *Joan knows how much I did for her baby, and now she's trying to make up for it. That's all it is.*

The next week, Joan came again. Peter held the baby, and even Val could see that his face softened when he looked into her blinking eyes. Peter—that hard-shelled, incomprehensible man.

Joan made Val a pot of tea and sat with her on the balcony, even though a cold wind was beginning to swirl around them. Inside, Peter sat with Dawn. Val could hear him singing to her, a strange, off-tune version of "Rock-a-bye Baby," but she didn't turn to look.

"You're alone here too much." Joan's voice, as always, cut through the air—unmerciful, unlovely. She continued, "I'm alone too, most days."

Val looked down and pulled at the fabric that bunched over her stomach.

The teacups rattled as Joan shifted in her chair to face Val. "Come home with us. I can help with the baby and we can be company for each other again. It'll be fun, like when we were little girls."

Val remembered the river. The way it smelled at the height of summer. The muddy banks where the bodies of fish that had died in the winter were exposed to the hot sun. The saltiness of eelgrass. The faint smell of chemical sewage from the paper mill upriver that was usually hidden by fog and rain the rest of the year. The rumble of trains speeding past every other day. Val and Joan, one small and the other smaller, sitting with bare legs on the steps of their back porch, sniffing the warm wind blowing up from the water and through the bush. Val never loved their house, but the river was something else altogether. It churned with the scraps of canning and log-ging, yet it still reflected the blue sky on sunny days and winked at Val if she watched it long enough, her chin resting on the rickety railing outside, her mind empty of all the debris from village gossip or a bad day at school. The river could be lovely. You just had to be patient.

As if Joan could hear Val's thoughts, she said, "Our house isn't so far from Burrard Inlet, you know. There's a beach there. Dawn would love it."

Val met Joan's eyes and nodded.

Val felt puffy with rest. She woke up before anyone else, her body jerking through the last cobwebs of a dream she couldn't remember. The baby wasn't crying yet. The early winter rain dripped off the eaves and onto the wide driveway lined with miniature spruce trees. It was still dark and the warmth of the bed cocooned her. Puffs of down-filled comforter formed in the crook of her elbow and the curve of her waist. Val fell asleep again, dozing as the overcast sky brightened. She was half aware of the wind shaking the Japanese maple on the front lawn, of cars slowly backing out of garages and heading toward the highway.

When she awoke a second time, she sat up stupidly at the sounds of Dawn whimpering in the next room. Val threw on a robe and slipped out of her bedroom, padding into Dawn's nursery, which, at the last minute, had been decorated by Joan with just a crib and a white dresser. As Val crept closer to the baby, Dawn began to wail. She kicked out her legs and stiffened her back when Val reached in to pick her up. Val changed her, tried to feed her, even held her to the window, whispering that this same type of tree lined the road where Val and Joan grew up. None of it made any difference. Finally, she screamed over Dawn's cries. "What do you want? I don't understand!" She leaned against the wall, too tired with the effort of shrieking to even cry herself.

Joan strode into the room and took the baby from Val. "What are you doing? Shouting at an infant like that," she scolded. Val stared as Joan wiped Dawn's face with a tissue from the pocket on her slacks and brushed her pinky against her mouth. Dawn's lips parted and, as she sucked on Joan's finger, her eyes closed and Val thought she heard her release a quiet chuckle.

"My car keys are on the hall table. When the store opens, you'll have to go and buy a soother." Joan turned toward the window and Val saw that, this time, Dawn opened her eyes wide and stared at the trees outside.

Weeks later, Val kneeled on the floor by her open bedroom window. No sound outside, not even the bang of a garbage can lid. If she listened hard enough, with her head craned to the right, she thought she could hear the swish of the highway, the sound of tires speeding through the rain. But she couldn't tell if what she was hearing was real or if she was making it all up because, otherwise, she would go mad, choked by Joan's wall-to-wall carpeting.

There was no music in the house, only a television in the family room that Peter turned on to watch the news. Dawn was asleep. To fill the silence, Val began humming a tune. Soon, her bare feet were tapping the carpet, and she stood up, twisting her hips, her arms above her head.

She closed her eyes, saw pin dots of light underneath the lids that she could trick herself into believing were stage lights, or the lampposts on Granville Street that glimmered yellow in the dark.

Val began to dance by herself every night after Joan and Peter and Dawn had gone to bed, her nightgown billowing around her legs. Her body remembered her old moves: the spin that helped unwind her skirt, the shrug that slipped one spaghetti strap down her arm. She opened the window as wide as it would go, and, as she twirled, the sharp air brushed past the hair on her arms and worked its way between her toes. Branches rustled together in the wind, and she pretended it was the sound of a rowdy crowd, cheering and clapping at every kick, every arched eyebrow. The rest of the house slept while her body vibrated, awake.

Val dressed carefully, sorting through her clothes until she found the right outfit, a grey day suit with navy-blue piping around the lapels and sleeves. She found Joan and Dawn by the living-room window, the baby nestled into Joan's lap.

"I'm going into town today, if that's all right," Val announced, fiddling with the clasp on her purse.

"Oh?" Joan didn't even look up.

"Yes, I thought I'd go and check on the apartment, maybe bring back a few things that I forgot to pack."

"How long will you be gone?"

"Since it's such a long drive, I thought I might stay overnight and come back in the morning. There doesn't seem to be any point to driving into town just to drive right back again." Val smoothed down a pleat in her skirt to hide her shaking hands.

"That's probably a good idea. Pick me up some magazines, will you?" Joan bent down to kiss Dawn on the forehead, her pale lips on the baby's white skin.

Val brushed her hand over Dawn's fine, floating hair. She swallowed hard and then marched out the door.

In the driveway, Val breathed in the cold suburban air, which smelled like frost. When she was on the highway, she could almost feel the heat from the electric lights on her head and the rise and fall of cracked sidewalks under her high-heeled shoes. The downtown streets were no place for a baby, of that she was certain. She pressed down harder on the gas pedal and smiled as the car surged forward.

The pounding of the drum was undeniable, and it bore its way into her body until her heartbeat was forced to keep pace. Val's blood rushed upward in waves, and she breathed hard as her fingers, sticky from a puddle of spilled beer, tapped the table-top. Around her, groups of men and women smoked cigarettes in long holders, shouted over the music to the waiters and lifted their drinks in a pool of light so warm that it seemed improbable it could be winter outside, where freezing rain hurled itself downward with such ferocity that it hurt to stand unprotected in the night.

The dancer onstage untied her gingham blouse and shook her breasts in their gingham brassiere at the audience. She wore a straw hat and freckles drawn in pencil on her cheeks. Val smiled. Milly the Country Girl. Young, with a rounded body. The men watched her sling her bra into the wings, wiggle her backside as she walked to the left to pick up a banjo. The band stopped, and she played "The Yellow Rose of Texas," singing so sweetly Val forgot that her breasts, except for a pair of pasties, were bare, white and full in the spotlight, and that her denim shorts were cut so high the curve of her ass hung past the frayed hems. The crowd stopped talking, their eyes on Milly.

A voice whispered behind her, "Val, is that you?"

She turned around in her chair and saw the manager of the supper club, sleek in a tuxedo, squinting at her through the shadows.

"Jim. Nice to see you."

"Everyone's been asking about you. Tell me you're back on the scene."

Val laughed and looked down at her hands. "No, honey. Just back for one night of fun."

An idea flashed across his face. "Come backstage with me. I'll get you a costume. We can set up a special performance. One night only with the Siamese Kitten!" He took her hand and pulled it in the direction of the stage.

Val remembered the wrinkles in her belly, the loose skin that sagged over the elastic of her underpants. She hadn't looked at her naked body in a mirror in months and knew the dimples in her bum from touch. Had she even shaved her legs? She pulled her hand back.

"I can't, Jim. I'm not ready. I haven't done anything to prepare."

"Come on, no one will know."

"Under those lights?" Val pointed at the spotlights and the bright white circles that swirled over Milly's body onstage. "They'll see everything."

Jim stood with his hands on his hips. "How's this? You

come back tomorrow night. We'll set it up. That way, you have time to do whatever it is you girls do to look pretty."

"Tomorrow?" Val felt the itch in her legs, the gooseflesh that could only be dissipated by the eyes of men watching her shimmy and grind and strut. "I'm supposed to be somewhere tomorrow."

He waved his arms around the club. "What could be more important than this?"

She could already hear the suspension of breath, the way a full room shimmers with silence when a crowd waits for something it has wanted for a very long time. She saw the sliver of light between the curtains and felt it slice through the darkness of backstage and burn as it touched her skin. She blinked.

"Tomorrow," she said. "I'll be here."

It was too easy. Val called Joan and told her that she needed to stay an extra day or two to sort out some financial matters she had forgotten about.

Joan didn't ask, perhaps because the baby was fussing, or perhaps because she recognized the lie in Val's voice, the same tone she used whenever she phoned home while on the road. "You can come back whenever you want," Joan said. "We're fine by ourselves."

She returned to the stage that night. Jim introduced her.

"Ladies and gentlemen, we have a real treat for you tonight. A special one-night-only event. Please welcome the incomparable Siamese Kitten!"

Men jumped to their feet and whistled. Even the women sat up straighter in their chairs, peering over heads for a better view of the stage and the inevitable spectacle of Val's return.

Before she stepped out through the curtains, she held the palm of her hand to her stomach, felt her breath coming sharp and fast. This was a borrowed costume with a swath of transparent fabric hastily sewn over the belly to conceal the marks her pregnancy had left behind. It had been over a year since she last danced in public. Everything could go wrong. She might ruin her flawless reputation.

She heard the audience fall silent. No impatient hissing, not even the shifting of legs or arms in boredom. No, they wanted her. Only she could deliver what they were expecting. She stepped through the curtains and waited a half-second before the applause started up again and enveloped her. It crawled over her skin in that singular way she didn't know she had been missing.

When she returned to Joan and Peter's house three days later, Joan proudly showed her how she had redecorated Dawn's room.

"Do you see the pink curtains? They're made of this new fabric, you know, and won't ever wrinkle. And I couldn't resist this little table-and-chair set. I thought Dawn could use it for tea parties." Joan laughed and picked up a tiny cup and saucer. "Who she'll invite to these parties, I don't know, but it was all so cute. Oh, and look. I thought we could use a good rocking chair by the window here, for night feedings. I always feel so comforted in a rocking chair, don't you?"

"It's beautiful, Joanie, really. Thanks so much." Even as the words left Val's lips, she wanted to run from this pink and frilled room to somewhere more familiar, somewhere with sticky floors and hard bar stools that made her ass cold and achy. When they went to the living room, she reached for Dawn, who sat solidly on the sofa, propped up with cushions, but the baby cringed and her lower lip began to tremble. Val pushed her hands back into her pockets and didn't try to touch her again for the rest of the day.

It didn't take long for Val's old agent to find out about her performance at the Cave, and he started phoning the house every day. "You've got to come back to the circuit, Val. Burlesque needs you. If you don't come back, we'll be drowning in these girls with no skill whatsoever. All they do is strip. You, my dear, have a *show*."

Val whispered into the receiver, turning her back to Joan, who listened with her arms crossed in front of her chest, her eyes gleaming palely in the winter sunshine. "I can't. I told you before: I have other things to do. I can't travel like that again."

"You could stay in Vancouver! There are plenty of clubs here. You'd be like the grande dame of burlesque, the resident queen of the strip. Come on, Val. You know you want to."

And she did, but she couldn't say it. "No. I can't."

"You can't stop me from phoning again. You'll rue the day you ever went back to the Cave," he said, with a note of amusement in his voice, before hanging up.

She woke up every night, itching to run out of this house and down the highway—droplets of mist collecting in her hair, her nose running from the cold breeze—until she reached the city. During the day, she and Joan did almost nothing, just fed and changed and soothed the baby, and then cooked supper for Peter, who only wanted to cuddle with Dawn in the armchair in his den, hardly noticing when Joan called him for dinner.

When she stood at the window one afternoon, looking out at the woods behind the house, her reflection seemed thin and bland. The shrubs in the garden squatted in the grass, substantial and unmistakeably green, while she was leached of colour, a poor imitation of her once green and gold self. The phone rang. It was for her.

At first, she went away for five days every three weeks, always returning on a Monday evening. Then she was away for a whole week and, later, ten days. Finally, she stayed away for two weeks, returning one morning with a bag of gifts for the baby. Val stared at Dawn—her pale skin, her golden hair. She searched for a trace of herself in her chin, her ears, even the line of her chubby jaw, but saw nothing, only a baby she must once have given birth to.

Joan saw Val's face, the restlessness in her eyes. Carefully, in a measured voice, she said, "Do you want me to keep her?"

It was a simple question, and Val knew the right answer. She was a mother, wasn't she? Mothers were supposed to be competent, unfailingly loving and calm. Mothers had no needs of their own; everything they did or said was for their children, not to satisfy their disgusting desires for the gaze of men. Mothers were clean and put together.

Val was a mother. But not the kind anyone wanted.

"If you don't mind, Joan, maybe I could leave her here for a month or so. There are still lots of loose ends for me to tie up."

Val left Joan's car to take the bus, bringing nothing except the carefully made quilt she pieced together when she was pregnant. Later, in her small apartment, Val rolled the quilt into a ball and carried it to bed with her, holding it close to her chest while she slept, waking when the afternoon sun flooded the room.

Kelly. That's what Joan started calling the baby, and soon the name Dawn was totally forgotten. Every third Tuesday of the month, Val woke up, a gnawing in her stomach. She clutched at her belly with both hands, eyes shut to the sunshine sneaking into her bedroom from a crack in the curtains. She knew that Joan was expecting her, as she did every month, and that, even though she was a failed mother, she must go and watch her daughter play and babble happily. There was no use in pretending that seeing Joan wipe the milk off Kelly's lips or retie a hair ribbon wasn't painful. Punishment wasn't punishment unless others could see. Val spent an hour and a half picking out her clothes and high heels and doing her makeup before boarding the bus to Joan's, shiny red lips on her powdered face. She knew the neighbours were watching, kept their eyes on her ass when she sashayed up the walk. She felt like laughing, until she remembered why she was there.

As soon as Kelly turned two, Joan started cancelling their visits at the last minute. There came a day when Kelly no longer recognized Val, and she cringed when she tried to hug her.

For a while, it was birthdays and Christmas. And after that, only at Kelly's elementary and high school graduations, or when Joan and Kelly drove into the city and ran into Val at a shop. Most of the time, Val didn't think about them but, once in a while, she felt that she might crumble, her skin and makeup and clothes nothing more than a thin, brittle veneer that covered up uncountable scars and underground fissures.

On bad nights, she stared into space, not daring to look at the studio photographs Joan had had done of Kelly and Peter and herself. The white wall or the black night sky was safer. Emptier.

For almost ten years, she continued to dance, wearing new costumes she had made to accommodate the extra weight around her thighs and hips. As time passed, she noticed how cold and dark it was in the wings, how brusque the managers were when the dancers asked for more light or a portable heater for the dressing room. The new girls seemed unprepared; their costumes looked cheap onstage, and, when they danced, Val could hear seams tearing as they struggled to keep time to the music. She pinned up the rips between sets, rubbed lotion on dry knees and put her arms around the younger girls to warm them up even as the cold seeped into the marrow of her own bones. She wondered if this was how people developed arthritis. When the MC announced their names to the audience, she pushed the dancers onstage, felt their clammy young skin underneath her hands, the fear vibrating off their bodies. Sometimes, she whispered, "You'll be fine, sweetie. The crowd will tell you what they want."

And when she looked in the mirrors as she stood beside these trembling, smooth-skinned girls, she could see what twenty-three years of dancing had done to her. She was forty-one, and the other strippers were half her age. Her maturity sat in the droop of her belly button, in the dark shadows under her eyes, in the wing-like looseness of the skin on her arms. She could feel her joints rubbing together, creaking as she tried to high-kick, grinding when she made a quick turn. If she had become a secretary, would there be this same damage? She might have been a woman who looked good for her age, who had spent her adult life in a cushioned chair instead of on stage floors that didn't give when she stomped through a routine.

Eventually, working nights both tired her and made it impossible for her to sleep through the light of morning. Besides, the circuit had changed again. When did it become titillating to look straight between a dancer's legs? To stare at the flesh without noticing the face? To scream with impatience if a girl tried to tease by slowly taking off one item of clothing at a time? The club managers told her that full nudity was what everyone expected these days. The province had even caved in and changed the laws so that girls could dance without their G-strings. Val supposed the bigwigs in government wanted more people in the clubs buying taxable liquor, and one sure way of keeping them there was bottomless dancers doing the splits onstage.

"But, of course," said the squat and bespectacled manager of the Penthouse, "you can keep something on. Your act is old-fashioned, and no one expects to see all your goods anyway."

When Val turned forty-four, she tried to be an agent for the dancers, but the scene wasn't the same. The government was giving out different licences to bars, which meant that they could hire girls to dance naked too, except these girls could dance to records instead of live bands and could strip all day if they wanted to. The clubs, working under the old licences, still needed musicians and could open only in the evenings. The cover at the bars was cheaper, the booze even more so, and crowds at the clubs disappeared, taking the dancers with them. More and more girls came to her in desperation, their pupils dilated from dope, their hands shaking because the Shanghai Junk or the Shangri-La was the last stop before they started hooking. Val saw how their stories might end.

"Honey," she said to one girl who had just turned eighteen and stood, shaking, in Val's office by the Granville Bridge, "I know a choreographer who can help you get a real act together, something really classy that'll make you good money in the long term. But you have to get clean, really focus on the dancing."

The girl sat limply in her chair. "I need a job, Miss Val. Any job. I have some bills that need to be paid."

And every other girl said the same thing until Val was tired of booking them into bars that played thumping, soulless music over scratchy speakers, and where they met men who paid them for other, more intimate jobs in the back seats of their cars.

So she left this new, raw-edged scene altogether. Eventually, she went to work at Woodward's department store, behind the lingerie and hosiery counter, where the shopping housewives giggled at her loud voice and the unceremonious way she handled their breasts when conducting a fitting. No one recognized her or seemed to remember the Siamese Kitten. Not the movie, not even her act. The customers saw only Val, with her curly brown hair piled on her head, her reading glasses balanced on the end of her nose. During the day, she was alone among the stockings and girdles. She could pretend she was still working for herself and that this little alcove on the fourth floor, with its peach satin slips that felt like water in her hands, was all hers.

Sometimes, the customers told her about their husbands or, often, their secret lovers—men they met accidentally, men who listened to them in ways their husbands never did, men who lived childless lives and were artists at heart. "Everything would be so much better if we had met fifteen years ago, when I was young and could still change," the women said. The words were sometimes different, but the meaning was always the same. "We could have had a free life, you know, and not worried about keeping up with the neighbours or whether we should get a new car." As Val hooked them into brassieres, they took deep breaths. "It could have been so wonderful."

In these women's voices, Val heard a small, barely perceptible note of cynicism. They knew that their lovers were as ordinary as the men they had married, and that it was marriage itself that eventually made everybody sexless. Val, a measuring tape around her neck, said nothing. She knew well enough that they didn't want to hear about Val's own encounters with men, the ones who were shopping for their wives but whose eyes travelled up and down Val's legs while she helped them, or the ones she met when she went out for a drink at the local pub. Rough men, sleek men, men who talked during sex.

On the five-year anniversary of her first day at the store, the staff threw her a lunchtime party. "Val," the store manager boomed, "is some broad."

He was the sort who would have tried to touch her from his spot in the front row, and she would have kicked him with the toe of her high-heeled shoe. But now, she simply laughed along with the others and raised her paper cup of fruit punch when he called for a toast.

She moved to the North Shore, where she set up a garden on her balcony and took the bus to the beach on her days off.

She liked to sit on a particular log—bleached white from years of sunshine and worn smooth by wind and climbing children—and stare at the waves coming in, one after another. The eagles flew over the treetops, and she could see the sea-wall in Stanley Park across the inlet and the people walking and biking and jogging in the distance. Some days, it was misty, and, when she put her hand to her hair, she felt the tiny drops in the curls around her ears. Other days, it was clear and cold, and the wind bit through her slacks and jacket until she was shivering, her arms wrapped around herself. And rarely, it was muggy and hot, when the only reprieve was the wind blowing off the ocean in gusts too few to be comfortable. But even here, she never stopped missing the thump of the drums that she once bounced to and the shimmer of the spotlight on her skin. Sometimes she would hum an old song until someone passed by and stared at her. She would pull her jacket tighter around her body and fall silent, feet unmoving in the rough sand.

It was at these times she wondered if she was leaving anything behind, if the boxes of costumes she had stored in Joan's basement or the obscure movie she had made actually counted. If her old life had left any footprint at all, or if it had all evaporated, the years like wisps of steam, the men for whom she danced now tottering in nursing homes, their memories not memories, only threadbare. There was only Dawn, and even she was now someone else.

PART FIVE

THE NURSE

1982

The beach is dark, lit dimly by the tall lamps that border the parking lot. Ahead of them, the blackness of the water and the sky and the cliffs has melted into one—flat and opaque. No seagulls call. No mosquitoes buzz. Danny can hear only the waves lapping on the sandy shore, and Val's soft breathing beside him.

"Does she know?" he asks.

"No. Joan and I promised each other we would never tell." Val's tired voice falters in the breeze.

"But didn't you ever want to?"

"She's a happy girl, Danny. You saw her. She's had a normal life."

Danny turns to Val. He can see the whites of her eyes, her hands clasped over her knees. "Normal. Is that what you wanted for her?"

Val laughs softly. "I suppose not. I wanted her to be Cyd Charisse, actually. Not very practical, is it?"

"Were you pregnant when I first met you in the alley?"

She nods. "I think so. But I didn't know it yet. When I saw you, all I could think of was Joanie's baby. Maybe I should have known that I was pregnant. It makes sense now."

Danny punches at the ground with a stick, poking holes in the grass and flicking dirt up and around them. His head feels heavy.

Val's voice cuts through the silence. "Honey, is there something you need to get off your chest? What are you keeping to yourself?"

He starts slowly, with long gaps between words, not because he is deciding what to say next but because he knows the next word, once said, will be final. *Dying, gay, alone, freedom, parents, the park at night, what will I do?*—all words he, in the brightness and tangibility of his everyday life, swallows deep inside his body. But with every second that he continues speaking, it grows easier. Phrases and clauses come tumbling out so rapidly that they generate a momentum of their own. He hears himself and understands that there might be nothing more to him than layers upon layers of secrets with no core underneath, or one that has been so neglected that it is unknown and indefinable. He slumps at the realization.

"Don't worry," says Val. "We all have our secrets. There's no shame in that."

Danny rips up a handful of grass and rolls it around in his hands until he is left with a tangled, damp ball of green. "The truth, Val. People keep telling me the truth is important." His voice cracks. "What if we need honesty more than anything?"

She snorts and puts a hand up to her curled hair. "What I need is a gin and tonic."

"I can't decide for myself, Val. Tell me what to do." He almost chokes on his own words.

"I can't do that," she says, touching his shoulder with her wide hand.

"Don't you think I have to change something, and be open with my parents, like Frank used to say?"

"Honesty," Val mutters. "Only stupid people tell the truth all the time."

Danny continues. "What if he's right? Shouldn't I tell my parents everything? Announce I'm gay and then it'll be all right?"

"What do you want me to say? That they won't be disgusted by you? That everything will be the same after you tell them, or that everything will be better? You know, Danny, it won't happen that way."

"I know," he whispers, throwing his warm ball of grass away into the darkness.

Val stands up and holds out her hand. "I'll make you a deal: the day you tell your parents you're queer is the day I'll tell Kelly I'm her mother." She laughs and straightens her jacket. "Nobody will like it, but you're the one who's obsessed with the truth." When he takes her hand and stands up, she nods curtly toward the car. "Now, come on. It's getting cold."

It's a fog, the kind of drinking that seeps into your eyes until you can no longer see distinctly, and all that's left are the vague outlines of objects, the solidity of furniture you once knew the names of. Red and yellow and green lights oscillate at the edges of your vision. You grow frustrated trying to see them directly because, every time you swivel your head, the lights simply dance to the side again and you wonder if you will go crazy from chasing them in this roundabout, disorienting game.

Danny lies on the surface of his balcony, the cold concrete biting through his clothes at the skin on his back and legs. He can hear Edwin crashing through the apartment, fingering all of Danny's things—his clothes, his dishes, even the pair of unused cross-country skis in the closet.

"Wine," Edwin yells. "Where the fuck is all your wine?"

Danny ignores him and rolls over on his side so that he is looking through the railing and down into the street. He knows that below there are bushes and cars, even the occasional person out for a nighttime walk. And yet it seems as if the entire world outside of this apartment and this balcony has totally disappeared, leaving behind shadowy lumps that in the darkness could be hunched-over fat men and their equally bulbous wives.

A few hours earlier, when Danny told Edwin about Frank, Edwin already knew. Danny was sure that Edwin was going to cry when he said, "I didn't want to tell you because I knew you loved him more than anyone. There's nothing you can do for him now." So bald, those words, and yet there was no other way to say those hard, painful things.

Edwin smacks the palm of his hand on the inside of the glass patio door. "What's this?" he shouts, waving a photograph in his other hand. "Pictures of strippers in their everyday clothes? Ridiculous, Danny. Sex sells, not fresh-faced girls in blue jeans. You're hopeless!" And he stumbles back into the living room, throwing the photograph on the couch. "You said you had wine, you stupid liar!"

Danny stares at Edwin's retreating body, the wideness of his shoulders, the slight waddle that hasn't changed since they were teenagers. They used to sit in Edwin's grandmother's musty house and eat from the box of stale Peek Freans that mouldered on her kitchen table for years. Edwin danced with abandon to pop music on the radio after watching *Club 6* on television to study the way the other kids bounced and shook. "How do I look, Danny?" he shouted over the tinny beat. "Am I cool or what?" He never seemed to notice that he had a round belly that jiggled when he writhed to the music, or that what was supposed to be a sexy expression on his face looked confused and a little sleepy. Back then, Danny thought he was hilarious. Here, in his apartment, not much has changed. Danny still thinks Edwin is funny, but that doesn't stop him from wishing Edwin could somehow stop attacking life and learn to softly nurse it instead. Now, they are drunker, hairier, with years of those built-up, unsaid things coating every square inch of their bodies.

It was Edwin who first said the words *I'm gay* and expected Danny to follow suit. Without him, those words, and the realization they held, might have remained buried, choked by the density of tangible fear.

A minute later, he hears the sound of something crashing to the floor, the unmistakeable rush of air on his face that means something has been disturbed. Something has gone wrong.

He stands up and steadies himself on the sliding glass door. As he makes his way into the hall, he sees Edwin crouching, his hands sweeping up the photographs that have spilled over the floor. Half of them sit in a puddle of red wine, their edges curling with moisture. A black box lies on its side, leaning against the bookcase.

"I'm sorry, Danny," Edwin starts, picking up a print and shaking it, sending droplets of wine flying through the hall and onto the walls. "I was putting that stripper photo away and I knocked the whole box over. I dropped my glass too. I'm sorry. Really."

Danny stares. All those prints, tinged red, dotted with dust from the floor that will stick to their surfaces and never come off. He'll have to buy more paper, develop them all over again. He rubs his forehead with the heel of his hand and closes his eyes. It's red underneath his lids, except for the bright white starbursts that explode one after another.

Edwin's voice again: "I can help you reprint them. I mean, I don't know how to do it, but you just have to tell me once. I'm a fast learner."

When Danny opens his eyes, Edwin is standing up, the empty black box in his hand. All these years, and Edwin hasn't magically learned subtlety or grown any thinner; he has only adjusted his clothes and transformed his fat into muscle. But in all the essential ways, he is the same boy with the silly grin who would never leave Danny alone, whose constant presence chased away all his other teenaged friends, who never understood when he wasn't wanted. Who now greets disease and death and love and dancing with martinis and silk shirts. Who never knows when it's time to stop.

"Danny? Please say something."

Danny slaps the wall with his right hand. "Shut up! Aren't you ever quiet?"

Edwin takes a step backward, not smiling for once.

"You ruin everything," Danny continues. "People are dying and all you can do is get drunk and mess up my apartment. I hate you! Do you understand?"

"Calm down. You need some sleep, that's all. I'll leave

now." Edwin turns and squints toward the front door, his eyes searching the hall for his shoes.

Danny reaches out and pushes Edwin on the back of the shoulder, propelling him forward. Before Edwin can say anything or even turn around, Danny has pushed him again, so hard that his face is crushed against the door. Quickly, Danny punches him in the back of his head. Danny's fist is pulled back, ready to hit Edwin again, when he hears him whimpering. A quiet, subconscious whimper, one that isn't even a cry for help, only the audible expression of pain. Danny punches the door to the left of Edwin's face.

Danny wants to crawl into bed with his throbbing hand and breathe in the air through the open window. But he stands, inches away from Edwin's hunched body, clenching and unclenching his right fist.

"What's the matter with you?" Edwin whispers, his face still mashed against the door.

"I don't know," he says, because there is no way of explaining his confusion, his fear of what lies underneath.

Slowly, Edwin turns around, and Danny can see the trail of tears on his cheeks, the snot now glistening on his upper lip. "I'm going to leave," he says quietly. "I'll call you tomorrow." And he turns the doorknob and walks down the hallway, one hand on the wall, the other wiping his face.

Danny walks back to the balcony and lies down. He rests his cheek against the concrete and briefly wonders if the tiny embedded pebbles will somehow burrow themselves into his face, appearing to others to be the pits and scars from teenaged acne or chicken pox. *It might be a relief,* he thinks, *to carry your marks on the outside, to be identified by sight as a dentist or a pianist or a man who loves men, or, more specifically, loves one man who is dying.* Then there would be no confusion, and those who might shun you would do so from the very beginning and you could walk through life without any surprises, knowing for certain who hates you or loves you. He feels his cheek beginning to settle into a dimple in the balcony floor. His left hand grips the railing but he is too drunk to pound on the wrought-iron bars, or to even wonder at himself, lying here like this, bruises starting to flower blue and yellow on his knuckles.

Chinatown is a place Danny avoids. Elements from his past hide in alleys and doorways, emerging silently when he walks by. They watch him with eyes full of reproach, frowning at his well-dressed self with his right hand wrapped in white bandages. In the alley behind the butcher shop are his father's high-school friends, sitting on overturned wooden crates, smoking, reliving their days as teenaged boys who were only starting to feel the crush of expectations they never met. On the stoop of the single-room hotel, a little girl with faded pedal-pushers clutches a blond-haired doll, eyeing the sweet red-bean buns in the bakery across the street. In the window of the busy noodle house on Keefer, a woman, her face so fallen and lined that she appears to be aching for sleep, mops the linoleum floor with dirty water.

But he can't avoid the neighbourhood forever. A bride he has been working with told him last week that she might want to have her photographs taken in Chinatown. She smiled when she mentioned it, her white teeth perfectly straight, her chin resting on her hands. "Could you take some test shots down there first, so I can see how it'll look on film? What I want is all that atmosphere, but I'm afraid it'll look too dingy," she said, and patted her smooth brown hair.

He walks up and down the sidewalks, his camera around his neck. When he's a block away from the curio shop, he crosses the street and peers past the parked and speeding cars, the old women with their wheeled carts and knitted caps. Through the window, he can barely make out his father standing by the cash register, talking to another man his age, who is leaning against the glass display case. As Danny creeps from one parking meter to another, the other man leaves, squints at the bright light outside and turns into the alley. It is Doug's cousin Uncle Kwan, or, as his patients know him, Dr. Lim.

Uncle Kwan. Beautiful wife. Big house in South Cambie. Vacations in Hawaii and California. And that big blue Cadillac.

Doug walks out into the sunshine, watches as the Cadillac eases out of the alley and drives slowly toward downtown, the top of Uncle Kwan's bald head visible above the seat. Doug's shoulders are hunched, and his hands hang loose at his sides, like stray threads dangling from a poorly sewn seam. The drooping of his head points to the years of his life wasted on racing and girls and late-night poker, a time that led to this current life of saving, always saving, rearranging cheap painted vases and bamboo placemats. Danny feels burdened with this flash, this sudden understanding. He stumbles down the street and into a parking lot, where he leans against a car and closes his eyes against the sunlight.

So much easier, he thinks, *to always know my father as only a father*. He rests his hands on his camera, feels the coolness of metal and plastic, the soothing solidity of the lens, the body, even the strap. He remembers the request for test shots, opens his eyes, and continues walking, briefly wondering if disappointment runs in families.

Danny parks the car outside his studio and steps out onto the sidewalk. Even though autumn is inching closer and closer, the early evening is still thick with heat, and he wipes his forehead with the back of his bandaged hand. A skinny man wrapped in a dark grey overcoat crouches to the side of the front door. As usual, Danny reaches into his pocket for spare change.

The man looks up and brushes the hair away from his forehead. It's Frank, standing up creakily, shivering even as he steps into the sunshine.

Danny rushes forward. "Are you all right? What are you doing here?"

Frank points a finger in Danny's face, jabbing at the air as forcefully as he can. "You told Cindy, didn't you."

"About what?" But he already knows.

"About me being sick, you moron. She freaked out and told the branch manager, who told the head office. They've forced me to quit, Danny." A dry, rattling cough emerges from his throat.

"I'm sorry, Frank. I didn't think. I didn't know she was going to do that."

Frank wavers in place, and Danny puts out an arm to steady him. Frank tries to shake him off, but Danny holds his elbow tightly.

"She wouldn't even look at me when I was leaving. Not one look."

Frank begins to crumple in Danny's arms; his knees buckle and he doubles over at the waist, his head falling forward. Danny pulls and hoists and manages to half carry, half drag Frank into the studio. He settles him in a chair and kneels on the floor in front of him, rubbing his bony hands in his own. Frank's hands are papery, the skin hardly like skin.

"The doctor said one more month. I have infections I've never even heard of."

Danny can't see anymore. Tears and snot drip down his face, onto the collar of his shirt.

"My mother wants me to move back in with her and Dad. I suppose I'll have to. What else is there to do?"

Danny's head pounds, one sickening thud after another. Frank leans forward and rests his forehead on Danny's shoulder, his back curved like a comma. Light floods through the window and Danny looks up, squinting until he can see the strange, ghostly outline of the sun itself. His eyes burn.

"I'll take care of you, Frank. We'll go back to your place and I won't leave you. I promise."

The silence is tangible. Danny imagines it like snow: white, cooling, not quite weightless. He feels Frank's body relax until he is like a cloth doll—limp, curled into Danny's embrace. He might be asleep, or so relieved of tension that he just appears to be. It doesn't matter as long as Danny can hold him up, their two selves so complementary it's hard to know whose body is whose.

The days begin quietly. Danny wakes first and kicks the covers off the couch where he has been sleeping. The light has been changing every day, growing thinner as September approaches and the days grow shorter. From the front window, Danny has been watching the roses in the front garden fade, dry and eventually float off into the wind, petal by petal. The sunsets, when you can see them at all through the smog, have grown streaky. Light bounces off the undersides of clouds well after the sun has disappeared behind the other apartment buildings to the west. Squirrels skitter by, acorns in their mouths, dodging the speeding cars. Every evening, Danny sniffs, imagining he can smell rain in the air, despite the continuing heat.

Frank coughs himself awake, and Danny hurries in to rub his back and prop him up while he sips from a glass of lukewarm water. Danny often feels there are no words to describe the evolution of Frank's cough, only that he is afraid Frank will one day cough up both lungs on the quilt and that they will lie there, raw-red and covered in lesions, while the two of them look on, unable to tear their eyes away.

They eat oatmeal and applesauce for breakfast as they listen to folk singers on the radio. Danny scrambles eggs with cheese for Frank as well, for the extra calories. Sometimes, Frank throws up at the table and then cries, saying, "I'm so sorry."

Once a week, Danny wraps Frank in sweaters and they take a cab to the hospital, where a doctor and a nurse listen to his heartbeat, ask him questions with lines of pity creeping across their faces. For a while, they were giving him chemotherapy injections, but these only made Frank sicker, so they stopped, and now they talk about making him *comfortable* and his *quality of life*. Danny knows these are code words for others that remain unspoken, others that, if uttered, would usher in a whole new feeling of finality, of waiting for the end. No one mentions AIDS.

Afterward, Frank's parents meet them at the café down the street. They are almost always there first, the sleeves of his mother's cardigan pulled down over her small, spotted hands. His father hunches over a hot cup of coffee, staring at an untouched Danish in front of him. He is quiet and only nods when Danny and Frank arrive, whereas she talks quickly, jumping from one topic to another, repeating what she's heard on the news.

"Did you know that these young people are trying to stop the seal hunt in Newfoundland? Baby seals, Frankie, with those big dark eyes, being clubbed to death. I can't bear to think of it."

She strokes Frank's hands across the table, inhales and exhales like a mouse catching its breath. Her eyes watch Frank as he sips his apple juice, search his face and neck for any change from the week before. While the rest of her jumps and flits, her eyes are grave and observant, taking in every line, every stray hair on her son's head.

Frank's father passes him a lottery ticket, saying in his low voice, "You never know when you might get lucky," before falling silent again, his thick fingers plucking invisible crumbs off the table and dropping them onto a paper napkin.

When they part on the sidewalk outside the café, Frank's mother holds his face in both her hands and smiles before linking arms with her husband and walking back to their car. Danny can hear the swish of her pants, the squeak of his clean white runners.

Last time, before they turned away, Frank's father put his hand on Danny's shoulder and murmured, "That's my boy, you know. I pray for him every day."

In the afternoons, Frank naps, and Danny returns to his own apartment to gather the mail and listen to the messages on his newly acquired answering machine. He shrugs at the urgency in people's voices, the shrillness in the messages.

"I need you to confirm, Danny. My wedding is in *two weeks*."

"I've been calling and calling. Where are you? Mom is worried."

"Are the prints done yet? I've been waiting for a long time."

"Call me. I know you're sorry. It didn't really hurt anyway."

"Danny? It's Val. We should talk."

When he returns to Frank's apartment, he lets himself in and creeps through the hallway in his socks. He watches Frank breathe, always slowly and sometimes erratically. He sleeps with both hands under his cheek and his mouth open, as if reciting a silent and sideways prayer. Danny sees the bones in his shoulders through the blankets and mentally calculates his dwindling weight. 152. 147. 136. Sometimes he wonders how much skin and bones and barely functioning organs weigh, thinking that Frank can't grow any lighter. But he does.

Usually, it's soup for dinner and a game of Scrabble before Danny helps Frank into the bathtub. He washes him carefully, scrubbing gently between all the wrinkles, every jutting bone. He dries him with a fluffy towel and rubs baby oil over his skin, over the rashes and Kaposi's sarcoma spots, over the boils that seem to multiply daily. Slowly, Danny buttons up Frank's flannel pyjamas and then they lie in bed together,

Danny's head resting on the wall as he reads out loud from the pile of library books on the floor. Frank stares at him, his eyes big in his thin face, chuckling when Danny reads something funny from his favourite comic-strip collection, tearing up a little at the sad parts in an old Russian novel. Eventually, he falls asleep, and Danny pulls the covers up and shuts the bedroom door behind him. He drinks tea in front of the television until midnight, when he undresses and lies down on the couch. In the morning, he can never remember if he's been dreaming or not, and this comforts him. He wakes with no trace of the night clinging to his face or body, and he can be satisfied with the morning and the long list of tasks he knows he will complete. After all, for once in his life he is doing exactly what he's supposed to.

THE MORNING

1982

There is so much that Danny could say that would be misunderstood and hurtful. He putters around Frank's apartment, answers his phone when he is asleep, massages his bony feet, which feel like bags of stones. Danny barely looks at himself in the mirror, seeing only the medicine cabinet behind the glass when he brushes his teeth.

If he could, he would say, "This apartment is so small. It's only you and me here." But he knows that if he were to ever say, "I need to get out," Frank would assume that Danny wanted to leave him to his illness and would tell him to go away forever before he could even explain. Danny longs to walk through the city, hear the truncated conversations of people huddled under awnings in the August heat, smell the grease through the back doors of restaurants, step carefully around the piles of goose shit dotting the lawns at English Bay.

Tonight, Frank sleeps on his back, a pillow behind his head and another under his knees. The apartment is clean. The laundry is folded and tucked into drawers. The doctors told Danny that everything must be washed regularly so Frank is kept away from opportunistic bacteria that could burrow their way into his skin and blood, could travel through his veins to every organ and every bone until the end products of their journey emerge on the surface as pus or abscesses. The hot-water bottle at Frank's feet will stay warm for another two hours, and yet Danny feels that he can't leave. What if he's out and the iron is still plugged in, or Frank reaches for the bucket beside the bed and it's six inches out of reach? Before he can dwell on all these possibilities, he slips on his shoes and leaves.

For the first time this summer, he feels a wash of cool air down the collar of his shirt. He walks around the perimeter of English Bay, sees two figures huddled in sleeping bags, the tops of their heads resting against a log. He wonders if they're in love or simply sleeping together for protection.

He continues up Davie Street, feeling the soles of his tan loafers sticking to the layers of grime and gum coating the sidewalk. Apartment buildings rise on the left and right. A bus rolls past, rumbling and snapping; Danny catches the face of a young girl through the window, her blond hair held away from her face with a barrette, her eyes flitting from tree to building to street sign. The street kids turn their faces away when he walks past and disappear into doorways and behind shrubs. He turns left on Granville, passes the pawnbrokers and sex shops before turning right into an alley. There, the same sign with the crooked letters, the same promise of THE BEST GIRLS IN TOWN!

He sits at his usual table in the back, directly opposite centre stage. There are only two other men in the club, both in light-grey suits, whispering in each other's ears as they drink Scotch on the rocks. Danny takes his beer from the waitress and smiles.

The club is meant to offer the same things over and over. There is always flesh, the curve of breasts against the torso, the soft folds of skin between the legs. The repetition is soothing, like chicken soup on a cold day; comforting, like a pair of socks worn to the shape of your feet.

The dancer twirls on a pole, her dark hair swinging behind her. She looks bored and tired, makeup only partially covering the puffiness around her eyes, the enlarged pores on her cheeks. Still, her legs are long and smooth, and she dances with poise in her six-inch platform heels. In and out of the shadows, she shows her body and hides it, smoothly moving to the music. Danny wonders how he would photograph her, how the hollows above her buttocks would appear in black and white, whether she would be flawless on film or appear even older and drier. Something glitters under the stage lights. Danny squints and sees that, around her neck, a thin gold chain with a seahorse pendant blinks every time she turns and fixes her disinterested gaze on the empty tables around him. A vestige of her real life.

When he leaves the club, he resists the urge to run back to Frank's apartment and hurries west and north, toward the park. The residue of cigarettes and beer sits like a skin over his clothes. To his left, the ocean. Above, thin smoggy clouds roll over themselves, changing shape in a darkly blue sky. Danny hears a boom and wonders if a thunderstorm is coming, if Frank will wake up, terrified by the crash and the crackling of lightning through the curtained windows.

He touches his hand to the rough bark of a spruce tree to feel the prickles on his palm. On the trail, dust floats up every time he steps forward. It hasn't rained in eight weeks and the ground beneath him isn't damp and spongy like it is in winter, when he feels he is walking on a breathing, fleshy body. Now it feels packed down, but covered in a layer of insubstantial gravel and powder that will cover his shoes and pants with a film of grey that smells both mineral and animal. He longs for rain.

If he finds someone here tonight, what will he bring home to Frank? A wayward, invisible germ on the sleeve of his polo shirt? The smell of another man so tenacious it won't wash off, and be smelled by Frank, who will under-stand, but whose understanding will make Danny feel smaller? Or will this be the time he catches AIDS through spit or cum or the unknown substances coating his one-night partner's body?

Cutting through the rustlings of the park comes a famil-iar voice. "Where the fuck have you been all this time?"

Edwin sits on a bench, his legs crossed and both arms stretched over the back. In his mouth hangs a bent cigarette.

The other men in the shadows have receded, and Danny is alone with Edwin in the middle of Lee's Trail, staring at Edwin's light-blue jeans and white runners.

"Well?" Edwin gestures to the empty spot on the bench beside him. "Are you going to answer me?"

Danny carefully brushes off the seat with his hand and sits. "I've been with Frank."

Letting his head droop, Edwin says, "That's what I heard. I didn't believe it, though. Poor Frankie."

"I'm not much of a nurse, I guess."

Edwin laughs. "That's not what I meant. He loves you, always did."

"I suppose. I sometimes wonder," he whispers, and the tail of his words is lost in the shifting of the branches around them. In a small voice he says, "Eddie, I'm sorry about that time. When I hurt you."

Edwin pats him on the shoulder. "I know. I'm annoying sometimes. I'm surprised you never punched me before."

"You don't need to joke about it. I'm really sorry. It was my fault. I don't know how you can even speak to me right now."

"We all love you, Danny. Even your parents." Edwin blows a line of smoke straight up, his head cocked back. "By the way, I saw them this morning at the shop."

"What were you doing there? I didn't think you went down to Chinatown so much anymore."

"My dearest mother sent your mom some ginseng from the homeland, so I was dropping it off." Edwin pauses to pull the cigarette butt out of his mouth and grind it into the arm of the bench. "They don't know where you're staying, and they were asking me if I'd heard from you. I said you were busy with work. Your mom worries, you know. I sometimes think she suspects."

In a blur, Danny sees his mother, wiping her hands on her apron, watching with her turned-down eyes as he and Cindy play with their paper dolls, the radio at top volume. And then Frank, struggling with the twisted blankets, calling for his own mother, hearing only the bounce of his voice off his apartment walls and nothing else.

"I have to go," Danny says. "Why am I even here?"

Edwin leans his head back on the edge of the bench and looks at the sky, now totally black. "To get laid; why else?"

"No, why now? I'm supposed to be watching Frank. I could even be hanging out with my mother. But no, I'm here."

"Listen, Danny. This stupid thing called AIDS is going to get us all sooner or later. And if not that, then a heart attack or a stroke or something. In the meantime, what do we have left? A fuck in the park, that's what. I might get hit by a bus, or I might live to be eighty. But if I can't get sucked off once in a while, then none of it matters much, does it?" Edwin's mouth twitches like he might laugh, and he searches his pockets for his pack of cigarettes.

Danny stands up. "I'm going back to Frank's."

Edwin mutters, the lighter held up to his face, "This is what we wanted once, Danny. To come here whenever we wanted; to be with any guy we wanted. For a while, that was enough."

The confusion in Danny's head doesn't clear as he

stumbles through the streets. His thoughts are unfinished, nothing more than a jumbled pile. AIDS. Frank. His mother. Cindy. Sex. He's tired of trying to sort it all out and wills himself to ignore the ugly mess. But disease and the prospect of death have a way of stirring it all together, like a bubbling, fetid soup. He wants to scoop out most of his brains, leaving behind only enough to function.

As the night air pushes warmly against his hurrying body, he visualizes the men cruising on the trail, their fingers linked. Two months ago, it would have been Danny looking for someone to fill an hour, someone whose face would live on in his memory, unencumbered by name or words or birthplace. And he would have been happy. Now, he can't stay in the park for more than twenty minutes. Now, it's not enough, but he doesn't know what he wants instead.

When he arrives at Frank's apartment, he rushes to the bedroom. Frank is still asleep, lying on his back as he was when Danny left. The rooms smell of pine-scented cleaner, and the dishes are drying in the rack. He steps into the shower, turning on the water as hot as it will go, until the fog in the stall matches the mess inside his head.

When they were children, Danny and Cindy often said nothing to each other. They walked their dolls across Cindy's bed, built an indoor tent with blankets and pillows when it stormed outside, pretended to cook with their mother's old dented pots. For hours, they silently smiled and nodded, dressed Paper Gina and Paper Adelaide in their evening gowns before sashaying them across the footboard to the same ball. As soon as Danny woke up in the morning, he could feel his sister on the other side of the wall, stretching under the covers, staring at the same morning light that was sometimes camouflaged by low, dense clouds, other times shining clear and thin through the windows and condensation around the sill. What was there to say when you already knew what the other was going to do?

Cindy is looking for him. This he knows without even thinking. He can feel her confusion, her fear that Danny might know it was she who suggested that Frank be forced to take a leave of absence. He can see her crunching in on herself, her shoulders curling forward, her hands twisting in her lap. He's angry, and he's sure Cindy knows it as she sits at her scratched, thinly varnished desk at work, as she rides the bus home, as she washes her office clothes by hand in the double-depth sink in the basement.

It's afternoon, and Danny closes the door to Frank's bedroom, where Frank is sleeping underneath two blankets and wearing flannel pyjamas over his long johns. Once in the hall, Danny looks into the bathroom, at the rubber gloves and toilet brush set out in the middle of the floor to remind him that he needs to clean it today. The phone rings.

The only calls Frank ever gets these days are the daily check-ins from his mother, and calls from his doctor's office reminding him of his appointment the next day. Danny checks his watch. Too early for Frank's mother, and he doesn't think Frank has another appointment for at least five days. He picks up the phone.

Even if she never uttered a syllable, he could tell who she is by the sound of her breathing, by that particular hitch in her exhale.

"Danny? Is that you?"

"Cindy," he says, "why are you calling here?"

"Is Frank all right?"

"No, of course not. He's doing shitty, if you really want to know. I'm paying his bills, cleaning the sores on his back, even holding him up when he sits on the toilet. Does that sound like he's all right?" His voice has reached that pitch where it will soon be incomprehensible; the sound of it panics even him.

Her words come out as half-sobs. "I didn't know."

"I don't want to talk to you anymore. Don't call here again."

Cindy half whispers, and it comes out like a hiss. "I called to say that I'm sorry. I didn't mean to get him fired. I just thought the bank should know, that's all. It's not my fault they made him leave. Why would I hurt him? He's my friend too."

"Some friend."

"Danny, I'm asking you to forgive me."

He turns to look at the closed bedroom door, wondering if Frank is awake and can hear what he's saying. "Fine. I forgive you."

"You don't mean it. I can tell."

Danny twirls the phone cord around his fingers and thinks about hanging up, but he can't.

"You know what?" Cindy's voice rises and she talks slowly, measuring every word she lets loose. "There's plenty for me to forgive too. How about you leaving me alone with Mom and Dad? How about you running away so you could live the life you wanted? What about me? Do you ever think that I might like something different too? Do you think I like living at home, having to explain where I've been every time I come home after nine o'clock? I'm almost thirty years old. How do you think that makes me feel? Or do you think about me at all?"

And Danny wants to say that he didn't know, but the truth is that he did. Everything she has said is true, but if Danny were ignorant, perhaps he wouldn't need to be forgiven. He knew he was leaving Cindy. He knew he wasn't trying to make his parents even a little bit happy. He knew that he was sacrificing his sister for his own imperfect freedom. As long as she never mentioned it, though, he could pretend that he hadn't run away and ignored the needs of everyone else. But now there is no such comfort.

"I'm sorry," he says. "Really."

"Good. Now we're even. I have to go." And she hangs up, the click of the line sounding tangibly final.

I'm sorry, I'm sorry, I'm sorry plays in his ears as he walks to the bathroom and picks up the toilet brush. He hears Frank rustling in the bedroom and he wants to yell, "Just a minute! I just need a minute!" But yelling would startle Frank, send his heart racing in a way that isn't good for anyone, so Danny sits on the edge of the tub and waits until Frank's voice begins calling through the door.

It happens so gradually—like the light changing from night to dawn—that Danny doesn't notice until the very end, until the change on Frank's face is almost complete.

They are in Frank's bed. Danny is curled around him, warming him with his own body. Lately, Frank has been unable to fall asleep, shivering no matter how high the heat is, no matter how many blankets cover him from chin to toes. Danny is dozing, falling in and out of sleep, waking when he hears a noise in the street, sleeping again when he realizes the noise is only a passing car, or the soft footsteps of a cat on the windowsill. Frank breathes quickly and then slowly, and the breaths themselves seem to skip and stutter, but Danny is used to this; he simply holds him tighter and puts his feet on Frank's icy ones.

For a time, their breathing in tandem soothes Danny, and he sleeps undisturbed.

He wakes suddenly and opens his eyes to see the pink light of early morning through the window. He sits up, propped on one elbow as he groggily tries to figure out what has woken him. There are no noises in the street outside, no thumping from the upstairs neighbours, not even the hum of the refrigerator. The silence is absolute.

And there it is, the thing that has shaken him out of sleep. The silence. The total absence of sound.

He leans over Frank, puts his fingers to his neck. Nothing. He turns his head toward him, holds his hand over his open mouth, hoping to feel the heat of his breath. Nothing. He touches his forehead. Cool, like a cup of coffee left out overnight.

Then Frank shudders, and a long, wheezing breath escapes from his body. His eyelids flutter, and he looks once at Danny, his eyes travelling over his face, stopping at his nose, his cheeks, his mouth. Danny holds his head with both hands, afraid to let go.

"What are you thinking?" Danny whispers. "Tell me."

Frank shudders again, and his eyes close. He grows limp, and his thin, thin body falls into Danny's. He lies motionless, his mouth still open, his head resting against Danny's stomach.

Strange how these things are always so quiet. Danny wonders why the earth isn't groaning underneath them, why thunder and lightning aren't crashing outside. Looking at Frank, being this close to the knife's edge, this close to an emptiness he has never seen before, Danny feels that he is being sucked away, as if a vacuum is pulling at him inexorably. He closes his own eyes and forces himself to count to ten before opening them again.

When Danny finally looks up, he sees that dawn has passed and the morning has fully arrived. As usual, he never saw the transition.

THE UNTOLD

1958

On a sweltering Saturday afternoon, Betty stood at the counter in the curio shop, turning all the bills in the cash register face-up. She was rarely alone here, but Doug had to help a friend move, and the children were at Uncle Kwan's, celebrating the birthday of one of his impeccably dressed daughters. Betty could never remember their names, mostly because their perfection left a gritty, bitter taste in her mouth. In front of others, though, she smiled and said her poor memory was the result of the girls' prettiness; who could tell them apart?

She sat on the stool, but stood up again when someone walked by the big front window. *Look busy*, she thought. *Do something.* Bending down, she spied a box of unsorted lacquered chopsticks, red and black and ivory. She lined them up on the counter and began matching the pairs, careful to check that each pair was the same length. She hummed.

Betty jumped and looked up when the bells on the door rang violently. This was no pretty tinkle from someone opening the door politely; this was the sound of someone pushing with all her body weight, someone unafraid to announce her arrival.

A tall woman, with sunglasses dangling from a gold chain around her neck, stepped into the shop. She wore a red shirtdress, tightly belted at the waist, and high, delicate, white sandals. Betty stared at the glossy brown curls brushed away from her face and clustered around the back of her head. She put a hand to her own black bobbed hair, which Doug had cut last week, making five snips and declaring that it looked finished enough for him.

The woman looked up and down the aisles, her eyes narrowing in the dim of the store.

"Can I help you?" Betty asked.

She stepped forward and smiled. Betty could see that a fine, translucent dust covered her whole face in a smooth, even layer.

"Yes, honey. I need some paper fans, the more colourful, the better. And since I'm here, I may as well stock up on some of those red silk slippers too. The men love those." She winked, and Betty fought the urge to wink back.

As Betty gathered up a pile of fans, the woman leaned on the counter and said, "I never tell any of the other girls about this place. I don't want them copying my act, you know."

"Your act?"

The woman inspected her red-painted fingernails. "I'm a dancer, sweetheart." She picked up a fan, unfolded it and began waving it at the base of her neck. "And not the respectable kind either."

Before Betty could say anything, this woman in red grabbed a second fan and struck a pose, holding one in front of her breasts and the other by her pelvis. She fluttered her hands and the fans seemed to magically hide and reveal all at the same time. She hummed a song Betty used to hear on the radio. Betty blushed, realizing that if this woman had been naked, she would have seen the side of her breast, the skin below her belly button.

Chuckling, the woman threw the fans back down on the counter. "I can tell you enjoyed that. You should come to the club sometime, catch my show."

Betty giggled, shaking her head. "Oh no, I could never do that."

"Why not? Lots of ladies come to watch us dance, and not always with their husbands either."

"Thank you for inviting me, but I am very busy. My children need a lot of attention, you know, especially my son." Inexplicably, Betty wanted to tell this woman something about herself, something that promised to be as revealing as the short dance she had just witnessed. She lowered her voice and leaned forward. "My husband thinks I baby him. Maybe he's right."

"Honey, you should just tell your husband where he can stick it. You're the mother here. You know what your kids need."

Betty swallowed a lump in her throat before answering. "I don't like to argue."

A loud laugh erupted from the woman's mouth. "You'll never get what you want until you learn to speak up. Trust me."

"Do you have children?" Betty asked, trying to change the subject.

The woman pursed her lipsticked mouth and looked out the front window. "No, not a chance," she muttered.

She continued to stare at the street until Betty began to wonder if she had gone too far. Or maybe the woman didn't want to buy the slippers after all. A car slowly drove by, and a beam of sunlight flashed off its windshield and into the shop's front window. Betty blinked.

When she opened her eyes, the woman's smile was brilliant. *How on earth does someone have teeth that white and still eat food?* Betty thought. On the counter was a neat pile of bills in exchange for the fans and slippers.

As she turned away, the woman said, "Well, if you change your mind, I'm at the Shanghai Junk for the rest of the month. They call me the Siamese Kitten. It's some show, I tell you." She pointed her finger at Betty's nose and, instantly, Betty felt guilty, as if that sharply manicured nail were ferreting out some unexpressed desire buried deep in her body. "I won't tell your husband. I promise." And she walked out, laughing, her heels on the wooden floor echoing through the shop.

—

Five days passed. Betty cleaned the big house in Shaughnessy with energy that surprised her. She found herself on her hands and knees, scrubbing the bathroom floor, alarmed at the mildew and dust that gathered in the rough grout between tiles. In the bedrooms, she flipped mattresses on her own, flinging them up and feeling a rush of air as they fell back on their frames. Mrs. Lehmann said nothing, just shook her head as Betty scurried into the kitchen for more hot water, her breath coming hard and fast.

As she was eating lunch, she ran a finger up her leg and wondered how it would feel encased in a fishnet stocking. How bright would a woman's skin be under harsh spotlights? Would the howls of men distract her or egg her on? Before the thoughts could form any further, Betty swallowed the rest of her sandwich and ran upstairs with a handful of newspaper to polish the mirrors.

That afternoon, she walked through Chinatown, intending only to buy a whole chicken and some fresh noodles. She didn't even have time for a short visit at the shop. But on her way to Superior Poultry, she circled the block that housed the Shanghai Junk. From the corner, she could see its neon sign, could even hear it buzz if she closed her ears to the traffic and concentrated. "'It's some show,'" she whispered, as she pretended to look at the mustard greens spread out on an overturned wooden box. The street merchant, a sharp-eyed old man, stared at her moving lips.

If she turned her head to the right, she would see the theatre's front door. But she was afraid to look, afraid that the place was spewing irresistible magic and that she would be drawn in, whether she struggled or not. Her hand in her jacket pocket grew hot, and she could feel the damp bits of lint lining the seams.

One look, she thought. *It won't hurt.* She stared at the black-painted door. And took a step forward.

Betty stood at the entrance, her hands clamped to her sides. Better to not draw attention to herself, especially here in Chinatown, where her husband's friends seemed to be planted everywhere—in dark doorways, leaning against brick walls that swallowed up their dark clothes. There was a small gap between the club and the building next door, and Betty slipped into it for a moment, her eyes travelling up and down the street slowly, looking for any trace of someone familiar. After several minutes, with her hands brushing the exterior wall, she backed into the Shanghai Junk.

The sensation: like floating. The cool air lifted the hairs on her arms.

A young girl (her hair was falling over her face, but Betty could see by the boniness in her shoulders that she was not a woman yet) sitting at the front desk muttered, "Fifty cents."

Betty gave her the coins, and the girl waved her through, her eyes fixed on the magazine open in front of her.

The doors to the theatre itself were closed. Double doors, the kind that silently swing both in and out. They were painted a dark red, too purple to look like blood, but alarmingly fleshy nonetheless. The foyer was empty. No one remarked on the small, motionless Chinese woman.

The doors opened, and Betty jumped backward until she was half hidden by a gold-painted pillar. A bearded man with a dirty hat and thick shoes walked out, rubbing his wide hands together. Through the open doors, Betty caught sight of a roving spotlight, then a flutter of red and yellow feathers. Before she could think any further, she took three steps and was inside. The doors closed behind her with a murmur of air.

The theatre was half full, and most of the men occupied the first eight rows of seats. A few dotted the seats in the back, but Betty spied a patch that was completely empty under the jutting balcony. She crab-walked into the middle and sat down.

It was dark, but everything glowed red and dark and thick—velvet curtains, rich wood, plush carpet beneath her feet. But these were details she noted only perfunctorily.

She looked up and there it was: the lit stage, the dancing woman dressed as a resplendent parrot, the men watching as if this woman were the only thing they could ever want to see, as if this performance, with the waggle of her hips, contained all their happiness. The dancer flashed a glitter-covered nipple, and a roar went up from the audience, a roar that belied the number of men actually gathered there.

The men reacted to every move she made. She flicked a finger, and a ripple of energy spread through the crowd. She walked the width of the stage, and Betty could see their heads following her. She performed a high kick, and a collective wave of approval surged through the seats.

Betty thought she could smell the arousal in the air, a burnt-skin odour that rose up from the seats and circled the room slowly like a thick soup. If she stepped on that stage, would the reaction be the same? Could the curve of her hips bounce to the beat and draw gasps from strange men, or even from her own husband?

She looked around, and drew the sleeves of her jacket over her hands. If anyone noticed her, they made no indication.

The spotlight twirled and spun, and Betty wished she could warm her hands in the light, watch her flesh turn white and blue and red with each change of a filter. The music pounded, and she thought about going home that night and dancing with the children, or waltzing around the living room with her husband. Preposterous, of course, but she smiled at the thought anyway: the house filled with the noise of stamping feet and the tinny music from their small radio. Laughter bouncing off walls and ceilings, rattling the windows and escaping into the night air, spurring the neighbours to remark, "That Lim family. Always having fun." Her own reflection in the glass, spinning and beautiful, so glowing and shiny that people on the street stopped and stared, unconsciously moving their heads in time to the music. It could be, couldn't it?

Another dancer appeared onstage, a blond woman dressed like Shirley Temple twenty years earlier. Betty watched for a few minutes, saw her body revealed bit by bit. She saw the look of irritation on her face, as if these men were mosquitoes, crowding her and impossible to swat away. Betty felt a headache coming on (that music, and the lights that seemed to pound at her just as loudly) and she remembered her children. She was a mother, sitting in a dark room half full of men, with naked ladies dancing in front of her. She looked down at the peanut shell–covered floor, her cheeks burning. How irresponsible.

She had groceries to buy and dinner to cook, a silent husband who would make his displeasure known in some other way if she was late. He might ignore the dripping garden hose, or leave his near-empty beer bottles on the floor, where they would inevitably tip over and form a sticky puddle she would have to clean up.

The twenty minutes inside this place would have to be forgotten, locked away in her brain. It didn't matter anyway; she would never be like these women, showing the intricacies of their bodies, or these men, displaying their desires for anyone to see. Her family didn't dance, and that was that. If she wanted something different, no one could know or guess, least of all her children. It wouldn't be a problem: half the time, little Danny stared right through her. He thought she wasn't interesting enough to hold his attention, and, while this occasionally made Betty sad, right now she considered it useful. The quiet, muddy-skinned mother couldn't possibly have music and dance and laughter ringing inside her body. Those things belonged to the beautiful people.

She buttoned up her jacket and stood, careful to keep her head down in case someone should notice her. As she was walking up the dark aisle, she heard a low and raspy male voice in the balcony shout, "Where's the Siamese Kitten? I want the Siamese Kitten." Betty stopped and scanned the crowd, but couldn't see who had spoken. She felt her shoulders droop.

She didn't know how she would shake off this fatigue. But today was like any other day, and there was food to be cooked and floors to be swept. Like always, she would hardly talk. She thought she might say something to her husband, just once, about Danny and how she knew he could still be the son they would be proud of, but then she thought that speaking up was something to be done sparingly. Best to save it all up for a time when she really needed to unleash what was on her mind. As Betty pushed open the door to the lobby, she took one last look behind her. The dancer onstage ripped off her skirt with a whirl of energy, but her face remained still, the lines clear but so, so tired.

THE MONEY SHOT

1982

Canada geese honk through the sky, and Danny's head is clogged with the late August sunshine. *Where is the fucking rain when you feel like weeping?* Danny shouts to himself over the din. Even if he cried, the tears would evaporate instantly. What, then, would be the point?

The funeral comes to him in bits and pieces. The priest droning in a voice that doesn't differentiate between speaking and chanting. Edwin standing with a group of men to the left, their eyes fixed on the casket. Frank's mother's grip hot on his arm. The relatives politely offering their condolences to Frank's parents, but not asking Danny's name or shaking his hand. The looseness of the skin in everyone's faces, but especially Frank's father's, who droops a little more with every passing minute until Danny wonders if he will topple into the grave; in the hole, at least, it would be cooler.

Danny looks back and sees Val, standing by herself with her hands clasped in front of her. Shadows from a maple tree dance across her face. When she sees Danny, she winks and nods. He feels swollen with the pressure of looking like he cares about the grief of others. Frank's mother's fingers are like claws, and he stays in his place. He turns back to the circle of people in front of him, and sees that they are no more than disparate groups, pieces of Frank's life that, without him, are nonsensical and unordered fragments.

He shuts his eyes and pictures Val as she was when he first met her, with her long, lean legs and her cigarette smouldering in the semi-darkness of that damp alley. There are things about that day he can no longer remember. Was it June or July? Had it been raining the night before, and did he peer at a familiar face in the theatre the day he went back, or was it a trick of the light, the shadows that morphed strange features into ones he thought he knew? He reaches further into his memory to retrieve small details, like the smell of the Sweet Caps in his hand, or the exact shape of the puddle he ran through on his way back to the shop. Frustrated, he pounds at his forehead. *I wish I'd had a camera then*, he thinks, *so none of it would be lost like this.*

Abruptly, Frank's mother pulls at his sleeve. He opens his eyes and sees that it's time to leave. There is a wake he must go to; one, in fact, he helped plan.

He pats her on the shoulder. "I'll meet you there," he whispers, and she smiles at him in a way that indicates only a bare satisfaction that nothing has yet gone wrong today.

He walks through the crowd. Edwin tries to stop him to talk, but Danny waves him away. Cindy, gripping her purse, stands by a large shrub and watches him stride across the grass. He breaks into a run until he catches up with Val's retreating body.

"Miss Val," he says, out of breath, "you're coming with me."

In his studio, under the lights that he wired himself and turned so that they would both show and hide at the same time, the satin wrapped around Val's body blinds him. Through his lens, she is smaller than real life, but the real-life Siamese Kitten cannot be seen in her entirety. Her red lips are a target. He focuses.

The small purple suitcase, still half open, has been pushed to the side. Val has only a stool to work with, but still, she vibrates. Buzzes even. Danny, for the first time since he was eight years old, is face to face with the costumed and powdered Siamese Kitten. She smiles, and he thinks it means either *I love you* or *I will eat you alive*. He shivers; her cool breath is blowing lines across his forehead.

The shots are flawless. No closed eyes, no drooping posture, no muscle untensed. Danny calls out, "These will be the greatest glamour shots ever taken."

He has not yet zoomed in on her face. From this distance, Val could be the dancer Danny first met twenty-four years ago. Beautiful and powerful and sexy, but not, somehow, the woman he now knows her to be.

"Miss Val," he says, "let's try something a little different."

He settles her on the stool and points the lights away. With a damp cotton ball, he gently wipes off the eye shadow, the glitter on her cheekbones and the powder on her nose until her face is almost bare. He is reaching for her mouth when Val says, "Leave the lips." Danny nods and backs away.

When he looks through the lens again, she is softer, her still-red mouth relaxed into a not-quite smile. The lines in her skin point to everything he has learned about her. Danny can see the house on River Road in the curve of her jaw. The lost babies in the hollows of her cheeks. The thorny bush she grew up with in the scar on her forehead. Even the years she spent on the circuit are embedded in the wrinkles that he might have expected to see on a woman fifteen years older. It's all there: frown lines, smile lines, a droop in her left eye. Yes, she is glamorous and beautiful, but hers isn't a fragile glamour; rather, it's the kind that has sprouted out of real flesh, the living, breathing mulch composed of her numerous pasts. They're all there, pulsing under her skin.

He hasn't said anything, but Val speaks anyway. "This will be all I have left, you know, of my life before. Everything else is gone."

The roll is finished and he straightens up. "I know," he says gently.

She doesn't cry, but he leaves anyway to go to the darkroom, in case she wants to.

When she sees the contact sheet for the first time, she runs her finger down each strip of tiny prints. She hunches over on her stool and considers every shot. With a half-smile, she turns to Danny and says, "I look *almost* young. Not so bad for an old stripper."

Danny places a stack of other prints in Val's lap, the photographs he took over several nights outside the club. She squints at them, her forehead wrinkling. But soon enough she sees the

neon sign in the background and recognizes the traces of heavy
stage makeup on the dancers, the apprehension on their faces
as they step out onto a street where the protection of bouncers and bartenders doesn't exist. Modern Red Riding Hoods,
picking their way through a forest consumed by city.

Val fans the prints out on the floor and places her contact
sheet beside them. "Do you see? They belong together,
Danny."

And they do. Each photograph is a girl transformed
from a dancer to the individual who walks through daylight,
but each carries the marks of the strip with her—streaks of
blush, a piece of stray glitter, the suspicion in her eyes as
she scans the street. And beside them, the Siamese Kitten,
the woman they might one day become. A dancer who carries the marks of her entire life on her face, who is both the
little girl dreaming of the city in her room with the thin walls
and limp curtains, and the woman strutting in pasties and a
G-string on stages from Idaho to Vancouver. There's no
separating them now.

Together, these photographs are a trajectory. Real girls
who dance for a living. A real woman who is defined by the
strip, but also by her lovers, parents and the boarding houses
she slept in. Together, they breathe near-tangible breath, feel
like skin—not costumes—in Danny's hands.

"You should do something with these," Val says.
"They're not doing any good sitting in a drawer."

She's right. Danny can see that this set of photographs
tells a lifetime of stories. There is fear and uproarious joy,
the smell of blood and missed connections. Everyone will
love them, and they could hang on a white gallery wall and

move people to think of their mothers or sisters or enemies, or the things they said that can never be taken back. He looks at the photographs once more, and it feels like he is about to throw off his unsuccessful, mediocre self and give birth to a brand-new, brightly coloured Danny who sings in the shower with gusto and smiles at children on the street. His skin tingles, feels raw and new and soft, in a way that seems baby-like, except that, as a child, he felt this open to the possibilities just once, when he was eight years old and met Miss Val for the first time and saw that even in ordinary alleys, glamour can smoulder.

He has been a disparate patchwork, none of his pieces contributing to a cohesive whole. What if this transformational moment doesn't last, and he fails to pull it all together? What will happen to him? The answer is inevitable and simple: he will never be anything but a collection of whisper-thin fragments, and he will die that way, sooner rather than later. He knows what he has to do, and he won't be afraid again. The real, lovely Val is the one with her history etched on her face. The real Danny, the one with no secrets, will be beautiful too.

Now that she has seen this set of photos, Val is the only one who knows everything about him. He feels as if the air has left his body, and he is on the cusp of filling himself up again, with breath or new places of beauty. Whatever he likes. He turns to Val. She of all people deserves his full attention on this night, at the end of a seething, unbearable summer. Sitting on a stool beside her, Danny pours two shots of whisky and rests his head on her shoulder, the satin like a kiss on his hot cheek.

—

Danny wakes up with a start at six in the morning. This is his apartment, his bed, the sound of one man living—and waking—by himself. He scratches his head and his fingertips are cold and clammy. He sits up and pulls open the blinds covering the window. The sky is a comforting grey, and mist blows in through the gap. He sees dark clouds to the west, a woman walking down the sidewalk with her head covered in a clear plastic kerchief, leaves falling from the maple out front as a squirrel jumps from branch to branch.

It's been ten weeks of unrelenting heat, of stickiness, of nights with no wind. Danny smells the coming rain, an odour so particular and so ground into his brain that the skin on his arms breaks into goosebumps in immediate recognition. Soft ground. Rainbow puddles of drain water and car oil. The continual drip from gutters and awnings.

He jumps out of bed and hums a nameless tune. It's September, and he can hardly wait to walk outside.

Val made the trip by herself, catching a bus over the Lions Gate Bridge and then a second that took her to Kitsilano, to the neighbourhood she and Joan lived in together when they first arrived in Vancouver years ago. Before she left, she called Joan. "I know why you did it."

The silence was crisp, like vodka seconds out of the freezer. Val couldn't even hear Joan breathing.

"He was going to leave you, wasn't he. When he figured out you couldn't have children, you panicked. Too bad for me, though. Did you think it was fate when you saw Dawn for the first time?"

Finally, Joan spoke. "It's Kelly."

Val laughed. "Of course it is."

Joan said, "I needed Peter. He was already sleeping with a girl in his office. What if she had gotten pregnant first?"

"What if giving away my baby had killed me?"

Joan let out a short, bitter laugh. "But it wouldn't have, Val. Even you must know that."

Now, as she steps off the bus and opens her umbrella, she thinks of Joan as hollow. Joan has worked so hard at maintaining appearances that there is nothing else, only the hard shell she created. Whatever she was before and underneath no longer exists, eaten away, perhaps, by herself.

She walks down Cypress Street, carefully checking the numbers of each apartment building against the note in her hand. It's a Sunday morning, and birds huddle in the trees and shrubs, ruffling the wet leaves as they hang, pecking at the aphids and spiders still crawling on the branches. She stops at a building on the corner and presses the buzzer by the front door.

"Kelly," she says into the intercom, "it's Auntie Val."

The front door unlocks and Val pushes through, pausing for only a second to look in the lobby mirror and touch up her lipstick. No need to worry. She looks perfect.

This day, the very act of standing on the front walk of his parents' house, has been something he has imagined over and over again. Like today, the rain is always falling and the call of seagulls slices through the air above his head, above the house, above even the power lines criss-crossing the sky. Today, the leaves on the trees lining the sidewalk have started to turn colour, some brown, some red, some yellow. He smells autumn, that sharp mixture of potential frost, mud and the burning of wood.

Cindy's shadow moves across the closed curtains. Her back is bent, and he remembers that she is only hunched like this when she's at home, when their parents are speaking to her and watching her with eyes fearful of her future life without them. He realizes he hasn't seen her in weeks, except at the funeral, hasn't even talked to her over the phone.

The sound of a metal spoon against the side of his mother's wok rings out. He can't stand outside forever.

Inside, Cindy's face looks drawn and jaundiced as she walks back and forth in the dull glow of the floor lamps. They say nothing to each other, only nod and look away. Danny wonders if Cindy is feeling guilt, if Frank's death sits in her thoughts like an immovable stone, heavy and distressingly unavoidable. Or if the grind of living with their parents—of seeing them every day, of listening to their silence punctuated only by Betty's mutterings over her unmarried children and Doug's grunts of displeasure over the electricity bill—has accumulated until that feeling of being trapped shows on her face, in the greyness of her skin, the droop in the corners of her eyes.

His mother strokes the line of his jaw with her square fingertips. After she returns to her cooking, he can smell the trace of ginger she left behind on his face.

Danny steps into the living room and stands near the window. Doug watches the news, and eyes Danny warily during the commercials. Outside, a brand-new BMW is inching into a parking space across the street. It reverses in, then pulls out, each time narrowly missing the bumpers of the economy cars ahead and behind. The windows are tinted, but Danny thinks he can see a professional haircut, a pair of reflective, designer sunglasses, even soft leather driving gloves.

"Some car," Doug says.

Danny turns around.

His father hasn't left the armchair, but his body is tensed, his neck stretched so that he can see over the windowsill. The legs of his cotton pants are rolled up, exposing his bare ankles and the tops of his feet before they disappear into his summer slippers. The stains on his short-sleeved shirt are mysterious—perhaps soy sauce, wood oil or dirty water from the rusty pipes in the shop. His hair, glossy with Brylcreem, is still forbidding.

"Yeah, it's pretty nice," Danny says.

Doug drums his fingers on the chair. "Too expensive to maintain. Too much car to handle. I was never much of a driver anyway."

Danny imagines his father as he might once have been. Slick hair, dust-covered pants, a cigarette hanging out of his mouth. The scowl on his face when he lost another street race and had to drive home in the produce truck, the smell of stray cabbage leaves drifting forward from the bed. He doubts they would have been friends had they met then, but that doesn't stop him from wishing he could have asked the younger version of his father what he really wanted. Betty and Cindy and this house? Or something else that required shiny cars and a house with a view of the ocean?

Danny nods. "Me neither."

Doug turns his head away from the window and looks at Danny's face. For a moment, Danny thinks that his father is trying to read him, but then Doug merely leans back in his chair and grunts.

"We have something in common, then," he says before he shifts his eyes back to the television.

Danny grins.

They eat, and only the click of chopsticks against bowls fills the kitchen. Cindy eats slowly, picking up one grain of rice at a time. Doug chews on a spare rib and spits the bone into a napkin, grimacing as he sucks the meat from between his teeth. Betty nibbles at a piece of *gai lan* and smiles at nothing in particular, her eyes unfocused. This dinner is the same as the ones they used to have when he was a little boy, some of them silent and uncomfortable, others peppered with Cindy's chirpy voice as she told the family the latest gossip from school. Danny settles into his chair, lifts his bowl to his mouth and readies himself for a long evening. All those years he stayed away, he carried his father and mother with him wherever he went, no matter how often he tried to pretend the opposite. There's no use in splitting up past and present, family and lovers, anymore.

Betty looks at him, cocks her head as she gazes at his mouth. Quietly, she asks, "Why did you not come home for so long? I thought you might come more often."

Cindy sits up, places her bowl on the table.

"I was helping a sick friend. I was looking after him."

"Such a nice boy you are, Danny. Who is your friend? Someone from school?" Betty smiles, holding her chopsticks in the air.

Cindy touches their mother's shoulder. "Don't be so nosy, Mom. Danny doesn't have to tell us everything." And she meets his eyes, alarm in the raising of her eyebrows, the wrinkling of her nose.

He looks at her face, at the little girl she used to be only partially hidden by the new, adult lines of her chin, her cheeks. That little girl who never let their father see Danny playing with their paper dolls, who turned off the radio to stop Edwin from dancing when Doug's car pulled into the driveway. *It's okay*, he thinks. *She can relax now*.

Out the kitchen window, Danny can see one white T-shirt blowing in the wind on the clothesline, forgotten in the rain. A howling begins around the house, and the clothespins give way. The T-shirt flies out of the yard, carried by the breeze but also beaten down by the drizzle. Danny watches as it floats upward and then falls, over and over again, until it blows out toward the end of the alley on one strong gust, where it pauses, suspended above the garbage cans and overgrown gardens. For a few strange seconds, it neither rises nor falls, only floats, almost motionless. But then, just as Danny opens his mouth to tell his parents that he's gay in a voice that he hopes will sound firm and irrevocable, the T-shirt plummets, plunging behind a fence, landing somewhere invisible, in a yard Danny cannot even picture from memory.

He meets his mother's eyes and sees her for what she is: loving, worried, hemmed in by the borders of this house and her family. He doesn't wish she were someone else anymore. He doesn't wish that for anyone.

"I have something to show you," he says, drawing out two small prints from his pocket. One is a photograph of Val in full costume. The other, an older one, is of Danny and

Frank from three years ago, standing at Prospect Point, the houses of the North Shore behind them. He fingers the edges before laying them carefully in the middle of the table.

ACKNOWLEDGEMENTS

To Amanda Lewis, Diane Martin, Louise Dennys, Marion Garner and Michael Schellenberg, for letting me crash the Knopf and Random House Canada party once again.

To my writing partners, June Hutton and Mary Novik of SPiN, without whom I would be despondent, devoid of ideas and irredeemably grumpy.

To Carolyn Swayze, whose gentle voice and rational advice have become mainstays of my writing life.

To Patricia Kells, for her continued enthusiasm in promoting my books.

To Lissa Cowan, Brendan McLeod and Andrea MacPherson, for commiserating with me over drinks, e-mail and swapped manuscripts.

To my friends at CBC Radio One, in particular Sheila Peacock, Sheryl MacKay, Stephen Quinn, Madeline Green, Jo-Ann Roberts, Ann Jansen, Jacqueline Kirk and Shelagh Rogers, for giving me an excuse to leave the house and reminding me that the world of books is always worth talking about.

To my family, especially my sisters Linda, Pamela, Tina and Emma, for helping me navigate the minefield of working motherhood. And to my niece Madeleine, for cheerfully babysitting a newborn infant while I finished this book, and for showing me the hidden gems of daytime television.

To Troy, Oscar and Molly, for giving me everything.

To the Canada Council for the Arts and its Project Assistance for Creative Writers, for supporting the development of this novel.

I used many sources in the research of *The Better Mother*, and have listed the ones I turned to again and again whenever I had questions about burlesque, HIV/AIDS or mid-twentieth century Vancouver.

The research of Becki L. Ross, now collected in her comprehensive book *Burlesque West: Showgirls, Sex and Sin in Postwar Vancouver*.

Fred Herzog, *Vancouver Photographs*.

Daniel Francis, *Red Light Neon: A History of Vancouver's Sex Trade*.

The Age of AIDS, a production of Frontline/WGBH, directed by William Cran.

In 2005, I saw an exhibit of photographs by a Canadian artist named Theodore Saskatche Wan (who changed his middle name to mirror the name of a small town on the Prairies) at the Vancouver Art Gallery. Many of his images moved me, but none moved me as much as his commercial photographs of exotic dancers. Wan died of cancer in 1987 at the age of thirty-three. I found myself ruminating on the fictional possibilities of his story, and soon developed a character named Danny. While Danny isn't Theodore Wan, I owe a great deal to Wan's photographs, which began this whole journey in the first place.

JEN SOOKFONG LEE was born and raised in Vancouver's Eastside, where she now lives with her husband and son. Her books include *The End of East* and *Shelter*, a novel for young adults. Her poetry, fiction and articles have appeared in a variety of magazines and anthologies, including *TOK: Writing the New City*, the *Antigonish Review* and *Event*. A popular radio personality, she contributes regularly to *The Next Chapter* with Shelagh Rogers and *Definitely Not the Opera*, and is a frequent co-host of the *Studio One Book Club*. www.sookfong.com